This Duchess of Mine

Eloisa James

This Duchess of Mine

AVON

An Imprint of HarperCollins*Publishers*

This is a work of fiction. Names, characters, places, and incidents are products of the author's imagination or are used fictitiously and are not to be construed as real. Any resemblance to actual events, locales, organizations, or persons, living or dead, is entirely coincidental.

AVON BOOKS
An Imprint of HarperCollins*Publishers*
10 East 53rd Street
New York, New York 10022-5299

Printed in the U.S.A.

This book is dedicated to Kim Castillo,
my wonderful assistant.
Not only does she keep my complicated life on track,
but her creative input is essential to my work.
In point of fact, she gave
This Duchess of Mine *its title.*
Thanks, sweetie!

Acknowledgments

My books are like small children; they take a whole village to get them to a literate state. I want to offer my heartfelt thanks to my personal village: my editor, Carrie Feron; my agent, Kim Witherspoon; my website designers, Wax Creative; and last, but not least, my personal team: Kim Castillo, Franzeca Drouin, and Anne Connell. I am so grateful to each of you!

I want to add a special thank you to Professor Lenny Cassuto, a brilliant chess player who has given me advice throughout the writing of this series. Dr. Cassuto designed Jemma and Elijah's final game, and even played it out in his head (though not blind-folded).

The village would wither, of course, without the cheerful support of my readers. One of the parts of being an author that I most enjoy is writing an "extra chapter" for each novel I publish, one that springs directly from my readers' responses to my work.

In the month or so after *This Duchess of Mine* publishes, please hop onto the Bulletin Board attached to my website (www.eloisajames.com) and vote for the chapter you wish I'd included in this novel! And if you'd like to read the "extra" chapters of earlier books, just look on the website under Readers' Menu.

Chapter One

Beaumont House
London Seat of the Duke of Beaumont
March 26, 1784

No one dressed to please a husband. At least, not in the Duchess of Beaumont's circle of acquaintances. One dressed—to be frank—to dazzle and amaze one's female friends. Or, if one were so inclined, to invite a seduction . . . to engage in an *affaire.*

Husbands were just there, like coal in Newcastle and pigs in the sty.

Which made it all the harder for Jemma, the duchess in question, to decide what to wear to seduce her spouse. After all, Elijah had been her husband for years. True, they had lived apart for some time, but now they'd agreed, in an alarmingly businesslike fashion, that after he returned from a fortnight spent at the Prime Minister's house, they would . . .

Would what?

Have a baby. Produce an heir, or at least go through the motions that would produce one in nine months.

Go to bed together.

They had come to that decision a year ago. When she had first returned from Paris, she was too angry to contemplate marital intimacies, but then somehow the fury drained away. Still, they kept to separate bedchambers. The humiliating truth was that Elijah didn't seem terribly interested.

First he said he wouldn't bed her until she finished her chess match with the Duke of Villiers, since everyone believed that the match was naught more than a cover for an *affaire*. Then, when she threw in the chess match, giving the win to Villiers, Elijah announced that he was going into the country with Pitt's wing of the government.

She couldn't imagine another man claiming that he was too busy to bed her. Too busy to seduce the Duchess of Beaumont?

Unlikely.

Jemma didn't think she was being overly vain, just realistic. It had been her experience that men were driven by lust above duty. And she had been assured by male attention from age sixteen that she was precisely what a lustful man would like to find in his bed.

She had blue eyes, hair of a deep golden color, a very elegant nose (she particularly liked her nose), and crimson lips. True, the crimson color resulted from lavish applications of lip rouge, but if one were lucky enough not to have a thin hard mouth, one might as well draw attention to it.

And at twenty-eight, she still had the allure of youth,

together with a sheen of sophistication and wit that no sixteen-year-old could command.

She even had all her teeth, to lower the subject to the level of cattle.

The problem, it seemed to her, was that to Elijah she was a *wife*, not a woman.

There was nothing sensual about the word *wife*. Jemma gave a little shudder. Wives nagged and complained. Wives wore little caps on their fading hair and suffered from broadening hips due to child-bearing.

It was mortifying to be a wife. Even worse, a wife whose husband was reluctant to take her to bed.

It was definitely a new, and rather disconcerting, sensation, to feel that she was more interested in bedding a man than the reverse. She was used to men trying to seduce *her*. During the years she lived at Versailles, gentlemen considered her ripe for the plucking, given that her husband lived in England. They swiveled before her to display a powerful thigh, flaunt an embroidered coat or an enameled snuff box. They dropped roses, plums, and poems at her doorstep.

She smiled, enticed, laughed, dismissed. She dressed to amuse herself, and to dazzle the court. She dressed for power and admiration. She certainly didn't dress to enchant men: she took that for granted.

But the whole process of making her *toilette* felt different tonight.

She wanted all the passion and energy her husband devoted to the House of Lords, to the fate of England. She wanted him to look at her with the same hunger that he showed for a new bill in Parliament. She wanted Elijah at her feet.

She wanted what she probably couldn't have. No wife had that.

Brigitte, her *femme de chambre*, popped into the room with a fistful of visiting cards. "All your beaux are below requesting to assist you in your *toilette*," she said. "Lord Corbin, of course, and Viscount St. Albans. Delacroix and Lord Piddleton."

Jemma wrinkled her nose. "I don't believe I shall admit anyone this evening."

"You shall dress *alone*, Your Grace?" The look on Brigitte's face was almost comical.

"I am never alone," Jemma pointed out. "I have your assistance as well as that of Mariette and Lucinda. A woman with three maids, each with such decided opinions, can hardly bemoan her lack of guidance!"

Brigitte's eyes narrowed, just for a second. "Indeed, Your Grace. Perhaps you plan a special *toilette* for the fête this evening. Shall I inform the gentlemen that you decline their counsel?"

But Jemma had already changed her mind, based on that little flash in Brigitte's eyes. Brigitte knew that the duke would be going directly to the king's fête. Servants talked . . . servants knew.

Jemma suspected that the house knew of her embarrassing, humiliating infatuation with her husband. In the last month or so she had taken to sitting in the library with a chessboard before her, waiting for Elijah to return from the House of Lords. She had started reading all the papers, with particular attention to accounts of the Duke of Beaumont's speeches. She was . . .

She was a dunce. She should behave as if there was nothing untoward about the evening. Her husband had been in the country for two weeks; that meant nothing to her. A fashionable wife would never even note the absence or presence of something as insignificant as a *husband*.

"It's just that I have a headache," she said, with precisely the right note of lament. "And Corbin and Delacroix can be so trivial. If only Villiers were here."

Suspicion vanished from her maid's eyes. "He would soothe your head, Your Grace. And he"—Brigitte dimpled—"is *far* from trivial."

Despite herself, Jemma smiled. "But Villiers would never lower himself to join a woman at her dressing. For one thing, I suspect that it takes him longer to dress than it takes me. I suppose I must needs admit Corbin, at least. How do I appear?"

Jemma was wearing a honey-pale corset, adorned with daring bows of sheer black ribbon. Brigitte darted about, pulling a lock of hair over her shoulder so it emphasized her white skin, dusting a touch of powder onto her nose.

Her hair, of course, was already built into a formidable pile of curls, though it awaited ornamentation and powder. One of her three French maids, Mariette, was a genius in that area and had spent two hours earlier that afternoon constructing a style fit for a royal occasion.

Jemma looked at herself again in the glass over her dressing table. To her mind, nothing suited her quite as much as dishabille, to be with her face painted, but her hair unpowdered, her legs showing through the frail lawn of her chemise. If only Elijah visited her at this time in the afternoon . . . but he never did.

Only strangers—or at best, acquaintances—thronged below in the drawing room, begging for permission to help her place a patch, or choose a gown.

Presumably husbands were uninterested in seeing their wives dress; their secrets were all known and the thrill of the unfamiliar was lost. Though considering that she and Elijah hadn't seen each other under intimate circumstances for nine years, one might imagine he felt a tinge of curiosity. The last time they had slept together she had been a gauche and, comparatively speaking, flat-chested twenty-year-old.

"If Villiers were below, would you admit him?" Brigitte asked, artfully spilling a box of ribbons onto the dressing table as if she were setting the stage for a play. She snatched up Jemma's silver-backed mirror and laid it carefully across the glowing strands of color.

"Villiers is dangerous," Jemma stated. Villiers was everything Corbin and Delacroix were not. He was a chess master, for one thing. His mind was as nimble as hers, and his machinations were not trivial, and—

And he wanted her.

Villiers's desire wasn't like the light emotions of the men waiting below. His desire was like a dark undertow, pulling at her along with the force of his charm, the wicked beauty of his smile, his French mother's delicious eyes . . .

Brigitte sighed, and the sigh said it all. "Of course, he's a Frenchman, and that changes everything."

"Only on his mother's side."

"Assez! Assez! C'est assez."

Brigitte was right. The French blood Villiers inherited from his mother was definitely *enough* . . . put together with an English manliness and strength. He was truly dangerous to a woman's peace of mind, not to mention her reputation.

"Only Corbin?" Brigitte asked, picking up the cards tendered by those waiting below.

Generally, a lady allowed two, three, even four gentlemen into the dressing room to help her choose patches and lace. To invite only Corbin would invite a scandal, but who could really believe that she was instigating an *affaire* with Corbin? He was Jemma's favorite partner for the minuet, her comfortable companion of an evening. A brilliant dancer, an exquisite dresser, a notable wit. And she had a shrewd feeling that he had as little interest in her as she had in him.

What if Elijah didn't bother to come tonight, for all they had agreed to meet this evening? What if affairs of state kept him from affairs of the heart?

Surely not.

Besides, one never had an affair of the heart with one's wife.

"Just Lord Corbin," she said decisively.

Brigitte nipped out of the room, down to dismiss the crowd and admit Corbin and no other, and set alive a small blaze of gossip about Jemma's preferential treatment.

A moment later Corbin paused in the door just long enough to allow Jemma to assess his costume, and to allow him to appreciate Brigitte's careful stage setting. The frank appreciation in his eyes was very soothing to Jemma's fraught feelings.

"I should like a glass of Champagne," she told Brigitte. "Lord Corbin, does that please you?"

"Absolutely," Corbin drawled. He was the son of a country lord, who likely was affronted, if not terrified, by his eldest son. Corbin's wig was a snowy perfection; his heels were higher than Jemma's and graced with large, floppy flowers; he was just saved from effeminacy by the breadth of his shoulders and by a rugged turn to his chin. He was dressed in a coat of antique rose, sewn with narrow cuffs of persimmon. His breeches were the same persimmon, and his stockings—

"Those stockings!" she cried. "Exquisite!" They were pale cream, with rose-colored clocks rising up the sides.

Corbin swept into a graceful bow. "I first saw a pair on Lord Stittle, if you can countenance it."

He sat in a chair at her side, the better to help her pick the perfect accoutrements for her hair.

"I would prefer not to imagine such a thing," Jemma said.

"I know, I know. I told him his thighs were too large. Or was it his feet? At any rate, it was only after sustained insults that I managed to wring the name of his hosier from him. William Low on Bond Street, if you can believe it. I thought Low carried only worsted stockings for country squires."

His eyes laughed, and Jemma felt fifty times better. "I must look my absolute *best* tonight," she said, hearing too late the fervency in her voice.

"Darling, you always look your best," he said, raising an eyebrow. "But always! Would I be your closest companion were you not the most exquisite duchess in London?"

"The reverse is true as well," Jemma remarked.

"Naturally," he said, grinning. "Speaking of which, do you care for this small accent on my chin? I spent the entire week in the country growing it, and by Thursday I was despairing of achieving an appropriate appearance in time for the king's fête."

Jemma looked at him carefully. Dazzled by his stockings, she hadn't noticed that he now sported the smallest goatee she'd ever seen, just an arrow of silky dark hair below his lower lip, fashioned into a wicked little V. "Yes," she said slowly. "I do like it, Corbin. You'll start a fashion. It makes you look older, and a bit dangerous."

"Ruinous in a woman, charming in a man," he said happily. "At least at my tender age. Dare I ask what makes this evening so fraught with anxiety? I do trust your plans have nothing to do with Delacroix. I had to elbow him out of the way to make my way up the stairs, and I don't like even to stand next to him; I'm afraid all that artlessness will rub off on me."

Jemma laughed. "Don't be cruel, darling. Delacroix considers himself to be the epitome of sophistication."

"One could call it adolescent greenness but for his advanced age. He tries so hard that I feel exhausted at the very sight of him. Such sincerity should be outlawed."

"You *are* cruel." Jemma picked up three or four ribbons and held them to the light, put them down again. Ribbons were too girlish for what she had in mind.

"Do you plan *la grande toilette*?" Corbin asked, catching the connotations of her gesture instantly.

"Therein lies my problem," Jemma said, waving a hand at her bed. "I cannot decide."

Naturally, Corbin rose to inspect the two choices Brigitte had laid out.

On one side was a lovely gown of a blue-green watered silk. It was embroidered with green roses, small ones, and the piquancy of the improbable flower made the whole costume all the more delicious. The skirts pulled back to reveal a gossamer underskirt in a lighter shade.

"In your hair?" Corbin asked.

"Roses to match." She tossed one to him.

"Exquisite," he said, inspecting it. "I gather the centers are made of emeralds and not green glass, Duchess?"

"Very small ones," she said, shrugging one shoulder. "Practically invisible."

"I am entirely in favor of luxury," Corbin said, turning the rose in his fingers. "Especially the kind that doesn't herald its worth."

"In truth, they were terribly expensive."

"And thus to be worn only by a woman who need not worry about finances. Though now I think of it, these roses should be worn by a woman deep in debt. Flaunting extravagance is the best way to assuage creditors' anxieties."

"I suppose that they are rather extravagant."

"A duchess's prerogative." Corbin moved to the other costume. "But if with the one gown you flaunt your extravagance, what exactly do you wish to flaunt— and *why*—with this gown?" His voice was silky, but delivered its insult for all that.

"It's the very newest fashion," Jemma said indignantly, coming to stand next to him. "A chemise gown. Queen Marie Antoinette has at least four, I assure you."

"Ah, but the lucky queen doesn't live in England." Corbin picked up the gown. It was made of a sweet flow of fabric in a pale peach, caught up here and there with bunches of pearls. Rather than being made of stiff satin, the cloth was as thin as a chemise—hence the name. It would barely skim her breasts, flowing down over her body like a delicate night garment.

"Are we so stuffy in England?" she asked.

"So *cold*," Corbin said. "In both senses of the word. My darling duchess, you will cause the women to thrill with rage and cause the men to thrill with something else. But meanwhile you will freeze."

"Freeze?" Jemma stared down at the chemise gown.

"There is nothing more unattractive than flesh dimpled with cold," Corbin said flatly. "And the king's fête takes place on his yacht. On the river. Unless you wish to spend the evening inside longing for a fireplace and a woolen shawl, you should wear the green gown. Which, by the way, is gorgeous."

"But—"

"And not so desperate," he continued.

Jemma whipped around. "I am *never* desperate!"

Corbin met her eyes in the glass. "Then why the desperation?" he asked gently.

"I am not desperate. I am . . . "

"Interested?" Corbin's eyebrow rose, and his smile was so amused that she couldn't help smiling back.

"In my husband," she told him impulsively.

She surprised him. He dropped into his chair with something less than his usual insouciance. "Your husband? *Your* husband?"

"No one else's," she said, adding, "I have never meddled with a married man." It was a frail claim to virtue, but all she had.

"I thought you had decided on Villiers," Corbin said.

"No." She didn't say that it was a near miss.

"Your *husband*. I don't even have the faintest idea what to advise you. I am shocked. Husbands are so—so—"

"Uninteresting."

"Of course, Beaumont is all that is admirable."

Jemma sighed. "I know." She picked up the chemise gown and held it against her body, looking in the glass.

"Essential to the future of the country, from what I hear."

"Tedious."

"I didn't say that! He holds deep moral beliefs, of course."

"He's my opposite," Jemma said dismally. She threw the chemise dress back on the bed.

"How clever of you to recognize it," Corbin said. "Life is so much more interesting when people understand how angels and devils differ. I hear His Grace is most sincere in the House. You can—" He hesitated. "—I believe you can trust *everything* he says." He sounded horrified.

"I know, I know," Jemma said, sighing again. "He's a veritable Puritan."

"We need good people," Corbin said firmly. "It's just a pity that they're so—so—"

"Good."

"I expect I feel so only because I myself am quite errant. I have never considered taking a seat in Parliament. Everyone—but *everyone*—wears those snail wigs. The ones with small crustaceans ranked around the ears like soldiers on parade."

"I can easily imagine you in Parliament," Jemma said, moving behind her friend so she could meet his eyes in the mirror over her dressing table. "You're certainly more clever than most of them. I'd much prefer to see you running the country."

He laughed at that. "I hope we are not friends due to some hopeless misconception about my character, Duchess."

"We are friends because you are funny," Jemma said. "And because you tell me the truth if my stockings are at odds with my slippers. And because you gossip cruelly about everyone and pretend to me that you will never do so behind my back."

"It's not a pretense. I can have room for only one

woman in my heart at a moment," he said, "and you are she."

Jemma bent and kissed his cheek. "We are admirably suited." She sat back down next to him.

"Except you are so serious this evening," Corbin pointed out. "So passionate."

"Are we allowed to be serious only about stockings?" she asked.

He thought about that longer than she thought necessary. "I am quite serious about scandal," he offered.

"But never about passion itself?"

He wrinkled his nose but his eyes were sympathetic. "Thank God, infatuation has never forced me into seriousness. A beautiful woman should never be serious, Duchess."

"Why not?"

"It implies that there is something you cannot have. And we who are not as beautiful prefer to believe that you have everything you wish for in life. That is the essence of beauty, after all."

"I feel myself growing plainer every moment," Jemma said. "Perhaps it is the curse of age."

"Age and passion!" Corbin looked faintly nauseated. "I shall have to ask your maid for a drink of brandy if you continue in this vein."

"So I should not wear the chemise gown," Jemma said.

"Absolutely not. In fact, given what you have just told me, the green silk may be a trifle too revealing in the bosom."

"For a husband?"

"For *your* husband," Corbin said. "The duke is . . . " He paused delicately. "Well, were Beaumont a woman, his skirts would be long and his neckline high."

Jemma thought about that and shook her head. "I can't transform into a Puritan wife in order to please Elijah. He'll have to take me as I am."

Corbin paused. "If you don't mind the question, exactly what sort of *taking* do you have in mind?"

"We need an heir," Jemma said.

"Of course. But that need not, in itself, involve passion on your part, and surely no anxiety. Though you might wish to put a bottle of brandy on the night table and take a surreptitious swig now and then."

"I want more than that."

"Thus the quest for passion?" Corbin asked.

"I'm a fool."

"You're not the first, but you set yourself such a difficult task, Duchess."

"You'd better call me Jemma," she said, rather grimly. "You're the only one who knows."

"I won't advertise it and you shouldn't either. So what you need is lessons in making a husband feel passion for his wife."

It seemed impossible, put so bluntly. "I'll wear the green dress."

"Seductive clothing will never work, not—"

"Not for Beaumont." She picked up a rosy ribbon and started wrapping it around one finger.

"If you wear the chemise dress, you'll likely just make him angry. Or embarrassed. After all, such flamboyant clothing is designed to make a man hunger for what he cannot have, and what he cannot imagine. But a husband . . . "

"Precisely."

"You'll have to surprise him," Corbin said. "Show him a side of you that he's never seen."

"I don't have any *sides*," Jemma said despairingly. "I

play chess; he knows that. We play together occasionally."

Corbin groaned. "Like an old married couple?"

"In the library," she confirmed. "While discussing the news of the day." But there was a look in Corbin's eye, a smile. "What?" she asked.

"You have something that he's never seen."

"What?"

"You are a woman with a *past*, Jemma. And better than that, you have a reputation."

She knitted her brow. "He doesn't like my past. And he never liked my wilder parties. Some years ago he paid me a visit in Paris over Twelfth Night. You should have seen his face when I informed him that all the gentlemen were to come to my ball dressed as satyrs! He refused, of course. Every Frenchman wore a satyr's tail, but Beaumont was in a frock coat, precisely as if it were not a masquerade at all."

"Naturally. And I've never heard a breath of scandal attached to the duke."

"He had a mistress, but no one considers that scandalous," she said, dropping the ribbon in a tangled heap back on her dressing table.

"Because it isn't. Mistresses are commonplace. And for a man of Beaumont's character, the presence of such a woman in his life must have been shaming after a time."

Jemma raised an eyebrow.

"They're *paid*," Corbin said. "Paid to play out the fantasies every man has in the back of his mind."

"Fantasies!" Jemma cried, revolted. "He had a regular appointment with her, in his chambers at the Inns of Court, at lunchtime yet. How could that possibly stem from fantasy?"

"That's just business," Corbin said. "He likely made the arrangement before marriage, and simply forgot to change it. How old was the duke when he inherited the title?"

"Oh, quite young," Jemma said. "Haven't you ever heard of the late duke's death? I'm afraid it was quite a scandal at the time."

"Of course! He died *in flagrante delicto* with—was it four women?"

"Two," Jemma said. "Only two. But I gather that The Palace of Salomé catered to rather specialized tastes, and it was the duke's favorite establishment."

"No wonder your husband made his mistress part of his public life," Corbin said. "Where better to prove that his tastes were not deviant than in his own office?"

Jemma's mouth fell open. "Elijah said he loved her," she added in a smallish voice.

"If you challenged him on the subject, he may have said that from rage. But it is very difficult to love someone whom one pays for the most intimate of pleasures. The money kills joy."

"You are rather terrifying," Jemma said, eyeing him.

"I try," Corbin said smugly. "Do you see what I am suggesting?"

"No."

"If you wish to rouse passion in a husband of so many years, I think you will have to show him the side of yourself that you have flaunted only in Paris."

"The chemise dress?" Jemma said, pleating her brow.

"No. That's boldly sexual. For Beaumont, you will have to be imaginative. Playful. Joyful. All the things that never, ever happen in the halls of the House of Lords, and certainly have never happened with his mistress. You need to be spontaneous, naughty, and fun."

"I can't imagine Elijah—"

"Having fun?" Corbin folded his hands. "Neither can I, Duchess. Neither can I. Therein lies your challenge. Oh, and I think he needs to *choose* you."

"Do you mean that I should encourage Villiers?" She wrinkled her nose.

"Perhaps. But I also mean that someone should flirt with the duke, someone as powerful and beautiful as you."

"You cannot be suggesting that I encourage another woman to court my husband!"

He shrugged. "No woman in London would dare do so unless you make it clear that you are uninterested, and frankly, indifference will only serve your cause. No man wants the woman who lies prostrate at his feet." Corbin's eyes drifted down to his feet, as if seeing feminine hands curled pleadingly around his ankles.

"I would never plead," Jemma stated.

"I am merely suggesting that you do not inform the world of your newfound passion. Let the duke come to you. Win your attentions from another man, if possible. Beaumont married at a young age, and for obvious reasons he never indulged in any sort of exuberant naughtiness."

"He did have a young woman pursuing him last year," Jemma pointed out. "Don't you remember Miss Tatlock?"

"The one you called Miss Fetlock? She of the long nose and abrasive intelligence? Please, Jemma. A true rival would have to be someone of your stature in beauty, wit, and status."

"His mistress's name was Sarah Cobbett," Jemma said.

"That speaks for itself, doesn't it? The poor man has experienced nothing but well-meaning intimacies with a woman graced by the name *Cobbett*. I am moved near to tears at the thought of it."

"Are you certain this is necessary, Corbin?"

"Absolutely. The man has never had women vie for his hand before. He will love it, if only because *you* are one of the two."

Jemma thought he might be right. "What makes you so wise?" she inquired.

"I take my pleasure in watching others," he said as a shadow passed over his eyes. "Some of us, like yourself, my dear duchess, fling themselves into the midst of life. Others, myself included, spend their time watching."

"I knew it," Jemma said. "You should be taking up a seat in Parliament and manipulating all the poor people like myself who never take the time to develop wisdom."

She'd never given much thought as to *why* Elijah was tupping his mistress on his desk all those years ago. It was simply the event that tore their marriage asunder, broke her heart and drove her to Paris.

But of course most men did set up their mistresses in houses in the suburbs. They didn't make appointments for them in their offices, appointments that every man working in Elijah's parliamentary chambers must have known about.

Brigitte entered with a silver tray and Champagne glasses.

"Thank goodness," Corbin sighed, accepting his glass. "All this deep thought is making me quite thirsty."

"I've decided on the green," Jemma told Brigitte, standing up so her maid could tie on her panniers.

"Two patches," Corbin said decisively. "A kissing patch near your mouth, and another below your eye."

The watered silk fell over her panniers with the gentle swish. The bodice plumped her breasts and pushed them forward. She raised an eyebrow to Corbin.

"Perfect," he said. "Delectable yet legal. And since you do not clash with my coat, I shall allow myself to stand next to you on occasion."

Jemma smiled at the glass. There was a small tendril of joy in her heart. "Crimson lip color tonight, Brigitte," she said.

"Naughty," Corbin observed.

An hour or so later, that is precisely how she looked. Her curls were powdered and adorned with green roses that glinted mysteriously from their emerald depths. Her eyes laughed above a small patch that drew attention to her crimson mouth. She looked naughty—not overtly available, not scandalous, but mischievous.

"You're perfect," Corbin said, rising to his feet.

"And you're a miracle!" Jemma cried, giving him a kiss.

Corbin's smile was smug. "I have always found it best to create my own entertainments," he remarked. "This evening should be truly interesting, Duchess."

Chapter Two

The Right Hon. William Pitt's country home
Cambridge
March 26, 1784

The Duke of Beaumont had been trying to extricate himself from the Prime Minister's house for the better part of an hour. A group of men, among the most powerful in the kingdom, had spent the last fortnight discussing strategies and laws, ways to thwart Fox's schemes and defeat his proposals, the case for and against every conceivable argument that a man could voice.

Elijah had spent the weeks fighting long hours for the causes he believed just, such as the ongoing effort to halt England's slave trade. He'd won some battles and lost others; it was the nature of politics to weigh inevitable failure against possible gains.

"I will convey your concern to His Majesty," he

said now, bowing before the Prime Minister, the Right Honorable William Pitt. "Tactfully, of course. I agree that it is perilous to hold a royal fete in such proximity to the hulks."

"Tell him that those floating monstrosities were never meant to be prisons," Lord Stibblestich put in. He was a florid man with eyes that glinted from the little caves shaped by his plump cheeks. His body was no more than brawny; his face was bloated in comparison. Even his nose appeared engorged in contrast to his shoulders.

Elijah bit his tongue rather than indulge the impulse to snap at Stibblestich. His Majesty was fully aware that the decommissioned warships anchored in the Thames were never meant to be used as prisons. The hulks were aging warships, as tired and broken down as the English navy.

But the presence of hundreds of criminals housed on those ships was a problem that His Majesty was not yet pleased to face. And in truth, Elijah knew it was the Parliament that should be finding a solution.

"There was an attempted prison break just last week," Stibblestich added shrilly, apparently under the illusion that he was saying something original.

"My butler informs me that your valet is recovering from his stomach ailment," Pitt said to Elijah, ignoring Stibblestich. "I will send him to London as soon as he is able to travel."

"I apologize for the inconvenience," Elijah said. "I know that Vickery is also grateful for your forbearance." He bowed again and turned to go. His carriage would go straight to the king's yacht, the *Peregrine*. Where . . .

Where he was due to meet his wife. Jemma.

Tired though he was, exhausted by a fortnight of late nights spent arguing, trying to get his own party to understand the unethical side of their deliberations, he couldn't wait to be aboard. Tucked into the corner of the carriage, he fell asleep, waking only when the wheels started jolting over London's cobblestones.

He pulled his watch from his waistcoat and glanced at it. He had forty minutes to board or the *Peregrine* would launch without him. The king had a mind to take his revels into the middle of the Thames and then float downstream, the yacht blazing with light and music pouring through the open windows.

At that very moment the carriage lurched and came to a halt. Elijah summoned his patience. London streets were crowded, and obstructions were common.

He waited two minutes before he banged on the roof. "What the devil is going on, Muffet?" he shouted.

"We're through Aldgate, but the street is blocked ahead, Your Grace!" came the shout back from his coachman.

Elijah groaned and pushed open the carriage door. The grooms were off the vehicle and standing at the horses' heads. A crowd was milling about the street, making it hard to see the source of the disturbance. "What's going on?" he demanded, pushing his way to the front.

"We're not entirely sure," Muffet said. "See, Your Grace, they've barricaded Sator Street. And they're still working on the blockade."

Sure enough, entry to the street was barred by a growing wall of furniture, beer barrels, and debris. People milled about cheerfully, handing up a stuffed armchair, ducking out of the way as a barrel came free and bounced around the street. There were a couple of small fires burning to the side, and what looked like a lively trade in baked potatoes.

"Anyone in charge?" Elijah asked.

"Not that I can see," Muffet said. "And Your Grace, it's going to be a proper mess getting ourselves out of here." He jerked his thumb, and Elijah realized that their carriage was merely the first of a tangled mess of carriages streaming in from outside London, now caught inside the city gate. Some people appeared to be backing their carriages, or trying to, but they were hampered by others who had apparently decided to scold their way to the front of the line.

Elijah glanced down at himself. He was dressed in full court attire, as befitted an event held on the king's yacht. His coat was a deep yellow-gold, embroidered with mustard flowers. His buttons were gilded. He would stand out in the crowd like a damned marigold.

He strode toward the flickering but bright light cast from the fires at the foot of the barricade.

The moment he came into the light, the cheerful calls and shouts died. A young man with lank black hair and a mouth like a trout's froze in the very act of hoisting a wardrobe to the top of the barricade. The sturdy fellow hauling it up recovered faster. "Evening!" he shouted down.

"Good evening!" Elijah shouted back. "May I ask for the reason for the barricade?"

"Riots in the city tonight," the man shouted back. He jerked a thumb behind him. "Limehouse ain't never been rioted in, and it ain't going to happen tonight either. We're not letting any of those hellhounds into our houses, nor yet into the square neither."

Elijah eyed the barricade. "It looks remarkably sturdy."

The man beamed. "Like I said, we've never been rioted in yet. I learned me barricading from me pa. We can put it up in under twenty minutes and we does it whenever we thinks it needful. The Watch knows," he added a bit defensively. "They're all back there behind the barricades."

"Is the rioting sure to happen tonight?" Elijah shouted.

"We've never been wrong yet. You'd best get your carriage out of sight. There's many a bastard in these parts would love to snatch those matched grays of yers, yer lordship." He started to haul on the wardrobe again.

"You put that up in twenty minutes?" Elijah bellowed.

"That's right," the man shouted back. He had the wardrobe now, precariously balanced on top of the armchair.

It was going to fall. Elijah moved back. It fell, with a great, splintering crash. Luckily the fish-lipped boy scrambled out of the way.

Elijah cast a glance behind them. The narrow street was entirely blocked by vehicles. Aldgate would be jammed for hours, if not all night.

If there was a riot, he would lose his horses. Unless . . . he eyed the blockade. Minus the wardrobe, it wasn't as high as it might have been. Six feet perhaps. He could smell the riot coming, smell it in the excitement of the men, in the frenzy with which they were piling up furniture, and in the utter absence of children.

"You!" he shouted up at the stout man, who was staring down at the wardrobe and cursing in an extremely creative manner.

"Got no time for chatter matter!" the man bellowed back.

"Get off the blockade. I'm bringing my horses over and my men as well. Clear space on the other side!"

Muffet appeared at his shoulder. "Your Grace, a carriage tried to back through Aldgate and the fool hit the wall and shattered his undercarriage. The way out is entirely blocked. You'll have to climb the barricade. You'll be safe on the other side, and the grooms and I will defend the coach and horses."

"Absolutely not," Elijah said. "I won't leave my men or horses behind. Given the situation on the street behind us, there's likely to be a riot started by this very blockade, if for no other reason. There'll be blood at some point."

"They'll never take down that blockade to let us in," Muffet said.

"They won't—and they can't," Elijah said, examining the complicated maze. It held everything from chairs to dining room tables, all bound together with rope in a haphazard way that looked as if it would take days to untangle.

"Take the horses out of the leads. I'll be damned if I allow them to be lost in whatever riot is about to happen. Pull the carriage over against that building. It'll probably burn, but I don't mind that so much. How many grooms do we have? Two? Send them together. Tell them to climb over that barricade and wait for the horses."

"We can't get the horses through," Muffet protested. "I can defend them, Your Grace. I have my pistols."

"I won't leave you," Elijah said. "And I must be on the king's yacht within the half hour. Take the horses from the coach and we'll get them to the other side."

"You can't mean to jump them!"

"Galileo will have no problem with the barrier, so you'll take him over. I'll go first with Ptolemy."

"It's too dangerous, Your Grace! Neither horse is trained for jumping. What if Ptolemy stumbles?"

"Nonsense," Elijah said. "I don't have time to quibble about it, Muffet. I have to ensure that these horses and yourself are safe, and then get to the yacht before she launches. If Ptolemy makes it over, you should have no problem; Galileo is the stronger horse."

A moment later the coachman returned with both horses. "James grew up in Limehouse," he said, "and he can talk his way through. I've sent him over."

"Good man."

"Your Grace—" Muffet began desperately.

But Elijah was already slicing the leads, cutting them to the length of reins. Then he was swinging up on Ptolemy. "I've an appointment with the duchess," he shouted down at Muffet. "Follow me."

He began backing Ptolemy, to give them enough space to gain speed. He felt like a boy again, riding bareback with Villiers through the meadows behind his estate, leaping anything they could find, turning around, and leaping it again.

Ptolemy was trained to draw a carriage, not be ridden, let alone bareback. He pranced madly, trying to pull his head free. Elijah wound the leads around his right hand and calmed the horse with his left. Once he'd backed as far as he could, he turned the horse's head back toward the barricade. It rose, a tangled maze against the houses, lit by leaping flames.

Ptolemy tried to buck again, but Elijah brought him down. Both horses were beloved and expensive, and he'd be damned if he would sacrifice them to a riot, let alone expose his men to the danger of trying to protect them.

"Steady," he whispered. "Steady."

Then he loosed the reins and Ptolemy leapt forward, obediently dashing straight for the barricade. Elijah judged the distance, accounting for possible defects in his abilities due to the shifting light, reached the exact spot, signaled—

Ptolemy leapt up, powerful rear legs throwing them into the night air. For a moment it seemed as if the snarled furniture was rushing toward them instead of the other way around; Elijah caught sight of a brass pole sticking out at an angle that could impale a horse's stomach. And then they were clearing the furniture, coming down with a hard jolt, a rush of wind, and a sharp snap of his teeth.

James was there, reaching up for the leads. Elijah tossed him the reins. "Keep them safe," he told the footman, who was quickly pulling Ptolemy out of the way so Muffet and Galileo could join them.

"It'll be no problem, Your Grace," he said, tugging his hat. "There's a mews just two streets over."

"I thought they were blocking a *square*?"

"Oh no, sir. They'll be barricading all of Limehouse, with a good eight thousand souls inside. Limehouse doesn't welcome strangers. It's known for that. Everyone who lives here knows that it's safe. See, there's the Watch."

Sure enough, London's finest were warming their hands over a fire. "I need to get to the Thames," Elijah told James, just as Muffet landed behind him, Galileo having sailed over the barricade with no problem at all. "I don't have the faintest idea where we are."

James chewed on his lower lip. "You'll have to go out by the barricade at Bramble Street," he said. "I'll give the horses to Muffet, Your Grace."

"You needn't—"

"You'll never make it without me," James said. "These streets aren't like the ones you're used to, Your Grace. They're scrambled up and people like it better that way. It's not far, but it's messy."

Elijah followed the footman from one knotty little street to another. There was a holiday spirit inside the barricades. The windows were all open, and people spilled out of the narrow tip-tilting houses, singing songs in a cant dialect that Elijah couldn't follow, shouting things to each other. They fell silent when they saw him, but not in a unfriendly way.

For the night, their enemies were not the rich, like himself, but the violent. The riot held everyone's attention, from the old men sitting outside boasting of foregone days and foregone barricades, to the young women frying up sausages in a lively trade.

Elijah had a strange, sudden wish that Jemma was with him. His expensive, delicious duchess would enjoy this strange evening. She would love to be following him through these streets.

The barricade at Bramble Street was a better one than the first. It was intricate but ordered. Men were handing up long pointed objects.

"What the devil are those?" Elijah asked.

"Spears," James said, weaving his way through the excited crowd toward the looming barricade.

"Spears? *Spears?*"

"They'll have a few guns, but in the dark, spears are a better deterrent. Though no one has attacked a Limehouse barricade in some twenty years. You'd have to be mad to do so," James said. "Stark mad, so most rioters hove off in other directions. It makes the men around here quite disappointed, really. They keep extending the barricade, in the hope that someone will prove foolish."

"How are we going through?"

The footman grinned, his face wild in the leaping firelight. "You'll see," he said.

It wasn't until they were in the shadow of the barricade that Elijah realized that there was, in fact, a small trickle of people making their way through a man-shaped hole in the bottom. "They'll only block the hole when they get word that the riot has started," James said, worming his way through the people. "Make way!" he shouted. "It's a duke here. Make way!"

Elijah felt like a fool, walking through the crowd in his brocade—not to mention his high heels and wig—but that was life as a duke. He'd resigned himself long ago to looking and acting in ways that most men found incomprehensible and that he, in the inner sanctum of his study, often found just as foolish.

He strode along, the heavy silk of his coat swinging around him, and the people fell back, letting him pass.

"We'd best make hurry," James said, almost pushing him through the hole. "They say it'll start soon."

"How on earth do they know?" Elijah asked. He checked his pocket watch. The yacht had taken up anchor. But he couldn't—*wouldn't*—miss his appointment with Jemma.

"They know," James said. "There's the Thames, Your Grace. I'll just ask one of the mudlarks about a boat. Wait a moment."

Some minutes later Elijah sent James back to guard the horses, in the unlikely event that one of the barricades failed, and he climbed into a rowboat owned by a man with the less than inspiring name of Twiddy.

Even hadn't he known of the Limehouse blockades, he could have guessed that something was afoot in London. Fires burned all over the city: not huge, uncontained fires, but small glowing ones, the kind that crowds of men gathered around to warm their hands, to talk and gossip.

Twiddy was a tired-looking fellow in a ripped coat who seemed to have only half his mouth at his disposal, since the other half was frozen by a nasty scar that split his face in two. "You're wanting the king's big boat," he said now, out of the right side of his mouth.

"Yes," Elijah said. "That is correct."

"Riots'll start any minute," the man said. His face seemed to sneer, though it was perhaps only because the left side was immobile.

Elijah thought of asking whether the authorities had been notified, and dropped the idea. They'd be dunces not to have noticed, even if they weren't officially informed. *Oh, by the way, Mr. Constable, sir, there's a riot due to start at ten o'clock tonight.*

He would make his way onto the *Peregrine*, inform the captain of the impending riots, and manage to get the yacht steered to a safe place. Then he would take his wife, bring her safely home, and that would be that. London could—nay, London undoubtedly *would*—burn, but if he could save Jemma, it would be enough.

That was what his world had shrunk to: from his grand plans for the poor and the disenfranchised, to a desperate desire to be home in bed. With his wife.

Twiddy pulled up his oars. "The yacht's gone toward the Tower of London," he said.

Elijah leaned forward. "The royal yacht?"

"It's down where the hulks are."

"Then make all speed after it."

Twiddy shook his head. "I can't do that, Yer Grace." He bent over and spat into the dark water lapping greasily at the small boat. The only light came from a torch burning at his back, affixed to the prow.

"I will pay you double," Elijah said, realizing the moment the words left his mouth that he'd made a mistake.

Sure enough, the man's face darkened and the immobile left lip pulled savagely down. "I stand to be arrested if I goes near the hulks, and I can't do it. Not for yer gold, not for nothing. I got two daughters at home."

"My wife is on that yacht," Elijah said. "Why will you be arrested?"

He spat again. "I'm demobbed."

A former soldier, Elijah translated. Which explained the damage to his face, but not why he couldn't venture near the hulks.

"Iffen a former soldier even goes near the hulks, they shoot him," Twiddy said. "Because it's me friends on those boats. Me brothers-in-arms. I stood with them, out there, and now they're shut up worse than chickens in a coop. I don't do nothing with the riots."

"The riots are coming from the hulks? Tonight?"

But Twiddy hadn't meant to reveal that, clearly, and his face closed like a trap.

"I must get to that yacht," Elijah said. "I will personally guarantee that you are not thrown in jail. I am the Duke of Beaumont, one of the highest in the land. *I must get my wife off that ship!*"

Twiddy stared at him, the left side of his face twitching slightly.

"I have a large estate in the country. If you wish, I will employ you there, and your children and wife can come with you."

"Wife's dead," he grunted.

"Then your daughters will be all the better for fresh country air and safety," Elijah said. "You sound like someone raised in the dells. Look about you, man! Is this the place to raise children?"

"Are you askin' me if I *choose* to raise my girls here?"

Elijah cursed himself silently. For someone with a reputation for a silver tongue, he was certainly awkward tonight. "I'll take you out of this," he said, sitting back. His heart was thumping in his chest, and he didn't want to think about that. "I'll take you to the country and give you decent work for decent pay. But you must get me to that yacht, and get myself and my wife off it."

"How's we to do that? Likely they aren't going to let someone like me draw up alongside the king's yacht. Not on a night like this."

"They don't know," Elijah said. "They don't know about the riots, or they've decided to ignore them."

Twiddy spat again.

Elijah felt like spitting too, but dukes didn't spit, and it was too late in life to start. A second later Twiddy picked up his oars and started silently moving them upstream again. He stuck close to the banks as they turned into the main cleft, clearly unnerved by the great floating prison ships anchored in midstream. There were redcoats on all the decks, Elijah was glad to see. Perhaps they would head off the riots.

They tooled silently along, the drip from the oars drowned out by the frequent howling shouts coming from the shore.

"It's up ahead," Twiddy finally said with a grunt.

Elijah leaned forward, braced on the gunwale, and

caught sight of the golden pearl that was the *Peregrine*. From this distance it seemed to be a glistening dream from a fairy tale, shimmering from the touch of a magic wand. But between them and the yacht floated two broken-down hulks, prisons for men who rotted in chains.

"Most of them don't live the first year," Twiddy said. It was like a curse under his breath.

Elijah had argued against the hulks for years now. "In fact, one-fourth die in the first three years," he said.

Twiddy's oars froze. "You know about them? I thought none of you even thought about them."

"I fought for a bill against using the hulks as prisons. I lost."

"A bill." He spat.

"In the House of Lords."

They drifted slowly past the first ship. The decks were thronged with guards. Clearly they, if not the king, knew about the impending riots, though whether they would be able to stop the conflagration hitting their own boat was debatable. One more ship lay between Elijah and the yacht.

Twiddy was edging along the shore, so close that reeds bent into the rowboat and brushed past Elijah's elaborate coat. *"Hist,"* he said, so quietly that his voice was just another shush from the reeds.

Elijah looked. The last hulk had no redcoats on the deck. It wasn't thronged with marauding prisoners either, though.

"Empty," Elijah breathed.

Twiddy shook his head. His oars came up and Elijah saw that his hands were shaking. Elijah took off his signet ring and handed it to Twiddy. They both stared down at the sapphire; it caught the light of the torch and sent back a flare of blue fire.

"Bring it back to me if we're separated," Elijah said. "Tell them it's my pass if you're caught."

Twiddy's hand closed on the ring and it disappeared into his clothing.

They were almost past the hulk, sliding up to the king's yacht on the far side. Music spilled from the deck and Elijah could see brilliantly colored forms meeting and separating. He watched as a plump woman laughed, tilting her head so far back that her tall wig was in danger of toppling.

Twiddy steered to the side of the yacht and threw a rope up to a servant, who reeled it in after a quick look at Elijah. "I'll fetch the duchess," Elijah said. "She'll see it as an adventure. We'll continue on—"

At that moment the yacht lurched, as if a giant hand had lifted it slightly into the air and thrown it back down.

"It's started," Twiddy said with a harsh gasp of air.

The black, silent prison ship, the one that had appeared devoid of life, had broken free of its moorings, struck the *Peregrine,* and rebounded away.

Elijah gave a mighty heave and pulled himself onto the deck. "Two minutes!" he shouted, looking down at Twiddy. The footman had run off, so he tied the rope from Twiddy's bark to the gold-plated railing and plunged into the throng of screaming nobles.

His heart was pounding and he forced himself to walk rather than run. Where was Jemma? He saw many he knew: one of the royal dukes; Lady Fibble fainting in the arms of her husband; Lord Randulf looking particularly idiotic, with his wig knocked askew.

He had to peer around high piles of white curls,

looking for his wife. She might wear roses and jewels in her hair, but never sailing ships or replicas of bridges.

There she was. On the other side of the crowd milling at the railings, waiting calmly. She must believe that there had been a small accident, he thought. But in his gut he knew that the silent, dark prisoners' warship, now coming closer to the yacht, wasn't accidentally drifting in the Thames.

Jemma was at the very end of the line to board the small boats for shore, her eyes searching the deck. Looking for him.

Then he was running toward her, twisting through the crush of people. They were flooding to the railing, which made it easier. The king's servants were lowering boats. He caught sight of His Majesty with a boatful of laughing courtiers, being rowed to shore, and still the hulk drifted closer.

Then he had her, gave her one hard kiss and pulled her back to the railing where Twiddy was waiting. The hulk was almost on the boat again. Noblemen were laughingly filling the boats that had come out from shore to rescue them, paying no attention to the seemingly dead ship.

"Why—Why, Elijah," Jemma said, breathlessly.

He picked her up and dropped her into Twiddy's hands as if she were no more than a load of laundry. Then he vaulted the railing himself and landed in the back of Twiddy's boat. There was no need to give the man orders.

Twiddy had an oar ready to push them away from the yacht. He jammed it back down into the water and threw his whole weight against the current to push them ahead of the two boats as quickly as he could.

"Elijah!" Jemma cried, just as a pistol barked.

"Down!" he shouted, and lunged forward, pushing her into the bottom of the boat and covering her with his body. Twiddy swore under his breath, rowing with all his might and main.

Elijah looked up to see the deck of the hulk thronged with prisoners. Five, or perhaps six, had taken a wild leap onto the deck of the royal yacht. A dilatory nobleman yelled and then fell into the water, making a fine splash. Twiddy gave another great heave, and the span of water between themselves and the yacht grew into a dark well.

Elijah let Jemma sit up. Her hair was tumbling about her shoulders, though she looked as beautiful as ever. The shore was brightly lit now, thronged with the king and his courtiers, with the little boatloads still coming ashore. And on the deck of the *Peregrine*, convicts waved their pistols and roared their defiance.

Twiddy shook his head and looked away, grunting at the force he put into rowing.

"The prisoners," Jemma breathed.

"You could have been hurt," he said. She was so beautiful. It wasn't her golden hair nor the color of her eyes, nor the lush shape of her bosom. It was the way her lips curled, the way her eyes laughed at him, the slender fingers she held out to him. He took her hand and carefully pulled off her glove. Then he pressed her palm to his lips.

The very touch of that small palm against his lips made his heart beat faster than it had while running, while jumping the horse, while diving into the boat.

"Elijah," she whispered, her eyes still on his.

And then she was in his lap, and Twiddy rowed away up the great River Thames while the Duke of Beaumont kissed his wife.

Chapter Three

Jemma looked flushed, happy and excited. More happy than Elijah had seen her look in . . . oh . . . forever. Perhaps since the early days of their marriage.

They didn't show each other joy, not anymore.

And she wasn't happy merely because they were away from the river, and safe on their way home. He caught her off the seat of the hackney and kissed her just because he could. And because the moment when she melted into his arms, when her arms came around his, wasn't anything he remembered from their awkward beddings years ago.

There was only one thought in his mind, beating through his body with the force of a tidal wave. The minute they entered the house, he would carry her up the stairs. The hell with any servants who might be watching. He would take her straight into his bedchamber.

Finally, after years, he was taking his wife. She was his again. His—

"We hardly know each other," Jemma whispered. She was seated on his lap, her head tucked into the curve of his shoulder.

"I do know you. Your name is Jemma, and you are my wife." And soon I mean to know you in another fashion, he added silently.

"We separated for nine years," she said, looking up at him. "We bungled our marriage before. I don't want to rush into this. It's important."

He bent his head and nipped her lip. "I promise you that I *never* rush."

She gurgled with laughter at that, and then fell silent again when he took her mouth with all the urgency in his heart. Time was finally on his side, had finally brought them together. It felt more important than life, even than death—

She interrupted that thought. "I've decided that we need to spend more time together. Almost as if we were courting, if that makes sense." He couldn't tell her . . . No. He *wouldn't* tell her.

"I'll woo you," he said, snatching up her fingers for a kiss. A horrifying thought crossed his mind. "Jemma, you're not suggesting that we shouldn't sleep together tonight, are you?" Every muscle in his body froze at the thought.

"No." She said it clearly, meeting his eyes. For all her sophistication, his Jemma was not the sort to banter when the subject was most important.

"Ah." He nuzzled her cheek, letting his voice fall to a seductive timbre. "Where will you be sleeping?"

But two could play at that game. She turned her face, caught his lips, breathed into the secret silence of his mouth. "With you." And then, again, even quieter: "With you."

Her eyes had turned a smoky blue, a color he would gladly look at every day of his life.

His heart stopped for a moment, kept going.

"But I shall woo you, Elijah."

"Women don't woo," he said, not really listening. He was trying to ignore the beating of his heart, as syncopated as the raindrops just beginning to fall on the roof of the carriage.

Her smile sent a flare of heat up his spine. "I have never paid much attention to that sort of rule. I do not need to be wooed, Elijah."

"And I do?"

She nodded. "You do. Could you perhaps take some time for yourself in the next few weeks? Persuade Pitt and the rest of them that the country will survive without your help?"

"I'm won," he said. His voice sounded dark and low. "Consider me wooed and won, Jemma. *Please.*"

She was laughing against his mouth, pulling away. "Not yet."

"I don't have a mistress, Jemma. There's no one to win me from, I promise you."

"It's not that. Though I am glad to hear—"

"Not since you discovered us on my desk," he said, coming out with the somber truth of it. "And no one else either."

Her eyes grew round.

"You see, I decided it was you—or no one." She seemed too stunned to speak. He bit back a smile. "Couldn't we consider me won?"

She cupped his face in her hands. "I'm wooing you because I want it to be different than it was nine years ago. Because you and I, Elijah, we will be together until we're old and gray."

It was one of the great acts of courage in his life to smile at her. "And how does the Duchess of Beaumont woo, when she puts her mind to it?"

"That remains to be seen," Jemma said. "I used to enjoy receiving poetry, but somehow I can't see myself breaking into verse. Perhaps we'll start with chess. We have a game left to play in our match. Don't you remember?"

The carriage was swinging around the corner. They would be home in a moment. Blood thrummed through his body with a dark promise of pleasure.

He forced himself to sound light rather than desperate, laughing rather than lustful. "How could I not? You owe me a last game. I seem to remember that there were a few rules attached to that game."

"We're to play blindfolded," she said. He could hear the faintest tremor of desire in her voice, just the promise of huskiness. But he meant to make her cry aloud with pleasure, grip his shoulders, beg for more.

"Blindfolded and in bed," he said slowly, tracing a pattern on her knee. He felt as if his fingers burned through her skirts, as if he caressed the pale perfection of her thigh instead of just rumpling her gown. "An unusual style of wooing, Jemma. But I like it."

"I believe you'll enjoy my wooing," she said, her voice as smug as a little girl with a pocket full of boiled sweets. "Perhaps I'll let you steal my pawns."

He was too hungry to consider her teasing, even to care about it. The carriage was finally, finally, coming to a halt. He curbed himself, drawing on years of self-control practiced in front of the House of Parliament. Of course he wouldn't throw his wife on a bed and leap on her like a wild dog.

Jemma left the carriage before him, bending down

to avoid striking her head on the door. Her bottom swayed for a tantalizing moment in the doorway of the carriage. Even given the absurd panniers she wore, the rounding of silk at her rump made him reckless, drunk with the need to touch her. He was in the grip of a raging passion that threatened to turn him into a man that he didn't recognize.

He didn't recognize her either.

In the flick of an eyelash she lost that edge of sensuality and hunger he saw in the carriage. She greeted Fowle at the top of the steps, looking regal, as if she hadn't just been rescued from a yacht at the very moment of disaster. As if she was as cool and uncaring as any other duchess out for tea.

Elijah took the steps two at a time. Jemma glanced over her shoulder at him as she handed her gloves to a footman. "I was just telling Fowle that Mr. Twiddy will be arriving tomorrow to—"

Since he'd lost his mind, he backed straight into the drawing room, grabbing her wrist and swirling her with him, slamming the door in his butler's face.

"Elijah!" Jemma said, sounding amused. "I assure you that—"

He swooped on her. Took her mouth with all the desperate wish he had to claim her, to make her *his*. In every sense of the word. He possessed her mouth, kissed her savagely, with all the fear he felt when he saw her on the *Peregrine*, standing there unprotected, without him. Anything could have happened to her. Anything.

"You're mine." His voice had nothing in common with a statesman's even tenor. It was deep, savage, knowing.

"I—"

He took her mouth again, stealing her words, telling her silently that she had no choice, that he would be the one to pleasure her, that the danger they had just gone through was only a shadow of what would happen if she ever tried to push him away.

"I let you go, years ago," he said.

"Yes," she gasped. Her voice had a breathy catch in it, an echo of desire that reverberated deep in his body.

"I will *never* let you go again." His voice grated with the truth of it.

She looked shocked. He didn't give a damn. Then she started smiling, and something deep inside his heart relaxed. That was a wicked smile. There was anticipation there . . .

"You can woo me tomorrow," he said, voice guttural, unrecognizable. "Tonight is another kind of event altogether."

She had been shocked but was recovering herself now. "So no chess?" Her pout said that she knew precisely what her deep bottom lip did to him.

"Jemma." He said it low and soft. His heart was dancing a wayward rhythm, and urgency gave his voice an edge.

"I must take a bath!" she said, laughing. He had her backed against the door, hunkering over her like a great beast.

"No."

"Indeed, Elijah, I must insist. I have been thrown into a boat and splashed with river water. I am . . . " She paused and gestured with mock horror. " . . . not myself." Vulnerability glimmered deep in those exquisite eyes of hers.

"You'd be beautiful to me if you were bathed in

mud," he said. "Let's call for the bath and I'll act as your maid."

Even in the dark, with no light other than that filtering through the windows, he could see a stain of color in her cheeks. "I bathe alone, always."

He bent closer. "After tonight I shall know every nook and cranny of your body, Jemma." His voice roughened. "Bathing will just hasten the process."

"You have a great deal of confidence in yourself," she said, looking a bit uncertain, not like the arrogant duchess who had ruled Paris with her wit and beauty.

He smiled. "You see? You're getting to know me better already. There's no need for a courtship between us."

But his wife was no malleable young miss. She pulled back. "I will welcome you in my bedchamber in one hour, Duke."

He couldn't protest again. They weren't children. His Jemma might have taken a lover or two in Paris during the years they were apart, but clearly she had granted the poor Frenchmen no real intimacies.

So he kissed her again. With all the knowledge he had that she was the only woman for him, that she'd been so for years.

With the knowledge that time was not his friend, and that if she took too long to woo him, he wouldn't be there for their last kiss.

Chapter Four

Jemma found it hard to formulate sentences, though luckily her maids were so excited about the riots that they didn't notice in the midst of their chatter.

One moment she was starkly terrified, and the next moment her whole body flushed with heat. It felt as if she faced a slide into some sort of delicious madness, a kind of wild state in which one had no concern for what others thought. She had an idea that Elijah was already there. Thinking of Fowle's startled face when Elijah slammed the door almost made her laugh aloud.

She was still in her bath when she heard a discreet knock. Brigitte bustled back into the room a moment later, her eyes shining. "We should finish your bath, Your Grace. The duke is requesting that you join him for a light supper in his bedchamber. The meal is already served and he has dismissed his valet for the night."

Brigitte's voice betrayed her excitement. For a

second all three maids froze, and then rushed into chatter about inconsequentials. Jemma rose and allowed herself to be toweled off. How strange it was that four women would all understand exactly what was to happen tonight and still say nothing of it.

The maids knew, of course, that she and Elijah had not slept together for years. They likely knew that she had returned from Paris due to the duchy's need for an heir; they almost certainly knew that she had a foolish infatuation for her husband.

Brigitte drew a nightgown from the wardrobe and held it up for approval. She had chosen Jemma's most extravagant, most French, most utterly delicious garment. It was made of a rosy silk so thin as to be translucent. The neck fell very low, and was embroidered with a thick tangle of red roses that called attention to her breasts.

She nodded, and Brigitte slipped the gown over her head. It followed the curves of her body and then flounced into a tiny train at her feet.

"I'll put roses in your hair," Mariette said, wielding a hairbrush like a sword.

"That seems rather elaborate," Jemma said.

"Just a rose or two." The maid smiled with a Frenchwoman's suggestive charm. "Nothing more than a little one tucked here or there."

Jemma looked in the glass and felt, not for the first time in her life, a bone-deep gratitude for her beauty. As an intelligent person, she had never allowed herself to fall into the trap of thinking that beauty made her a person of greater worth.

But if one had to face appallingly frightening—and yet exciting—events, it helped to be beautiful. It gave one backbone. Her hair fell in lazy honey-colored waves down her back, and the little roses gave her the look of a wanton matron prancing off to some sort of pagan holiday. The kind that involved spring woods and satyrs, Jemma thought, seeing the pink high in her cheeks.

"Quite nice," Brigitte said, coming forward again. "A patch, perhaps? Just one?"

"I am preparing for bed, not a ball," Jemma protested.

But Brigitte wasn't listening. "Just there," she murmured, pressing a small velvet patch just above the corner of Jemma's mouth. "The *bisous*—the kissing patch. And a touch of lip color."

Jemma reached for her favorite pot of color, but Brigitte presented her with another. "More rose than crimson this evening, Your Grace."

It truly was a strange life, one in which her maids dictated the color of her lips and the flowers in her hair. She turned and gave them a huge smile. There was no need to speak, after all. They were servants *and* friends, and in their eyes she read the hope that her evening would be a pleasurable one.

"I suppose," she said, "that I should join His Grace before our meal cools. You may all retire for the night."

They curtsied and left, unspoken encouragement floating in the air behind them.

Jemma took a deep breath. Now it came down to herself and Elijah. Their marriage had been an embittering, desolate thing so far. But it had changed—and they had changed. The night could be one of joy.

And tenderness. She had learned in their years apart that while pleasure was desirable, tenderness was far more rare, and far more valuable.

She straightened her shoulders and opened the door to her bedchamber.

Elijah came awake all of a sudden. He always did. The slide into unconsciousness was like drifting into darkness. Generally when he woke after one of these spells, it was to find himself staring into the frightened face of someone who thought he was dead. That was a bracing sensation.

Then he would find his heart beating wildly in his chest, trying, one had to assume, to catch its rhythm again, keep itself going.

When he had fainted in front of the House of Lords, he had woken to find a shocked Lord Cumberland shaking him. The Duke of Villiers had actually slapped him on finding him in the library. Once he awoke in an armchair to find Fowle shouting in his ear. The butler had backed away, dull red rising in his cheeks.

But this was the worst.

Jemma's face was utterly drained of color. Her fingers, wrapped around his wrists, were trembling.

"I'm so sorry," he said, after a moment.

"Oh my God." Her voice wobbled like a child's. "Please, tell me this is a bad dream."

He managed a smile.

"It's your heart," she said. "Your heart . . . your heart is faltering, just as your father's did."

"I'm not dead, Jemma. I'm almost accustomed to these spells now. I could live for years like this, fainting occasionally."

He lifted his hands, and her fingers fell from his wrists. She was kneeling by his chair, just where she must have thrown herself. Elijah put a hand on her hair and a small rose tumbled into his lap. Like the roses one throws into the grave at funerals, he thought with a wrenching twist of self-pity.

She still hadn't moved. "Oh God, Elijah, this can't be happening."

"I didn't know how to tell you." Her hair was warm, thick and springy against his fingers.

"How long have you known?"

"Since I fainted in the House last year."

"But—we—"

He wrapped a hand behind her neck and gently pulled her toward him. "Come."

"Don't exert yourself!" she cried, terrified.

"There's no need to fear that. The attack is over." He reached down and scooped her up, sitting back with his wife curled into his lap.

"I can't believe it!" she said a moment later. "I won't believe it. You're so young and we were going to have children and grow old together."

He put his cheek against her hair. "Life should not be measured by time. The only thing that counts is how one uses the time one has."

"You knew before last year, before you summoned me home from Paris, didn't you?" she asked suddenly. She was shivering in his arms as if a frigid wind were blowing through the room.

"My father died at thirty-four. I'd have been a fool not to question my ability to live much over that date."

"When did you understand that?"

"When I was eight years old."

"No, no." She was moaning it, her hands clutching his shirt.

"It drove me," he said. "It was a passion, to make sure that my life came to something."

"Because your father's didn't."

"He had no time. I hated him for a while. But then I realized that he hadn't my advantage. He had no idea. He was young; he might have proved himself a man had he lived another forty years."

"Life allowed him to be foolish. Oh, Elijah, you never had the chance to be foolish. I'm just so—so sorry."

They were silent a moment. Jemma's eyes were dry, and fierce, like those of a mother hawk. "If you die before me . . . Well, whenever you get to where you're going, Elijah, you sit down and wait for me."

He laughed at that. "What do you envision? A bridge?"

"I'm thoroughly unimaginative. But I want to find you waiting for me."

"I will wait for you," he said, kissing her again.

She swallowed. "Does it hurt?"

"You mean, when I fall asleep?"

"That was no sleep," she said. "But yes."

"Not at all. It generally happens when I sit down. It's as if the darkness just gathers itself up and comes over me. There's just a little pain when I wake up, that's all."

"Your heart?"

"It works hard to bring me back. And it does bring me back, Jemma. In that sense, the attacks are no worse than they were a year ago: I wake up every time."

"Don't be so brave," she said, her hands moving quickly. "I can't bear it; I can't bear it."

He put a hand on her cheek but didn't know what to say. Words came to him easily when he was in front of the House of Lords. But he became tongue-tied at the most important moments of his life, and all of those were with his wife.

"There's nothing to be done, Jemma. I shall just live until I can't anymore. People die unexpectedly every hour." Unfortunately, his attacks were always followed by a headache, and he could feel its iron grip tightening.

"I don't believe you when you say it doesn't hurt, Elijah. Your eyes are tight."

"I have a headache. Fowle has something for it."

She was up in a flash, ringing the bell for his valet. "Fowle knows?"

"I meant to tell you. Eventually."

"Who else?"

"Vickery."

"And Vickery didn't tell me!"

"I wouldn't allow it. Villiers."

"You told *Villiers* and not—"

"No. He found me one day, in the library." Elijah stood with some difficulty, given that his head felt as if it were a blacksmith's anvil, pounded by blows from a sledgehammer.

"Sit down," Jemma said. She came back and pushed him a little. "You shouldn't be up."

"Physical exertion is necessary," Elijah told her, brushing her mouth with his. "I have lived past my father's life span because I am fit."

"How do you know when an attack is likely to happen?"

"I have begun to entertain the idea that they result from moments of sudden, great exertion. The time I fainted in the House, for example, I felt passionately angry about my subject. And this evening, when I saw you on the yacht, I was so alarmed that my heart lost its rhythm."

"You must stop being so exhausted." Her eyes brightened. "You could stay in bed!"

Elijah smiled wryly. "That's not a cure, but a prison. The attacks don't happen constantly, Jemma. I likely won't have another one for a week." He rolled his head from side to side, trying to ease the pressure that clamped his forehead. "I've found that taking exercise is very helpful. If my heart begins to beat irregularly, I can head off an attack by going for a ride. Forcing my heart into a regular rhythm helps it remember the correct pattern."

He looked down at her. "I have every belief that marital intimacy will achieve precisely the same effect."

But she just scowled at him. "Have you seen a doctor?"

"There's no point to that."

"I don't agree!" she said hotly.

"No one's found a cure for a broken heart," he said. "Not in any sense of the word."

She did cry then, and he found himself cursing his heart, not for the fact that it was broken, but for its ability to break other hearts.

Chapter Five

March 27

Jemma rose the next morning with the emptiness that follows grief. The night before, she had forced Elijah to drink a posset, and then left. She had returned to her room, plucked a few wilted roses from her hair, washed her face, changed into a nice cotton nightdress—and cried for hours.

Not that crying did any good. She came to only one conclusion: Elijah *must* leave his work with Pitt. The unremitting work and frantic pace could not be good for his health.

Likely Elijah was right in his assessment that he wasn't going to die today or tomorrow. But if he dropped the frenzied pace and the extraordinary hours of work generated by the House of Lords, he might be alive in a year. Or five years. Or . . .

She dressed carefully, avoiding Brigitte's eyes. The

household knew of their master's heart problem now, of course. There was a distressed silence perceptible in the very air.

Elijah wasn't in the breakfast room. When Fowle announced that His Grace had been summoned to an emergency meeting at the chief magistrate's office, Jemma felt rage swell into that empty place in her heart.

"Did the duke leave a note?" she asked, and knew the answer already, of course.

Fowle cleared his throat. "Since the messenger came at dawn, His Grace merely asked me to give you his most sincere apologies."

Elijah was killing himself. And for *what*? So the government of England would run more smoothly for one day, or even a week?

"He was not entirely certain what time he would be able to return," Fowle continued, laying a carefully ironed copy of the *Morning Post* before her.

It was absurd to feel this angry at Elijah. And yet— how could he simply leave without a word, after what had happened last night? What if he died during the day? Would he leave her without a kiss, without a word? Realizing that thought would just lead to tears, she cut it off.

"My husband said he wouldn't be home for the evening meal, didn't he, Fowle?" she asked, hearing the peculiar deadness of her own voice.

"I'm afraid that His Grace did indicate the possibility that he would not return until late tonight," Fowle replied, jumping straight to another subject with the adroitness of an experienced butler. "The duke left instructions with me about sending Mr. Twiddy to Swallowhill, should that person present himself today.

The butler at Swallowhill has told me of the difficulty he has retaining garden laborers. I am sure he will be grateful for the help."

So Elijah had not forgotten Twiddy, though he appeared to have forgotten his wife. Anger burned in Jemma's chest.

The butler put down another paper. "I have also the *Morning Chronicle*, Your Grace. They are comparing the riots to the Gordon Riots four years ago. Though thank the Lord, there were fewer casualties and the Clink is unharmed."

Elijah had looked so exhausted last night. He was utterly delectable even tired, of course. His dark eyebrows and dark eyes emphasized his cheekbones, giving him the raw beauty of a marble statue of a Roman statesman. Or perhaps it was the expression in his eyes: all that serious passion in the service of good had chiseled his face.

If he had been in the room, Jemma would have screamed at him like a common fishwife.

Couldn't he be selfish for once? He *must* give up his seat in the House of Lords. Corbin was right, though for the wrong reasons. Elijah needed to enjoy himself, rather than get up at dawn and leave for pressured meetings about riots and floating prisons.

She stared blindly down at the paper, reading one sentence over and over again. It was the beginning of a piece about a hoax carried out near St. Paul's Cathedral. *Convinced that the devil had taken up residence in his sitting room, Mr. Bartlebee gave a conjurer a gold chain to exorcise the unwanted guest,* she read. And then read it again.

And then finally moved on to the next sentence. *Mr. Bartlebee's son Jeremy was equally convinced of the devil's presence . . .*

How could they have children now? When Elijah was a child he had had white-blond curls, which implied that their children might have had the same. A darling young boy with Elijah's beauty and his serious eyes drifted in her mind's eye. Her throat tightened and she turned back to her buttered toast.

There was nothing she could do—*nothing*. The knowledge was bitter in the back of her throat. Even the idea of playing chess felt horrible, like fiddling as Rome burned. She was desperate to find a plan, something she could do to help.

The only thing she could come up with was paltry indeed. If her husband didn't have very long to live, then it was up to her to make certain that he enjoyed every moment. That meant following Corbin's plan. Wooing Elijah. Winning him from another woman. Or was Elijah supposed to win *her* from another man?

She found herself staring at the account in the paper again. Given the lingering smell of sulfur, the constable asserted that a devil of some sort had paid a call to the sitting room.

She could not flirt with another man merely so Elijah could win her. The falseness of it curdled in her stomach. Even if he had cheerfully jaunted off to work, without even bothering to leave her a note, she could not flirt with someone merely for fun. Surely she could orchestrate a seduction—or an attempted seduction—of Elijah. There was only the matter of determining her rival. He knew all the English ladies of her acquaintance, and anyway, they were—

She froze, the toast halfway to her mouth.

For the eight years that she lived in Paris, she had had one great rival, the Marquise de Perthuis. Their sparring matches were known throughout the city.

They competed against each other in fashion, in dress, and in manner. They excelled at insulting each other under the mask of an apparent compliment.

The marquise was now in England, and Elijah hardly knew her. Louise was consummately witty, but not so beautiful that she made Jemma's liver curl. The question was only how to drive the marquise to Elijah's side.

It wasn't an easy proposition. The marquise cherished her milk-white reputation. Jemma knew it wasn't for the sake of virtue itself; Louise was so besotted by her loose fish of a husband that she likely never even looked at another man.

The only way Louise would dance to her tune would be out of rage. That posed a challenge: to convince the marquise to attempt a seduction of Elijah, without that lady having the faintest idea of her intentions. It would be a fiendishly difficult task. Machiavellian, really.

Jemma finished her toast, forcing herself to read the paper's account of the prisoners' riot. Before recapture, the prisoners had burned a number of houses, though they were barred from a large area of the city due to the forethought of the citizens, who had defended themselves by erecting impenetrable barriers.

The *Morning Post* issued a challenge to the mayor of London and to Pitt's cabinet: How had it come to pass that common citizens had to defend themselves, using brooms and trash cans? Why wasn't the Queen's Royal Regiment called in to quell the violence of these criminals?

Jemma couldn't bear to read any longer. It just made her think of the speeches Elijah would undoubtedly be called upon to make in the House. She threw the paper aside and rose.

"I must be at my most elegant," she told Brigitte a moment later. "I shall go to visit the marquise. I caught a glimpse of her on the king's yacht last night, so I know that she is currently in London."

Brigitte's eyes widened and she set to work with the concentrated fervor of a lady's maid whose work would be judged by the best—her rival *femme de chambre*. A few hours later Jemma tripped into the marquise's drawing room, fit to dine with Queen Marie Antoinette herself.

She was wearing, unusually for her, a wig. Unlike the rather tatty and (she felt) dirty wigs that she commonly saw in ballrooms, hers was made of white curls so delicate that they shone like spun sugar in the morning sunlight. They rose to an exuberant height, but rather than supporting an entire birdcage with its songbird or anything of that ridiculous nature, Mariette had simply tucked a few pale blossoms among the curls.

With it she wore an exquisite morning gown of the same pink as the blossoms, the skirts caught back to show a deeper, rosy underskirt with a border of amber gold. The *pièce de résistance*, to Jemma's mind, was her shoes: delicate high-heeled slippers in rose-colored silk, with tiny gold buckles.

She had been seated a mere twenty minutes before the marquise appeared. Jemma rose, dropping into a short curtsy. It was a signal honor, indicating that she was overlooking their difference in rank. The marquise fell into a deeper curtsy, the sort that recognized the delicate compliment Jemma had just given her, and topped it with an expression of deep respect.

Finally they managed to seat themselves, on opposing sofas, naturally, given the width of their skirts.

The marquise was even more elegantly attired than was Jemma. As a matter of course, the marquise never wore any colors other than black and white, a rather eccentric notion that complemented her dark eyes and hair. This morning her gown was white and embroidered with elaborate swirls of black silk.

Jemma thought about that costume while they went through the motions of drinking tea and chatting about the riots. Hadn't Elijah once said that the marquise looked like a chessboard?

"How do you find yourself?" Jemma asked, watching the marquise over the edge of her teacup. "The last time I saw you, you were on your way to Lincolnshire . . . " She allowed her voice to trail off in a tactful invitation.

The marquise's eyebrows drew together. "I did locate my husband, or at least where he had been. There was a village where he stayed with this—this *putain* that he followed to England. I made my footmen inquire."

The pained edge to her voice made her humiliation clear. "Apparently he and the woman were together, and then he suddenly left. She stayed a mere day or two longer—"

"At least they are no longer together!" Jemma exclaimed. "He left her."

"Yes." Louise's tone lightened. "The villagers were very clear about that. Henri simply left. He must have been desperate to get away from her; there was some talk that he discarded his clothing in the inn where they were staying, though I don't hold with that notion. Henri is not the sort to travel without proper *accoutrements*. I expect he went back to France."

She picked up a lemon tart. "I found it hard to believe that he ever left France for this woman, even in the throes of the deep *love* he felt." She spat the last sentence.

"Will you follow him across the Channel directly?" Jemma enquired.

"Absolutely not," the marquise said. "Can you imagine? He might think that I pursued him to England because of some anxiety about his degenerate activities." She magnificently ignored the fact that she had followed her husband for just that reason. Instead she gave a careless shrug. "I couldn't be less concerned about what he does, and he is perfectly aware of that fact. I shall stay here for as long as I please. London is an enchanting place, of course."

Jemma translated that statement into a declaration that Louise would stay in London just as long as necessary to assure that her husband dared not question her presence in this country.

It was time for an insult, one ruthless enough to send Louise directly into a towering fury. Jemma shook open her fan and held it so that it covered the lower part of her face, as if she were preparing to say the unsayable. Fans were so useful to the art of the insult. She pitched her voice low and confidential. "My dear marquise, if you'd ever like some guidance in the matter of husbands, you need not do more than ask."

Louise narrowed her eyes. "Advice of what sort, *dear* duchess?"

"It's a mere suggestion," Jemma said. "But have you considered altering your—" She waved her hand as if she couldn't even think of the word.

"My what?"

"We must be frank between ourselves, must we not?" Jemma said, lowering her fan to chin level to bestow a lavish smile. "I mean, of course, between close friends like ourselves."

"*Naturellement*," the marquise said, every inch of her rigid body showing just how much she disliked frankness.

"You wear the most sophisticated costumes in the French court. Your *ensemble* is only equaled by that of Marie Antoinette herself. Your face is always exquisite, your—"

"Exactly so." Coldness sliced through Louise's words.

"And yet." Jemma sighed. "One cannot ignore the fact that you look . . . oh just slightly . . . like a chessboard, dearest marquise. What man wants to sleep with a chessboard? You do not dress like a woman who wants to seduce, but like a woman who wants to impress. To be noticed." Then she added, as a kindly afterthought, "Though you are, of course, a *most* beautiful woman."

Louise appeared to be grinding her teeth.

"My husband never strays," Jemma said, closing her fan. "And why is that, Marquise? Why is that?"

"It certainly isn't because you yourself have remained chaste," the marquise said flatly.

"Alas, that is so true," Jemma said. "So, so, so true. And yet my dearest Elijah never wandered during all the years I lived in France, never even looked at another woman. I wish for nothing more than for you to have the same happiness." Her smile was guaranteed to scrape the marquise's nerves like the squeal of rats in an alley. "Dear friends should always look out for each other's best interests."

"So you believe that Henri took this woman to Lincolnshire because he dislikes my *élégance*?" One had to admire the marquise's command over her voice. She conveyed withering scorn with nothing more than a shading of tone.

It was time to move in for the kill. "My husband," Jemma said, "never, but *never*, looks at another woman. And why is that, my dear marquise? It is not only because my clothing is perhaps, shall we say, just slightly more graceful than your dogged wearing of black and white, but also because I do not wear my heart on my sleeve."

Little white marks had appeared on either side of Louise's nose. "This English term . . . I do not know it. Where is my heart?"

"Out for everyone to see. You never flirt. You stay to the side of a ballroom and gaze at Henri with your heart in your eyes. You—"

"So now my heart is in my eyes?"

"Of course, most people do feel sympathy, though there are always the unkind who mock. You might try to seem a bit indifferent, my dear. A passion so flamboyant is bound to garner pity."

"Ah," the marquise said. "Pity."

"Elijah never looks at another woman," Jemma repeated, a bit worried about whether she was overdoing it.

But the marquise's nails had curled in such a way that strips of delicate paper shredded off her fan.

"*I* know!" Jemma said, sitting up as if suddenly inspired. "You might strive to create a bit of a scandal here in England. Something that would cause a rumor to fly home to Paris, convincing your husband that he is not the only one to enjoy himself with matters of the heart."

Louise gave a savage little laugh. "You don't think

that I should have trouble finding someone willing to overlook my chessboard?"

"Oh, no, no, no," Jemma cried. "You mustn't take me too literally. When you say chessboard, it truly sounds as if I meant you were *flat* in the bodice, and of course I would never say such a thing! I have no doubt but that many men are delighted with a, shall we say, more modest offering." Her eyes gently slid away from the marquise's entirely adequate bosom, as if she were excusing a serious flaw.

She continued, "Of course, women can be so cruel to each other. Why, the other day a bumbling lady of my acquaintance referred to you in the most disparaging terms—she is really hopelessly ill-bred—oh yes, I believe she mentioned a bird. Could it have been a crow?" She gave a shrug. "At any rate, I defended you. I told her that you were the only woman I considered to have the wit and charm to rival the great courtesans."

Louise drew in a sharp breath.

"I mean that as the greatest compliment," Jemma added. "You could have any man you wished. If you put your mind to it."

She paused. "Other than my dear Elijah, of course. He is so *very* devoted."

"I don't care for English men," the marquise said, chomping down on a lemon tart. "For the most part they are quite brutish in their manners. Their bows are too unformed, too unrefined." She waved her hand in the air. "They lack that sense of *élégance* that characterizes the French court. The beauty of the French poise and discretion."

"While your point about elegance is absolutely fair, some Englishmen have a kind of masculine *beauté* that

I find appealing," Jemma said. "I have always thought that my husband, the Duke of Beaumont, looks rather like Gerard de Ridefort, but with less affectation. And you know that Marie Antoinette herself called de Ridefort the most beautiful man in Paris."

"Your husband," Louise said broodingly. "Dear me, I remember the strangest rumor. But I am sure it is no more than that." She opened her fan and waved it just below her eyes.

Jemma shrugged again. "Any scandal that involves the duke is surely untrue."

"I know!" the marquise cried. "'Twas the reason why you moved to France, all those years ago. The foolish man declared himself in love with someone else."

"His mistress," Jemma said, her tone pitched to perfect indifference.

"But what an excellent decision you made to come to Paris. I remember the first year when you arrived; you had no poise, none of the charm that comes with sophisticated taste. And now look at you!" Louise raised an eyebrow. "So much older, and yet still with that sprightly, artless mode of dressing."

"I learned so much in Versailles," Jemma said. "Why, you have no idea how innocent I was. I truly believed that the duke loved his mistress. I can hardly believe that I was so foolish as to flee to another country over a matter as paltry as a husband's lover!"

The marquise took a moment to compose herself. "Dear me, all that agitation for a mistress," she said, fluttering her damaged fan vigorously.

"I was very young."

"How fortunate that you retain your memory. So many people find it difficult to think back over that many years."

"Of course, I am very possessive," Jemma added. "What is mine, is mine. I would naturally consider it the worst of insults if a woman dared to approach my husband. Even though my husband merely *thought* he loved his mistress, I could hardly contain my anger. Very childish of me, I know. In Paris I learned that the way to my husband's heart was to ignore his unrefined behavior."

The marquise picked up her third tart. "I consider mistresses to be part of a man's world, a necessary adjunct, as it were. They parade and trade them the way women might trade fans. They are necessary to their sense of—I don't know the word in English—*amour propre?*"

"Their sense of vanity," Jemma translated. "Yes, I suppose you are right. But I was young and rash, and so I fled to France. Luckily, Elijah quickly learned his lesson. His eyes never stray to other women. I credit that to the fact I went to France and had a few dalliances of my own. He learned that what is sauce for the gander is even better for the goose."

"I fail to see how your dissipated behavior turned him into a saint," Louise said acidly.

"Ah, well," Jemma said. "Just think, Marquise. Your husband has never had to worry that *your* affections were caught by another man, one who would be a worthy competitor to himself. No, he is free to stray about, to fall in love, to act as foolishly as he wishes—confident that you will be at home waiting for him."

The marquise chewed her tart rather savagely. "I would never lower myself to his level!"

"I expect you have never met a man whom you considered his equal," Jemma said soothingly. "I myself am so fastidious about a man's appearance that I could not countenance your husband's adorable way of finishing every scrap of food that strays onto his plate. He has such an appetite! It's admirable in a man, of course," she added unconvincingly.

"Do you dare to suggest that Henri is fat?" Louise inquired.

"Of course not, of course not!" Jemma said. "Why, a man his age *should* have a belly. It shows gravity of purpose. Seriousness. That sort of thing. Please do continue to eat, Marquise. I myself never eat sweet things in the morning."

They both looked down at the plate. "Dear me!" Jemma said. "I hadn't even noticed they were all gone. At any rate, as we were saying, I do admire your husband. He's so modest . . . of course, he has much to be modest about."

There was a rigidity about the marquise's jaw that suggested to Jemma that perhaps she should stop before a plate broke over her head.

She sprang to her feet. "What a lovely conversation this has been. I would give you the name of my mantua maker, but I never share her address, even with my very closest friends. She's by far the best in London, and if I pay her three times the price, she plucks gowns literally out of the air. I've had a gown made for the following day!"

Louise managed a good show of indifference. Of course, half of London knew that Jemma frequented the establishment of Madame Montesquieu, on Bond Street.

"I do hope to meet you again soon, Marquise," Jemma said blithely. "We go to Vauxhall tomorrow night . . . well, I believe I've never seen you there. Do you not care for it?"

"In fact, I had long planned to pay it a visit," the marquise said. "Does one not wear a domino there?"

"Always."

"Then no one would note my odious clothing," Louise said with a marked snap. "I look forward to it."

Rather than curtsy, Jemma delivered the *coup de grâce*. She held out her hand to be kissed.

Of course Louise bent her head over her hand with utmost grace. But her eyes swore revenge. Jemma left smiling.

She couldn't control everything. She couldn't control her husband's erratic heart. Elijah was important to the government and she was important to no one.

But she had her own rather particular skills.

Chapter Six

On the way back from the marquise's house, Jemma remembered that she had one problem left to solve in Francesch Vicent's *100 Chess Problems*. She handed her pelisse to Fowle and headed directly for the library and her chessboard.

"Your Grace," the butler said. "You have callers."

But Jemma was already living inside the game. "I can't talk now, Fowle. I'll just be in the library for a bit."

"Your gloves," the butler said, a wry smile in his eyes.

"Oh," Jemma said, pulling them off.

"The Duke of Villiers awaits," Fowle said, to her back.

She turned about, feeling a pulse of extreme annoyance. "Villiers is here? What on earth is he doing here?"

"The duke paid you a call," Fowle said. "Since the drawing room had a number of ladies waiting in it—and they are still there—he requested to be placed in the library. In front of the chess set."

"Ah," Jemma said, smiling. "I think those callers had better take themselves off, Fowle." She paused for a moment. "Do they know of Villiers's visit?"

"I believe not."

"Excellent!" She turned to the library. "I am suffering from a terrible headache, Fowle. Do give my apologies to all my visitors. And you might bring a light luncheon in an hour or so."

As she walked into the room, the Duke of Villiers rose from the chessboard. Villiers was an odd mix of fashionable and its opposite. He disdained the mania for wigs, wearing his hair tied back in a ribbon, unpowdered of course. And yet he dressed as magnificently as she did.

In some ways, Villiers was the opposite of Elijah. He had none of Elijah's startling beauty: his face was too rough to be courtly, and his eyes too cold to be alluring. He cared nothing for the world's opinion, let alone its salvation. He had never taken up his seat in the House of Lords; as far as Jemma knew, his sole passion was the one she shared: chess.

Jemma actually felt a pulse of envy at the sight of his coat, an emotion rarely inspired by men's attire.

"You've outdone yourself, Villiers," she said, by way of greeting. "Cream silk with interlocking chains in cherry embroidery. I've never heard of such a coat. No, I've never dreamed of such a coat."

Villiers fell into a bow as magnificent as his garment. "I dreamed of it, though my tailor complained. It seems he feared I might become besmirched by dirt or spotted by rain."

She laughed. "Rain would not dare spot His Grace, the Duke of Villiers?"

"Dirt is something that happens to others," he said,

with that wicked laughter in his eyes. "Like sin and bankruptcy."

"Alas, if you hope to avoid the blemish of sin," Jemma said, sitting down before the chessboard, "I am not the one to give you an education."

"But that is one of the things I love about you," he said amiably. "The only thing I am certain about is the art of dress. Since you dress exquisitely on your own, I need not bother with advice. I do like your wig this morning."

"Delicious," Jemma agreed. She was wondering whether to speak to him of Elijah's heart. Better not. She might cry, a truly horrific thought.

She began swiftly rearranging the chess pieces. "The last time I spoke to you, Villiers, you flatly refused to play with me. I hope that your current position opposite me indicates that you have revoked your ban on the game?"

"Your husband tells me that you have decided to forfeit the final game in our match," he said, sighing.

Jemma looked up quickly. "You discussed our match with Elijah?"

"The final game was to be blindfolded and in bed," he said mournfully. "How it pains me to give up the prospect. You can have no idea."

"But I am throwing the match! You win. Surely that makes you just as happy as being blindfolded."

"To my astonishment, I find it does not," he said, looking faintly surprised.

"In that case, I will give you the pleasure of playing a game," she said, promptly putting the pieces in order. "You may be White, as it agrees with your coat."

"My coat is the color of rich cream," he said with a delicate shudder. "Not White. I abhor white silk, and satin of that hue is even worse. It reminds me of angels. Saints. That sort of thing."

"I don't see anything wrong with angels," Jemma observed. "I've always liked the idea of feathery wings, though perhaps not halos. They sound like a particularly awkward kind of bonnet."

"Then you will like the reason I've come to see you," Villiers said, moving a pawn forward. "I am considering a bid for a halo of my own."

"I'm shocked," Jemma murmured. They played for a moment in silence. Villiers brought forward a rook and she challenged one of his pawns with her bishop.

"I have a problem," Villiers said, not even pausing before he brought a knight into the contest.

Jemma raised an eyebrow. "You, the Great Villiers, has that most plebeian of all human conditions—a *problem*?"

He sighed. "It's a particularly tedious conundrum, or I wouldn't bring it up."

"They all are. Although I was of the opinion that unmarried men with no encumbrances had the fewest problems of any."

"Alas, I seem to have acquired a few encumbrances, though, as yet, no wife," Villiers said thoughtfully. "I have fallen into respectability without noticing."

"Fallen?" Jemma said with a chortle. "Given those illegitimate children of yours, you should boast of the opposite."

"Vulgar," he said. "Unworthy of you."

Jemma grinned at him. "I find vulgarity so refreshing. From what I understand, children *are* a problem. Though surely the illegitimate type, tucked away out of sight and mind, cannot present very many problems?"

"My thought exactly." His long fingers played with the pawn she had just knocked from the board.

"But?"

"If you remember, while I was very ill following my regrettable duel last year, I made a promise about my children."

"The deathbed promise! Oh, the very worst kind."

"Adding unkindness to vulgarity," he said with mock severity.

"Precisely," she said. "To whom did you make that promise, anyway? I don't remember hearing that any church folk were tenderly waiting by your bedside."

"It was to Miss Charlotte Tatlock."

Jemma made a face before she could stop herself. "No Puritan. Miss Learned Fetlock."

"The same one who spent too much time adoring your husband," he confirmed. "I asked her to marry me, you know."

"I am glad she didn't accept you," Jemma said with satisfaction.

"Who said she didn't accept me?"

"At my Twelfth Night ball I walked into my own sitting room to find her passionately clasped in the embrace of your heir. She wasn't nearly interesting enough to kiss him *and* marry you."

"Then why did you fret about whether she would be successful in pursuit of your husband?"

"I wasn't fretting. I would never do something as bourgeois as fret."

"You were fretting," Villiers said. "Eyeing poor Elijah the way a rat eyes cheese. A true dog in the manger, in fact. 'I don't care to have him, but no one else can either.'"

"Let's go back to your problems," Jemma said, taking his rook.

"As it happens, I received a missive this morning informing me that my heir has irresponsibly and inappropriately married Miss Tatlock by special license."

"Very romantic," Jemma said.

"Your tone is distinctly unkind. Unsympathetic, in truth. Do you know that is the second of my fiancées to marry by special license?"

"My brother's wife and now Miss Tatlock. Tut tut, Villiers. Is that the problem you wish me to solve? Finding you a fiancée who will actually stay with you, rather than dash off with a swashbuckling passerby?"

"There's no need to enjoy my plight quite so much," Villiers said, moving a pawn forward. "And no, I don't care for a wife. I have other pursuits in mind."

Jemma caught her breath. He looked up at her, his hand still holding the chess piece, and there was no mistaking which pursuit he was thinking of. All of a sudden her laughing friend was gone; his eyes were smoldering. She raced into speech. "Your problem? What is it?"

He didn't speak for a moment, letting her know that he saw her flimsy evasion. She couldn't help it; the flicker of amusement—and recognition of desire— in his eyes made the corners of her mouth curl into a smile. But there was nothing in her smile that betrayed Elijah. Nothing.

"Children," he said. "I promised Charlotte that I would find her the perfect husband. She showed no faith in my abilities, and insisted that if I managed the task, I would have to turn father, when she turned wife."

"And she just turned wife!" Jemma cried. "You are caught, Villiers, fairly caught!"

"I thought you were going to call me Leopold. I'm sure we had reached that pitch of intimacy."

The air stilled in the room again. She fled back to the subject at hand. "The question is, what did she mean by turning father?"

"She said something about learning the children's names."

"You do support them, don't you?" she asked, knowing that he did. Even if he didn't entertain guilt, Villiers would never shirk a financial responsibility.

He nodded.

"I gather that you need to understand the word 'fatherhood.'"

"I'm finding the parameters hard to determine."

"I don't believe I ever met your father. Mine taught me to play chess."

"I could do that," Villiers said, something easing in his expression.

Jemma sneaked a glance at him under her lashes. "My father taught me how to fight off an unwanted suitor, and threatened to kill me if I failed."

"Dear me," Villiers said languidly, taking one of her knights. "How very violent."

Jemma felt a prickle of irritation. Her father had been rightfully impassioned on the subject of rakes like Villiers. "Most of what he taught us we learned from living with him. Fatherhood involves propinquity."

Villiers didn't even flinch. "The children are—"

"How many children are we talking about?" Jemma demanded. And, when he didn't answer, "You do know the number, don't you?"

"Of course. But there are complications."

Jemma swept a bishop off the board. "Such as?"

"Six," he said.

"*Six?* You have *six* children out of wedlock?"

His eyes focused on her fingers, still holding the bishop. "Considering the number of women I have made love to in my life, it seems a not inconceivable number."

"*Inconceivable?* Who's vulgar now?"

He blinked. "An inadvertent pun, I assure you."

"I thought you had perhaps two children."

"Six."

"You need to be more careful," she scolded.

"Yes."

"Didn't you ever give a thought to the lives of those children, born out of wedlock? Or their mothers, bearing children without marriage lines?"

"No."

It was Jemma's turn to move, but she hesitated. She felt a bit sick. She liked Villiers. Leopold. She really liked him. She had even—

"I am a duke," he said. His voice was like dark velvet, impenetrable. "Why would I give a damn about that sort of thing?"

"At least you pay for them."

"I could support a foundling hospital, and you would applaud my virtue."

"I didn't expect you to populate your own orphanage," she said, her voice coming out more sharply than she intended. "It's despicable to think so little of the women that you—"

"Bed," he supplied. "I think a great deal of some women I bed. Or hope to bed."

But this bit of gallantry was forced, and she flashed him a look of contempt.

"What is the difference between six and two?" he asked.

"One child out of wedlock is an error. Two suggests carelessness. Three—and six—is simply wrong. Wrong."

There was something in those dark eyes of his that made her anger diminish.

"You understand that, don't you?"

"You simply don't appreciate the mental cast of a duke."

"Don't you dare tell me that your children's mothers were lucky to be impregnated by you, simply because of your rank!"

There was a brief smile in his eyes. "No. I meant that I was brought up to think that everyone below me was unworthy. That my inherited money, power, and title gave me the right to do just as I please. And as it happens, I dislike French letters and I honored my dislike for some years."

"There's nothing honorable about that," Jemma said scathingly. "You're lucky you don't have fourteen children! Who are they?"

"The children?"

"The mothers. I know that a child of yours was born to a gentlewoman, Lady Caroline Killigrew. And that you refused to marry her."

"In fact," he said, "that particular girl is not mine."

"You mean she doesn't count as one of the six?"

"She does, but merely because she is in my care. I told you there were complications."

"Of course the girl is yours. Lady Caroline told everyone. And her father told my Uncle Edmund that you admitted to bedding her and then refused to marry her. Everyone was so sympathetic and—" She met his eyes and caught herself. "My God. So who was the father?"

Villiers shrugged. "I have no idea. I certainly never bedded her. I think she must have been desperate. It seemed to me that as a gentleman I had to play my part in the script she had written."

"Perhaps she hoped you would be forced to marry her."

"I don't think so. If she wanted to acquire a husband, she would have accused someone of lower rank, someone who would be glad of the large dowry her father would offer."

"Saved by your dukedom," Jemma said. "And yet you played the hero."

"Hardly," he said dryly. "I refused to marry her. I merely restrained myself from pointing out the fact that I hardly knew her. She, for her part, did a wonderful job of lurking at the side of ballrooms and staring at me tragically, until her father whisked her off to Canada. The child was sent back to England a few months later with a quite disagreeable note about my role in its upbringing. What on earth could I do except accept her as my own?"

"You don't know where the mother is now?"

"Why should I?"

"Good point."

"So her child is one of my six."

"Who are the five remaining mothers? Nightwalkers, all?"

He waved a hand. "Play your piece, Jemma. I intend to win. And no, there are no nightwalkers among them. I have a great deal of respect for myself, and the risk of disease in those encounters is appalling."

"You're splitting hairs," Jemma said, moving her king. "Call them courtesans, if you wish."

"Their station in life is irrelevant," he said with

emphasis. Just as she hoped, he was focused on the conversation and didn't appear to notice that her remaining bishop would soon have his queen.

"I wouldn't agree, given that they are rearing *your* children. And I imagine they aren't teaching the children chess. Just imagine all the useful lessons the girls are learning."

"In fact, only one child is being reared by her mother," he said.

"Oh? Then who cares for the others?"

"My solicitor makes sure that the children are well cared for."

"You don't know."

"Why would I? Do you—"

"If I had a child, I would know where he was!"

"So far, we have two items on the fathering list," he said, sighing. He was being surprisingly calm. The old Villiers, the pre-nearly-dead Villiers, would have stalked from the room long ago. "Ascertain who is raising them, and teach them chess."

"I do believe you ought to take them in yourself, as we discussed a few weeks ago," Jemma said, baiting him. "Although I must admit that I thought we were talking of two children at that point." She moved a pawn, calculating the number of moves remaining before she seized his queen.

He looked up. "You were joking then, and I trust you are now as well."

"Absolutely not! Is your hand on that pawn because you intend to move it?"

He looked down with a slight frown and moved the piece.

"Children ought to live with their parents. It's part of the duties of parenthood."

"Don't be a fool. I have no wife."

"Didn't the Earl of Ballston take in at least twelve illegitimate children?"

"He had a wife."

"A couple of the illegitimate children were hers, by all accounts. So, what we need to do is find you a wife . . . just the right kind of wife."

"The kind who won't object to my children, you mean, because she has some illegitimate offspring of her own?"

"It would serve you right," she said, breaking into a laugh at the look on his face.

"You think I should *live* with these children?"

"Well . . . no." She moved her bishop. "Check and mate."

He stared down at the trap she'd set. "Christ! You distracted me!"

"But it was so delicious to see your face when I suggested that you move the children into your house. Delicious!"

He blinked at the board and looked at her. "I might take in one child."

"*What?*"

"I could take in one. Do you think that would be enough?"

"Enough for what?" Jemma stared at Villiers as if she'd never seen him before. "I was merely trying to win the game. And I won. Do you wish to trace your mistaken move?"

He shrugged. "No. You won. If you'll excuse me, I must think."

She sprang to her feet. "Think about bringing illegitimate children into your house? I was only joking, Villiers! Truly. No respectable woman will marry you under those circumstances. I should never have said such a thing."

He rose and came one step toward her. He was tall, almost as tall as her husband, and she had to tilt her head up.

"I don't want to marry a respectable woman," he said. Slowly.

Oh God. There was something in those black eyes of his that she'd never seen before. They had been flirting for almost a year now, ever since she had returned from France and challenged him to a chess match . . . A match that was never finished, and never would be. A match designed to end in bed.

"Leopold," she whispered. "You mustn't—"

"I must be serious," he said. "You're married. You're married to my childhood friend, Elijah. And Elijah—" He seemed to change his mind and took a breath. "He's got you and I haven't. I'm just saying, Jemma, that there aren't a lot of places a man can go after he has met you."

Jemma felt the pleasure of that compliment deep in her gut, in her backbone, in all the silly places that a person can feel a compliment. And she knew why, too. Somewhere in her was still the forlorn young woman, desolated to find that her husband enjoyed the company of his mistress over that of his wife.

She shook her head. She would never be unfaithful to Elijah again. "We plan to have a child," she said, pretending there was nothing wrong with her husband's heart.

"I already have some children, and I think it's time I came to know them." Villiers stepped back, and she found herself reaching out a hand without conscious will. His tone was so sad and yet so self-accepting, with that flare of humor.

"You will fall in love with someone, Leopold. Someone will steal your heart before you notice it." He shook his head. "I plan to visit Vauxhall tomorrow night; come and I will introduce you to the loveliest women of my acquaintance."

He bowed, said all the right things, and left.

Jemma sat in front of the game board for a long time, thinking that Villiers had changed. After finishing a game of chess, they used to play it backwards, dissect it three or four different ways, argue over moves. Now he'd walked away after she'd played the oldest, silliest ploy in the book, distracting him with a lively conversation.

The thing that made her uneasy, made her sit staring at the discarded pieces, was that she knew what was in his eyes when he looked at her. Not that she'd seen it all that often.

It wasn't something he was supposed to feel. Not for her. Not for . . . not for anyone, except his wife, when he had one.

Chapter Seven

By evening, Elijah had not yet returned to the house. Jemma ate in solitary splendor at nine; she dallied over her meal until ten and then retreated to the library. She fiddled with a chess problem and went over the household accounts.

But in reality, she watched the clock. She felt torn in two: one moment desperate just to see Elijah, the next torn by resentment and a furious determination to make him leave the House of Lords.

When her husband finally walked into the library, his face gaunt and exhausted, she wanted to throw herself into his arms, at the same time that she wanted to rail at him. Fortunately, she didn't have to choose: the presence of Fowle and the footmen made either an impossibility.

Elijah bent over her hand, kissing it as if she were the merest acquaintance. Fowle bustled across the room before they could exchange a word, followed by three footmen carrying a small table, covered dishes, and china.

Jemma walked back to her seat, feeling as if she were walking on broken glass. She, who was never at a loss for words, was struggling to formulate even the most trivial comment. They sat in silence as Fowle set the table before Elijah, uncovered a beefsteak, and poured him a glass of wine.

"If you would be so kind as to leave the dishes, I will serve myself," Elijah said.

Fowle pursed his lips in a scandalized kind of way, but Elijah sent him from the room with one look.

"How was your day?" Elijah asked as the door closed behind Fowle and the footmen.

Jemma took a sip of brandy. "Oh, quite enjoyable," she said lightly. "I paid a visit to a friend in the morning, and I beat Villiers at a game of chess in the afternoon."

A shadow crossed his eyes. "How is the duke?"

"Fine. Though he confessed that he has six illegitimate children."

Elijah's hand froze, a piece of steak halfway to his mouth.

"Six," Jemma repeated. "What's more, he did not actually father Lady Caroline Killigrew's child. Do you remember all the fuss when he refused to marry her?"

Elijah nodded.

"It was astonishingly generous of him to allow that story to circulate. He said that he felt it was the gentlemanly thing to do."

"Not an impulse he feels on a daily basis," Elijah said dryly.

"Only Villiers would be so careless of his reputation that he allowed himself to be besmirched by a young lady he hardly knew."

"It is the privilege of the uncaring." There was a bit of a snap in his tone.

"He's a great deal more sanctimonious than he allows. I believe that he finds a reputation for immorality useful."

"He makes being on the side of the sinners look extremely attractive," Elijah admitted, pulling off a cover and putting a helping of plaice on his plate.

"Whereas you make being on the side of the saints look very exhausting," Jemma replied, seizing the opening.

He looked at her over the table. "I know what you're going to say."

"Then I shan't ask it, because there's nothing worse than a nagging wife, saying the things that one knows already."

His smile made her heart beat suddenly faster. "I quite look forward to being nagged by you."

"You mustn't give me encouragement of this sort," Jemma said, striving for a flirtatious tone. "We've lived apart so long that you've forgotten what a shrew I can be."

"You were never a shrew," he said, his voice low. They stared at each other a moment. "You didn't even scream at me after walking into my office when I was—with my mistress."

"I didn't?" In all honesty, Jemma couldn't remember anything but Sarah Cobbett's yellow hair, hanging over the edge of Elijah's large desk.

"You just looked at me, your face white. You dropped the picnic hamper you held, and you fled."

Jemma gave him a little smile. "Don't think I'd be as silent again. If I ever encountered such a scene now, I would bring the walls down around your

ears." But she said it knowing perfectly well that
Elijah would never do such a thing again. That he'd
changed, and she'd changed, and no woman stood
between them.

"The look on your face was like a dagger," Elijah
said.

"Surely, you—"

"I'm not exaggerating. I'd seen that look before."

"You had?"

He waved his fork at the walls. "You've taken down
all the evidence."

Jemma blinked at the walls. She'd had them repan-
eled and painted a dark crimson while they were in
the country for Christmas. "They were oak," she said
confusedly. "I would hardly call that evidence of a
crime, though they were rather old-fashioned."

"A large and detailed picture of Judith and Holofernes used to hang directly before my father's desk,"
Elijah said, returning to his plate. "It was a particularly
vivid tableau in which Judith waved Holofernes's sev-
ered head with a distinct air of glee. I think my mother
liked to believe that it would force my father to notice
her rage, but I doubt she succeeded. He was not an observant man."

"Your mother was angry about your father's mistress?" Jemma asked cautiously.

"Something of that nature."

The conversation was not going where Jemma had
planned. The former duke's dubious intimacies were
interesting, but not relevant.

"In truth, I had a horrid day," she said abruptly.

Elijah immediately put down his fork. "I am very
sorry if the state of my health caused you any distress."

"Distress?" For a moment she couldn't continue; it felt as if her throat were closed to words. "I was quite unkind in the morning to a woman who is an acquaintance, if not precisely a friend. And I topped that piece of goodwill by goading Villiers into taking his illegitimate children under his own roof."

"He can't do that," Elijah said, frowning. "Even his rank won't inoculate him from becoming a pariah. What were you thinking, Jemma?"

"I wasn't thinking." She raised her chin, willing herself not to cry. "I was so angry at you for leaving this morning without even a note, that I behaved—" Despite herself, her voice wavered. She swallowed and continued. "I behaved like the worst sort of person, determined to win in both encounters no matter the damage I caused."

"*Win?* What on earth did you hope to win from your friend?"

"It's unimportant, and I'm afraid that that friendship is at an end."

"It was most unkind of me to leave you no personal message, particularly after the shock of last night. I apologize." His eyes were warm and sympathetic. "I shall not behave in such a discourteous way again."

She was a shrew and he was the perfect husband. "Thank you," she said. "But I do have a request."

"I believe I can anticipate you," he said, raising his wineglass to his lips. "I know we need to have a serious discussion; of course, you wish to address the question of an heir. The next duke. I have already informed Pitt that I will not be available tomorrow." His eyes caressed hers. He clearly meant to spend the day in bed. With her.

"In fact, that is not my request," she said carefully,

trying not to dwell on the cold-blooded fashion with which Elijah referred to the question of children.

"Oh?" He raised an eyebrow.

"I would ask that you give up your seat in the House of Lords. For your health."

The words hung in the air. The sensual warmth in his eyes disappeared as if it had never been, and she was faced by the consummate statesman. Being Elijah, he didn't dissemble. "The government faces ongoing prisoner riots, a coming election, an impoverished citizenry. Fox and the Prince of Wales risk the health of the entire nation with their drunken exploits; the king seems unable to rein in his own son. I could not consider such a drastic move."

"I would not argue with their need for you," Jemma said. "But I wonder that you need *them*."

"I'm afraid that I don't follow your point."

"I have no doubt that the Prime Minister faces a difficult year. But Mr. Pitt seems to me to be amply, if not eagerly, able to take on those challenges. In fact, he was elected for just that purpose. But you, Elijah, were not elected."

"Responsibility is not incurred only from election." His eyes were grave but utterly resolute.

"Your heart is giving out because of the pressure of being roused at dawn to argue problems that most of your peers merely read of in the papers, if they bother to do so. Villiers never took up his seat in Lords. When he was so very ill last year, after his duel, he recovered in bed."

Elijah put down his wine. "We are very different men. The ethical compass of Villiers's life is bounded by the chessboard."

"You are not listening to me," Jemma said, feeling

her hold over her temper slipping. "Villiers nearly lost his life last year, but he is here today because he retreated to his chambers. Had he pushed himself out of bed at dawn under the mistaken impression that there was no one else able to deal with a public furor, he would be dead."

Elijah's jaw was set. "Surely you are not suggesting that I live the remainder of my life in bed? Lying flat, as Villiers did in the grip of fever? Perhaps playing a game of chess now and then?" He pushed his plate away, the food half-eaten.

"That seems an exaggeration."

His tone was courteous as ever, but she could see the leashed fury in his eyes. "You suggest that I should treasure life so much that I preserve it, as a fly in amber? That I should add to my allotted minutes by staying on my back, by giving up every ambition I had to do something of value with those minutes?"

"You needn't—" Jemma began, only to be overridden by the steady voice of a man used to shouting down a chamber full of howling statesmen.

"In fact, you would have me become a man like Villiers, a man whose children are negligently scattered about the countryside, a man who cares for nothing but his next game of chess. Though perhaps you consider that an unjust appraisal. After all, Villiers does care about his appearance. So I would be allowed sartorial splendor and chess."

Jemma straightened her back, trying to force air into her lungs.

"I could walk about with a sword stick and make absolutely sure that every man on the street understood that I was a duke, a man who by the fortune of birth considered himself just under the rank of the

Archangel himself. Without lifting a finger to gain that status." He picked up a silver cover and put it precisely on top of one of the serving platters with a sound like a slap.

"Let me put this as clearly as I can, Jemma." His mouth was a straight line. "I will shoot myself before I become the man that Villiers is."

"You are unkind," Jemma said, hearing a slight shake in her voice and hating it. She wasn't used to battles of this nature. In fact, she never argued with anyone but her husband. Her sanctimonious, infuriating husband.

Elijah obviously heard the tremor in her voice. He rose, walked to the cabinet and poured two tiny glasses of ruby-colored liqueur. Then he returned and handed her one. "It's made by monks in France, from cherries. Or cherry blossoms."

Jemma took a taste and choked. The liqueur burned to the bottom of her stomach.

"The particular pastimes of the Duke of Villiers are not relevant," he said, sitting down again. "But he and I are very different men. I cannot conceive of a life in which I drift around London, impulsively stopping for a game of chess with a friend. Or did you summon him this afternoon?"

He waited, one eyebrow up. Jemma shook her head.

"So the duke happened by and you spent a delightful afternoon together, sharing a bit of light banter about his bastard children, a bit of flirtation, I have no doubt."

Jemma heard the naked anger in his voice with a shock of surprise. "You couldn't be jealous of Villiers! Not after I gave up the chess match with him."

"Jealous of a man who spends the afternoon telling my wife how beautiful she is?"

She opened her mouth and he held up a hand.

"Tell me that Villiers didn't compliment you, Jemma. Tell me that, and I'll acknowledge myself a fool."

She was silent.

"He's in love with you," Elijah said flatly.

They were at some sort of queer crossroads. "That doesn't mean that I would be unfaithful to you. With Villiers or any other man."

"I know that."

She took another sip of liquor. It was like a fiery stream of sugar. She hated it.

"Last night Fox called out the Artillery Company and told them to open fire on rioting citizens in Lambeth, his district," Elijah said.

"That's terrible," Jemma murmured.

"I have no doubt it seems a remote problem. But tell that to the young mother whose babe was shot in her arms last night, when she thought they were safe inside her own house. A stray bullet from the company."

"I am deeply sorry for that poor young woman," Jemma said. "But must you be so self-righteous, Elijah? Listening to you, one would think that you are the only thing stopping Fox and Pitt and everyone else in the government from turning to a snarling mass of savages. Your sense of importance seems a trifle overblown. After all, you too gained your position due to an accident of birth. Or do you think that you would have the same influence, the same power, were you not a duke?"

She couldn't read his expression. There was nothing in his eyes. "Has your opinion of me always been this low?" he asked. He sounded curious, as if he were asking about a preference for peas over potatoes.

"I do not have a low opinion of you," Jemma stated. "I merely suggested that you might wish to rethink the extent of your personal capacity to cut short the world's injustices, including Fox's authorization of an artillery man who accidentally shot a child. Did you personally sanction Fox's unfortunate decision?"

Anger flared in his eyes, and she welcomed it. There was nothing worse than a dismissive Elijah, the statesman who made her feel like a fool easily quelled by a patronizing word or two.

"Do you want to know what happened today, Jemma?" he demanded. "Do you really want to know?"

"I wait with bated breath," she said.

"I suppose your sarcasm is warranted. I can imagine it is much easier, and certainly pleasant, to stay at home and win a game of chess."

Jemma sprang to her feet and walked quickly to the fireplace. She turned around a moment later, certain that she had her breathing under control. She'd be damned if she started panting from pure rage. "Given that women are allowed no part in government, your insults are not only unkind but unfair."

He had risen to his feet, of course. Elijah would never sit while a woman stood. "I apologize. That is an entirely valid point. In that case, let's not talk of your day, but of Villiers's."

"Oh for goodness sake!" Jemma exclaimed.

"The duke spent a delightful afternoon telling you a sad tale of his children, and his newfound resolution to be a good father. Rousing your sympathy and your interest, he opened his heart. True, he lost the game of chess, but he gained so much more in becoming closer to you. Closer to you than he is to any other person on this earth, I expect."

His tone was dispassionate. Jemma took a deep breath. "Either you believe that I will be unfaithful or—"

"You're a fool if you think that infidelity is a matter of bodies alone, Jemma!"

His insult burned in her stomach. "I have *always* thought that infidelity took forms beyond the obvious! From the moment I—"

"I know. I know. From the moment you found me on the desk with my mistress. What you have never understood is how unimportant that relationship was compared to one of true intimacy."

"If you're trying to say that you and I were truly intimate all those years ago, I must disagree."

"No, we weren't. In fact, I expect that you and Villiers are now better friends, more intimate, and in sum, more loving to each other, than we were in our early marriage. And yet I know perfectly well that you and Leopold have never entered a bedchamber together."

Words burned on Jemma's tongue, but Elijah didn't wait for her to formulate a response.

"Let me make this very clear. I would not wish for the duke's pleasant afternoon, idling away his time and yours, even should I die tomorrow. I realized when I was eight years old that either I could die knowing that my life had changed the world around me—or I could die like any trout on a string, leaving the world precisely as it was before I was born. I chose not to be that sort of person, and you will *never* be able to turn me into Villiers. Never."

"I didn't ask you to become Villiers!" Jemma cried.

"I merely thought that even in the face of the world's injustices, there might be a point at which a man is allowed to retreat from the fray. It's not that you would eke out your remaining moments in bed, but that this life is actually killing you."

"I consider that unimportant," Elijah said, after a moment.

"Your life is *unimportant*?"

"I have always known my life would be short. Why should I betray everything I hold dear in order to gain a few extra, lazy minutes?"

She stared at him, unable to even begin a sentence.

"I see that you would prefer me to throw away the world to stay at your side," he said, restlessly walking away from her, across the room.

"I would—"

Never had Elijah interrupted her so many times. He swung about and faced her. "We are too old to prevaricate, Jemma. I have no doubt but that after I am gone, you and Villiers will find great happiness together."

"How dare you say such a thing!"

"I dare because it is true."

"You suggest that I am simply waiting for you to die!" she cried furiously. "You insult me as well as Villiers!"

"Leopold is my closest friend in the world," Elijah said quietly. "Even when he and I were estranged, I still considered him so. The fact is that I have never been and cannot become the charming companion you deserve. But my disinclination to nurse my health doesn't mean that I am afraid to acknowledge that Villiers would be a better mate for you."

"I cannot believe your arrogance," Jemma said. "As you see it, I will prance away from your grave and turn directly to my partner in lazy crime, living the rest of my life in happy indolence?"

"Your characterization is not helpful. What you call arrogance, I would call logic." He took another quick turn and stopped just before her. "I am merely trying to be honest with you, Jemma. It would be patronizing of me to not share my opinion."

"I see," she said, striving to get a grip on her temper. "But just to make certain that I understand your point of view: although you consider Villiers to be a lackwit, you have every belief that I will turn directly from your grave to his arms."

"Poetically put," he said dryly.

"Moreover, you refuse to take any action that might prolong your life, preferring instead to gallop recklessly toward that grave without a thought for—for those you leave behind."

"I think of you, Jemma."

"Do you? Why? I am nothing but a frivolity ensconced at home, a woman who can be quickly dispatched into Villiers's arms the moment your brief candle burns out."

"Not only poetic but Shakespearean."

Jemma turned sharply and stared out the dark window, biting her lip savagely to control tears that caught at the back of her throat. Her heart was beating heavily, in harmony with her new—and wretched—understanding of her importance to her husband.

"I truly wish that I could be the man you'd prefer." His voice came from somewhere behind her.

She controlled her voice with an effort. "I wonder, Elijah, that you bothered to summon me from Paris at all."

He cleared his throat. "I do not understand your

bitterness, Jemma. If you don't wish to marry Villiers, you won't do so. I merely—" His voice broke off and suddenly his large hands were on her shoulders, turning her around to face him. "Damn it, Jemma, the truth is that I envy him. I envy him your cozy afternoon, the chess game, the sympathy in your eyes, the affection between you."

Jemma angrily dashed a tear away. "You just scorned such intimacies!"

"I am not made to be a courtier."

What could she say? That she'd been fool enough to think that he was falling in love with her?

She leaned her head back against the cool dark window behind her. It wasn't Elijah's fault that his honor came before his wife. She should admire him for it. God knows, the world admired his nobility.

She opened her eyes again and looked at her beautiful, honorable husband. That same stupid, foolish man who thought to pass her over to Villiers like a package that might spoil if left in the rain.

"I am sorry to have caused you distress," he said. She could tell he meant it.

"Distress." She had to swallow. "Yes, well, I suppose that goes along with a dying husband." The words fell harshly from her lips, and he flinched.

"It needn't be like this between us," he said, his hands sliding from her shoulders to her hands. "I thought we were . . . "

"We were what?" she inquired.

He didn't reply. His eyes were the dark blue of a midnight sky, too beautiful for a man.

"You seem to consider me an appendage of the estate," she said, charging recklessly, miserably, on. "A cow to be passed from hand to hand."

"Jemma, you are growing hysterical—"

She interrupted him. "Allow me the grace to finish. Since you consider nothing in life to be more important than your work, the question of an heir cannot truly perturb you. You have known for more than a year that your heart was unstable, to say the least, and yet you refused to bed me until I finished my chess match with Villiers."

His mouth tightened. "It was for the good of the child. I wouldn't want the world to think that my heir was not of my blood."

"Then I shall make this as clear as you have your refusal to leave the House of Lords. I will not sleep with you, Elijah. I am no brood mare, available for breeding during the spare moments you are not with Pitt or the chief magistrate."

"Jemma!"

She raised an eyebrow. "Yes?"

"I have been longing to sleep with you." The words were halting. "As much as if you were a drink of water in the desert."

Elijah was not a man who wanted to reveal a vulnerability, ever. When she didn't answer, he kissed first one of her palms, and then the other. His touch burned. "We desire each other, Jemma."

"No," she said stonily. "Or rather, yes. We do desire each other. But that's not enough, Elijah."

He dropped her hands. His eyes were shaded, dark and impenetrable. "Then woo me."

"*What?*"

"I understand courtship. I see it in the House of Lords every day. It takes an elaborate courtship to convince a man that his opinion is wrong. That he has made a grave mistake in backing the slave trade, or the tax on wheat. If you are right, and I am spending my time in a fruitless effort, then convince me."

"In the five minutes you spare me on your way to the House of Lords?"

"Are you giving up?"

She narrowed her eyes.

"I thought you never gave up. I thought you always wanted to win. I thought you were my equal in that, Jemma."

"I cannot work miracles."

"I'll give you time. I have dropped some of my committees." He was watching her closely. Her thoughts were tumbling between inconsolable misery and irritation. "I want what you give to Villiers," he added.

That made her head snap up. "Oh for God's sake, Elijah—"

"Please. Woo me."

"Elijah, I don't *woo* Villiers."

"Please." He caught up her hands again. "Please. I am not going to the House of Lords tomorrow. Allow me to accompany you?"

"Where?"

"Wherever you are going. Whatever you are doing."

"I shan't go out and save the world, or even one prisoner tomorrow, Elijah. It's Thursday, and that means I shall go to the flower market."

"Will you woo me even though I am a fool who enrages you?" He asked it quietly, but she heard the strain in his voice.

"You make me so angry." The words spat like fat in the fire. But she found it impossible to harden her heart entirely. She was too infatuated. Of course, it was only infatuation.

She put a hand to his cheek. It was faintly bristly,

male, so different from her own. Elijah said nothing, so she let her fingers spread over his cheek, turning her touch carnal. One touched his lips, another the arch of his cheekbone. He closed his eyes, and his dark eyelashes lay against his cheek like the shadow of sin.

"I won't sleep with you. I won't go to bed with you merely to have an heir. Your cousin can inherit for all I care."

"Will you sleep with me for another reason altogether?"

What was she supposed to say? *When you want me more than you want to save the world?* That would never happen. The intrinsic fabric of Elijah's soul, the whole construction of his life, meant that he could not give her what she wanted. Some part of her heart grieved, and another part craved him even so. His kisses. That affection she had interpreted as love.

When he opened his eyes, his voice sounded hoarse and guttural. "You are *mine*, Jemma. Do you understand that?"

Then, suddenly, she understood. In fact, she couldn't imagine why she hadn't seen it all from the beginning: the way Elijah insisted on playing chess with her only after she and Villiers started a match. The way he refused to sleep with her—until after she finished the match with Villiers.

All along she had been in a relationship in which Villiers and her husband were the opposite poles, and she had been too stupid to realize it.

"I'm yours," she said, hearing the heavy sadness in her own voice.

"You sound . . . "

"But you are not mine, Elijah."

And she left the room before he could say more.

Chapter Eight

March 28

Jemma had barely arrived downstairs the next morning before her husband appeared. He looked better for having slept past dawn, she thought, watching him descend the stairs. A man of such physical beauty never looked truly haggard; his bones carried it. And Elijah had been given great gifts: a nobleman's chin and a statesman's eyes. A beautiful, mobile mouth.

She had decided to woo—with the understanding that her husband's emotions were bound in a rivalry with Villiers that she could never challenge. She would woo with no expectation of winning, but simply because every moment that she kept Elijah from Lords was healing for his heart. Even if she secretly thought that those same moments would break *her* heart in two.

"Where are we going?" he asked immediately.

Elijah, she thought, had spent far too much of his life expecting that every day would be life-changing.

"We are going to the Covent Garden flower markets. It's a humble errand, such as duchesses sometimes do, when they feel like being useful. Which," she added candidly, "isn't terribly often."

He handed her into the carriage, and being Elijah, didn't look in the least bored.

A mere half hour later they were wandering among stalls of flowers, hawkers shouting on all sides.

"Violets," Jemma said, halting next to a great tub of the small flowers.

"Ah, those purple ones," Elijah said, staring down at them. "I've seen them."

"Don't you know what violets are?"

He shrugged. "Not particularly. Why should I?"

"Botanical studies? General knowledge?"

"No." He didn't seem to mind the gap in his knowledge either.

She plucked a bunch of velvety small flowers and held them to his nose. "These are violets."

"Quite acceptable," he said. "Shall we take the lot?"

"The whole bucket?" She laughed. "No. They're delicate. These will last only a day or so. This kind of pleasure comes best in small bunches, a bit by the bed, for example. To take so many would be extravagance. You, Duke, have accused me of extravagance on occasion, but in truth I am quite economical."

"I don't remember accusing you of extravagance," he protested.

"I believe it was in Paris. You were not happy with the cost of my crystal forest, remember?"

"Hundreds of pounds a tree," he said, remembering. "But then . . . the king loved it."

"And the crystals were promptly sold back to the merchant from whom we bought them. At a discount, naturally. But violets die, and cannot be resold."

She took a few violets from the bunch and tucked them into his coat. "There. Now you don't look as severe."

Elijah glanced down at his black velvet. "Do I look too severe?" he inquired.

"You look like a statesman. But the violets give you a more debonair air."

"Would you prefer that I take to wearing coats like Villiers's?"

He sounded so dubious that she burst out laughing. "Villiers would never give you the address of his embroiderers, Elijah, so you are quite safe."

He caught her gloved hand and brought it to his lips. "You called me Elijah."

Jemma could feel herself growing a trifle pink. "I often do."

"We're in public."

"We're—We're married," she said, hearing the slightly breathless quality of her voice and cursing herself.

"I don't believe my mother even knew my father's given name," he said, putting her hand down.

Jemma handed the rest of the violets to a footman. "These and another bunch, please, James." Then she tucked her hand through Elijah's arm. "I'm quite sure she did. Likely she simply chose not to use it in your hearing. Do you suppose that your mother might pay us a visit? Or—" She hesitated. "—ought I to have paid her one? I suppose I have been a sadly neglectful daughter-in-law."

"If my mother wished to see you, she would have

sent you a command, informing you of her decision,"
Elijah said. "What are all these white ones?"

"Apple blossoms!" Jemma crowed. "Oh, I love these.
It means spring is truly here. And those are white
cherries. I think we should have a huge amount in the
drawing room, don't you? These are boxwood."

Elijah sniffed the boxwood and actually took a step
back. "I think something died."

"Boxwood doesn't smell as beautiful as it looks,"
Jemma agreed. She nodded to James. "We'll have a
largish amount of the white cherry, thank you." She
drew Elijah on, out of earshot of the footman. "Do tell
me, Elijah, should I pay your mother a visit?"

"We could do so together," he replied, with a notable lack of enthusiasm. "It's like visiting the king, you
know. We'd have to petition a visit. She hasn't summoned me in some two years." He thought about it.
"Perhaps longer."

Jemma stopped. "She might be ill!"

"Oh, no. She writes me once a week. Strategy is her
métier. She has given me remarkably good advice on a
number of topics over the years. Though she tends to
be far too inclined to insult," he added. "She is always
counseling me to ferocity."

The fact that his mother's primary decorating idea
had been to strew the house with lurid depictions of
Judith holding Holofernes's bloody head meant the
dowager duchess's forceful tendencies were no surprise to Jemma. She bent to look at a pail of bluebells.

The old man selling the bluebells looked like a tattered and rather furry owl, all eyes and beak. "Grew
'em on the dung heap," he said to her. "I's always has
the first and best bluebells in London. It's the dung
that does it. Ha'penny a bunch, if you please."

Elijah looked down at the bluebells with the first real interest he'd shown in the market. "Why do you suppose that is?" he asked the man. "Could it be that the dung generates heat?"

"Me granddad said it was because there's nothing richer than the dung of a horse fed on grain."

"Dung heaps do generate heat, though. Sometimes they combust. Perhaps this flower enjoys heat from above and below." The man didn't roll his eyes, because one didn't do that to a nabob wearing a velvet jacket.

"What are these flowers?" Jemma asked. He had a bucket of tall, showy flowers that resembled bluebells, but with heads the color of violets.

"Don't touch those," the man barked.

"You are speaking to a duchess." Elijah's voice was all the more commanding for being utterly even.

"They're some sort of pisin."

"Pissing?" Elijah asked. "A pissing flower?"

"Pisin!" the man said, annoyed. "Dead Men's Bells, they're called. And they're pisin!"

"Poison," Jemma supplied. "And yet they're so beautiful. Do you grow them for an apothecary?"

"A doctor. He takes whatever I grows. Some sort o' medicine he's cooking up." The old man gave a sudden cackle. "Don't mind taking his brass but I'll be slumgubbered if I'll take any o' his medicine!"

"Surely it doesn't kill by the touch," Elijah said, his voice still sounding annoyed.

"For all I know, you'll reach down an' eat one," the man said stubbornly. "There's chillen have died o' that. You can die even from drinking the water one of these has been sittin' in."

"I'll put bluebells down the dining room table,"

Jemma decided. "We'll take at least half of those, if you please, James," she told the footman.

Elijah plucked a few of the nodding bluebells. "They're the perfect color for your hair," he said, looking down at her. He tucked them on top of her ear. "Your hair is the color of . . . something yellow. I'm not very good at compliments."

"Egg yolks?" she said cheerfully.

"Drowsy sunshine," he said, tucking another flower into her curls.

"How lovely," she said, startled. "Like poetry."

He smiled at her and pulled her arm back into his. "Perhaps I shall write an ode to you. That is what courting couples do, do they not?"

"Well, I've never heard of a woman writing an ode to a man," she said with a gurgle of laughter. "But I could try. I'm afraid I'm sadly unimaginative. It's the chess player in me."

"For Jemma, whose hair is like drowsy sunshine," he said, "and whose eyes are like . . . are like . . . "

"Marbles?" she suggested, laughing.

He glanced down at her. "I can see that you have no gift for romance. I shall have to take control of this wooing business."

"Absolutely not," Jemma said. "You have control of far too many things. I am in charge of our wooing. To-night you are going to Vauxhall."

"*I?* Don't you mean *we*?"

"I shall be there, masked of course. You will have to find me."

He groaned. "Jemma, I'm an old and respectable duke, too old to—"

"Elijah, what are you saying? You're thirty-four! When's the last time you went to Vauxhall?"

"Not long," he said, extremely unconvincingly.

"I've never been there with you," she said. "And I can't imagine you going alone. Did you visit before we married?"

"I took up my seat at age twenty-one," he said. "I had no time—"

"No time! No time for one of the most . . . I must say, Elijah, it's a good thing that our parents arranged our marriage when we were young. At this rate, you'd have become a curmudgeonly old bachelor without even entertaining the thought of marriage."

"Not after I had seen you," he said.

She felt that, like a drop of joy, all the way to her toes.

"You didn't look so pleased to marry me at the time," she said, keeping her voice light. "I was quite infatuated with you, as I'm sure was painfully obvious. But even infatuation couldn't disguise the fact that you were less than pleased to be married."

"I was fascinated by power," he said. "It took me the way strong drink takes other men. My father had disgraced himself, you know."

Jemma cleared her throat. "Do you refer to the unfortunate circumstances of his death?"

"That, of course. But also in the House. He took up his seat, God knows why. He clearly must have had no interest. And he led a group of men who took delight in delaying measures, in frolicking."

Jemma frowned, uncertain what he meant.

"If a bill was being debated, they would stand up and make long, frivolous arguments in favor or against, switching their argument halfway through sometimes. They would introduce new bills, arguing for things like providing every man in the country with free French letters, or providing all whores with lessons in Eastern dance."

"Oh."

"There were enough of them so that they effectively killed several bills, and caused no end of embarrassment to men who were trying hard to do the work of government."

"It must have been difficult to take up your seat after that," Jemma ventured.

"They—my father's friends—were still around, you see. They hailed me as Bawdy Beaumont. They thought I would continue in his vein, play the young Bacchus to their frolics."

"Well, you didn't."

He smiled ruefully. "I didn't. But it took time, and much thought and scheming, to play down my father's reputation and the House's expectations for me. I'm afraid that marriage wasn't terribly important under those circumstances. In fact, as I recall, the months before our marriage were particularly fraught, as I was finally establishing myself as a voice in my own right. I could hardly concentrate on anything else."

Jemma cleared her throat. "I really should apologize."

He bent over and tucked the bluebells into her hair again. His hand lingered for a moment. "They were slipping."

"I know that my scandals, in France and here, caused you embarrassment. But I had no idea that you were contending with something like 'Bawdy Beaumont,'" she said. "None. I promise you that I would have been discreet, Elijah."

"I didn't share my travails with you, did I? I never told you about my daily problems."

"No," she said. "I remember asking about your day, and you would tell me the events being discussed. I wanted to contribute somehow, but of course I knew nothing."

"It took me a few years to think clearly about the early days of our marriage, but then I remembered. You would lie next to me in the morning and ply me with questions. And I was such a fool that I was eager to be in the House already. I had no time for you. That was one of my greatest stupidities, Jemma."

"You had other concerns."

"I deserved to lose you. And I did."

"I'm here now," she said, smiling up at him. "And I'll be at Vauxhall tonight, masked, of course. You *do* have a domino, don't you, Elijah?"

"I believe so," he said. "Will you wear a domino as well?"

She nodded.

"What color?"

"That is for you to find out," she said, laughing. "The first lesson in courting is to be able to identify the woman you wish to woo!"

"But you are wooing me," he said rather smugly. "I shall just wait until a beautiful woman in a mask approaches me and begins a flirtation."

"You do that," Jemma said, laughing.

He eyed her suspiciously, so she gave a little shrug. "Of course you'll be able to identify me immediately, Elijah. Who else would try to flirt with you?"

Chapter Nine

The Duke of Villiers, known to himself as Leopold and to everyone else as terrifying, had made up his mind. The one woman he really wanted, Jemma, wasn't his to win. His old friend Elijah had her, and for all Elijah's ideas that he might follow his father's early death, Leopold didn't think so.

At any rate, some small foolish part of him wanted to be loved by someone who hadn't loved Elijah better.

After all, the first woman he loved in the world had been a winsome barmaid by the name of Bess. But once Elijah crooked a finger, she traipsed after Beaumont without a backward glance.

'Twas all the fault of Villiers' face, no doubt. It was a harsh type of face, and not softening with the years. The silver streaks in his hair didn't help, and neither did his great beak of a nose. In fact, he looked like the damned beast he was, and the hell with that.

He was done with women. He revised that thought.

Not done with women until—God forbid—his loins withered. But he was throwing away the idea of a good woman, by which he meant a marriageable woman. Not that Jemma was ever marriageable, given that she was married to Elijah.

So, not marriageable, but otherwise a woman like Jemma. A woman who was worth giving a damn about.

Villiers was very good at dismissing his little black moments. He generally took that sort of emotion and shoved it away with a pungent curse.

His butler, Ashmole, entered the library. He had been in the household for years and grown slope-shouldered and sunken as he grew old. His skin was the color of a wilted celery leaf.

"Would you prefer a pension or a cottage?" Villiers asked, before Ashmole could say anything. He asked him periodically, as a matter of course.

Ashmole gave him the ferocious look of an aging vulture, all bony beak and chin. It struck Villiers that he would probably look the same in *his* seventies. It was an unpleasant thought.

"Why would I do that?" the butler replied. "Just when you're having a fit of the vapors and planning to make things interesting around here?"

Villiers eyed him. There was something distinctly disadvantageous about inheriting a butler who had spanked you as a lad, ignoring the fact that you were the future duke and focusing merely on your sins to do with stolen blackberry tarts. The man had never formed a proper sense of awe. "You look like something that fell off a tinker's cart."

"You look like a damned parrot," Ashmole retorted. Then he pulled his shoulders back, which signaled that their charming preliminaries were at an end. "Your Grace's solicitor, Mr. Templeton, awaits Your Grace's pleasure."

"Send him in," Villiers said. "And for God's sake, go take a nap. I don't want to frighten Templeton by the thought you might expire while handing over his cloak."

Ashmole retired without a word, which meant that he would take a nap, and knew he needed it. Villiers sighed. It was just as well that he hadn't the faintest inclination to invite anyone to visit his house.

Templeton was a miracle of legal sobriety. His long, jutting chin had surely never lowered to emit laughter. Given his superior attitude, it was hard to imagine him taking a piss. He looked like a mourning bird hatched from a somber black legal tome, and due to be buried in the same.

Villiers nodded, indicating that Templeton might stop bowing and take a seat. "I've decided to house my bastards," he said without further introduction.

Templeton blinked. "I assure Your Grace that they are housed."

"Here."

Templeton was the sort of man who had a huge desk containing at least forty pigeonholes. Each of those would be assigned to part of the duke's estate: bastard children likely off in a lower corner somewhere, in a position of shame. The horror in his eyes surely resulted from a confusion of pigeonholes.

"Your Grace?"

"Collect them," Villiers said briefly. "Wait—isn't there one of them living with its mother?"

Templeton coughed. "If you'd given me some warning, Your Grace, I would have brought the list."

"There aren't that many, for God's sake," Villiers barked. "Surely you know their situations?"

Even a duke could read the criticism deep in Templeton's eyes.

"I handed those children over to you," Villiers said.

"They are well cared for," Templeton said, a little bluster entering his voice. "You can find no fault in the record."

"I'm not looking to do so. I've simply changed course. The children are coming to live here. All but, perhaps, the one who lives with the mother. I'm not having any mothers."

Templeton cleared his throat, took out a small notebook. "No mothers," he said weakly.

"Should be easy enough to round them up. Simply go to their addresses, relieve their current minders of responsibility, and bring them here."

"Here?" Templeton looked around the room a bit desperately, his gaze skewing upwards.

Villiers had to admit that his library almost veered into a parody of himself—but then, so did he. Last year he'd had the vaulted ceiling painted with a riotous mural depicting life on Mount Olympus. He had long thought of Greek myths as a storage house for the male imagination (Jove's seduction of Danae in a rain of gold coins was a particularly efficient fantasy). It struck him as amusing to house his literature collection in a room that implied it was all about the bed.

Jove was here, there, and everywhere. Now a bull, now a swan, but always in pursuit of a lushly nubile (and naked) nymph. He had instructed the artist to forget the idea of painting any of those little Italian cupids, the ones with limp, small penises, and concentrate on breasts instead.

The painter had taken to his task with a great deal of enthusiasm. Villiers was still discovering new breasts that he hadn't noticed previously.

Templeton clearly did not approve. Unfortunately for him, Villiers didn't give a damn about his opinion.

"That will be all," he said, looking back down at the papers on his desk.

"Your Grace," Templeton implored.

Villiers layered his voice with a combination of irritation, annoyance, and possible violence. "Yes?"

"Who shall care for these children?"

"Mrs. Ferrers will manage them. You might mention it to her. She'll hire some nursemaids or some such, I've no doubt."

Templeton gulped.

Villiers raised his eyes again. "If you're afraid of my housekeeper, Templeton, just let me know and I'll inform her myself."

Templeton rose to his feet, regaining a semblance of dignity. "I bid Your Grace a good morning," he said, bowing.

A thought struck Villiers. "Templeton."

"Yes, Your Grace." Bowing again.

"Would a sensible—nay, a charitable—person believe that I ought to recover these infants myself?"

Templeton's mouth hung open.

"I wonder what Miss Tatlock would say?" Villiers mused to himself.

"Miss Tatlock?" Templeton stammered.

"Actually, her name is now Mrs. Dautry, since she married my heir," Villiers murmured. "I *did* give you that letter, didn't I? Yes, I surely did. With instructions to change the details of my will, I believe. I am quite certain that the line of descent is now assured. She

will likely produce any number of clucking infants—
and all within the bounds of wedlock, which is surely
more than I can say for myself."

"Yes, Your Grace—that is, I am aware of that, Your
Grace."

"She would think I should fetch the children
myself," Villiers said, making up his mind. "Very well,
Templeton. Send me a note in the morning with the
relevant names and addresses. I shall try to fit it in. I
have a very busy few days ahead of me. I promised the
Duchess of Beaumont I would visit Vauxhall tonight;
I am promised for several games of chess at Parsloe's,
and now this."

He lowered his chin.

His solicitor's voice was a predictable squeal, but
there was an extra edge of scandalized horror there.
Villiers heard it with interest. Why should his solicitor
be afraid at the idea of him rounding up his illegitimate infants?

"Your Grace *cannot* mean to—"

Villiers fixed him with a look. "I can indeed," he
said softly. "And on second thought, I should like that
list delivered to me within the hour, Templeton."

Templeton scurried from the room.

Chapter Ten

Later that evening

The Marquise de Perthuis was feeling miserably uncertain. "This costume makes me feel like a circus performer," she told her companion, pulling her purple domino more tightly around her body.

"You look ravishing," Lord Corbin said, bracing himself as the carriage went around a corner. "I promise you, Madame la Marquise, everyone at Vauxhall will think that you are utterly exquisite."

"But isn't this Vauxhall a place of ill repute? I seem to have been told something like that. I remember now; it was Balthazar Monoconys. He said there was a miscellany of persons there and a wench in a mask asked him, in the most familiar way, if he would drink a bottle of mead with her."

Lord Corbin leaned forward and patted her hand. "It is true that without the affectation of black and white, you are alarming beautiful, marquise. But I will ward off anyone asking you to share a bottle."

"Do you really think this color suits me?" Louise was aware that she shouldn't reveal her insecurities to Corbin. But he was so sympathetic—and besides, she had seen him exchanging intimacies a thousand times with Jemma. First, she planned to usurp Corbin, and next, the duke himself.

"Absolutely. That bluish-purple is perfect for you," Corbin said. "Black is too harsh. It can have an aging effect."

The marquise was silenced by that revelation. Though she would never forgive the Duchess of Beaumont for her grotesque impoliteness, perhaps it was just as well that she had discarded her penchant for black and white.

She smiled at Corbin. "What does one do at Vauxhall?"

"We'll take a table near the orchestra," he told her. "There's a raised building in Moorish style that you'll find very interesting. And truly, there's no need for concern. I shan't leave your side."

That would never do. *"Mon Dieu!"* she cried, snapping open her fan. "I am not an *enfant* who needs to be coddled, Lord Corbin. In fact, I am hoping to see a particular friend of mine."

He didn't look in the least insulted by this revelation. It was just as she suspected: Corbin understood that he had no real hope that she, a marquise, would take his charms seriously. He was very attractive and well-dressed, with an easiness of manner that made him seem almost French, but still . . . if she, the Marquise de Perthuis, decided to stray from the marital bond, it would not be into the arms of a man of his rank.

"You see," she continued, leaning forward as if confiding a deep secret, "the Duke of Beaumont and I are *dear* friends." Corbin was a notable gossip, which was one of the reasons she had chosen him to escort her. All of London needed to know of this night.

"My goodness," Lord Corbin said with his charming smile. "I must compliment you, Marquise. I confess that I viewed the duke as something of a Puritan. But of course, no man is invulnerable before a woman of your beauty."

"You are too kind," the marquise said, settling back on the seat and rewarding his compliment with a smile.

"Do you find the duke an easy conversationalist?" Corbin inquired. "I'm afraid that I know little of the state of the government, and he, of course, is an expert."

"I never discuss such matters," Louise said. "For one thing, I never read the English papers. I am not very good at reading the language, and they're so depressing, always. It's the same with the French papers, but at least I can understand the words."

"I absolutely agree," Corbin said. "These newspaper people write only for themselves, and with no thought about what is really interesting in life. It's a wonder anyone reads them at all."

"They are always writing about obscure people," Louise said fretfully. "Savages and the like."

"I can't abide reading about the Americas," Corbin agreed. "They sound quite unsanitary. And full of people murdering each other for the most extraordinary reasons."

"No, I refer to savages living in the next street," Louise corrected him. "If you believe the French papers, there are astonishing kinds of people anywhere one looks. The papers positively delight in telling one loathsome details about poisoners and the like. It's enough to make one quite nervous about the cook."

"How exceedingly thought-provoking," Corbin said. "And boring. I expect the Duke of Beaumont is very glad to have a change of subject when he talks to you."

"Naturally," Louise said, wondering just what she should talk to Beaumont about. Perhaps she should have perused the *Morning Chronicle*.

"If you don't mind my asking, what *is* the duke's familiar name?" Corbin asked.

Louise narrowed her eyes at him, but he gazed back innocently. "I never address any man by his first name," she pronounced.

"My apologies!" Corbin cried. "I recall the Duke of Villiers addressing you as Louise . . . "

"I myself do not engage in such intimacies. At any rate, Villiers is my cousin. He's not a man."

"Contrary to what everyone thinks," Corbin said, sounding delighted.

When the carriage stopped, Louise tied on her mask and they strolled toward the center of the park. There were some young couples embracing rather ardently in the shade of the poplar trees.

"It's nothing more than one might see in the environs of the Bois de Boulogne," Corbin said, after she pointed out this vulgarity.

"I have never entered the Bois de Boulogne," Louise remarked. "And now you tell me that, I never shall."

Corbin immediately commanded a supper box in just the right spot with a minimum of fuss, ordering two bottles of Champagne and a plate of delicacies.

"*Two* bottles?" Louise said, trying to adjust her mask so she could see a bit better.

"We might as well make ourselves comfortable," Corbin said. "I'm afraid that the Duke of Beaumont does not appear to have arrived yet."

"I didn't come only for that purpose," Louise said loftily (and untruthfully).

Corbin didn't seem to mind. "I should hope not. It doesn't do for ladies to track men down like hunting dogs. It would make my whole sex far too vain to even know of the possibility."

Louise took a desperate swallow of Champagne. "These masks make everything rather difficult," she said. "I certainly hope I recognize those people I know."

"There is no need for introductions at Vauxhall," Corbin assured her.

She digested that in silence. Truly, the English were a different race than the French. No French nobleman would attend an uncouth event of this nature. Still, she ought to be polite, since Corbin was kind enough to accompany her. "Those lamps shaped like stars are quite beautiful," she told him. Corbin filled up her glass again, and she clutched it like a precious elixir. "Do you see any sign of the duke?"

"Not yet."

"Look at that!" Louise exclaimed. "I do believe there are courtesans here." The woman in question had thrown off her mask, if she ever had one.

"Dear me," Corbin replied. "That is an elegant dress. I wonder if she knows that her entire bosom is visible?"

"Of course she does," Louise retorted. "One doesn't skimp cloth in that particular area unless one has made up one's mind to do so. I must admit that I've never seen the *demimondaine* very close. Of course, one jokes about people such as the Comtesse de Montbard, but there is a difference."

"Yes, the countess is liberal with her affections but entirely free," Corbin murmured.

"I wonder how they phrase the request for money," Louise said, drinking again. "I would be quite embarrassed at the need to price myself, so to speak."

"I suspect they are used to it," Corbin said in a companionable sort of way. They sat in their small box and observed the dancers for a time. Then Louise found herself watching a very tall man with an air of natural command and a beautiful profile, even masked. There was no question: the Duke of Beaumont had arrived.

"I beg you to excuse me for a moment," she said, rising. She swayed a bit but caught herself. "I see a friend of mine. I'll just take a glass of Champagne with me."

"I will be right here," Lord Corbin said, with just the right note of reassurance.

Louise headed directly across the dance floor. The duke appeared to be in a veritable nest of courtesans, and she thought she ought to make haste. The duchess was certainly wrong about her husband's faithfulness. But then, Louise thought with a pang, she'd had the same illusions about her own husband.

"Peter, what on earth are you doing here?" Jemma said, sliding into the marquise's chair as Louise wavered away from the table. "You find yourself in the midst of a play of my making, though now that I think of it, it's entirely appropriate. You instigated the plot, after all."

"My dear duchess," Corbin said, kissing her fingers, "I must compliment you on your efficacy. I certainly didn't think that you'd be able to bring about a courtship of your husband within twenty-four hours."

"I wasn't entirely sure the marquise would take the bait," Jemma confessed. "But I thought Vauxhall offered many opportunities for that sort of encounter. Where is Elijah, anyway?"

"He's directly across from us. I rather think that's a courtesan he's speaking to."

"Do give me a glass of Champagne, darling. This *is* fun for Elijah! And now comes Louise."

"Oh my, she is truly unsteady. It must have been that third glass of Champagne. How was I to know that she had such a light head?"

"What on earth is Louise doing?"

"She's winding herself around your husband," Corbin pointed out. "You'll have to stop giggling, Jemma, if you want me to believe that you are sober."

"You may believe whatever you like. Did she just throw herself into his arms?"

"I think she might have tripped on her cloak."

"Well, he's holding her very tenderly," Jemma observed. "You don't suppose Elijah thinks she is I, do you?"

"Not now that he's holding the marquise," Corbin said cheerfully. "You weigh at least a stone more than she does."

"Thank you very much!"

"Your weight is nicely apportioned in the chest area. Men tend to notice that sort of thing."

"Well, at least he got her back on her feet. He's laughing," Jemma said. "Elijah is laughing."

"Ah, the Puritan bends." Corbin poured a little

more Champagne into Jemma's glass. "We must have a drink to the—"

"You drink," Jemma said, getting up. "I'm going to rescue my husband. The marquise just kissed him on the ear, and that was *not* part of the plan."

She pulled her mask straight and sauntered toward them. The marquise was draped against Elijah's right side, looking muzzy but determined, and an unknown lady was draped on his left, looking considerably livelier and just as determined.

"Hello," Jemma said as she sauntered up, pitching her voice deliberately in the hope that Elijah would think she was yet another stranger.

She couldn't tell whether he recognized her or not. "Hello," he said politely, and then turned back to the lady on his left. "I'm afraid that I don't dance very well, but it's kind of you to ask."

"Every gentleman knows how to dance," Jemma said, moving closer. The marquise had her head resting on Elijah's arm.

"I know how to dance," Louise said, clearly recognizing Jemma as she straightened immediately. "And what I'd like to do is dance with you!" She smiled up at Elijah. "Because you're beautiful. I'm very, very fond of beautiful men. You probably didn't know that."

A muscle moved in Elijah's cheek, and Jemma thought he was close to breaking into laughter. Which was better than becoming swamped by desire.

"I can teach you how to dance," said the crimson domino on his left side. She had a husky voice that promised a lot more than dancing lessons.

There was definitely a cocky glint in Elijah's smile now, Jemma thought.

Jemma put a hand on her hip and pitched her voice

to be as inviting as that of the stranger with the husky voice. "Men have been known to cry if I refused to dance."

Elijah looked expectantly to his left, to the crimson charmer. Her eyes were narrowed and she was examining Jemma inch by inch. "There are some people who aren't worth dancing with because they're too hoity-toity to have a good time."

The marquise stepped away from Elijah with nary a waver and gave the crimson domino a scathing look. *"Une allure honteuse."*

"What did she say to me?" the woman demanded.

Elijah very courteously translated. "I believe she called you a shameless jade."

"What?"

But with one triumphant glance, Louise neatly turned Elijah about and hauled him into the throng of dancers.

Jemma's mouth fell open.

"Christ's toenails!" the crimson cloak said. "I had him all set, and then that drunk wobbled out of nowhere, and now she took him! It's because she is French."

"Really?"

"Men all think that Frenchwomen are on their knees half the night," she confided. "The worst of it is that he was a nabob." She grinned at Jemma. "And he had big hands. I was looking forward to dancing with him."

Jemma turned about and surveyed the assembly.

"You'd best look elsewhere," the crimson cloak said consolingly. "She had him from the start, I could tell. She made a couple of remarks that made him laugh. And she had herself draped on him. I got only one feel but it was a nice one."

Jemma blinked at her.

"Love's dart, so they call it. But this was a great deal thicker than a dart," she added, with a naughty laugh. "Ah, well, it wasn't for my benefit." And she wandered off.

Jemma's eyes narrowed. She didn't like to think of that woman touching the dart in question. She turned back to the dancers. Louise seemed to have sobered enough so that she was dancing a reasonable approximation of the minuet, but as Jemma watched, she tripped and fell into Elijah's arms. He was laughing.

Jemma ground her teeth.

Enough!

Chapter Eleven

Dancing in Vauxhall, at this hour of the night, did not resemble the parallel activities that took place in the ballrooms of Versailles and St. James. The music sounded the same; a large orchestra was sawing away on its raised platform. But the dancers' movements were entirely more intimate.

Some people seemed to know that the minuet being played at the moment was generally danced in a formal pattern; others seemed to consider it more of a country dance. No one bothered trading partners: why pass your partner to the hand of another if it meant you might not see her again?

Only the Puritanical would insist that those at Vauxhall were drunker than those in elegant ballrooms. Elijah had seen whole rooms full of bluebloods reeling from an excess of punch. And those same Puritans couldn't honestly call the dancers more lascivious, since lust coursed through the noble soul with the same fury as anyone else's.

The primary difference, Elijah decided, was that whereas noblemen danced in patterns, those who came to Vauxhall danced in pairs. And pairing allowed for a certain proximity that encouraged groping.

Not that he felt the slightest inclination to approach his partner in that manner. He had recognized her immediately, though without any particular pleasure.

He was supporting the Marquise de Perthuis with one arm, while dancing a lamentable version of the minuet, and wondering where on earth Jemma had got to when he realized that his wife was standing at the edge of the floor, tapping her foot in an irritated fashion.

He swiftly turned the marquise in a circle so Jemma didn't catch his delighted grin.

"Goodness me," the marquise said, "you are very quick on your feet!"

"It is because you are so beautiful," he said to her.

She looked up at him rather owlishly, and Elijah thought that in fact she actually did look beautiful. Maybe it was due to being inebriated. Generally the marquise's rigid personality precluded anyone from thinking she was beautiful.

It was an odd thought, because rigid was what Jemma had always called *him* when they quarreled. As well as hidebound, moralistic, and tedious. He looked down at the marquise uneasily. Moralistic people were quite dislikable . . . though he never thought of himself in those terms.

She took a deep breath and shook her head a bit. "I do believe that I might have drunk a trifle more Champagne than I ought."

"We all indulge at times," he told her, looking around to see where Jemma was now. She would be very annoyed to see how closely he was holding the marquise, though in fact he either had to grasp her tightly or let her slip to the ground.

"I never indulge," the marquise told him. "Indulgence is the province of the devil. My mother said so and I'm sure she was always right."

She seemed to be brooding about something, so Elijah twirled her again so he could see the space where he had last seen Jemma. She was still there, but no longer alone.

A red-haired fellow in a tired blue domino and matching mask was bowing before her. He looked like a sailor on leave. He had the rakish air of a young man of the town: not a gentleman, not a farmer, but something in between. Elijah began edging the marquise backwards through the crowd.

"Do mind my skirts," the marquise said. "I must say, have you ever seen so many dissolute women in your life?" She seemed utterly fascinated. "I love it here. Had I known, I would have come long ago. You must have been to Vauxhall many times."

"Hmm," Elijah said. The blue cloak was leading Jemma onto the floor, and she was smiling up at him in a way that sent a flare down Elijah's spine. A moment later he had maneuvered the marquise so that he was shoulder-to-shoulder with his wife.

From the lavish and delighted smile Jemma was giving her partner, she knew perfectly well he was there.

He set the marquise to turn a gentle circle and leaned in toward Jemma's ear. "I want you." His voice was somewhere between a whisper and a growl.

She threw him a glance from those laughing, wicked eyes of hers. The man in the blue cloak hadn't noticed and drew her in the opposite direction. He had red whiskers, a look that Elijah found extremely unattractive.

Now he was bending his head, to say something clever, no doubt. Jemma was laughing. Elijah saw her throat ripple and was seized by a blind wave of lust. He wanted to lick her there, to lick her whole body, feel the vibration of every muscle when she—

Belatedly he remembered the marquise and took her back on his arm. She was growing slightly more sober the longer they danced. "You know, Beaumont," she pronounced, "I expect my husband Henri adores this place."

"You do?" Elijah had met the Marquis de Perthuis only once, but he remembered a man with a longing face, the face of someone who wanted more than dissolute dancing. He looked like a frustrated painter, or an inventor of some kind.

"He hates being a marquis. He has all sorts of revolutionary notions about the *noblesse* and the *canaille* being alike. Can you imagine?"

Elijah could imagine quite easily. The marquis was a man who hated himself, and apparently he extended that dislike to his entire class. The marquise went on, telling him about her husband's strange proclivities, while he steered her through the crowd and back over next to Jemma. That fellow she was dancing with was entirely too familiar for Elijah's comfort. He was looking at Jemma as if she was a tart ripe for devouring.

Elijah could sympathize. Jemma looked succulent and sweet, like a peach. But she was *his* peach. Finally he managed to get the marquise jostled into the correct position so that he was shoulder-to-shoulder with Jemma again. The marquise was still talking, though Elijah had lost track of the subject.

Elijah Tobier, Duke of Beaumont, was never vulgar. Even when in the company of men who indulged in coarse jokes at women's expense—or at their own—he invariably smiled, but always remained silent. But now all nature of coarse words surged to his lips, though he didn't want to share them with a roomful of men, but with only one woman.

He leaned over and brushed her hair with his mouth, and whispered something extremely vulgar that only she could hear. He turned away, but heard her choke and laugh.

The marquise was pouting, so he bent his head down to her again.

"As I said," she repeated, "he met this woman at a meeting with le Marquis de Lafayette. She helped Henri translate an American document, a declaration of some sort, into French. Can you imagine?"

It was surprising. "It would have been easier had he fallen in love with someone of my stature," the marquise said dismally. "Because she would understand—" She waved her hands. "All of it, she would understand all of it. As it was, this woman demanded that he leave with her. Leave!"

"And did he?" Elijah enquired.

"He did." She nodded vehemently and tripped on her cloak again. Elijah neatly caught her and put her back on her feet. "He left with her, and he left me. *Moi!*" She widened her eyes.

"An absurd decision," Elijah put in.

"I am a leader in Queen Marie Antoinette's court," the marquise announced. "My clothes are talked of by everyone. I have never marred my reputation, even with the slightest slur. I have never contemplated an excess."

"An excess?"

"You know."

He didn't, but it hardly mattered. *"You* are my first excess," she stated.

He blinked down at her. "I am an excess?"

"Of course. Shall we go have some more Champagne?" she asked, seemingly forgetting that he hadn't been with her from the beginning. "There are several bottles on our table."

"Are you here with a party?" he asked, more than willing to return her and pluck Jemma away from that sailor she was dancing with.

"Of course," the marquise said with a frown. "I'm here with you. And you and I are . . . " She struggled for the word. " . . . seducing each other."

Elijah's mouth fell open. "We *are*?"

"I have not decided exactly how far I shall allow the seduction to continue," the marquise said loftily. "It likely depends on the Champagne." She looked around with a little puckered frown. "This wooing was quite easy once I had a glass or two. I should like some more. I believe I shall fetch it myself." And with no further ado, she left.

Elijah looked after her for a moment, but a gentleman was hailing her to join him at a table to the side, and she wasn't swaying quite so much anymore. He wondered briefly how the marquise found herself at Vauxhall, and then swiveled to find Jemma.

She was still dancing. Her partner had either had too much to drink or was simply too lusty for his own good. He was trying to pull Jemma against his body. She stepped precisely on his foot with her sharp heel, and the sailor stumbled back.

Of course Jemma had fended for herself in Paris

for years. She didn't need him. The recognition of it turned his mouth into a hard line. She didn't even leave the floor after her partner's attempt at a kiss, just kept dancing with that blackguard as if nothing had happened.

"What a distinct—and surprising—pleasure," said a voice at his ear.

He didn't bother turning, just kept his eyes on Jemma. "Villiers."

"What are you watching with such— Ah, the wife."

"She doesn't realize the man is drunk."

Villiers laughed. "Jemma strikes me as a woman who will always be able to ascertain the extent of a man's inebriation."

On the dance floor, the gallant leaned over as if he were trying to gobble Jemma's ear and she neatly evaded him.

"Why the devil doesn't she simply leave him there alone?"

"Because she's having too much fun putting on a drama for you. The cruelest thing you could do would be to turn away."

That wasn't a possibility. Turn away while another man tried to paw his wife? Never mind the fact that he had known quite well that she was having *affaires* while living in Paris. That he deliberately hadn't followed her to Paris for three years—no, four—until rumor reached him that she'd had a week-long fling with a young fool named DuPuy.

It was her *right*, after what he'd done to her. He owed her.

But it was different now.

Now he was going to have to kill that fool she was

dancing with. Even as they watched, the red-haired sailor leaned toward her again, trying to catch a kiss. He was going for her mouth— He was—

A strong hand caught him. Villiers. "Just what do you think you're doing?"

"Going to retrieve my wife," he said tightly.

"You can't be involved in a fight," Villiers said.

"Why the hell not?"

He hesitated. "You're a statesman."

"That hasn't stopped most of the men I know from brawling."

"You *know* why."

Jemma seemed to be fending off her swain with her elbow, so Elijah frowned at Villiers. "What are you talking about?"

"Your heart," Villiers hissed. "You should be at home resting."

"The devil with that." Out of the corner of his eye he saw the man swoop in again. He was bigger and stronger than Jemma. She was trying to push him away but—

Elijah was next to them in a second. He grabbed the man's shoulder and caught one glimpse of his surprised face, red lips pursed in a kiss, before he hit him so hard that the man rose slightly in the air, landed hard, and skidded on his bottom to the edge of the dance floor.

There was a chorus of little screams as dancers scrambled to get out of the way. The ruffian climbed to his feet. "What'd you do that for?" he yelled, furious. "I wasn't doing anything that the trollop didn't want me to do! Who the hell are you? Her protector?"

"The husband," Elijah said softly. "Just the husband." He could see the man shifting his weight from foot to foot, trying to decide whether to lunge at him.

"I'm glad I don't have a wife like that!" he bellowed.

The crowd was interested now, forming a circle around the swell in the velvet domino and the red-haired sailor. There was a murmur of approval at that comment.

"It's hard to keep a wife where she belongs!" someone shouted.

The red-haired man grinned. "Especially if she's not satisfied at home. This one was looking for company."

Elijah's fists clenched and he stepped forward, just one step. "No woman should be handled in such an uncouth manner."

A shrill voice agreed. "She got the right to dance with whoever she pleases without paying with her reputation!" It was a burly woman in the front of the growing crowd.

"An' he's got a right to fight for his wife, light-skirt though she be!" someone else shouted.

Behind him, Elijah could hear Jemma's help-less laughter. He made the mistake of smiling at the sound.

"You're laughing at me! I did nothing to your wife but what she welcomed. She's worse than a light-skirt. She's a—a . . . " Maybe it was the look in Elijah's eyes that dried up his words. Without bothering to finish his sentence, the sailor lowered his shoulder and charged like a bull, catching Elijah square in the chest.

Elijah was expecting a blow to the face because that was how the men fought in the boxing salon he regu-larly visited. He barely managed to keep to his feet, and the man was rounding about, ready for another charge.

In one lightning quick moment, Elijah calculated the rate of speed of his attacker and his relatively lower height, drew back his fist, and waited for the man's chin to connect with it.

Over the sailor went, out cold.

The *thunk* that resounded through the night air was followed directly by an unmistakably official bellow. "Now what's all this, what's all this?"

"Ah . . . the watchman," Villiers said softly.

Elijah turned his head. "You're at my shoulder?"

Villiers shrugged. "He might have had a brother. How are you feeling?"

Elijah waited a split second, shook himself, and started grinning. "Stupendous. Where's Jemma?"

"Fool," Villiers muttered, stepping forward.

The duke made an imposing figure. A plain domino would never do for Villiers, of course. His was of black velvet with a border of pale lilac. His silver cane looked exactly like the sword stick it was. The crowd stopped chattering when they saw him.

He prodded the fallen man with the tip of his boot.

"Drunk," he announced.

The watchman frowned. "I was informed there was a fight and I think I heard . . . " His voice died out.

The cold look in Villiers's eyes could have graced the devil himself. "You must have been mistaken." He looked around at the bystanders. "He *was* mistaken, wasn't he?"

Vauxhall might attract those of different backgrounds, but it wasn't limited to the stupid. "Drunk as a sailor," the burly woman in the front said promptly. "Only person drunker would be my old da, and he ain't here tonight."

"Humph," the watchman said.

"I suppose someone must drag him away to sleep it off," Villiers said, sighing. "For your trouble." There was a gentle click, the kind made by guineas passing from one hand to another.

"Now, now!" the watchman shouted briskly. "No need to stand about gawking at this unfortunate inebriate."

Jemma was standing to the side, still giggling.

"You are a reckless wench," Elijah said, taking her hands.

"I'm not," she protested, but her eyes were alight with laughter.

"You enticed that man to kiss you."

"If I wanted to make you jealous," she said with a delicious pout, "I could do far better than that."

"Yes?" He pulled her mask over her head.

"Villiers is here."

"I saw him."

"I could—" She broke off in a little grunt. "What are you doing?"

Without further ado, he picked her up and threw her over his shoulder. "Going where I can chastise my errant wife."

There was an enthusiastic shout behind him. "That's the way, square toes! Keep the missus in line!"

Elijah turned. "I shall, thank you . . . Villiers!" he called.

"You couldn't be an acquaintance of mine," Villiers said. "Are you the local dockworker?"

"The Marquise de Perthuis is here somewhere, unless she's fallen into a drunken stupor. Will you escort her to her house? I must take my wife home."

Villiers bowed and disappeared.

"That's the sauce!" someone shouted. "Give her a bit

of the home remedy and she won't be flirting with the first jackanapes she sees!"

Jemma was laughing helplessly. Her hair had fallen around her face and she couldn't see anything. "Elijah," she gasped.

"In a moment," he said politely, walking off.

"I had too much Champagne to be in this position," she said a second later.

He put her down immediately. By then they were in one of the shadowed lanes that spread out from the orchestra pavilion and were lit only by infrequent lamps.

"I'm afraid I've lost track of where we are," he said. "The carriages don't seem to be in this direction. Did you have a great deal of Champagne?"

"This is the Dark Walk," Jemma said, sitting down on a bench. "I suppose I shouldn't have flirted with that ginger-haired fellow."

"Why not?" he said agreeably.

"It was rather fun, knowing that you were watching."

"Though of course *he* didn't know that."

"He shouldn't have tried to kiss me so roughly."

"He had reason to think that you welcomed his advances. After all, you stayed on the floor with him."

"Well . . . You're making me feel shabby, Elijah. I hate it when you do that!"

He reached out and pulled her into his lap in one swift movement. "Let's discuss the rules of marriage."

"The rules of marriage!"

"You're not to kiss anyone else."

"No?" She must have recovered from her shame, because she gave that one word a deeply wistful tone.

"Never again."

"I shall think about it."

His arm tightened. "No thinking. No kissing."

"Then I get to tell you the second rule of marriage."

"All right."

"You have to care if someone is going to kiss me. While dancing or elsewhere." She whispered it.

"I—"

Jemma laid her head against his chest, so she couldn't see Elijah's eyes. "When I went to Paris, you didn't follow. I cried every night for months, but inside, I thought you would arrive any day. Then I decided that you couldn't come while Parliament was in session."

He groaned.

"But then Parliament went into recess, and friends wrote me and said that you had gone to Kent, to the Earl of Chatham's estate. I thought perhaps you couldn't escape the work," she said, relentlessly.

"But I never came."

"You never came."

"I couldn't."

She didn't say anything.

"And not because of work. Because—Because it wasn't my right, Jemma."

"Your right to do what?"

"To follow you. *I'd* broken our marriage. I'd done just what my father did to my mother, over and over, without even realizing it. I'd broken your heart and your trust."

Jemma thought about reassuring him, but it was all true. "So why didn't you come after me?" She sounded like a little girl.

"I waited."

"Waited for what?"

"Waited until you had found someone."

"But I didn't want anyone!"

His arms tightened. "You had the right."

"It hurt to see you with a mistress. It was heart-breaking when you said you loved her. But the real heartbreak came when I realized you didn't even care what I did. That I meant so little to you that you didn't bother to visit for years."

"Three years, ten months, and fourteen days."

The only sound was that of a sleepy, confused lark, somewhere deep in the park. Jemma straightened up so she could see Elijah's face. *"What?"*

"That's how long it took you. You finally had an *af-faire* with DuPuy. It lasted only—"

"It lasted three days," Jemma said. "You knew that?"

He nodded. "My friends were as assiduous in let-ter-writing as were yours. And of course the fact that DuPuy had fallen so deeply in love with you was con-sidered tantalizing news for your husband."

"So you came that Christmas."

"I came as soon as the Parliament recessed. I had this foolish notion . . . "

"What?"

"That it would all be fine. But you were furious at me. And I—I found that for all my reasoned decision that it was your right to have an *affaire*, I wanted to throttle you."

"The things you said drove me to more excess."

He ran a finger slowly down the slope of her cheek. "I know. I came again the next year, but . . . "

"We didn't fight as much," Jemma said, remem-bering.

"You thought I was moralistic and boring. And I was. You had become so sophisticated and beautiful. I had ruined everything, and I didn't know what to do. So I went back to England, back to the House. But I never took another mistress, Jemma. I mean that."

"I'm stunned," she said. She kept searching his eyes, but it was too dark and she couldn't see them well.

"The third rule of marriage," he said.

She put her arms around his neck, feeling a huge wrench of emotion that she wasn't even sure how to name. "What is it?"

"We never let anger or the sea stand between us again."

It was too sad, all that time lost. She couldn't even smile. Her throat moved, and then he was kissing her and she could have sworn that the same sorrow was in his mouth and his touch, in the way his hands twisted into her hair. Finally the sweet deep pleasure of his mouth made all the rest of it fade away.

After a while he unwound her arms and stood up, slowly putting her on her feet. "I need to get my duchess home safe," he said. "You will be glad to know that I am not attending Pitt tomorrow. I would be happy if you would accompany me."

"What shall we do?"

"Nothing as colorful as the flower market."

"Dear me," she said. "Shall I dress in black?"

"It's not a visit to the cemetery," he said. "But perhaps it would be best to avoid being very extravagantly duchess-like."

"I shall eschew my jewels."

"And no wig."

"A hard bargain," she said, smiling at him. "But I suppose I can be seen outside the house in such a pitiful state without my reputation suffering overmuch."

Chapter Twelve

March 29

"We're going to Cow Cross," Elijah announced the next morning.

"Where's that?"

"In Spitalfields."

Jemma blinked. Spitalfields was one of the poorest areas of London, a tangled mass of grimy tenements and questionable businesses. Cook shops there followed no regulations and regularly were accused of serving rat stew, but who would know, since the entire district had the odor of cooking onions and aged chicken fat?

No duchess entered Spitalfields. In fact, Jemma would have ventured to say that the only ladies who entered Spitalfields were of the missionary variety, tough by nature and likely carrying defensive weapons to boot.

"I'm taking you to a house that is not as beautiful as the flower market but just as interesting," Elijah said, acting as if he had said nothing much out of the ordinary.

"Is Cow Cross on the outskirts of Spitalfields?" Jemma asked, knowing she was a coward.

"In the very center." He helped her into the coach. "Cow Cross is a tiny lane, bounded on one side by a sewer ditch and the other by Simple Boy Lane. Most people don't know these streets exist," he pointed out, which was something she knew quite well herself.

"I can't say that I've had the opportunity to call on anyone in Simple Boy Lane," she said. "Who lives there?"

"Cow Cross is the home of glassblowers, for the most part," Elijah said.

"Glassblowers. And?"

"My father owned a house there, which I inherited."

"*You* own a house in Spitalfields?" She was stunned. Moralistic Elijah, champion of the poor?

"I can see that you think I should have torn it down."

She chose her words carefully. "I am surprised to find that you are a landlord in such an area."

"Someone must be," he said reasonably. Then he relented. "In fact, I don't rent rooms."

"An orphanage?" she said, her frown clearing. Of course Elijah would be involved in good projects.

"No children," he said. "And you might not like it once you learn more of the place. I inherited it from my father, and I maintain it. But it is shameful, all the same."

"If it's shameful, why don't you sell the house?"

"It's also complicated." A moment later he added, "We own the Cacky Street Glassworks."

"Oh," Jemma said uncertainly. "Is that a large establishment? In Spitalfields?"

"It is certainly located there."

He seemed to be in a fierce mood, and she wasn't quite sure what to do. One good thing about being separated for the past years was that she hadn't had to deal with anyone's moods but her own. If she were in a bad mood, she stayed inside and played chess against herself until she felt better.

But what did one do with a grumpy husband? She stole a look at Elijah, but he was frowning out the window. Already the streets were growing smaller and grimier.

After a moment she took off her gloves and removed the diamond her mother had given her. It wasn't that she didn't trust Elijah to protect her, but there was no need to be foolish. She dropped it neatly into the pocket next to her seat.

"Will Muffet wait for us?" she asked.

"Of course. Though we may wish to take a walk."

Take a walk in Spitalfields? She had done very daring things in her life, as she saw it. She had ridden a horse bareback, once. She had left her husband and presented herself to the Court of Versailles before she understood how to look truly expensive (and thus irreproachable). She had provoked a woman into attempting to seduce her husband.

But she had never put herself deliberately in the way of bodily harm. Her native intelligence included a keen sense of self-preservation.

Out the window, everything looked slightly foreign. The shops were jammed together like an old man's teeth just before they fell out: dingy, leaning, doubtless full of holes. She could see alleys snaking away to the left and right, but buildings bent over them, so the sunshine disappeared a foot or two from the entrance. The darkness looked rusty, as if it had solid mass.

She cleared her throat. "Elijah."

"Yes?" He was staring sightlessly out the window, as best she could tell.

"I've never been into Spitalfields."

"I'm perfectly capable of taking care of you."

She bit her lip.

"It's quite safe," he added. "Of course, Spitalfields would not be a wise place to enter at night. But it's not as if hordes of savages roam the streets, Jemma. Spitalfields is simply a place where the very poor live. And they are trying, rather desperately for the most part, to find their next meal, rear their babies, afford a blanket or two."

"I hate it when you do that," she said crossly.

"What?" He honestly looked surprised.

"Make me feel so shabby."

"I don't mean to."

"I suppose you can't help it. Don't you ever get tired of being so *good*, Elijah? Of always—"

His face looked forbidding now. "Always what?"

"Knowing the right thing to do?" *Being better than the rest of us frivolous mortals,* she wanted to say. But she didn't dare.

"I am neither better nor worse than the next man," he said, biting the words. "I have compromised on issues where I felt bitterly that the better option—the kinder, more ethical option—was being tossed to the side."

The carriage rocked to a halt. "Don't be frightened,"

he said, holding out a hand to her. His smile helped. "I do believe you'll find yourself interested, Jemma. And I need you to know of this place."

"Why?" she asked, just as the footman opened the door to the carriage.

"You'll have to carry on," he said, rather obscurely.

But Jemma knew instantly what he was referring to, and her heart hiccupped from fear. Then she pulled herself together. She had the blood of three arrogant duchesses running through her veins. She could certainly survive a visit to Spitalfields.

They stepped out onto a street that was presumably made of cobblestones, but if so, the stones were buried under a thick compost of rotting vegetables. It felt like a springy blanket under her feet, as if made of horse hair.

"The carriage won't fit in Cow Cross," Elijah said, tucking her arm under his. "It's just down there."

Cow Cross was one of those little alleys that lurched suddenly off the street as if it were a hare fleeing a fox. This one broke left and then faded into the same rusty darkness as the alleys she'd glimpsed from the carriage.

"You see?" Elijah said, sounding amused. "No one is lurking in Cacky Street, hoping that a duchess with a jewel in her slipper will happen by."

That was true enough. She didn't see a single person, only a great congregation of ravens sitting atop a dilapidated house. They looked down at the two of them in a disapproving fashion, as if they were preachers in ragged blacks, squawking at the incongruity of a ducal carriage in Cacky Street.

"Where is everyone?" Jemma asked. She had the mistaken idea that the poor lived in the street. That was how they were depicted in the papers: cooking, sleeping, fighting in the open. But Cacky Street was empty, just a twisted, shabby street dozing in the sun.

"Sleeping," Elijah said. "Working." He glanced at her and there was a gleam of something in his eye. "Making love. If you're not rich enough to have a hundred rooms, you know, you find yourself curled up next to the missus of a morning and that gives a man ideas."

Jemma ignored him. "Where are your glassworks?"

"Down to the left," Elijah said, his face closing again. Somehow she'd asked the wrong question.

"Well," she said brightly, "shall we continue to Cow Cross?"

Once they entered the lane, Cow Cross wasn't as dark as it had seemed from Cacky Street. A bit of sun managed to sneak past the buildings that leaned and wobbled toward each other like tipsy matrons sharing secrets. Elijah stamped down the lane as if it belonged to him, which, for all Jemma knew, it did.

The lane curved to the left and then stopped. "This is it," he said.

It was the biggest house in the street, though that wasn't saying much. And it was definitely in the best repair. Of course, it would be, since it was Elijah's. There was a large door with a rusty knocker, but Elijah simply pushed it open.

"I stopped begging them to lock the door years ago," he said to her.

"Why don't they wish to?"

"If someone really wants to come in, they'll come regardless of a lock. It's Spitalfields. So they prefer to channel visitors through the door. It saves on wear and tear. Ah, Knabby, there you are."

A small stout man was coming toward them, squinting in the gloom of the hallway. "Yer Grace!" he said happily. "Now this is truly a pleasure. You're here for the birthday, of course. May I say what an honor it is that you remembered such an event? Cully will be happy, but happy indeed!"

Jemma could tell that Elijah had no memory of a birthday, but he didn't say so. Instead he drew her forward and said, "Mr. Knabby, may I present my wife, the duchess?"

Knabby blinked at her uncertainly. "A duchess," he said. "A woman!" Then, as if he suddenly remembered the protocol, he bobbed something between a curtsy and a bow.

"A pleasure," Jemma said.

"What a lovely voice," Knabby said, cocking his head to one side. "Yes, it sounds like a duchess. I shall remember that, indeed I shall. So *that* is what a duchess sounds like!" He wasn't squinting due to the dark, Jemma realized. He had a permanent squint.

Jemma looked up at Elijah. "Knabby has lost his sight," he told her.

"I see a bit, I see a bit," Knabby put in. "Light and shadows, really. Better than many."

"I am sorry to hear that," Jemma said. She knew Elijah had to be involved in a charitable project. It was so like him. But her smile died at the hard look in his eyes.

"Knabby lost his sight because he worked in our glassblowing factory," Elijah said, and his voice was flinty.

Knabby had turned and was making his way briskly along the dark corridor. "Do come along to the birthday!" he called. "Oh my yes, I was a glass-blower, m'lady. Is it my lady? Or is there something else I should be a-calling her? Is she a grace as well? Or duchess lady?"

"You may call me whatever you wish," Jemma said, picking up her skirts and following him.

"Do you wish to give me a report, before we go to the birthday party?" Elijah asked Knabby.

Knabby stopped suddenly, and Jemma almost ran into him. Then he started jabbering so fast she could hardly follow. "Nibble's wife has been staying with him for a spell, but they do fight something terrible. So I moved them to the back of the house where no one can hear her a-beating on him."

"Beating on him?" Jemma said, unable to stop herself.

Knabby turned his face toward her. "She's a devilishly strong woman, and if you give her a saucepan, she can make a right rumpus," he said. "Especially when he's been in the drink. 'Course, Nibble isn't easy either. Many's the time that my hand has itched for a saucepan, if you take my meaning."

"How's Waxy doing?" Elijah asked. "Waxy is a quite elderly gentleman," he told Jemma. "He must be around sixty now, isn't he, Knabby?"

"Well, he has his lung problems. He has those. But his daughter's been visiting him regular-like, with a couple babes in tow, so he's right as a flea in a cup of tea."

"Has the doctor been coming weekly?"

Knabby started down the hall again. "A waste of your ready that is, Yer Grace. A waste of the ready. There's nothing the man can do and we're all happy. Though he did pull a tooth for Cully the other day."

"Cully is well?"

"Fair to middling. Of course, it's his birthday today, so he's in the drink already, though I hate to say it. But that's Cully." He stopped just outside a tall door. "They're in the courtyard, enjoying the sun. But I should tell you that the foreman stopped by and we'll be having a new man with us, any day now. The name is Berket. Can't say that I remember him very well, but he was beginning when I left, I expect."

"There's room enough?" Elijah asked.

"More than enough! We've got that room from when Lasker left us, a month ago that's been. And there's Nicholson's room open still, and another one too, when Miss Sophisba ain't choosing to stay there. She's here today and will be glad to see Yer Grace."

"Anything you need, just send a boy to Towse," Elijah said. He glanced down at Jemma. "Towse is one of my solicitors."

"We need nothing," Knabby said merrily. "We admired them fruits as you sent from yer conservatory, Yer Grace, but to tell the truth, none of the men would eat them. They're set in their ways, and they're not adventuresome, if you know what I mean. The children snapped them right up, though."

"Who is Miss Sophisba?" Jemma whispered as Knabby opened the door. "And—"

"You'll see," Elijah said, and there was something so grim about his voice that Jemma stopped talking.

At first sight the small courtyard seemed to be hosting a children's party, but after a moment Jemma realized that there were more chickens than people, and though both groups were making noise, the three children chasing a puppy were winning the contest.

"Now look who's come to celebrate Cully's birthday,"

Knabby announced. "The duke is here, you group of lazy scubblers!"

The courtyard was dominated by a circle of dilapidated armchairs mostly occupied by men, all of whom turned toward Knabby's voice. And all of whom, Jemma realized immediately, were blind.

They were a curious bunch. For one thing, not everyone had chosen to put on clothing. Two men were entirely without trousers; their scrawny white legs stretched out in the weak sun. One of them had a beard so long that it was tucked into the waistband of his apron, which he wore, incongruously, on top of a plaid coat.

There were two women, one a hard-mouthed matron whom she assumed must be Mrs. Nibble, as she looked precisely like someone who wielded a mean saucepan.

The other must be Miss Sophisba. She was younger, and while not exactly pretty, she had the air of someone who made an effort. Most of that effort involved lip rouge and improbably golden hair. It appeared to be directed toward attracting male attention, which seemed odd, given that no one could see her except Mrs. Nibble. And Mrs. Nibble was definitely not the sort to enjoy crimson lips and yellow hair.

One of the half-naked men stood up. "Get up, ye flea-bitten knabblesquabbers," he bellowed suddenly. "The duke's here. You should be on yer feet and doing the pretty! It's my birthday and I'll have everything in—in—"

He sat down suddenly. Knabby was definitely right. Cully had been in the drink, and never mind the fact that it was morning.

"And the duchess is with me," Elijah said easily. The

frown had dropped from his face and he looked as genial as if he had entered a tea party in Kensington. "I've brought along my wife, the prettiest duchess in all the kingdom."

"I wish we could see that," the bearded man said, staring into space. "I've never seen a real duchess. Though I did see the queen once. She had a fearsome wig, the queen did." He elbowed Mrs. Nibble. "Is there a wig, one of those tall ones?"

"She's wearing a velvet dress," the older woman told him. She had risen and given a quick bob of a curtsy and then sat back down directly. "She doesn't have one of those wigs on her head. I think she has her own hair, but with some powder on it, like nobs wear."

Elijah had strolled over to wish happy returns of the day to Cully. Then he stopped at the next chair and started a conversation about the riots. Jemma felt she had to do something. She couldn't just stand about like a fool. So she moved toward the two women. Miss Sophisba promptly jumped to her feet, looking terrified.

"Are these your children?" Jemma asked. "They're delightful." Which was not the truth. They were too dirty to give anyone a sensation of delight. But they looked cheerful and well-fed.

The older woman had lumbered to her feet again. "*She* don't have any children." She jerked her head derisively.

Miss Sophisba ignored her. "They belong to Knabby's sister. Or perhaps his niece. At any rate, she's a cloth-dyer, which is prodigious hard work, and so the children spend the days here. Usually Waxy's grandchildren come along later in the day, too. His daughter works in the mews, and so she drops them here."

"Don't they go to school?" Jemma asked.

"Not most of the time," Miss Sophisba said with a shy smile. "It's not something most people hold with, here in Spitalfields."

"I don't think there is a school in Spitalfields," Mrs. Nibble said. "Not in my time, anyhow."

"Oh dear," Jemma said.

"Those are loverly gloves," Miss Sophisba said. "I've never seen anything like them."

"Would you like to try them on?" Jemma asked readily. She ignored Mrs. Nibble's snort and pulled them off.

"I couldn't," Miss Sophisba gasped. But they slid over her small dirty hands as if they'd been made for her.

"You may have them," Jemma said, smiling at her.

Miss Sophisba paled. "I couldn't!"

"No, she couldn't," Mrs. Nibble said grimly. "Her husband'd have 'em off her in no more time than it takes to dock a whore." Suddenly she looked self-conscious. "If you'll excuse the expression, milady."

"I could hide them," Sophisba said. "An' just look at them now and then, when I was here, like."

"Aren't you here all the time?" Jemma asked.

"Only when her husband is thrown in the Clink," Mrs. Nibble said. "Then she doesn't have to be on her back, you see, and his dukeship is nice enough to let her stay here."

"You keep them for her, Mrs. Nibble," Jemma said. She let just enough of a duchess tone creep into her voice so that Mrs. Nibble blinked. "Whenever Miss Sophisba is in residence at Cow Cross, she can wear them."

Miss Sophisba was stroking the gloves as if they were

alive. "I'd be that thankful," she breathed. "They're the most beautiful thing I ever saw in my life."

"And you shall have this handkerchief for your trouble, Mrs. Nibble," Jemma said.

Mrs. Nibble frowned. "I don't need no bribe to keep them gloves for her. I'm not a person to cast her aside, just 'cause of what she does."

Jemma's handkerchief was woven of Belgian lace and embroidered in the middle with a very elaborate white B, for the Duchy of Beaumont.

"That's a B," Mrs. Nibble said, turning the handkerchief this way and that. "My name is Bertha."

"It's not a bribe," Jemma said. "It's a gift."

"This place is a gift," Miss Sophisba said, clutching the gloves. "Does you know that, Miss Duchess?"

"You don't call her that," Mrs. Nibble said. "Mrs. Duchess maybe, or 'my lady.'"

A boy ran by, shrieking like a teakettle in a way that signified he wanted to be noticed. And just to make sure he was, he dropped a handful of smallish wooden balls at Jemma's feet.

Mrs. Nibble took after him with an enraged howl. Jemma bent down to pick up the boy's balls, since he was currently being rapped on the head by Mrs. Nibble, though thankfully not with a saucepan.

"How clever!" she exclaimed, turning it over. There was a human face carved into the ball, a face with a laughing, stubby nose and eyes that seemed to twinkle with amusement. She picked up another, which turned out to have the face of a wicked little demon with pointed ears and sharp chin. A third was a round-faced woman.

"Pie makes 'em," Miss Sophisba said. "See, he's always carving." She gestured toward a man in the circle. Pie was holding a tiny sharp knife and flicking at a piece of wood. A steady stream of shavings flew out to his left and right.

"But he can't see!"

"He sees with his fingers, he says," Miss Sophisba explained.

Jemma walked over to Pie. "These are absolutely wonderful," she said, dropping one of the balls in his hand so he knew what she meant.

He grinned. "The wood tells me, that's all. The wood tells me what's inside."

Elijah appeared at her side. "Pie was a master glass-blower."

"We all were," Knobby said cheerfully. "Only the best for the Cacky Street glassblowers. There's quite a wait list," he told Jemma.

"To work in the factory?" she asked.

"His Grace here won't take any apprentices, 'cause he says they're too young to decide about whether to give up their eyesight. But those of us that has already got the skills, well, there's nowhere else anyone would want to work 'cept for Cacky Street."

"Because of this?" she said, looking around.

" 'Course. All paid for, see, and nice to boot. Food we have, and enough to spare over and share about. Wives if we want 'em with us, and if they want to come. It's always warm, even in the coldest months."

Elijah was rocking back and forth slightly on his heels. "It's the least we could do," he said, his voice harsh. "We're responsible for taking your sight."

"Oh no ye ain't," Pie said unexpectedly. " 'Twas the glass that took my sight. All that lovely, beautiful glass, and I wouldn't have had it another way. See, when you blow, the glass tells you what's inside," he said, moving his face in the general direction of Jemma and Elijah. "That's what the duke here never understands, for all he feels to blame and such. It's glass that's our mistress. I thought I'd go mad at first, when I had to stop blowing. Then someone gave me a knife and some wood and I was away. Thought I'd go mad," he repeated.

"We have one of Pie's glass bowls," Elijah said. "In the drawing room."

"Not the green one with the fluted edge? Mr. Pie, that is an exquisite bowl," Jemma said.

He beamed. "She called to me and I just brought her out, that's all. And now she lives in a duke's home." His hands kept moving over the block of wood he held in his lap and then he started flicking away at it again with his knife. "Can't do better than that."

"Happy birthday again, Cully," Elijah said.

Cully genially waved a bottle in their direction and hiccupped.

"I gave him a bit of the best today," Knobby said. "Seeing as it's his birthday. That's the best gin."

Elijah took Jemma's ungloved hand. "Goodbye, everyone."

The men all turned their heads and chorused goodbye; the children ran by screaming. Miss Sophisba waved her gloves shyly, and Mrs. Nibble glared from her chair next to Nibble.

"They're blind because of the Cacky Street glass-blowing factory," Jemma said as soon as they were back in the carriage. "Which we own."

"There's something in the glass that ruins the eye," Elijah said. "The doctor thinks it's in the smoke. It's not good for their lungs either. They don't live very long. We've lost two in the last six months."

She was silent.

"You likely think I should close the factory," Elijah said.

"No—"

"If I close the factory," he interrupted, "it won't stop people from buying glass. And if I sell the factory, there won't be anywhere for the workers to go once they're blinded. The run of them from the other factories end up in the poorhouses."

"Elijah . . . "

"I thought I might move the house to the country, where there would be air and cleanliness, and I could get a decent woman to live in and cook for them. But they hated that idea. They like living in Spitalfields, with all their old friends dropping by for gossip and a chunk of bread. We feed half the neighborhood."

"Elijah . . . " she repeated.

"Knabby has a cook shop deliver meals. I probably shouldn't allow Sophisba there but she keeps the men happy—"

"Elijah!" She touched his cheek and he finally focused on her.

"Yes?"

"I think it's a wonderful house. I think you've done exactly the right thing. I have just two suggestions."

"You do?" His eyes lightened. "You don't think I should—"

"I don't think you should change anything," she said firmly. "But perhaps you could hire a young woman to play with the children and even teach them to read."

"We could do that easily enough," he said, looking surprised.

"And you should fix up some sort of head . . . piece, with glass in the front, so the blowers don't get smoke in their eyes."

"What?"

"Pie could carve a sort of helmet, like a soldier's helmet. And there could be something in front, oh I don't know what, something. And then some glass, so they could see the glass to blow it, but their eyes would be protected."

He stared at her.

"You could try," she suggested.

"Damn," he said.

"Elijah! I've never heard you swear." She started laughing.

"Damn and double damn." But he said it slowly, thinking.

"I have a question. What do you mean that Sophisba keeps the men—happy? How exactly does she . . . "

Elijah wasn't listening. "I can see what you're suggesting. It would need light wood. Or leather. It'll take thinking." He looked up. "Sophisba is there only when her husband's in the Clink. When he's out, he makes her work the streets. She's Mrs. Nibble's daughter, you know."

"No!"

"She has her own room. I don't believe she actually performs personal services for the men. But she makes them happy."

"Because she's a young woman."

"She flirts with them." He reached out and picked up her hand. "I like your hands without gloves, Jemma. And I love your idea about the helmet. I think we can make that work."

"You can figure it out, and then make sure that all the glassblowing factories start using them," she said, beaming at him.

"What I want to do is flirt with the most beautiful

duchess in London," he said, turning her hand over and placing a kiss in the middle of her palm.

"I flirt best over a chessboard."

"Then chess it shall be," he said. "Do you ever play out of doors, Jemma?"

"Chess? And a picnic, you mean? That sounds lovely."

"I must be at my chambers in the morning. But I could arrange a picnic for the afternoon." There was a world of meaning in his voice.

"No," she said, shaking her head. The carriage came to a halt. "I have an appointment for tomorrow afternoon, though you're more than welcome to join me. Parsloe's is holding an open session of the Chess Club and I intend to become one of the members."

"They allow women? How marvelously forward-thinking of them." A footman opened the carriage door.

"Not at all," Jemma said. "I believe that it was entirely in error. They simply never thought that a woman could possibly play chess. Until the redoubtable Mrs. Patton came along. You do remember her from our Twelfth Night party, don't you?"

"Eccentric and thoroughly intelligent," Elijah observed. "With a sharp edge to her. Mrs. Patton told me that the House should be ashamed of itself for ignoring a Quaker bill outlawing the slave trade, and she was right."

"Mrs. Patton realized that there was nothing barring a woman from going to an open session and simply playing everyone there until she won a spot."

"Which she did," Elijah said, laughing.

"She took herself there for a visit last year. No one can join until they win all offered games at an open session. I shall do so tomorrow," Jemma said serenely. "And you are welcome to try for a spot as well."

"I assume the open session is to replace a deceased member? As I understand it, Parsloe's ruthlessly maintains its members at one hundred precisely. In that case, we cannot both successfully join the Chess Club tomorrow."

Jemma took Elijah's hand as she stepped down from the carriage. "I shall ask Fowle to make sure there is a particularly lovely meal tomorrow night, so as to assuage your disappointment."

Elijah loved the look in her eyes. It was just too bad that he was going to have to puncture her expectations. "Aren't you fond of gooseberry tarts?"

"They are my favorite."

"Fowle, do inform Mrs. Tulip that Her Grace will be in need of comfort tomorrow night," he told the butler.

"Pride goeth before a fall!" Jemma said, but she was laughing as she climbed the stairs.

The footmen were all staring. Elijah paused for a moment. "Whom will you bet on, Fowle? And don't try to tell me that the household won't engage in a very lively series of bets if Her Grace and I both try for a spot in the Chess Club."

Fowle raised an eyebrow, ever the imperturbable butler. "I could not bring myself to bet against one of mine own masters," he said, bowing.

"In that case?"

"The Duke of Villiers," Fowle said.

"But he is already a member."

"Just so."

"You mean that unless one of us *wins* the tournament, we won't become a member?"

"I'm afraid that His Grace has been responsible for keeping many aspirants from joining Parsloe's. I believe that in fact there are only seventy-three standing members at the moment."

"Good lord," Elijah said, startled. "Do you happen to know how many people have managed to beat Villiers and join Parsloe's?"

"Mrs. Patton joined after His Grace did not attend an open day," Fowle said. "But Mrs. Patton has beaten him thereafter. There's many a man who has rued the day that His Grace decided to join the London Chess Club."

"You're a positive fount of information, Fowle."

Fowle bowed. A butler of the very best caliber would count it a failure not to anticipate all the questions his master might ask. But he never anticipated the duke's next inquiry.

"Do you think I should lose?"

He blinked. "Lose, Your Grace?"

"To the duchess."

The duke appeared to be perfectly serious. It was the first time Fowle had been asked to give marital advice, but he drew himself upright. "Absolutely not," he said. "Her Grace would be appalled."

"Thank you, Fowle."

The butler was still staring at the duke's back, trying to remember the last time he saw his master smile like that, when Beaumont paused on the stairs and turned. "You know, Fowle . . . "

"Yes, Your Grace?"

"If I were you, I wouldn't put your wages on a bet in favor of the Duke of Villiers."

He was grinning again.

Chapter Thirteen

March 30

$\mathcal{P}$arsloe's, on St. James's Street, was a rather nondescript establishment for an organization that wielded such power over the hearts of English chess players. Elijah stepped down from the carriage and held out his hand for Jemma. Perhaps forty people were jostling for space around the path leading to Parsloe's, held back by some annoyed-looking footmen.

"May the best man win," she said to him.

"That's her, all right," came a shout. "That's the duchess! Look at that hair!"

Jemma's twinkling smile disappeared from her face and she began walking up the path, suddenly looking like a duchess rather than a mere woman. As if duchesses were a breed apart, Elijah mused, following her up the path. Beings whose hair towered and who walked as if their feet were not quite touching the ground. Jemma did it brilliantly. She looked sublimely beautiful and outrageously expensive.

Belying Elijah's assessment, a portly woman in a tattered stole said, "She's not wearing *that* many joowels."

"She wears them on her slippers," Elijah told her.

The portly woman's mouth fell open but nothing came out of it, even when the sharp-nosed woman behind her said, "Mrs. Mogg, you be talking to a duke!"

"Why on earth are all of you here?" Elijah asked Mrs. Mogg, seeing that Jemma was inside the door and beginning the lengthy process of removing her pelisse, chip hat, gloves, and all the other *accoutrements* worn by a duchess out-of-doors.

Mrs. Mogg didn't seem able to summon words, so her friend spoke up. "It's all over London. A duke and a duchess are going to battle another duke for a place in this here club."

"They won't let anyone watch the game," Mrs. Mogg said, finally opening her mouth.

"It'll take hours," Elijah said. "You should come back around . . . oh . . . four of the clock."

"Elijah!" Jemma called.

"She's calling you," the sharp-nosed woman said.

"Just like I might call my Henry," Mrs. Mogg said, still staring at Elijah. Her tattered stole rose and fell with her breaths, giving its little fox head the odd semblance of life. "I'm putting my money on you," she breathed.

Elijah was used to accolades from his peers in the House of Lords, and he bowed just as deeply. "You do me too much honor, madam."

She gasped, and the fox rose into the air, looking as if its sharp glass eyes were about to blink.

Elijah went inside, thinking that he really had to speak to Fowle. A betting circle within Beaumont House was one thing, but involving greater London in such foolishness wasn't appropriate.

The upper floor of Parsloe's opened into a large ballroom, now dotted with small tables and chairs. Hopeful members faced the wall, Elijah realized immediately; club members faced into the room and seemed to pride themselves on playing with a certain éclat.

"Mr. Parsloe has been kind enough to allow us to eschew the opening round of play," Jemma said to him.

The head of the Chess Club bowed. "It is the least I can do, given Your Graces' famed skill at chess."

"I don't see Villiers," Elijah said, scanning the room. He was disappointed. It wouldn't be a true battle unless the duke showed up.

"His Grace never attends before the late afternoon," Mr. Parsloe said. "By that point all the first and second round plays will have been completed. There's a hierarchy of play, you see, and members are accordingly rated first, second, or third tier."

"Villiers?" Elijah said, eyebrow up.

"Strictly third tier play," Parsloe said, "though he does do the honor of dropping by the Chess Club frequently and engaging in play with whomever is available. His Grace is the top-rated player in the club."

"What fun this is!" Jemma cried. "Well, dear Mr. Parsloe, please do give me an opponent."

Mr. Parsloe hesitated, but three or four gentlemen were already bounding toward Jemma. Lord Woodward Jourdain was in the forefront, but he was elbowed to the side by Saint Albans, who swept Jemma off to a table.

"The duchess will be fine," Elijah said, rocking back on his heels. "Could you find me an opponent, Parsloe?"

"Of course, Your Grace. Please forgive me: it's just that we have only one female member, and I wasn't quite certain—"

"Her Grace will neither expect nor desire special treatment," Elijah assured him.

"Lord Woodward would be an excellent partner for Your Grace," Parsloe said, after one more look at Saint Albans and Jemma. "He is a second tier player who tends toward eccentric but lively play."

Elijah bowed. "I would be honored." Two minutes later he knew he had the man, but it was amusing to see how quickly he could bring the game to a halt.

Jemma generally found Lord Saint Albans to be a bit of a dunce, but with an acute eye for clothing, which she truly appreciated. Today he wore a high wig, paired with a coat of iridescent turquoise silk. Obviously, they could not begin the game without a preliminary discussion of their attire. His enameled buttons; her overskirt *retroussée dans les poches*; even her laylock slippers were admired.

She didn't expect much of the game. But it turned out that Saint Albans's clever—albeit often vicious—comments sprang from a quick mind. Of course she won, but only after a bit of delicate manipulation with her rook.

"That was quite fun," she told Saint Albans, who was blinking down at the board as if surprised. "I thought moving your King's Knight to Queen's Bishop Three was inspired."

"You did?" he asked, and then, pulling himself together, "Your skill at chess is remarkable, Your Grace.

You beat me in only eight moves. That has *never* happened before."

She smiled at him. "Should I play someone else?" There was by now a deep circle of observers around them.

Mr. Parsloe appeared. "A win, Your Grace? May I suggest that you take Lord Feddrington for your next opponent?"

"I'm rated higher than Feddrington," Lord Wigstead pointed out.

"I need you to play another opponent," Parsloe said, bearing him off.

"I much enjoyed Lady Feddrington's ball last fortnight," Jemma told her opponent as a nimble-fingered footman replaced all the chess pieces.

"Chess isn't as much fun as dancing, eh?" Feddrington had the jovial look of a man who thought a woman didn't truly have the brains to play such a cerebral game as chess.

"I'm looking forward to playing you," Jemma said, meaning it.

"Your fame precedes you," Feddrington said, "but maybe I can still teach you a thing or two. I beat that fellow Philidor when he was here, and he's reckoned to be the best that France has to offer."

One of the bystanders snorted, and Feddrington threw him an unfriendly look. "Of course, Philidor beat me a time or two as well. Chess is like that. Even the best can't win all the time."

Jemma smiled and moved a pawn. A short time later Feddrington was frowning, and the circle of onlookers around her had grown deeper. "I call that a smothered mate," she told him sweetly. "And speaking of mates, how is the duke faring?"

Mr. Parsloe appeared to escort Feddrington from the seat across from her, and the footman leapt to action, resetting the board.

"His Grace has just won his second game," Mr. Parsloe said. "He is now playing Mr. Pringle. May I introduce your next opponent, Dr. Belsize? Dr. Belsize is one of our very best players in the second tier."

Dr. Belsize was a cheerful-looking gentleman wearing a pair of large spectacles. "I do believe we've met," Jemma said, racking her brain.

"I'm afraid not," Dr. Belsize said. "But I have common enough features, Your Grace. One nose, two eyes, all the rest of it. People often think I'm a long-lost uncle."

"You're a scientist! I heard you give a talk at the Royal Society."

"I'm honored to think of Your Grace as a member of the audience. And now I am unsurprised to find your interests extend to chess, unlike many of your fair sex. I find that science and chess are intrinsically related."

Mr. Parsloe inspected the board and stepped back. Jemma knew within a move or two that Dr. Belsize was a formidable opponent. There was actually a moment when she hesitated, thinking she would have difficulty disentangling herself if he . . . but that was thinking five moves ahead, so she made the play.

He missed the opportunity, and the chance to make the game a truly competitive one. Jemma swallowed a little sigh. This was why she preferred not to play strangers, for the most part.

"You are now on to the third tier," Mr. Parsloe confirmed a few minutes later. "Would Your Grace wish to rise and refresh yourself, perhaps?"

Jemma stood up amid a chorus of congratulations.

She looked around for Elijah, and spotted him sitting opposite a man with a mustache like a kitchen brush. "What's the next step?" she asked Parsloe.

"Third tier games are played strictly by hierarchy," he said. "Since you last beat Mr. Belsize, who is rated number sixteen, you will play the next available player with a lower number."

"And His Grace?" she asked, nodding at Elijah.

"Should the duke win this match, he will be rated above Mr. Pringle at number twelve."

Jemma swallowed her annoyance at the fact that Parsloe had been giving her opponents at a lower level than he gave to Elijah. It was up to her to prove her skill; she could educate the Chess Club by beating her husband, not to mention Villiers.

Two hours later she had just tidily vanquished another opponent when Villiers made his appearance. She was seated facing the wall, and surrounded by a circle of onlookers. She didn't have to raise her eyes to know of Villiers's arrival, however. The men to her left suddenly melted away.

And there was Villiers: hair unpowdered, naturally, and tied back with a ribbon. He wore a coat of deep cinnamon, embroidered in black. His heels were high and his legs muscled. She smiled to herself and made a final move.

"Checkmate," she told her stunned opponent.

As she understood it, there remained only two players between herself and membership. Jemma smiled sweetly at her latest victim, stripping off her gloves to wiggle her fingers.

Mr. Parsloe was looking slightly distraught. "Your Grace," he said to Villiers, "the Duke of Beaumont has beaten Mr. Potemkin, which means that the duke now challenges you. The Duchess of Beaumont will play Mr. Potemkin in the meantime."

Jemma rose from her chair and held out her hand for Villiers to kiss. "I advise that you beat my husband with all due expediency. He's deeply cunning, for all he possesses an honest face."

"I shall take your advice to heart," Villiers replied, bowing with a gorgeous flourish of his coat.

"And then I shall beat you," Jemma said, letting it all go to her head for a moment.

Villiers gave her his customary cool glance. "You are, of course, welcome to try."

Jemma sat down again, dismissing Villiers from her mind. Mr. Potemkin must be a redoubtable opponent, she thought, rated as he was, at number two behind Villiers. The last thing she wanted was to be cut from the tournament now.

Mr. Potemkin turned out to be a Russian man with a shy smile and a brutal style of attack. His weakness, Jemma discovered, was greed. Through a series of brilliant sacrifices, allowing him to pile her pieces on his side of the table, she closed mercilessly on his queen.

And won.

Mr. Potemkin didn't blink at the board. Of all her opponents, he was the one who had followed every move, understanding the advantages, the positions, the possibilities.

"You are brilliant," he said in a heavy accent, rising to his feet and bowing deeply.

"That was a beautiful game," Jemma said. "I thank you for it."

Then she turned to Villiers and Elijah. She had been left to win the last game without audience, as the entire population of Parsloe's was watching with bated breath as the two dukes battled it out.

She strolled over and the men parted before her like the Red Sea. She saw at once that Villiers had control of almost all of Elijah's pieces, certainly all the rank and file. The audience was murmuring to each other, convinced that Villiers had yet again brought down an applicant to the Chess Club.

"At this rate, we'll never have a new member!" Feddrington said clearly.

But Elijah looked amused. She *knew* him, knew that look of deep satisfaction in his eyes.

She turned back to the board with a frown. There wasn't a sound in the whole building as Villiers reached forward one hand, marked with a deep ruby-colored signet ring, and took a pawn.

Suddenly, she saw it! Villiers would be forced to capture Elijah's bishop. Elijah raised his eyes and smiled at her. Two more exchanges, and then Villiers, still silent, moved his queen. Elijah reached forward, moved his knight again.

"Checkmate," he said, his deep voice as unruffled as his face.

The crowd broke out in a sound somewhere between a howl and a squeal.

"You trounced me," Villiers said, staring at the board. "Damn well trounced me." He looked up. "Your play has improved since we were boys."

Elijah shrugged. "I've played the occasional game with the duchess. I suppose her brilliance has rubbed off on me."

Mr. Parsloe was bowing deeply before Elijah. "Your Grace, may I welcome you to the London Chess Club? It is a true honor . . . you are the first new member in some years. In fact, since the Duke of Villiers did us the honor of joining the club."

"I'm likely not to be the last," Elijah said. "After all, my duchess has yet to play the Duke of Villiers."

"We are free to admit more than one member," Parsloe told him hastily.

Villiers was kissing Jemma's hand again. "Ah, what a pleasure to play another Beaumont. I feel as if I am virtually a member of the family."

Jemma sat down. "And just like the dramas that recur in the best of families, I fully intend to eviscerate you."

"I have often remarked how grateful I am to have been spared a sibling," Villiers said.

The footman backed away, and Parsloe quieted the room with one look. Jemma moved her pawn to King Four. In the last year, she and Villiers had played a number of games. They were matched in daring, she knew. He was an inventive player. In order to win, she needed to think far ahead.

He steadily built up a nest of pawns. Jemma watched. She could do herself no good by dashing into a counterthreat without thinking it out first. But finally . . . finally . . . she saw it. A brilliant combination, only seven moves ahead.

For the first time, she raised her eyes from the board. Elijah was standing to her right. Their eyes met and she saw that he knew, he'd seen the possibility, he approved.

Marriage, she thought, was a very strange thing.

She won.

"You will come to me for supper," Villiers said, speaking under the roar of excited voices replaying every move. "No, no, I insist. I absolutely insist. I am, after all, dejected. Positively melancholy. I *never* lose."

"You don't look it," Jemma said, cocking her head to the side.

"My natural dislike of losing is warring with my knowledge that I will now be able to enjoy excellent games on a more regular basis."

"We'd be happy to join you tonight," Elijah said.

Jemma glanced from one man to the other. For childhood friends who hadn't spoken in years, they were rapidly mending their fences.

"Damn it, Villiers, you must be off your bacon today," Feddrington roared. He might have slapped Villiers on the back, but the duke was the sort of man not even Feddrington would dare to touch.

Villiers cast him a look under heavy-lidded eyes. "You wound me, Feddrington."

"We all lose sometimes," the man said, smirking. "But here's a question. The duke and the duchess have both beat Villiers, and he's rated first in the club. So who's first?" He turned to Parsloe. "Are they to play each other?"

"Doubtless we shall play each other on many occasions," Elijah said, smoothly cutting in before Parsloe could name him number one, as Jemma was certain he was about to do. "As it happens, my duchess and I intend to play the final game in our rather widely publicized match in the very near future."

Villiers gave a little crooked grin. "The duchess had an equally publicized match with me some months ago, but she threw over the game. Shall we assume that she fights to the end with you?"

"Such is the nature of marriage," Elijah said.

"We shall make the outcome of the duke and duchess's match the key to rating these two players," Villiers said, laying down the law. "Should the duchess win, she will become number one, and vice versa."

Jemma always meant to win her final game with Elijah. Now the only thing that stood between her and victory was her refusal to bed her husband, because for all that Elijah seemed to enjoy their wooing, she had no real expectation that he would come to understand her point of view.

She could bear being ranked number two. "Tonight," she said to Villiers, and swept from the room.

She found herself in the carriage, waiting for Elijah, who was engaged in conversation with a couple of elderly women. "Did you know them from somewhere?" she asked curiously once he joined her.

"Not so to speak," Elijah said. "Mrs. Mogg was kind enough to bet on my winning the game with Villiers, so I felt I had to give her the news in person. She has a shilling sixpence riding on my beating you as well," he added.

Jemma smiled. "I do hope that she has some money laid aside for a rainy day. Because that shilling is lost."

Elijah leaned over. "Pride goeth . . . " he said softly. Suddenly the air in the carriage changed, and every nerve in Jemma's body jumped to attention.

"Elijah," she breathed.

The duke was a man who knew when a game was won, without even being played. Anyone who had seen the look in his eyes after he beat Villiers would have recognized his face when the duke and duchess stepped from the carriage in front of Beaumont House.

The duchess looked pink-cheeked, disheveled, and a little dazed.

The duke was smiling.

Chapter Fourteen

London town house of the Duke of Villiers
15 Piccadilly
That evening

"*I* haven't been here since Villiers was on the point of death," Elijah commented as they walked up the steps.

"I've never been here," Jemma said, wondering if she ought to hand her pelisse over to the duke's butler. He looked extremely old and frail; the weight of it might knock him to the ground. Elijah saved her the decision by taking off her pelisse and handing it directly to a footman.

"His Grace and his guests are in the sitting room," the butler proclaimed, tottering ahead of them.

Jemma walked into the room and almost checked her step. Villiers had invited the Marquise de Perthuis. And this was not the marquise who would be recognized in the Court of Versailles either. Rather than her customary frizzed, crimped wig, styled to be nearly as wide as it was tall, the marquise was clearly wearing her own hair, albeit powdered. It was dressed in loose ringlets all over her head, with some flowing down each side.

What's more, she had eschewed her black-and-white attire for a chemise gown, precisely the style that Corbin had declared too sensual for Jemma to wear. The marquise's gown was made of pale hyacinth blue lustring so delicate that the fabric floated behind her as she turned to rap the gentleman she was speaking to on the shoulder with her fan. He turned his head and Jemma realized it was Corbin. But she couldn't help noting that the marquise looked utterly delectable and outrageously sensuous.

"The marquise looks much better sober," Elijah remarked. "Shall we?" Not even waiting for Jemma, he walked forward. The marquise's roguish smile turned to something else, something delicious and intimate.

Jemma's mouth tightened. Given the way the marquise's bodice dipped in the front, Elijah could probably see her nipples.

Villiers appeared at her elbow. "Dear me," he said, an obvious thread of amusement in his voice. "Did I misstep by inviting my dear cousin to dinner? You seemed to have achieved civility, if not friendship, in the past."

"Of course, your cousin is always a charming companion," Jemma said, watching Elijah bend his head to the marquise again. She was flirting with her fan now, eyeing him over the edge. Jemma had to admit that the marquise wielded a fan like a deadly weapon.

Wasn't this just what she wanted?

Of course it was! She snatched her own fan, shook it open with a snap and sailed forward. She might not be wearing a chemise gown—in fact, she was wearing a dress of silver muslin that covered every inch of her bosom—but she was still the Duchess of Beaumont.

"How lovely you look!" she cried, by way of greeting.

The marquise dropped her a curtsy that had the marked benefit of presenting all three gentlemen— Villiers, Elijah, and Corbin—with an excellent view of her breasts. "As do you," she said, her tone a little breathless. "I *adore* muslin; I always have. Why, I was married in a dress quite like that." She smiled innocently. "Though of course that was quite a while ago now."

Jemma knew that if she narrowed her eyes, it would honor that insult. "It is hard to countenance how old we have all grown, isn't it?" she asked, knowing full well that the marquise was only two years younger than she. "We must make a pact never to try to dress with the *joie de vivre* of the very young. There's nothing worse than a matron in a dashing style that only the youngest of women can wear with confidence."

"Confidence is so essential to beauty, isn't it?" the marquise replied, neatly turning Jemma's insult on its head. "*I* think there's nothing worse than an anxious woman. There can be nothing more aging than desperation."

"Dear me," Villiers said, a wicked smile playing around his mouth. "You both look rather purple in the face. It must be the heat from the fire. Madame la Marquise, do let me move you away from this annoying heat." And he scooped her away while Jemma was still planning her next riposte.

Elijah was called away to greet Lord Vesey, so Jemma turned to Corbin. "Just when did she transform into such a hussy?" she demanded.

Corbin's eyes were dancing. "Only after the second glass of Champagne. Although that gown she is wearing suggests that the real marquise has been hiding behind all that black-and-white. I find myself very interested in what her husband will make of her transformation."

"He's back in France," Jemma said. "Spared the sight of his wife wearing a gown that a demirep might find too debauched."

"She's downing a third glass of Champagne," Corbin said thoughtfully. "I never should have bought those two bottles at Vauxhall. Do you know, she's been telling me the last twenty minutes that she wants to visit the gardens again tonight?"

"She and Villiers look quite good together," Jemma said. "They have that same sort of French insouciance."

"Which you need to practice," Corbin said. "You looked like a disgruntled little spaniel when you were watching her flirt with your husband."

"I never look like a canine!" Jemma cried.

"One who lost her bone," Corbin added.

"This was your idea," Jemma said glumly. "I don't think it's working very well."

"That's because you have to move to the second part of the plan: in other words, the point at which you cut out the marquise and start flirting with Beaumont yourself."

"Oh, hurrah," Jemma said. "I don't think that Elijah is even interested in flirting. He's such a straightforward type of person—"

"He's doing a good job of it now," Corbin pointed out.

Jemma whipped her head around. The marquise had escaped from Villiers and was standing in front of Elijah. He was laughing. "She can be very witty."

"You wanted formidable competition," Corbin said firmly. "You have it. She's witty, a little tipsy, and making it all too clear that she is available."

Jemma felt herself grinding her teeth. "Well, *he's* not available."

"I suggest that you amuse yourself for a time before making a move toward your husband," Corbin said. "It's not considered appropriate to glower at your spouse. Remember, there's nothing more aging than desperation."

Jemma sighed. "I'll talk to Villiers."

"About chess, no doubt?"

She nodded. "I expect he's seething over that combination move I managed this afternoon. We can talk it through."

"Make it look as if you're flirting with him," Corbin said, by way of farewell.

Jemma pranced up to Villiers without even glancing over at Elijah. Her host was leaning against the fireplace, staring down into the fire. "Don't tell me that you're truly suffering pangs over losing those chess games," she said.

He straightened immediately. "Actually, I wasn't even thinking of them."

She smiled at him over the edge of her fan. "You played very well. I almost regret cancelling our blind-folded game."

She'd seen him look at others with a glance so cold and indifferent that it paralyzed; he had never looked at her that way before, but he did now. "Don't shame yourself, Jemma."

And, when she opened her mouth to spit back at him, he raised a hand. "You don't wish to find yourself in bed with me, blindfolded or otherwise. To pretend otherwise is to cheapen the friendship we have managed to build."

He looked directly at her. "Which I treasure. I have few friendships."

She stepped forward involuntarily and held out her hand. He stared down for a moment as if he didn't understand what to do. Then his large, warm fingers curled around hers. "I'm sorry," she said. "I shouldn't have behaved in such an insincere fashion."

"I suppose there was a reason for it," Villiers said, throwing a glance across the room toward where Elijah was talking with the marquise. Jemma could hear her soft giggles.

"So have you really known the marquise since she was a young girl?" she asked brightly.

"She was an awful little thing, as you can imagine."

"I expect she was one of those children who never smudged her dress and was adored by her governess."

"She was as small and round as a shrub, one of those shrubs that looks innocent but is kitted out with thorns. I remember playing spillikins with her, and when it appeared she'd lost, she picked up a stick and tried to stab me in the chest."

Jemma laughed.

"She did!" Villiers protested. "I can imagine that you were a little devil as well."

Jemma realized that their hands were still linked. But what did it matter? It was a small dinner, and she just heard Elijah laughing at another of the marquise's sallies. Obviously, he wasn't worried about her intimacies with Villiers. "I was charming," she told him. "Whereas *you* were undoubtedly a dreadful boy."

He looked at her from under his long eyelashes, and she felt that odd pulse of alarm again. "True enough," he said, leaning a bit closer. "Fierce, bad-tempered, and, I realize now, inconsolably lonely."

"Oh, Leopold," she said, her hand tightening on his. "I'm so sorry you were lonely."

"It was hardly a wretched existence. I amused myself by giving the servants assigned to me a terrible time. The only person who could control me at all was Ashmole, my butler."

"The same butler you have now?" Jemma asked.

"He used to spank me on a regular basis," Villiers said. "He was fearless, for all that he was just a footman then."

"You know, you're not as bad as you let everyone think," she said.

"Don't get ideas about my sainthood," he replied with an indifferent glance. "I keep Ashmole here because I can't be bothered to pension him off."

Jemma laughed at that, and reached up to tuck back a strand of Villiers's hair that had fallen from the ribbon tied at the nape of his neck.

"So how long will you allow the marquise to trifle with your husband?" he asked. "It seems like a strange type of parlor game. Clearly you feel strongly about her behavior."

"Elijah needs to have fun," she told him. "I have decided that he has been far too serious all these years."

"Just how much fun do you intend he should have? This is all sounding alarmingly depraved."

"Not that much fun!" Jemma said, rapping him with her fan. "I can't believe you could have such a dissipated thought."

"Oh, I have many dissipated thoughts," Villiers said lazily. "They're practically my stock in trade. I think I'd better tell Ashmole to move supper forward. My cousin has drunk an alarming amount of Champagne, and the last thing I want is a drunken *très-coquette* losing control of her stomach."

"Your hair is still falling out of its ribbon, Leopold." Jemma tucked the lock behind his ear before she turned about, flipped open her fan, and began to saunter across the room. The marquise may have been half dressed, but she considered herself unrivaled in the art of flirtation.

Fifteen minutes later she had woken to a signal truth: she could certainly flirt, but only if the man in question showed interest.

The marquise and Elijah were tucked together on a small sofa. While Elijah stood up when she approached, there was something careless in the way he looked at her, and he immediately excused himself and sat down again, which was so extraordinarily rude that she could hardly believe it had just happened. Elijah was *never* rude.

Jemma stood in front of the sofa for a moment like a gauche debutante. "Do allow me to join your conversation," she said, managing to keep her tone calm with an effort.

Elijah glanced up at her. "Of course," he said, blinking as if he'd forgotten she was there at all. "I shall pull up a chair for you."

The moment he stepped away to bring a chair, she seated herself beside Louise. "How are you tonight, *dear* marquise?"

Louise eyed her a little blurrily and then smiled. "I am enjoying myself. Your husband is the sweetest, most attentive man I've ever met."

"I can imagine—" Jemma began, but then Elijah reappeared with a chair.

"We were discussing foolish antics from our childhoods," he said. His eyes slid directly past Jemma and focused on the marquise again. Perhaps on her bosom; Jemma couldn't quite tell.

"Villiers and I were just discussing the same thing!" Jemma said gaily. "He insists that he was an extraordinarily naughty boy as a lad."

At that, Elijah finally looked at her. "Give me the boy and you give me the man," he said. There was something remarkably cold in his tone.

"Were you naughty?" she asked him, fanning herself slightly. This conversation was not going precisely as she had planned.

"Between the two of us, I expect that you would win that particular ribbon," he said.

"I was a bit of a madcap," the marquise put in.

"I can't believe that," Elijah said, his tone caressing. "You are, of course, lauded for being exceptionally stylish, but also for your irreproachable reputation."

The marquise giggled and fluttered her eyelashes at him. "I assure you that I was a bit of a romp. My mother despaired of me. Why, I had a wild infatuation with Villiers. I took every opportunity I could to flirt with him, though my mother made it as difficult as possible."

"Women have always shown an attraction to Villiers," Elijah said. "It's astonishing, from a logical point of view."

Jemma realized there were undercurrents to the

conversation that she wasn't grasping. Elijah leaned forward and took the marquise's fan from her hand, acting as if Jemma wasn't even sitting there. "This is exquisite," he said. "A lovely dancing scene. It can't have been a gift from Villiers, of course, given as it is more coquettish than debauched."

"As if I would accept a gift from Villiers," Louise said, seemingly remembering her finicky disposition for a moment. "I am a married woman, Your Grace!"

"I have accepted many such small gifts," Jemma put in. "Villiers gave me an exquisite fan last year . . . dear me, I wonder what could have happened to it? It was one of my very favorites." She knew quite well what had happened to it. Her husband had taken one glance, thrown it to a footman, and she never saw it again.

"Perhaps he'll give you another," Elijah said. "My dear marquise, you appear a bit flushed. Shall we find you another glass of Champagne?"

Jemma opened her mouth to say that further Champagne was inadvisable, or something along those lines, but the marquise had already bounded up from the sofa and was flouncing away on Elijah's arm before she could formulate the sentence.

Leaving her alone on the sofa.

"How the mighty are fallen." Villiers plumped himself down next to her and handed her a glass.

She turned to him and to her horror felt tears rising to her eyes. "He's angry for some reason, that's all."

"Drink your Champagne," Villiers said. "Of course he's angry. Elijah has no interest in my cousin, a sweet little drunken duck of a woman. Don't be a fool."

His tone was bracing, and the Champagne helped too. "He doesn't want to flirt with me," Jemma said a few minutes later, rather sadly.

"That makes two of us," Villiers said. "Perhaps he wants something more than a light flirtation with you. You are his wife, after all."

"But I intended to *woo* him this week," she said desperately.

"Men can take only so much wooing. Not that I've experienced much of it."

"That was the point. Elijah never had a chance to have the fun of flirting with a seductive woman. It was supposed to be *fun!*"

"Are you sure that Elijah considers it fun?"

"Well, he's certainly having a lovely time at the moment," Jemma said, drinking some more of her Champagne. She could see them across the room, standing close together and seemingly examining something in one of Villiers's cabinets.

"I don't think he is. If you want my opinion—"

"I don't," Jemma interrupted.

"He doesn't want to flirt with the marquise, or with you either. Elijah is a serious man, Jemma. You have to understand that if you intend to love him."

"I—I—" Did she love him?

"You don't know him very well."

"Neither do—"

"We were the best of friends for ten years," Villiers said. "Elijah was never any good at just tumbling around in the mud, for example. He always had to be building something, planning a town or an invasion."

"He didn't play?"

"He has never liked to play. It's not in his nature."

"He plays chess," she said, defending him.

"He likes games of strategy. You might want to take that into account before you get your feathers too ruffled tonight. Now . . . speaking of chess."

Jemma didn't want to speak of chess, but it was better than watching her husband laugh with another woman.

"We might view this all as a giant chessboard," Villiers said.

"So?" All right, she couldn't stop watching. Did Elijah really have to touch the marquise on the shoulder in that intimate manner?

"Obviously, I am the Black King," Villiers said.

Finally she looked at him. He had that wicked little smile of his. "And I?"

"The White Queen."

"That makes Louise the Black Queen," Jemma pointed out.

"And Elijah, as always, the White King." Villiers sighed, but his eyes were laughing. "I told you I was becoming a saint, didn't I?"

"Just what do you mean by that?"

"I shall sacrifice myself," he said, rising and bringing her to her feet. "The Black King sweeps the Black Queen from the board. It pains me to do it. It's been such a day for losing at chess. I can hardly countenance my own defeats."

Jemma watched from the side of the room as Villiers nimbly drew his cousin from Elijah's side. She didn't approach Elijah, though. He didn't like to flirt, and his temper was uncertain. At dinner, Villiers sat at the head of the table, flirting outrageously with the marquise, who looked prettier every moment.

Elijah was engaged in a lively discussion with Lord Vesey about Pitt's India Act. Jemma and Corbin discussed the plate of fruit that the Duchess of Guise had worn atop her wig during her recent visit to London.

"I preferred Lady Kersnips's stalks of barley," Corbin said. "And you are not listening to me, Your Grace."

In fact, she was eavesdropping on Elijah's conversation. Lord Vesey was inquiring about the aftermath of the riots. "I was in the office of the chief magistrate day before yesterday," Elijah replied. "Did you know that Lord Stibblestich is the liaison between the House of Lords and the office of the magistrate?"

"I can't bear the man," Vesey grunted.

"Stibblestich's response to the riot is to suggest that they should all be shot."

Corbin was listening as well, and he cut in with a comment. "The papers adamantly concurred with that sentence. I had not heard there was dispute about the matter at all."

Elijah's gaze brushed over Jemma and turned to Corbin. "Stibblestich doesn't stop with the rioters. You see, the prisoners were bound to die anyway. The hulks breed disease and despair, and they would likely die within a few months, saving the price of the rounds of lead needed to shoot them. The hulks are not prisons; they are effective ways by which the government of England can dispatch large numbers of unwanted men."

"That is reprehensible," Jemma said, pulling his attention back to her.

"Stibblestich maintains that since the rioters had nothing to lose by rioting," Elijah said, "we must be more aggressive in order to deter future riots."

"He can't mean to torture them before shooting them!" Vesey said.

"No. He suggests we take all male members of each man's family into custody as possible accessories to crime. And place all those men on the hulks," Elijah continued relentlessly. "Every one of them. Elderly fathers, brothers, brothers-in-law, and male children over the age of eleven."

His eyes slid away from Jemma as he turned to Vesey. "Yes, eleven. He has specified that age."

"I always thought he was a blackguard," Vesey grunted. "His father was the same. Hope you managed to head him off, Your Grace?"

"Luckily, while Stibblestich doesn't give a damn about the opinion of elected officials, he's still cowed by my rank."

"Oh God," Jemma whispered. That was what Elijah had been doing at dawn, when he left her without a note.

He turned away as if he were too tired, or too disgusted, to even look at her any longer.

Corbin launched into a meandering monologue that touched on everything from the newest hats to the price of shoe buckles, as Elijah and Lord Vesey continued their conversation.

"Surely this meal is almost over," Jemma said, interrupting Corbin a moment later. "It seems endless."

"Not even the rather extraordinary sight of our host flirting so outrageously with the marquise helps your ennui?" Corbin asked. "Her husband will learn of this by next week, even if he is in France. Just look how Lady Vesey keeps peering at them."

Well, that was what the marquise wanted. And in a way, the Duke of Villiers was an even better person for such a rumor, as Henri would never believe that Villiers wouldn't seduce his wife, whereas Elijah's Puritanical reputation might blunt the marquis's jealousy.

"I have such a headache," Jemma said, truthfully.

"I'm afraid that the dear marquise probably feels worse," Corbin said thoughtfully. "She's looking quite white. And swaying. Oh, dear."

In the fracas that followed the Marquise de Perthuis's collapse from her chair, Elijah appeared at Jemma's shoulder. "You look exhausted."

Wonderful, Jemma thought. She looked like an old hag compared to the luscious, drunken marquise. "In truth, I should like to go home," she said, rising.

Elijah was nothing if not efficient. Two minutes later they were sitting in the carriage, heading home in total silence.

She spent most of the trip reminding herself that there were many reasons that people didn't like being married, and this just proved their point: spouses suffered black moods, and one simply had to endure them.

"Will you retire directly?" Elijah asked, helping her off with her pelisse after they entered the house.

The only thing she wanted was to get away from all these emotions that she didn't understand. "I was intending to repair to the library," she said. "I have a new chess set that I'm eager to try out."

He prowled after her, without saying whether he would play or no. Fowle had set the chessboard by the fire. The pieces were made of gorgeously carved ivory and jasper, each one a small work of art.

Jemma sat down quickly. "Isn't it lovely?" She picked up the king. He was standing with one leg forward, arms crossed, a ferocious scowl on his face. His body was dwarfed by his crown, which loomed over him: a remarkable sphere, carved with open work.

"You see," she said, holding it up, "if you look inside you'll see another sphere, and another, smaller and smaller."

Elijah took it from her while she looked at a knight. He too was the embodiment of rage: riding his horse with a small hand raised above his head in a posture of utter fury.

"Where did you acquire this?" he inquired.

"Oh, it was a gift," Jemma said. "Look, Elijah, the rook has a tiny person inside the window."

"Would you say that I am a restrained person?"

Jemma looked up. Her husband sounded as if he were speaking through clenched teeth. "Yes, of course I would, Elijah."

"In short, my face never takes on a seething expression like that on the face of this king."

She was starting to wish that she had just gone to bed.

"This is a gift from a man, isn't it?" Elijah said, still with that curiously flat intonation.

"If you are planning to boil with rage over that fact," she said, "I believe we should cancel our game until tomorrow."

"This chess set is worth a small fortune."

Jemma put down the piece she was holding and rose to her feet.

"I know exactly who sent it to you. And I won't have it."

"I find this display of matrimonial jealousy somewhat surprising after the lavish attentions you paid to another woman this evening," she said. "Not to mention her bosom."

"Don't be a fool."

"Don't call me names!"

"You know, and I know, that the kind of relationship the marquise and I have—if one could even call it that—was limited to a mild flirtation."

"It certainly didn't look like that to me!" Jemma interrupted.

"Whereas you and Villiers only exchanged commonplaces?"

So that was the problem. "It *was* different," Jemma said. "We talked of chess."

"I saw the two of you together," Elijah said. "Do you know, Jemma, that I am besotted?" He was speaking between clenched teeth.

Her heart thumped. "Is that a compliment?"

"It means that I can't stop watching you. It means that I watched you near the fireplace, touching Villiers, smoothing his hair, talking to him. That was no ripe, easily dismissed flirtation between a drunken woman and a man she decided to compliment!"

Jemma opened her mouth but he swept on.

"May I ask exactly why you set that woman to flirting with me? I felt as if I were a steak on a string, being dangled before a dog. Just what did I do to deserve that, Jemma?"

"How did you know?" Jemma cried. "It wasn't supposed to be a *punishment!* I was trying to give you some fun! I thought if another woman wooed you, it would be fun for you!"

"Do you want to know the truly ironic thing about this?" Elijah asked.

Jemma was fairly sure she didn't want to know, but he didn't wait for her to answer. "I told Villiers to go ahead with his seduction. I told him to try his best, because I was winning you."

"Oh for Christ's sake!" Jemma said, losing her

temper entirely. "You discussed me? You discussed *which one of you could have me*? Were my feelings in the matter ever taken into consideration at all?"

Elijah held up his hand. The chess king stood on his palm, arms folded, glaring. "I told him to go ahead and court you, and look what happened."

Jemma frowned.

With one swift movement, Elijah hurled the white king straight into the fireplace. It shattered against the bricks. Jemma gasped, but by then the white queen was also in shards. Words choked her throat, but rather than utter them, she just folded her arms and waited. It was too late for the set. Once the king was gone, the set was gone.

She would have thought that Elijah might get tired of it, but no. Every single ivory piece smashed against the back of the fireplace, followed by the black pieces. They smashed more easily; she had to suppose that chalcedony was brittle.

Then her husband turned back to her. "Now is my face calm and reasonable?" he demanded.

"No."

"I have my limits, Jemma. I will not watch you and Villiers express your—your love for each other in front of my very eyes. You played with his hair."

"But—"

"You held hands with him. In front of a dinner party of some six persons. In front of your husband, you took his hand! I am a *man*, Jemma. You are mine, not his."

"I belong to no one," Jemma protested. She felt extraordinarily tired, and rather sad. This all confirmed her notion that Elijah's relation with Villiers was far more important to him than that with his wife. "May

I inquire why my chess set had to go the way of the fireplace?"

"You know why."

"Because it was a gift from a man?"

"Not any man. Villiers. I lost my temper—" He caught himself, looking surprised. "I lost my temper because—"

"Villiers didn't give me that chess set," Jemma said. She folded her arms across her chest.

"Of course he did. He—"

"Lord Strange sent me the chess set."

There was a moment of silence—and she enjoyed every second of it. Finally, Elijah said, "I apologize. I'm sorry about the damn chess set, Jemma. But you can't behave like that in front of me—"

"Why not?"

"Because—Because you're *mine.*" His eyes claimed her with the same ruthlessness as his words.

"Am I yours because you care about me, or because you don't want to share anything with Villiers?"

There was a moment of stark silence in the room. "Why on earth would you think such a thing?" he asked finally.

She turned away, picked up the poker and stirred the shards in the back of the fireplace. "Because it is true. Because your possessiveness has more to do with Villiers than with me."

"Not so. I cannot share you with *any* man, Jemma. I cannot." The words seemed wrenched from his chest.

"Good night, Elijah."

He caught her arm as she turned. "Tomorrow?"

"Surely Pitt is demanding your presence?"

"I told him I would be unavailable."

"You mean . . . in the future? You told him that?"

"No! I cannot simply put aside everything that is important to me, Jemma."

She flinched.

"I didn't mean it that way," he said quickly.

"There's no need to qualify. I understand what you find important." She felt an overwhelming sweep of exhaustion. "I suppose I can plan a diversion for tomorrow." Her tone was bleak rather than bitter, which was a triumph in itself.

"I can't bear it when you look like that," Elijah said, his voice savage. Then his arms were like steel bands around her and his lips took her mouth, hard and demanding. He lifted her off her feet, wrapping her in lust and desire.

There wasn't a sound in the room, in the world, except for their hard breathing and little murmurs or groans. Only a tinkle from the jeweled flower in her hair striking the ground woke Jemma.

"No," she said. And then a bit stronger: "No, Elijah."

His voice sounded thick and strained. "Why not?"

She pushed away. "I won't—I can't. I just can't."

He made a hungry sound in the back of his throat. But he let her go. "Let me be with you tomorrow."

Suddenly she remembered where she planned to go in the afternoon. It was as if life itself was conspiring to break down the last protection she had against him. She knew instinctively that going to bed with her husband would break her. It would leave her vulnerable to utter despair, not only because of his passion for work. But because when his heart—

Her throat closed and she turned. "I must go to bed."

"Please."

Elijah never begged.

"All right," she said, not turning around as she almost ran for the door, intent on reaching her room before she wept. "You may accompany me. I have an appointment at three in the afternoon. I leave an hour beforehand."

Outside the room, she took a shaky breath and concentrated on climbing the stairs. Elijah was stripping away her defenses, one by one. And unless she was fortunate, tomorrow's excursion would break down the very last of them, leaving her broken.

She knew she wasn't being logical, or even fair, given that she was his wife. She'd returned from Paris explicitly so her husband could bed her and create an heir.

It was practical. The honorable thing to do. And yet terror caught in her throat at the very idea. It had all made sense before . . .

Before she loved him so much.

She ran all the way to her bedchamber, but even so, a footman saw the tears on her cheeks.

Chapter Fifteen

March 31

E lijah turned over from a confused dream in which Jemma was riding a white horse far ahead of him, disappearing into a wild, bramble-strewn forest. He was calling to her to wait, but she was too far ahead—

"Wake up, damn it," a cold voice said.

He opened his eyes to find Villiers standing by his bedside. Vickery, his valet, was hurriedly throwing open the curtains.

As always, Villiers was magnificently dressed, from his coat to his snowy neck cloth. "You're a deep sleeper," he said, tapping his sword stick.

"It's early." Elijah pulled himself up in the bed. Then he added, "I'm shocked. I thought you were the sort who didn't rouse until ten of the clock at the least, and after that would take the morning to dress."

"I don't," Villiers said, all evidence to the contrary.

Elijah squinted at the windows. It couldn't be later than seven or eight. Jemma had promised to take him with her at two o'clock.

"Stop smiling in that nauseating fashion," Villiers barked. "You make me feel ill. I'll wait for you downstairs. We have an appointment in forty minutes, so make your *toilette* a brief one."

"Appointment?" But he was talking to an already-closed door, so he swung his legs from the bed.

Vickery was nervously pulling clothes from the wardrobe. "Will you wear the velvet today, Your Grace?"

The coat was black, like most of Elijah's clothing. "I need an appointment with my tailor," he said. "I no longer wish to look so funereal."

"Yes, of course, Your Grace." He drew out stockings, boots, a shirt.

"You don't appear as nervous when *I* am in a hurry to go somewhere," Elijah observed, pulling on smalls.

Vickery actually shivered. "His Grace the Duke of Villiers is so proper, so rigid in his dressing and clothing!"

Elijah waited.

"Perfect in every way," Vickery added, his voice hushed. "And his valet . . . everyone knows Mr. Finchley is the best in London." He sounded as if the man were an alchemist who could turn lead into gold.

"Is Villiers so difficult to dress, then?" Elijah pulled pantaloons over his stockings.

"Everything—but everything!—must be perfect," Vickery said. "He has been known to tie his neck cloth fourteen, fifteen times. A fresh cloth each time, you understand. And everything next to his skin is the finest linen. Once he threw a pair of smalls out the window because they were inadequately ironed."

"Bloody absurd," Elijah murmured. "Do you iron my smalls, Vickery?"

His valet looked offended. "I iron only your neck cloths, Your Grace. I cannot trust anyone else with those. A laundry maid irons your intimates, of course."

"We have a maid just for ironing?"

"Several," his valet said, kneeling to help him slip on his boots. "Her Grace, naturally, has some three personal maids, as well as a laundry maid who works only with her garments."

"Half of London," Elijah marveled, "toiling away simply to keep two people adequately dressed."

Vickery was holding his wig. Elijah looked at it with distaste. "The Duke of Villiers never wears a wig," he pointed out.

"Never. His Grace sets his own fashion." Vickery's voice was reverent.

Elijah sighed. He wore his hair extremely short to accommodate a wig, and he had to admit that after so many years, he hardly noticed it anymore. He popped it on his head and accepted a walking stick.

"We have no time to break your fast," Villiers told him, when Elijah joined him downstairs.

"Just where are we going?" Elijah asked, taking his hat from Fowle.

But Villiers waited until they were in the carriage. "I've made an appointment with the best man for hearts," he said, rapping on the door to signal his coachman to take off.

For a moment Elijah thought confusedly about breakfast meats, then the penny dropped. "My heart?"

"You're obviously not bothering to deal with these unpleasantries yourself," Villiers remarked. "I find myself constrained to play the role of nursemaid. And it doesn't suit my personality."

"Presumptuous of you," Elijah observed, keeping his temper.

"A truly presumptuous friend would tell your wife," Villiers said. His voice was so oiled and cold that he could have been speaking to his worst enemy.

"She knows."

"Ah. That explains a great deal about the last few days."

"Your interference is quite unnecessary," Elijah said.

"You shouldn't have saved my life, as my valet believes you to have done. Then we'd both be rid of each other."

"You are charming in the morning."

"This is not morning," Villiers retorted. "This is the tail end of the night."

"You haven't been to bed?" Elijah peered at him. Villiers appeared immaculately groomed. His hair was tied back in its usual velvet ribbon, and there wasn't a crease on his neck cloth.

A small smile played around Villiers's mouth. "I was entertaining a lady."

"Not the marquise?"

"Louise was in no state to be entertained by anyone."

"Louise?" Elijah repeated, at a loss for a moment.

"The Marquise de Perthuis," Villiers said, sighing.

"I don't need to see a doctor, for hearts or otherwise," Elijah said flatly.

"Did you faint yesterday?"

"Not for three days," Elijah replied. "Perhaps it will all go away."

"And pigs will fly, etcetera," Villiers said with a wave of his hand. "People have accused you of many things, but never of cowardice."

Elijah digested that. "There's no point."

"It may well be that he'll tell you that you have a rare fainting illness, and cure it on the spot."

Elijah snorted. "My father died of a defective heart, and mine is going the same direction."

Villiers's face grew so forbidding that Elijah didn't continue. "In that case," he said coolly, "you will do your wife the favor of tidying up your affairs. Perhaps we could have your coffin measured this afternoon, since you are so determined to die in the near future."

"My affairs are in order," Elijah said icily.

"Have you updated your will?" Villiers paused, then added deliberately, "In the event that you have no heir, of course."

Elijah felt his heart, stupid defective instrument that it was, give a great thump.

Villiers continued, ruthless to the end. "Who is to put your affairs in order if you die intestate? Not I."

Elijah's only reply was unprintable but heartfelt.

"The same to you," Villiers said serenely, and then they kept silence until they reached the doctor's offices.

Dr. Chalus was large-headed and bald. His wig sat on top of a stack of books; more books cluttered the floor and all the chairs. His offices were hung with blood-purple curtains, as if he didn't see enough of the color during the day, and they smelled distinctly of cabbage.

Villiers strolled in and after one pained glance focused on the doctor's shiny pate.

"Do sit down," the doctor said, not bothering to look up. His servant paled, moved closer and repeated shrilly:

"The Duke of Villiers and the Duke of Beaumont. Two *dukes* are here to consult with you."

Dr. Chalus hummed, deep in his throat, and finally looked up. His eyes were bloodshot and tired, and for the first time, Elijah felt a bit of hope. The doctor looked like a man working as hard to cure hearts as he himself was to cure the ills of English governance.

"Your Graces," he said, looking singularly unimpressed by their presence in his office. "What can I do for you?"

By fifteen minutes later, though, it was clear that Chalus was having no more luck solving heart problems than Elijah had had in the House of Lords. "Your heart is beating irregularly," he said. "I can hear it clearly. At the moment it is quite fast."

"What can you do for it?" Elijah asked, already knowing the answer. The doctor's eyes were far too sympathetic for his liking.

"I have had small successes here and there," he told them. "I am working on a medicine that will force urination when a patient has dropsy. I believe the swelling we call dropsy indicates the heart is about to give out. But your ankles are quite normal."

Elijah nodded.

"From the sound of your heart, you may have a spasmodic defect, something wrong on the right side.

Which is unusual: generally one hears problems with the left side. That may explain . . . "

Dr. Chalus's voice died away and he looked as if he were listening to an argument only he could hear.

Villiers cleared his throat.

The doctor shook himself. "Your heartbeat is tumultuous, but you are perplexingly free of some of the symptoms I would expect. Perhaps a structural defect on the right side would explain why you are not suffering from dropsy. I would love to know . . . "

"How could you determine it?" Elijah asked.

Chalus shook his head. "I can't."

"Then how do you gain your knowledge?"

"Through autopsy of the dead," the doctor said, backing away to his desk. "And for the most part, those patients who are wealthy enough to realize that they should see me are not inclined to allow me to examine their bodies after death."

Elijah nodded. He had no such inclination himself.

"You have no idea how frustrating the study of medicine can be. The only bodies I am able to examine are those of criminals. And when a man has been hanged, it is readily obvious why and how he died. That is not helpful in the study of hearts. You'd be surprised," he said, turning to include Villiers in the conversation, "how infrequently criminals suffer from dropsy."

"I can imagine," Villiers said.

"There is nothing that can be done," Elijah stated. He felt a remote airiness in his head, though it was nothing he hadn't surmised himself.

Dr. Chalus was sympathetic enough. "I don't have anything to offer you that isn't, frankly, a palliative. I am currently having some success by inducing my patients to inhale a vapor infused with fungi, or mushrooms. But as I say, I am trying to find a cure for dropsy, and you show no signs of that."

"Surely you are not the only physician studying hearts?" Villiers said briskly. "Who are your colleagues? Who else is experimenting with such medicines?"

"Darwin, of course," Chalus said. "Erasmus Darwin. But frankly, I consider him a fool, and his recent publications have been rather weak. There's a fellow that we're considering admitting to the Royal Society. He's had some luck, I believe . . . " He went over to his desk and began rummaging about the great sheaves of paper.

Elijah wasn't even listening. Villiers was right. He had to prepare his estate. He should summon his solicitor tonight.

"How much time do I have?" he asked abruptly.

The doctor paused. "You present an unusual case, Your Grace."

"Surely you can give me some sort of estimation."

"You are fainting, you said, for short periods of time. Immediately upon vigorous exercise?"

Elijah shook his head.

"He was in a fistfight at Vauxhall last night and seemed in the pink of health afterwards," Villiers said. "But I found him unconscious, sitting in a chair one afternoon."

"I was tired," Elijah said. "Tired. If I'm very, very tired, and I sit down . . . "

"You're rather lucky," Dr. Chalus said. "Most patients can't tolerate vigorous exercise and you seem to be the opposite. How often does this occur?"

"I have these episodes perhaps once a week. More so if I am deeply exhausted."

"I recommend avoiding exhaustion, though I'm sure that has occurred to you as well."

"And?"

"Perhaps you have a month, perhaps a year. I apologize, Your Grace, but I can no more name the day of your death than I can entice a chicken to sing."

He went back to scrabbling among his papers. "Ah, here it is. William Withering. He trained in Scotland, though I believe he lives in Birmingham. He published a very interesting study of fungi; the *Witheringia solanacea* was given his name as a result."

"And?" Villiers prompted.

"In more recent months he's had some remarkable results giving a reduction of *Digitalis purpurea* to heart patients. I have that piece here somewhere. Aha! You may keep that," he said, handing the papers to Villiers. "As a member of the Royal Society, I can easily obtain another copy."

He turned to Elijah, who was putting his coat back on. "I should be very remiss," Chalus began, and stopped.

Villiers raised his head. Elijah nodded at the doctor and spoke for him. "You wish to tell me that I might not have a month. I might die on your very doorstep."

"Death is an unwelcome visitor," the doctor said. "We might any of us be struck down by a wayward coach in the street outside."

"True," Elijah said. "True." His lips felt numb. It was one thing to know of his father's fate and to surmise the same of himself. It was another to hear it so bluntly stated.

Villiers was bowing, so Elijah did the same. They walked out onto an ordinary street, in the ordinary sunshine.

"I'll send a coach to Birmingham," Villiers announced.

Elijah hesitated, and said nothing. There were some advantages to having known a man since you were both boys. There was no stopping Villiers once he took that tone.

"I have to write Jemma a letter," Elijah said suddenly. "I promised that I wouldn't leave the house without a personal note." He smiled rather crookedly.

"This qualifies," Villiers observed.

"I'll write the letter when I get home and put it in the desk in the library, bottom left drawer, the locked one. Will you give it to her?"

The word sounded as if it came from behind clenched teeth, but: "Yes."

"I need at least a week," Elijah said. "God, but we haven't slept together yet, Leopold. And I want it to be joyful. I couldn't bear if she was afraid I would topple over, a corpse from the very act."

"You are far more fit than your father was. He was quite robust, if you remember."

"Plump," Elijah corrected.

"I expect that made exercise more of a danger." Villiers leaned his head back against the velvet seat and closed his eyes.

"You finally look tired," Elijah observed.

"You could always do as I do," Villiers said with his coldly amused smile.

"And that is?"

"I see no point in sleeping if my partner is willing and energetic."

"She must be *very* energetic," Elijah said, raising an eyebrow.

"Her name is Marguerite. She is a widow still in

the throes of mourning her elderly husband, or so her family thinks. They expect her to pray at his grave at least two hours a day."

"Goodness."

"She tells me that the graveside is much more bearable after one of my visits," Villiers said.

"Be careful. She'll want to marry you."

"Nay."

"They all want you," Elijah said, amused. "The great Duke of Villiers . . . one of the richest men in the kingdom, and one of the most successful at evading the parson's noose. You pose a challenge, Leopold, and that is the most dangerous of all positions to be in."

Villiers shrugged.

"You don't mourn your fiancée, do you?" Elijah asked. "The one who ran off with Jemma's brother?"

"I want what you have."

There was the stark truth of it, in the open between them. "I know," Elijah said heavily.

"*Not* Jemma," Villiers stated. "But a woman of her intelligence and beauty, who looks at me the way she looks at you. If I had what you have, even for one day, I believe I might die happy."

"Christ," Elijah said. "I—"

"Then don't let your jealousy make you into a fool." Villiers's voice grated.

"Christ," Elijah said again.

They didn't say anything else until the carriage drew up before Beaumont House. Then Leopold opened his heavy lidded eyes and met Elijah's. "You asked me once to keep wooing Jemma so that I could be there when you died. I would ask you to release me from that promise. I love her. But not in the way you supposed."

His words were sure and steady, and fell on Elijah's soul like a healing balm. "Have you forgiven me, then?"

"For which of your multitudinous sins?" Villiers asked, the sardonic bite back in his voice.

"For stealing your Bess those years ago . . . for turning my back on you."

"Oh no," Villiers said. "I'll mourn the loss of my barmaid until death."

Elijah blinked.

"You always were a fool," Villiers murmured, closing his eyes again.

"Be careful," Elijah warned.

"Or what?"

"I'll leave you a note as well." He laughed aloud at Villiers's revolted expression.

Chapter Sixteen

That afternoon

"Where are we going?" Elijah asked, handing his wife into the carriage. It couldn't be a fashionable destination because as far as he could tell, Jemma was wearing small side panniers if any, and she certainly wore no wig.

She must have forgiven him for the tempest of the previous night because she smiled teasingly. "It's a secret. I've already instructed Muffet as to our destination."

For the last nine years he had punished himself for having no wife—or rather for having a wife in France. He had ignored the pleasantries of women who sought his company, avoided the eyes of women who sought money . . . satisfied himself alone, in his room. Infrequently and unhappily.

Now he felt like tinder about to flare. The curve of

Jemma's lower lip, the faint scent of roses that clung to her skin . . .

"You never used to like perfume," he commented, climbing into the coach after her. He thought of sitting beside her, but even without large panniers, her skirts still filled most of the carriage seat.

"I rarely wear scent. I did today only because when I'm naked, I feel more protected with perfume."

Her words seared Elijah's body and he heard his own hoarse voice as if it were another man's. "We're going to be *naked*?"

She smiled, the eternal smile of the Sphinx. Obviously, she had said all she intended. He spent the rest of the journey tormenting himself by imagining her soft and smooth, creamy white and delicate . . .

"Don't look at me like that!" she said crossly just as the carriage stopped.

"I can't look at you any other way," he said to her back as she descended from the carriage.

Elijah descended onto a cobblestone street in a part of London he didn't recognize. It wasn't even a part of London whose smell he recognized. He knew the smell of coal that hung around the Inns of Court, and the smell of cloth dyes down by the Thames. Hyde Park's sooty poplars had no odor, and so the park smelled mostly of dust and sweaty horses. He knew when he was in Smithfield from the odor of dung that spread from it like a fetid gift. Limehouse, where the riots didn't take place . . . Limehouse smelled like the sea and the cheerful poor, like baking bread and buckets of urine thrown into the street at night.

But this street smelled like lilacs in a country garden. They were standing before a wall with a small door. An old wall, made of round stones and sand that looked old enough to date to the days of Henry IV, or even earlier than that.

He looked at Jemma but she wasn't going to tell him anything, obviously. So they stood there in the street and smelled lilacs drifting from somewhere, while a footman rang the bell hanging by the door.

A little monk in a rough-woven white robe opened the door. *That* was interesting, and not what Elijah expected. He hadn't thought clearly, but the question of nakedness jostled in his mind into a pleasant anticipation of sin, skin, pleasure . . .

A witch's brew of sensual experience that monks had no part of.

"As you requested, Your Grace," the man said, bowing. "The baths are ready."

Jemma stepped forward. "We are most grateful, *Frater.*" His grizzled head quickly disappeared back through the door.

Elijah grabbed Jemma's arm. "There are no monks in England," he hissed. "I'm quite sure that Henry VIII did away with them."

She smiled. "That wasn't a monk. He just looked like one."

"Then what is he?"

She drew him forward. Inside the old walls there was a great muddy courtyard made of ill-kept pavement though which poked blades of grass and stunted weeds. Lilacs grew in a tangled mess against the wall, pale flowers opening in the first signs of spring. Wild garlic had sprung up around the lilac, adding a touch of pungency to the air.

The door closed behind them. Across the courtyard, square-cut pillars rose to the level of a second floor. Most of the roof was still there, but to the right there was nothing but rubble. Ahead of them the "monk" vanished into the maze of pillars. For an old man, he was remarkably nimble.

"Come on," Jemma said, taking Elijah's hand.

"Where are we?" Something was nagging at Elijah's memory but he couldn't bring it to the surface. Swallows were diving and reeling in the open courtyard, flying around the standing pillars, under the roof, and out the other side.

"A Roman *balineum*," Jemma said.

"Baths," Elijah said, puzzling it out. "I thought they'd been torn down. Or fallen down, years ago."

"Just forgotten."

"What do we do next?"

"The baths are this way." She led him among the pillars, curved to the right, and a floor paved with half-cracked and dingy blue tiles appeared. There had been mosaics there once. A single blue eye stared up at Elijah from a fractured tile, the curve of a lion's tail from another.

Jemma descended broad shallow steps and the air turned hazy. She walked ahead of him through a warm mist that clung to her hair and turned her pelisse from a rich ruby to a dimmer mauve.

Then they came out into the bath. It was very large, filled with clear water from which rose tendrils of steam. The room had walls of varying heights on three sides, and was sheltered on the fourth by a great bank of overgrown lilacs. There was no sign of the small monk. Without hesitation, Jemma walked around the bath and stood on the other side. He began to follow her, but she shook her head.

"It's divided into men's and women's baths, don't you see?" She pointed down into the clear water. The tiles on the bath's floor were intact, and clearly divided in two. He could see there must have once been a separating wall, but it had either disintegrated or been torn down.

The men's side, where he stood, depicted a battle scene, a confusion of rearing horses and spears. The women's side, where Jemma stood, depicted women bent over spindles, listening to a harp player.

Jemma smiled at him and took off her pelisse, dropping it on a bench. Underneath, she was wearing a much simpler garment than usual, one that laced in front. She began unlacing it as Elijah tried to pull himself together.

"We're—We're bathing."

She inclined her head, raising one finger. "Separately. As befits a holy place."

He looked around. "Holy?"

"Dedicated to Apollo. The Roman god of medicine."

"How on earth do you know of this place, Jemma?" He was astounded. He wouldn't in a million years have pictured his sophisticated, urbane wife frequenting a run-down ruin of a bath house. Under the water, brilliantly colored tiles glinted like fish scales sliding against each other. The spring air was just cold enough that steam drifted between them occasionally, like a transparent curtain.

"How is it heated? When did you first come here? Who was that man? And—where is he now?"

"He's down below, tending the fires," she said.

And the questions failed in his throat because she had finished unlacing and, with a simple gesture, slipped off her gown. She was wearing neither a corset nor panniers. Her petticoats must have been part of her gown, because now she wore only a chemise, and Elijah could see the lines of her hips, round and lush, the slender curve of her waist, the beguiling weight of her breasts.

"Jemma," he said hoarsely.

She raised her arms and began pulling pins from her hair. It fell around her shoulders and below, the shining sleek color of old gold. She was the most beautiful woman he'd ever seen in his life. She would have made Apollo cry with desire.

Lust slammed into him along with an urgent, male, possessive claim. She was *his*, damn it. She was his wife, and he hadn't had her, hadn't been with her, hadn't taken her—

He tossed off his wig. He wrenched off his coat and threw it on the bench behind him, pulling his shirt over his head—

Caught sight of her fascinated eyes through his lifted arms. He stayed there for a moment, arms crossed over his head, one hand holding his shirt.

"I truly have to stay on my side of the baths?" he asked. Elijah looked down at himself. Taking vigorous exercise at the boxing salon made him feel better after long nights of useless talk. So he supposed that his chest was more muscled than those of many gentlemen.

And . . . it seemed she liked that. Jemma's mouth was a perfect ruby circle. He bent over, slowly, and pulled off his boots.

"I should take *everything* off?"

She nodded.

"Everything?"

She cleared her throat. Damn, but he was enjoying this. "Everything," she said firmly.

"But you haven't."

She looked down at herself as if she'd forgotten that her body existed. "I thought I'd wear my chemise," she said, and then looked at him again.

"Then I suppose I could wear my breeches."

He unbuttoned the top button of his waistband, watched her eyes. There were some wonderful things about having been married so long. One was that neither of them was a virgin.

"You've changed!" she blurted out.

He unbuttoned another button, lazily. "How so?"

She sketched a shape in the air. "I know the shape of your body. I know you, Elijah. I could—for years I could feel the shape of your shoulder, and your hip, in my fingertips."

His desire cooled for a moment, iced by regret. "God, I'm—"

But she overrode him. "But now you're so much—so much larger. Your shoulders . . . your height. You must be—"

The stab of guilt in his heart was gone and he was laughing, laughing at the surprise in her voice, at the potent thread of desire in her eyes, at the way she was staring at him.

He undid the fourth and last button. "Aren't you curious about the rest of me?"

"You may undress," she said regally. A wave of steam rose from the pool and turned her into a nymph, glimmering in her white chemise.

He waited until the air was clear, until she could see every movement of his hands. Then he pulled off his stockings and turned his back.

She made a little muffled sound, and he turned around again, hands still on his breeches. "Did you say something?"

"No . . . " She was laughing too, but the laughter rode on a wrenching wave of desire. He turned his back again. "Yes! Don't do that!"

This time he turned with his pantaloons wrenched down just a bit. He knew the front was tented. And he knew that when it came to male equipment, his was larger than most.

"How long were we together, all those years ago?" he asked her.

She dragged her gaze from his front. "Two weeks? Three?" One shoulder rose.

"I think it was more. A month, perhaps."

"I'm sure there's one part of your body that hasn't changed," she said, one corner of her mouth quirking up in a wicked smile.

But he felt as if *he* had. As if the very sight of her turned him mad with lust. And he'd never been mad with lust. Not for his young wife whom he hardly knew. Not for Sarah Cobbett, his unimaginative, if reliable, mistress.

"Don't stop now," Jemma called, and there was something in that throaty call that shook loose a different Elijah than the man he knew.

He let his eyes range over her, linger on her breasts. Then he hitched down his pantaloons again, pulling his smalls with them. He knew she was watching, so he put his hand down his front and gave himself a slow caress.

He heard a gasp of laughter from the other side of the pool and met the eyes of his wife, felt that roaring, purring rage of lust through his body again. He had waited a long time to feel that, and perhaps its strength was ten times greater for the wait. He kicked off his pantaloons and stood there, letting her see what his side of the marriage brought her. Wondering, if the truth be told, about those famed *affaires* she had had while living in Paris. Two, he had heard, or perhaps three.

He thought, at the time, that it was her revenge, and her right. He had destroyed her dignity and her faith. She had the right to do the same. But she'd chosen puny fellows to have *affaires* with, men who would never challenge her on any front.

Jemma pulled her gaze away without saying anything and began testing the water with her foot, one slender toe poking into the warm water.

"Not in your chemise, I would hope?"

She didn't listen, of course. Jemma was unlikely ever to listen if the advice went against what she wanted to do. He waited while she walked down the steps into the bath, enjoying the curve of her hips, the pink glow of her skin, the way he could dimly see cloth clinging to her legs as she went deeper.

To his disappointment, she sat down on a middle step, the water swirling around her waist. The tips of her hair, thrown back over her shoulders, trailed in the water.

He moved down his flight of stairs. The water was as warm as a baby's bath. It was unfortunate that in his state of lust even the gentle lap of the water drove him into more of a fever.

"Jemma," he said hoarsely.

"Yes?" She was leaning back against the steps now. Her white shift was turning transparent as the wavelets touched it. He could see her long slender legs sprawled on the steps, slightly askew. It was enough to make his blood pound in his chest.

Now the water was lapping at her breasts.

"So I stay on my side of the pool, and you stay on yours," he said.

"Yes."

"But I came here to know you better."

She opened her eyes, and the look in them should have been outlawed, just for the better good of all mankind. "We can talk," she suggested.

"Jesus," he muttered.

"You go ahead," she said.

"What?" He felt drugged, as if the air was disappearing from the pool.

"Teach me something about yourself," she said. Her voice was soft but her gaze scorched him, lingering, admiring.

"Jesus," he said. But his hand moved toward himself.

Fascinated, she lost her position for a moment and slid deeper into the water, just enough so her breasts were submerged. She pulled herself out, but the cloth had turned transparent, painted onto her body.

Elijah didn't want to be touching himself. He wanted to be touching her. He couldn't stop looking under the water, at the shadow between her long graceful legs. His hands slid down his body.

"Can we come back here whenever we please?" he asked.

She seemed so fascinated by his hands that it took her a moment to respond. Then she lifted her eyes to his, and he nearly grinned to see that they'd turned smoky. His polished, sophisticated duchess was gone, leaving a woman whose cheeks were stained rosy and her eyes dark with desire, rather than by cosmetic art.

She cleared her throat. "Did you ask something?"

"I was just saying that we could return in the future," he said. There was something in her dazed expression that made joy pump through his body with the same urgency as lust. It occurred to him that however those Frenchmen had wooed his duchess, they hadn't woken her to her own sensuality. He would wake her.

"Of course," she said. "It's just a matter of sending a footman over the day before to request the baths to be heated. The caretakers support themselves, you know, so they're always glad of visitors."

"How on earth did you find this place?" he asked conversationally. He spread his legs, enjoying the way his muscles flexed. He was built like a bull, much to his valet's disapproval, inasmuch as it made his pantaloons strain over his thighs in an inelegant manner. Jemma didn't seem to mind.

"My mother enjoyed the baths," she commented, rather absently.

Elijah ran a hand up the inside of his thigh. His manhood jerked, desperate to be touched, desperate for more than a touch, if the truth be told. "This doesn't seem like a maternal sort of place," he said.

"Umm," Jemma said.

"Why did your mother bring you here?"

"It's an old custom," she said, obviously struggling to come up with the right words.

He ran his hand over his own length, threw back his head with the pleasure of it.

"When a young girl reaches womanhood . . . "

"She comes here?" Elijah's hand tightened involuntarily at the idea of Jemma as a mere wisp of a girl. Shy, slender—

Jemma had never been shy. He revised that. A rebel of a girl . . .

She was still talking about old customs, and Apollo's baths. "What were you like at that age?" he asked her.

"Romantic. I believed in fairies, and magic healing springs."

"Is this a magic pool?"

She shook her head. "One finds a magic spring in the depths of a dark wood, only after toiling for miles over hills and catching one's hair on brambles."

"Is that experience talking?" he said lazily.

"My nanny was a great one for fairy tales. Aren't you going to continue?"

"Continue what?"

She waved her hand toward his thighs.

His hand slid back to his shaft. "Would you like to watch?"

"I never have," she said. "Seen anything of that nature."

"But you have pleasured yourself?"

"What do you think?"

"Absolutely," he whispered, and cleared his throat. "Without question."

She smiled.

"Will *you* demonstrate?" he asked.

She seemed to turn even pinker. "No. Not—"

"Not?"

"Not today."

But he felt as decadent as a Roman god. "That old monk won't show up, will he?"

She shook her head. "He would never come near the women's baths. We'll leave without seeing him again."

Elijah's hand tightened on himself. "I'm thinking about you," he said, hearing his voice fall into a deeper register. He kept his eyes on hers and let words slip from his throat . . . earthy, sexy words that a respected statesman like himself would never utter. Sentences, fragments, that dropped into a little groan, about suckling her breasts, spreading her legs, where he would kiss her . . . what she would taste like . . .

She looked boneless, lying back in the warm water, staring at him. He went on, using his gift for language to describe exactly how he would spread her legs, open her for his gaze and his mouth.

"But you never kissed me like that!" she blurted out.

Somehow he had closed his eyes, lost in the pleasure, and opened them to find that she was sitting up, eyes narrowed. He stilled his hand, though it nearly killed him to do so. "I've never kissed any woman in that fashion," he said bluntly. "I was too young and stupid, when we were first married, and I had no inclination with Sarah. My relations with her did not include her pleasure." The sourness of that was in the back of his throat. "Not that she was uncomfortable," he added.

The thought was demoralizing, and just like that, his personal weapon drooped.

Jemma stood up and moved down the remaining stairs. The water came to just the level of her breasts, so it looked as if the water was caressing them. Was she coming to him? Breaking this foolish rule?

She walked until her pink toes touched the line between the men's and women's baths. Then, suddenly, she ducked under the water and came up a drenched nymph, a denizen of the seas, sleek and beautiful.

Elijah was down his stairs in a moment, across the water so fast that he caused a minor tidal wave. He didn't have to look down to realize that his weapon had leapt back to full life again.

"Surely kissing is allowed in the baths," he suggested, leaning forward.

She shook her head. Wet, she looked mysterious, her eyes dreamy. He could see the romantic girl who came to the baths with her mother, the young wife in love with her husband, though it was an arranged marriage, and one where he paid her precious little attention to boot.

"No touching," she said, and that wicked little smile was back. "So . . . "

She was within his reach. His hands itched to shape the soft weight of her breasts, take a nipple into his mouth, run a hand down her sleek back. His heart was pounding—

His heart was pounding, but regularly. In tune.

He didn't care.

"You seem to have ideas that you didn't attempt when we were married," she noted.

"We *are* married," he said hoarsely.

"You know what I mean. We were—" She waved her hands in the water, and drops fell on her breasts, like the caresses Elijah wanted to give her.

"Strictly under the covers," he said resignedly. "I was very young, you know. And stupid. That goes without saying. And I was also very afraid."

That surprised her.

It was killing him to stand just before such a luscious body, *Jemma's* body, and keep his hands at his sides. His cock strained forward, as if unable to obey the command to stand still.

"Did anyone ever tell you how and where my father died?" he asked.

He hated sympathy, but not from her. It warmed
something cold and miserable in his heart.

"He was entertaining some ladies," she said carefully.

"The Palace of Salomê," he told her. "We managed
to keep some of the details from becoming public."

"I know there were two women."

"The true scandal wasn't the women," he said, resigned to telling her everything.

Her mouth dropped open. "A man?"

"No. But my father was—" It was difficult to force
the words past his throat. "—he was tied to the bed.
His tastes were peculiar."

"Ah."

"It took me a while to realize that engaging in more
than the strictest interpretation of the act didn't neces-
sarily include a spanking."

She laughed. The sound was delicious, charming,
inviting. Shocking. "I'm sorry," she said, giggling. "But
the idea of someone spanking *you*, Elijah, is absurd.
You're such a *duke*. Even now, even naked." She waved
her hands.

He looked down at himself. "I look like a man, nothing more, nothing less."

"No." She shook her head, laughing. "It's the way
you stand, as if you own the ground you stand on.
And the way you hold your chin. There's something
powerful about you, Elijah, bred in the bone."

"Something rigid, you mean." He was resigned to
being his hidebound, moralistic self. It was probably
too late to relax.

"I suppose I won't try to tie you to the bed with my
corset strings, then," she said.

He blinked for a moment and then realized she was

laughing again. At him. His hands twitched, ready to lunge at her, pull her to his side of the baths. "I'm absurd, aren't I?" he said a moment later.

"No! It's just that . . . well, I always thought it might be fun to . . . "

"You did?" He stared. "You want to tie me to the bed?"

She was blushing.

"No!"

But there was something in her eyes, something secret and delicious, something that turned intimacies into shared pleasure between a man and a woman rather than a horrid act, fraught with disgust.

"My mother probably shouldn't have told me all those details," he said. He made little waves with his hands, for the pleasure of seeing them lap her breasts.

"How old were you?"

"Seven? Eight?"

Jemma looked appalled. "She told you the details of your father's death just when it happened? *All* the details?"

It had never before occurred to him how damaging that had been. His mother hadn't just told him of the circumstances of his father's death; her voice had vibrated with disgust and revulsion as she detailed the women, the leather the former duke wore, the humiliating truth of it.

Jemma apparently could see it in his face. "That was very wrong," she observed. "No matter how egregiously your father behaved, she should have protected his memory in front of his only child."

"I think she couldn't control her anger."

There was a moment of silence, a contented moment

in which Elijah felt as if his childish disgust and fear were being washed away in the warm water.

"Did any of those Frenchmen ever tie you up?" he asked cautiously.

Just like that, her face turned pink again. "Of course not! And there weren't so many. You make it sound as if I had hundreds of lovers! There were only two."

"I know you didn't." He doubted he would ever feel comfortable in that position, but he could suddenly imagine winding a soft ribbon around Jemma's wrists. Tying her to the bed so that his oh-so-sophisticated wife couldn't stop him from doing whatever he wished to her body.

She must have read his thoughts in his eye. Her hands came up to cover her breasts, as if she were suddenly protective.

"No," he said, tired of the limitations she set. The next second he had her in his arms, her soft body pressed against his. In between ferocious kisses, he told her all the things he would do to her once she allowed him to join her in bed.

With a pile of ribbons.

"Jemma," he said finally, raising his head from her mouth, running his hands down her back to her round bottom. Pulling her against him roughly. "If you truly insist that we should not be intimate in this bath, then may I accompany you to Beaumont House? And may I join you in your bedchamber later this evening?"

Jemma felt as if the steam were rising from her body, rather than from the water. Elijah's eyes blazed down into hers with the same steady strength as his hands, holding her close against his demanding body.

"Yes," she whispered. She knew it would break her heart, but she couldn't steel herself against him any longer. If she were truthful, it was already too late . . . it was far too late.

He was the man she loved. The man who loved honor more than his life, and certainly more than his wife. There was nothing she could do but allow him to revel in his conquest.

But Elijah surprised her. He ran his hands up her back with an achingly soft touch, and then moved back, away from her. The water felt like ice touching her thighs, her belly, the places where his skin had caressed hers. "Yesterday you said no."

He was so beautiful, with his grave eyes and marked cheekbones. "It's a woman's prerogative to change her mind," she said, guarding her tongue so she didn't make a fool of herself and confess to loving him more than her life.

More than he loved his own life.

His smile was more intoxicating than wine, sweeter than honey. And because, after all, he was a man, it was more than a little triumphant.

Chapter Seventeen

Later

"Lady Banistre holds a charity ball this evening," Jemma said, entering Elijah's study. She thought she knew what his response would be but . . .

Elijah, intent over a document on his desk, looked up absently. "What did you say? I apologize, I'm writing—"

"Is it important? Shall I come back?"

"I can finish it later," he said, putting blotting paper over a sheet as she sat down on the arm of his chair.

"Oh," she said, taken aback by how quickly he covered his work. Not that she wanted to see it, but . . .

"I'm afraid that I must pay a quick visit to my solicitor," he said. "I may not be back to the house before the sun sets."

Jemma wrinkled her nose. "How tedious. Can't it wait?"

"Alas, no. I thought we might play chess this evening."

"Chess?"

"In bed," he added casually.

Her mind reeled. "You wish to play the last game of our match? Tonight?"

He looked up at her calmly, every inch the duke. "I think we should put the Chess Club out of its misery, and solve the question of who is the first-rated player."

Jemma felt herself growing pink, remembering their agreement. "Blindfolded?"

His smile caused a fever in her blood. Without saying a word, he toppled her into his lap. But there was something different about his kiss, she thought dimly, something savage and despairing, something—

"Elijah," she said, struggling against the strength of his arms. "What is it? What's the matter?"

"I'm just writing a difficult note," he said, kissing her eyebrow. "It has made me ill-tempered, and I apologize."

"Oh."

"So our chess game begins tonight, Duchess. At eleven o'clock. I will give you one hour to try to win, blindfolded or no." His teeth showed very white when he smiled. "And then I shall win."

Jemma sniffed and turned up her nose. "Pride goeth before a fall, *Duke*."

"You will fall before me," he said, his smile a blatant challenge. "Backwards."

Her breath caught at the blatant masculinity of him. The two French lovers she'd taken, years ago now, had both been secretive and circumspect, thrilled by the fact that the woman called the most beautiful Englishwoman in Paris had chosen them. They lavished attention on her.

They didn't command. They weren't arrogant or possessive. They were *grateful*.

One could say they weren't dukes, and leave it at that. But the title didn't explain things, Jemma thought. The title didn't explain Elijah, and the way he was looking at her.

"I just don't understand," she whispered, saying it again, even though he'd explained before. "You let me go so easily, years ago. What changed?"

"It wasn't easy to allow you to go." The muscles in his jaw stood out. "I followed you to Gravesend, did you know that?"

She shook her head. "You said goodbye the night before, if one could call it that. I remember exactly what you said. If it was my decision to go to France, then you would not stand in my way."

"I couldn't sleep. Finally, I got in a carriage for Gravesend, arrived at dawn, and questioned the captain to make sure his ship was tight and safe. Then I waited."

"You didn't!"

"I stood on the pier where you couldn't see me. You—"

"I cried," she said.

"You were crying as you walked onto the ship," he said flatly. "I knew then that I had ruined everything, ruined our lives. But you had the right to go. It was your choice, and I had to give you that choice."

"I wish you hadn't," she whispered, wrapping her arms around his waist.

"If I hadn't, I'd be no better than my father."

"I don't see that. You could have told me you were sorry . . . I would have stayed."

"That would be to treat you as my possession. It would have been unethical."

She started to laugh, caught against his chest again, listening to his heart. "And now?"

"But now you're mine," he said, growling it. His arms tightened. "And Jemma . . . "

"Yes?"

"You needn't wear clothing tonight."

The smile in his eyes was pure arrogance. "I just don't understand," she said, staring up at him. "Maybe I never will understand. What if I said that I wanted to play chess with Villiers tonight instead of you?"

There was an instant flare deep in his eyes. "Don't think you will *ever* walk away from me again." His voice was soft, low.

Jemma had supper in her room, followed by a bath. Two problems came to her mind, and both stemmed from her memories of the first weeks of their marriage. In retrospect their intimacies had been, well, dull. She might not have had many or lengthy *affaires* in Paris, but to her mind, one learned most about the bed from talking to other women, anyway. And she had learned a great deal.

But meanwhile Elijah had dismissed his mistress and stayed at home by himself. Would he abhor her for the knowledge she'd gained? What should she do, and when should she pretend ignorance?

What if he became enraged, disgusted, thinking her nothing more than a light-skirt? She'd heard many times of women kissing men intimately, for example, though she had certainly never felt the impulse herself. But it felt different when she thought of Elijah. Even thinking of him in the baths made her feel flushed all over.

She would—yes, she *would* like to—

She couldn't. The hard-headed side of her brain, the side that had successfully negotiated the intrigues that characterized Versailles, knew it deep down. Unless she played this adroitly, Elijah would feel a prickle of discomfort, a prickle of unease.

She had been an unfaithful wife, for all he kept saying that he allowed her to leave him because she "had the right."

On the very verge of a panic, she stopped herself.

She was no timid mouse, to be frightened by a man's emotions. She was Jemma. And if she'd had an *affaire*, it was more than half the fault of Elijah and his stiff-necked moral thinking that drove her away, by showing such cold indifference. What sort of senseless man waits to visit his wife until he knows she has taken a lover?

The thought was steadying, bitter though it was.

She would simply be herself. In bed and out of bed. She was too old to claim a virginity she no longer had, and too experienced to pretend that she wasn't interested in pleasure. In fact, she had a veritable passion for it.

And if there was one thing she remembered clearly about their early couplings, it was that there hadn't been quite enough pleasure for her. It was, after all, easy enough for a man to satisfy himself, but it seemed to be harder for women.

If she pretended to some sort of naiveté, she would risk finding herself in the position of a disappointed woman: in short, without what the French called *le petit mort*. And that was unacceptable.

She rose from her simple meal, feeling composed. Delicious though she found Elijah's tone of command, he would simply have to learn to take instructions.

"I'll serve a small collation to His Grace tonight," she told Brigitte. "He comes to my room for chess."

"I know, Your Grace," Brigitte said. "All of London knows . . . finally the chess match will be over!"

Jemma was taken aback by that. It was bad enough that the household would encourage the bedding of its master and mistress, but all of London?

"Because of the wagers," Brigitte explained, catching the look on her face. "There are so many bets placed on the match between yourself and the master. Fowle says that the entire London Chess Club is riveted to learn the outcome. There are only two women in the Chess Club, you know, yourself and Mrs. Patton."

"I've heard as much," Jemma murmured.

"The majority are betting in favor of you, Your Grace," Brigitte said happily. "And if you win the match, you will be the top-ranked player!"

"I shall win," Jemma stated. She had spent years playing herself at chess—with the twist that she played Black (for sin), and Elijah played White (for virtue). Or rather, since Elijah was in England, and she in France, she imitated Elijah, playing White. She knew his style of play: he had foresight, courage, and an uncanny ability to corner an opponent and smash his—or *her*— resistance.

"How should you like to manage the game?" Brigitte asked rather tentatively. "I mean, with the two of you blindfolded . . . how will you manage the pieces? Shall you call the moves to me and I shall make the moves you request?"

"Oh no," Jemma said absently. "Luckily Elijah and I are both masters."

Brigitte looked confused.

"We don't need a board," she said, smiling at her maid. "We'll play it in our heads."

"In your *heads*?" Brigitte had obviously never considered such a thing.

"Unless His Grace feels he hasn't had enough practice to keep the board in his head," Jemma said, grinning.

She had no idea whether Elijah had ever played without a chessboard, but he could do it. He was one of the best players she'd faced in her life, better than the French genius, Philidor, better (sometimes) than Villiers. Though to her mind, Elijah, Villiers, and herself were fairly evenly matched.

No, that was a lie.

They each had different strengths: Elijah his steady, rational forethought; Villiers his sweeping battle plans; she her moments of brilliant and beautiful play.

But they had weaknesses too. Elijah would always find himself misled into questions of virtue. It was a passion for him: to carve life into black and white, good and evil, right and wrong.

It was all in the chess game.

Even blindfolded and in bed . . . She had to raise the stakes.

She knew exactly how Elijah saw tonight's game: as a means to an end, the end being her body and her bed. He would try to win, but what he really wanted was the last click of the pieces.

Whereas chess had been her dearest companion in the years of their separation, and it would be so now.

What she needed to do was turn the chess to her advantage by distracting him.

The slow smile on Jemma's lips would have given Elijah pause, had he seen it.

"Brigitte," she said.

"Yes, Your Grace?"

"There are a few other things that I will need for the evening, if you would be so kind."

Chapter Eighteen

Jemma was curious about one thing in particular: what would Elijah wear when he appeared at her door? On reflection, she decided he would be fully dressed. To appear in a dressing gown would lack a gentleman's discretion, given the household's focus on their chess game.

For her part, she put on an utterly delicious nightgown. It was made of delicate silk in a cream color, lined with lace and covered by a matching wrapper. It was only when she was lying down, and the neckline shifted in a certain way, that one suddenly had a glimpse of a gorgeous cherry silk lining. That was something she had learned from a circle of Frenchwomen, years ago.

"Surprise him!" an older woman had laughed. "Wear a sweet-natured gown, and underneath, a harlot's scarlet. Play the innocent and then the rascal." She followed that advice with a few earthy suggestions involving the male anatomy, none of which Jemma had tried . . . but none of which she was opposed to trying.

Her face paint was so artfully applied that only a man of Corbin's perception would have known she wore any. Her hair didn't have a speck of powder. It fell over her shoulders, gleaming like bottled sunshine.

"His Grace will be a happy man," Brigitte said, pausing before she left for the night.

Jemma looked up, surprised. "Thank you! Though you and I know better than he how much of my beauty comes from Signora Angelico's brilliant designs, not to mention my favorite lip rouge."

"I don't mean that," Brigitte said. "I mean because you—you are interested in this evening, no? You—"

Jemma sighed inwardly. Could life become yet more embarrassing? "Yes."

Brigitte smiled brilliantly. "He is lucky."

Elijah appeared precisely at ten, which Jemma thought showed a healthy level of enthusiasm for the game, as well as—no doubt—what would likely follow it.

He was fully dressed. Naturally.

She opened the door, well aware that the candles placed around the room cast an extremely flattering light on her skin.

Being Elijah, his eyes didn't drop from her face. Instead he strolled into her room as if they were in the drawing room. He looked at the delicate little table set up by her bed, the delicious morsels Mrs. Tulip had sent up, the carefully draped scarves she'd chosen to serve as blindfolds.

To her utter surprise, he started laughing. "I feel as if I just happened into one of the great courtesan's apartments."

Jemma bit her lip, and then smiled swiftly. "Should I demand a payment before, or trust on your gentleman's honor to provide payment after?"

"Oh, before," he said gravely, walking toward her. There was something in his eyes that cured the hiccup in her heart, the pulse of shame she felt at his first comment.

"May I kiss you?" His question was so simple, and so—so Elijah.

She swallowed hard and said, "Only if I might return the favor."

He bent his head then, and gave her the kind of kiss that no man gives a courtesan. Or a mistress. Or anyone who is paid for the most intimate of pleasures. It was a kiss that started with a brush of the lips and a silent question.

A courtesan couldn't have answered, because she wouldn't have been able to read all the hundreds of ways that the question came to Jemma: through the touch of his hands on her shoulders, through the controlled stillness of his mouth, through the very tilt of his head.

"Yes," she said, telling him silently as well, brushing his bottom lip with hers. "Yes."

He pulled back and looked in her eyes and then just folded her into his arms. It was as if they could try their wedding night all over again.

That first time, they hardly knew each other. She was terribly infatuated with him; he seemed barely to have registered her first name.

It was all different this time.

He let her go without another word. She took his hand and asked, "Will you blindfold yourself . . . or would you like me to do it?" She hesitated. "And Elijah, if this reminds you too much of your father's predilections, we could simply skip the blindfold. It was a silly idea anyway."

"Never," he said, and the grin on his face had nothing to do with the sorry fate of his father. He picked up a swath of pink silk that she had chosen for its exquisite match to her gown. "I'll just put this on, shall I?"

A moment later it was tight around his eyes and she was laughing helplessly, watching as he bumped into the end of the bed and stretched his arms out, trying to catch her.

It wasn't until he accused her of unfairness that she picked up the unadorned white scarf she'd chosen for him. He had caught her by then and was laughingly trying to pull her toward the bed.

The world disappeared once she tied the scarf around her head. "Goodness," she said.

"It's odd, isn't it?" Elijah's lazy, happy voice came from somewhere to her right.

"Are you on the bed?" she asked uncertainly.

"Yes. Lying here imagining you stumbling about the way I did."

"Wretch!" she scolded, turning and walking toward his voice, hands outstretched. She bumped into the bed and fell forward.

Strong arms scooped her up and placed her next to him. "I should have taken off my boots," he said thoughtfully. "Would it be cheating to start over? I'm not sure I can manage that with the blindfold."

"Yes," she said, wiggling about until she was fairly sure she wouldn't fall off the bed.

"You forgot something too." There was a thump that sounded like a boot hitting the ground.

"Not the Champagne," she said. She knew exactly where she was—on the left side of her bed at the head—and that meant the little table with the glasses of Champagne was just at her hand. Which it was. She just managed to touch a stem with her fingertips and then wrap her hand around it.

She realized that she could even sip Champagne.

"You forgot the chessboard," he said, amusement dark in his voice. "Dear me, we'll just have to think of something else to do."

"We don't need a chessboard! Are you—" She put out an arm. "Are you returning to the bed?"

The mattress sagged a bit, answering her question. "Yes."

"I shall give you a glass of Champagne."

"We can always move to my bed after this one is drenched," Elijah said cheerfully.

She managed to put her own glass back on the table and pick up his. Their hands bumped, but the glass was saved.

"I shall drink the whole glass right now," he said in her ear. "Otherwise I can't answer for its safety."

"I should like to see you as tipsy as the marquise," she said, trying to find her glass again.

"What are you doing?"

"I'm just—" There was a tinkle, then the sound of shattering crystal. "I was just trying to find my glass," she said sadly.

"The bottle is still there. Don't move." He reached over her and apparently managed to grab the bottle. "I suppose I'll just have to serve you."

"Oh? And just how do you plan to do that?"

"Like this." Suddenly she felt a warm, large hand on her hair, running like the softest caress she could imagine over her forehead. One finger paused on her nose, and was replaced by a kiss.

Another finger traced her lips, and a kiss followed.

"Imagine that," he whispered. "Anywhere my hand can go, I can find with my lips. The possibilities are . . . limitless."

She couldn't help giggling, but the truth was that being blindfolded made her feel uncertain. She had never, ever, made love without constantly checking the effect of her body on her partner—whether it was Elijah, all those years ago, or her two French lovers.

In fact, her pleasure came more than a little from that, from the sense of control and power she got as a man eyed her breasts. As she adjusted her legs, just a little, and he let out a muffled groan. As she watched a man's eyes darken with lust so he looked as if he were in pain.

But now . . .

Blindfolded, she felt vulnerable, as if all her skills, her power, her attraction, were gone, along with her sight.

"I feel strange like this," she whispered. "Maybe we should stop, Elijah."

His fingers were on her lips, followed by the cold smooth edge of the Champagne bottle.

"I don't drink from bottles!" she squeaked.

"Tonight you do." His voice was a purring command that made her feel even more vulnerable.

She drank. It gave her the oddest sensation, as if her senses narrowed to the icy, sparkling feel of the wine in her throat. Elijah wasn't touching her, but she could sense him there, his breath stirring her hair, his body just next to hers. He smelled delicious, like spice and soap and clean male.

"Enough!" she said, trying to regain her sense of control.

She heard a clink as he put the bottle down. "Now let me see if I understand the parameters of the game. We're going to lie here, next to each other—after all, the rules demand that we stay in bed—and imagine the chessboard in our heads."

"Yes."

"I've never played chess without a board," he said thoughtfully.

"You might lose," she said.

He nuzzled her ear and she jumped. "Or . . . *you* might lose."

"Of course, that's true as well." Suddenly she felt just the brush of his tongue. "Elijah!"

"I feel as if we'll be lying next to each other, like those medieval tombs."

"What?" He was distracting her, playing with her ear. His thumb was tracing circles on her throat.

"You know, the tombs where Lady Whatsit and her husband lie next to each other in marble effigy, staring straight up. I think they usually have their hands arranged in prayer. Is that what we're to do . . . at least until the game is over?" His voice dropped at the end of the sentence.

"Um," Jemma said, trying to pull herself together. But she felt entirely unbalanced. She was stretched out on the bed, so it wasn't as if she could fall off. Elijah was playing with her, as if she were one of the treats arranged next to the bed, but she felt immobilized by her sightlessness.

"Doesn't this bother you?" she said, turning her head toward him even though she couldn't see.

"No." She could tell from his voice that he felt perfectly normal. "How do you feel?"

"Alone," she said uncertainly.

"You're not alone." There was a thread of laughter in his voice that made her cross.

"I'm not enjoying this," she said, reaching up to take off the scarf.

But he knew, somehow. He suddenly rolled on top of her, and a large hand trapped her hands over her head. "You're changing the rules," he whispered, running his lips over hers.

His body was hard. The silk of her nightdress might not even have been there: she could feel every button on his pantaloons, the weight of his thigh muscles, the bulge of his private parts.

The horrible, unbalanced uncertainty of being unable to see transformed into something else, something unbearably erotic. His hands were over their heads, holding hers. She should have felt even more powerless . . . but it was the opposite.

Slowly she stretched up against him, rubbing like a purring cat. She didn't hear his low groan so much as *feel* it, with every fiber of her being. "This is better," she said. "So: you're White, and White moves first." She raised her hips slightly.

"We need some rules." His voice had darkened, deepened.

"I thought the same thing."

"What do you have in mind?"

"Every time a player loses a piece, he or she gets a boon, a request. She can ask for whatever she wants."

"Is what you're doing now a boon?" His voice was a

low rumble; she was finding that rubbing against him made her feel happy.

"Indeed," she said demurely, subsiding flat on the bed again.

"*Every* piece? That could be—"

"Twelve. Or as few as five. It depends on how well you play."

"It depends on how well I can keep the board in my head, you vixen," he said, nipping her lower lip.

She gurgled with laughter.

"And now that I think of it," he growled, "your play is marked by rushing all over the board and knocking my pieces off."

"But I also frequently win through wild sacrifice."

He had kept still, so far, just allowing her to rub against him like a friendly cat. Now he pressed against *her*, just enough so she felt the strength of him. Her body instinctively sought his urgency, her legs cradling him.

Her mouth opened with the shock of it, and his lips covered hers.

Their kiss was devouring, fierce, indulgent, slow. He released his hold on her hands, and she wound her arms around his neck.

Slowly, Jemma realized that the best kisses are always blind. She tasted Elijah, let him explore her mouth, make his mark. She could feel what he was doing . . . she could feel what was happening.

Her gentlemanly husband had disappeared. The man on top of her was no gentleman. He wasn't her Elijah, her safe, ethical husband. He seemed to her like a highwayman, an outlaw, come to savage an innocent maiden, the kind of man who thrusts his tongue into a lady's mouth and then comes back for more.

The kind of man who suddenly pulls away, without a word. She felt him rise to his knees, and then a breeze as his coat flew to the side. She lay still, wildly excited, imagining Elijah as she'd seen him in the Roman baths.

His shirt followed. "Touch me," came a growl at her ear.

Jemma grinned. She deliberately clasped her hands behind her head. "Did you win a boon?" she asked. "Because to the best of my belief, White goes first and you have yet to make a move."

He groaned and bit off something that sounded like an oath, except that Elijah never swore. "Pawn to King's Four."

"The same," she said. "Pawn to King's Four."

"Christ," he said. His breathing sounded ragged. "I need to concentrate. I can't think." He was still braced above her, his strong knees brushing her body on either side.

She laughed. "I can't see you!"

"I know that," he muttered. "But you're not afraid of the blindfold anymore."

"No."

He moved away. "I'm sitting up against the headboard," he said a moment later. "Why don't you join me?"

Jemma sat up cautiously. Now that he wasn't touching her, a sense of inadequacy and vulnerability flooded back. "Where are you?" There must have been something tremulous in her voice, because his arms wound around her a moment later and he hauled her into his lap.

"Right here," he said. "Holding you."

And just like that, she felt fine again. "Your move," she said.

"Wait a moment." He felt around and came up with the bottle. His fingers touched her lips and then the lip of the bottle followed. "Drink," he commanded.

She let the Champagne cool her throat. He pulled the bottle away and drops ran down her face and neck.

His fingers were there, feeling the cool drops, and a moment later his tongue followed. "Elijah," she breathed. He lapped the drops of wine from her throat, and a shiver went through her whole body, clenching her thighs.

"You like that?" he asked.

"Your move," she repeated, shaking the feeling away.

"Pawn to Queen's Four," he said.

She answered instantly. "Pawn takes Pawn."

He gave a groan, but there was laughter in it. "Do I have to give you a boon, or do you give me a boon? I forget."

"You lost a piece, so you have a boon."

"How detailed may I be?"

"Very detailed," she said, mentally lining up her next four moves. She planned to sacrifice three pieces in a row. And she planned to be *very* detailed in her requests, and she'd be tremendously surprised if Elijah managed to keep track of the game after that.

"I would like you to touch me. Touch my chest."

She could feel her smile all over her body. "I would be happy to do that. Why don't you lie down?" Since she had been in his lap, she ended up lying on top of him when he pushed himself flat.

She spread her hands over his chest, feeling the warmth of his skin under her fingers. His chest was wonderful, all hard muscles and textures that were entirely different from her own. But it wasn't enough to touch him with her fingertips; her breasts felt full and heavy. She leaned down, her lips grazing his face. The delicate silk of her nightgown slid over his body like water. He didn't make a sound.

"Do you like this kind of touch?" she whispered.

His answer was gasp and a prayer. "Yes." His hands were running through her hair, skimming over the blindfold, and everything she couldn't see on his face and couldn't hear in his voice, she *knew* from the tension in his hands.

"Good," she murmured throatily, coming back to a sitting position. His hands fell to her hips and tightened there. It was odd and wonderful to be unable to see. She found his nipples, brushed them gently and then dealt them a rougher caress with her thumb. Still he said nothing, though she felt a tremor quake through his body.

"Queen takes Pawn," he said. His voice sounded far too controlled for her liking.

Carefully she rolled off his body, a little afraid she would fall off the bed and end up ignominiously sprawled on the floor.

"Your request, milady?" he asked. "I am at your command."

"My nightgown," she said. "Will you take it off?"

There was no fumbling from him. She lifted her arms over her head, expecting the whisper of silk, but instead strong hands clenched at her neckline. With one fierce ripping sound, she suddenly felt the kiss of air on her skin. He pulled the cloth away from her, without a touch. Still, she could feel him towering beside her.

"Knight to Queen's Bishop's Three," she said, her voice a hungry whisper.

"Queen to Queen's Rook's Four."

Jemma pulled herself together, quelling the hunger for his touch. "Knight to Bishop's Three."

"Knight to King's Bishop's Three."

How could Elijah's voice sound so untouched, so steady? "Bishop to Bishop's Four," she continued, pushing her voice above a whisper. The chess game in her head grew more complicated. Elijah was playing defensively, but brilliantly. She attacked, preparing to safeguard her king by castling. Elijah responded, attacking one of her knights. The dance of chess pieces became ever more intricate as they moved about the board.

"Pawn takes Pawn," he said some moments later. "Milady?"

She felt a little dizzy. "I have a two-part request."

"I'm not sure that's legal," Elijah said. His voice was husky and dark, and ran like brandy through her blood. He didn't sound like Pitt's opposition in the Lords, like the bright young hope who would save the English nation.

"I'd like you to—to touch my breasts, just as I did your chest." She'd never said such a thing out loud, and she had to steady her voice. "If you would be so kind. And I want you to tell me what it feels like."

"Tell you how it feels for me?"

"Talk to me," she said, sliding flat and stretching her arms above her head to the wooden headboard. "Tell me what you feel, since you can't see my breasts. I loved what you told me in the baths."

She felt maddened with desire, waiting for the touch of his hands. When finally—finally!—she felt strong hands cup both breasts, she let out an involuntary moan. And when he started moving his thumbs, she found herself shaking, her breath coming fast.

"Tell me," she gasped.

"You have the most beautiful breasts in the world," he said, and the guttural sound of his voice told her everything she needed to know. He was being a little rough now, and she couldn't help twisting up against his touch. "I can't feel well enough with my hands to describe you, so . . . "

His lips set trails of fire across her body. He spoke the whole time, talking of sweet curves and cherry something, but she wasn't listening. Without her eyesight, her body seemed to have taken over. She couldn't stop moving, twisting under his hands and his mouth, begging silently.

It was hard, surprisingly hard, to remember the chessboard. But she did, and they played on, until:

"Bishop takes Knight," Elijah said, his voice dark and sweet.

"My turn," she said with a gasp, breaking free. She found his head with her hands and pulled him down to her lips. "Kiss me," she breathed.

Elijah's kisses were like words. This kiss was a rough caress, a controlled warning from the pirate king to the maiden. Tremors of fire crept down to Jemma's stomach.

"Queen takes Bishop," she said, shocked to hear the hunger in her own voice.

"I'll take a kiss like this," he whispered, and he thrust his hardness against the cradle of her legs. Their kiss was like a fire in the blood. Jemma found herself instinctively arching against him.

"Pawn to Queen's Rook's Three," Elijah murmured.

Then she tried to remember what move should come next. She knew it all . . . she knew the next move. But just when she almost remembered, Elijah ran a hand down her body and her mind went blank. Was it a pawn she meant to move? To take his bishop, perhaps?

He stretched toward the table, and his body shifted deliciously against her. She was thinking about that, and trying to ignore the urgent signals her body was sending, when she suddenly gave a little scream. Elijah must have drunk from the Champagne bottle because cold lips slid across her throat.

Her skin felt as if it were burning. "No," she gasped, turning her head toward him.

"It's not your turn to ask for a kiss," he said, laughter running through his voice. "Not even if you beg, Duchess."

"I never beg!" Jemma said, instantly remembering the move she planned. "Knight takes Bishop. Your boon."

A cold tongue ran shockingly up her throat.

"Oh—"

His lips trailed fire and ice across her cheek and hovered at the corner of her mouth. She opened her mouth, but his lips evaded hers. "I'll have you begging," he said. "That's what I want, more than a boon."

"Oh—"

"Rook takes Knight," he whispered in her ear.

The very sound of his voice turned Jemma's legs to sweet fire. She tried to think of the next move, the one that was going to smash his game and win her the top spot in the Chess Club. He was braced over her, nuz-zling her chin. He smelled wonderful, like clean male. His lips were tracing patterns on her cheeks.

She couldn't think. The only thing she wanted to do was tear off the blindfold and run her hands into his hair. Kiss him again, and again.

"Your move!" he commanded. She didn't answer, and she felt his ripple of laughter as clearly in her body as in his.

Jemma suddenly realized something that she should have known all along.

There are times where winning at chess doesn't matter. She loved Elijah. She loved him with all her heart—and that meant that she wanted him to win. Or rather, she didn't care. She didn't have to win every game of chess.

"You win," she said huskily, and gave him a free kiss, one that had nothing to do with boons or chess pieces.

"You win," she repeated. Then she reached up de-liberately and pulled off her blindfold.

Only to meet Elijah's dark, smiling eyes.

Chapter Nineteen

"*Y*ou're not blindfolded!" she gasped.

"I cheated." He rolled off her body and sat up.

Jemma pulled herself to a seated position as well. "You—*You* cheated?" She couldn't believe it. Not only had Elijah the Perfect Paragon cheated by untying his blindfold, but he didn't seem in the least repentant. "Why did you remove your scarf? Wait! I've been running my fingers through your hair! I should have known—"

He was laughing outright. "You must have been distracted."

" But *why*?"

"I don't want to win." He leaned forward to brush his lips across hers. "I took my blindfold off the moment we began the game. I didn't want to miss even a moment of watching you."

She scowled at him. "You should have told me!"

The look in his eyes was tender and rough at the same time. "You're so beautiful," he said. "I never really saw you when we made love before. You were always under the blankets."

"I watched you," she said. "I used to lie very quietly and pretend to be asleep while you dressed. Remember? We would sleep in the master chamber then."

He glanced indifferently at the walls of her chamber. "No difference."

"The difference is that you've come to me."

"I'll come to you anywhere," he promised.

"Just come, and I'll be happy," she said, giggling.

But he didn't laugh with her. "I don't remember you coming, all those years ago."

Jemma was torn between the delicious feeling in her body and a small tingle of embarrassment. "I didn't."

"Tonight, will you tell exactly what you like?"

She felt a blush starting. "Well . . ."

"Do you mean to tell me that the reputation of Frenchmen is exaggerated?"

It was embarrassing to admit. "Perhaps." She might as well be hanged for a sheep as a lamb. "I never—I didn't stay long enough—I—"

His mouth twitched and she realized he was laughing. Laughing! "I'm trying to tell you something important!" she protested, giving him a little push.

"I should have known it. I was in England, suffering the tortures of the damned because I was so convinced you had discovered far better lovers than I."

"I didn't drop them because our intimacies were unsatisfactory," she said, shaking her head. "It was because of you."

"Of me!"

"I always felt that I was betraying you. I would

decide, in the most cold-blooded way, to have an *affaire*, but it never seemed to work. They were so tedious, and the bedding wasn't terribly interesting."

"We were fools, Jemma."

"Was there something you learned from your mistress that you would like me to try?" she said, clearing her throat.

His eyes were serious now. "There are things I'd like to try, but none of them came from poor Sarah. I think perhaps we need to talk about her, since we keep circling the subject."

She bit her lip, but she wanted to know.

"A mistress appears with her private parts oiled, Jemma. Did you know that?"

She could feel her eyes widening. "So that a man—"

"Precisely. Before we were married, I did try to give her some pleasure. I would touch her breasts. She was a good woman, and I was fond of her. But after I married you, I lost all enjoyment in it. I used to simply take her. With few words, and with all possible speed."

Jemma bit her lip. Her body felt suddenly cold. "We both made some terrible mistakes. I should have fought for you. Instead I simply ran away."

They stayed silent a moment. "Would you like to just—sleep tonight?" he asked, finally. "This has undoubtedly made you feel rather ill." His eyes were black with self-recrimination, somber.

"Are you going to sit there and feel bad about a woman who was paid a fortune to make love to a man who had one of the most beautiful bodies in England," Jemma asked, "or are you going to make love to your wife?"

His mouth softened, but still he just looked at her, as if there were something more she had to say.

So she slid down onto her back and said, "Of course, we still need to talk."

He nodded.

"I'll tell what I learned in France." Elijah frowned, and she added hastily, "Not from my two lovers. I'm afraid those encounters were less than inspiring, which was undoubtedly my fault since I was both cold and apathetic."

His eyes definitely looked less somber now.

"I learned a great deal from French*women*," she said dreamily, running a hand down over her breasts.

"I want to hear every word," Elijah said, leaning over her, but not touching her.

"Did you know that women love to be kissed, *here*?" Jemma asked, running a finger straight down her belly and below.

"I've heard as much. And I would love to experiment." The throaty pleasure in his voice was entirely genuine.

"And did you know that some men enjoy a woman's kiss—" She let her eyes drift down to the relevant spot. "—almost as much as they enjoy other acts? And that sometimes a woman's pleasure is increased if her lover strokes her at the right moment?"

His eyes looked wild, like those of a man at the very limit of his self-control. "Jemma, are you done talking now?"

Without pausing to give her answer, she turned over on her stomach, came up on her knees, and turned her head to look at him over her shoulder. "I just wanted to say that an old Frenchwoman told me that this was the best position in which to conceive a child."

Elijah made a hoarse, strangled sound in his throat and flipped her back over. Then he was looming over her, on his knees, looking into her face. "It's going to be all right, isn't it?"

She cupped his face. "I *love* you."

The words seemed to fall into the room like a blessing, like cool rain in summer. His throat worked and then he said, "Ah, God, Jemma, do you really?"

"More than life," she said simply. "Elijah?"

He was staring down at her as if she were made of pure gold. "Yes?"

"Would you mind very much if we made love now? Because I think that I'm about to go out of my mind." Her whole body was prickling and tremors kept running through her legs.

A corner of his mouth quirked up, and a hand settled on her breast.

It felt so good that she twisted under him, gasping, and finally managed to say, "I need—"

"This?" His lips replaced his hand, but it wasn't enough. They had been playing for hours, and she was mad for him.

"I need you." Her voice sounded childish to her ears, so she wound her hand hard into his hair and pulled his mouth to hers. She said it into the sweetness of his kiss, "I need you *now*."

The Duke of Beaumont was a man whom many in the English government had come to trust. If you told him there was a desperate need for something, no matter how difficult or impossible, he would do his best to satisfy you.

Without saying a word, Elijah reared above her and a thumb stroked down her most delicate part.

Jemma twisted under him, crying out. His voice was as deep as the devil's itself, without a trace of the controlled statesman about it. "You are exquisite." His hand caressed her so that she arched again.

"Elijah," she whispered, and then lost track of what she was saying because his lips followed his hand. His tongue sent wild sensations rocketing through her body. She closed her eyes as if the blindfold were there again. Elijah was ruthless, controlling her desire, driving her higher and higher, closer and closer.

Finally, finally, he pulled back, pushing her legs even farther apart. "Open your eyes, Jemma," he growled. *"Look at me."*

She could no more disobey him than she could fly to the moon. *"Please,"* she finally gasped. "Elijah!"

She was small, and he was large, yet he stroked into her as if they had made love every night for years. It felt as if he were coming home, as if no time had passed. A dark pleasure burned down her legs, making her cry out.

The passion that gripped her had nothing in common with what she remembered of the awkward couplings of their early marriage. She had been unsure and embarrassed, those days, biting her lip to keep silent so he wouldn't be disgusted. Now she could no sooner control the moans flying from her lips than she could leap from the bed.

Yet still their rhythm didn't seem entirely right. He would thrust, and then she would arch up at the wrong moment. They bounced off each other rather than moving in unison.

Elijah stopped moving.

"No," Jemma gasped. There was a lovely, building heat in her legs, more intense than she'd ever experienced, and she was desperate to chase the sensation. "Please, please don't stop!" She shuddered and arched against him again.

"You're leading, Jemma," he said, his voice hoarse.

"What?" She blinked up at him.

He deftly pulled her arms over her head and imprisoned them with one hand. "Let me," he said through his teeth.

But she didn't understand, even when he stroked forward again. It was so lovely that the heat seethed in her legs and she cried out.

Elijah stroked forward again, long and deep.

It was so intoxicating that she twisted up against him any way she could. She couldn't stay still.

He made a noise that was somewhere between a groan and a laugh and dropped her hands, pulling her hips up so her legs wrapped around him and she couldn't move.

"Elijah!" she cried, shocked by the vulnerability of her position. But he wasn't listening, just moving, and suddenly she got it, and pushed back against him at just the right moment.

"Yes," he said, between his teeth, his eyes intent, fierce. He kept moving *that* way, hard and deep, and she arched toward him frantically, at the right moment. The fire in her legs was spreading and making her seethe and tremble.

Elijah was looking down at her the whole time. The look in his eyes, the raw possession, made the feelings in her body spiral tighter and tighter.

"Jemma," he said, deep and hard as his body, and

she wrapped her arms around him and broke the way thunder cracks in the sky, into a before and after, into the Jemma-who-had-never and the new Jemma.

He came with her, into the fury and the heat of it, and the only thing she heard was one word, and it wasn't love, but *mine*, and that was good enough.

Chapter Twenty

April 1
Morning

Villiers looked with some distaste at the page delivered from Templeton's office. It contained a neat list of eight names and eight addresses. Why eight, one might ask? He, of all people, knew that he had six children. Or rather, to be precise, he had five children and was paying for six.

Yet the list explained nothing. There was an ominous feeling to it, as if Templeton, his little rat of a solicitor, had disappeared into a hole from which he wouldn't be re-emerging. And if that were the case, Templeton had likely taken a good amount of ducal coin with him.

Either the list implied that he now had eight children, which explanation he rejected, or two children were unaccounted for in a welter of addresses.

He sighed and summoned his coach.

The first address was a house in a respectable area of Stepney. He considered instructing a footman to knock on the door and simply fetch the child, but thought better of it. This was the place where lived—the very thought made him clammy and slightly nauseated—his firstborn son.

The woman who answered the door was pious, by the look of her. But there was a hint of spice in her eye. Villiers deduced that she had settled for piety when she couldn't find something more lively.

"Good morning," he said. "I am the Duke of Villiers. Are you Mrs. Jobber?"

"Huh." She was clearly nonplussed by the appearance of a duke. Though of course Villiers did not fool himself that there were any in the kingdom who looked more ducal than he. This morning, he was wearing pale rose velvet and could have graced the king's court with ease.

Instead he was standing before a battered-looking little house. The irony was not lost on him. One might wear all the velvet in the world and still discover that one's children were living in a small house in Stepney.

"I've come for my son," he said to her.

A flash of pain crossed Mrs. Jobber's eyes. "You're taking him?"

Of course she would have come to feel affection for the lad. Of course she would. It was what any reasonable parent would prefer. "If you would be so kind," he said, bowing.

She stepped back, holding the door open, so Villiers left his footmen outside and followed her into the shadowy house. It smelled like flour and apples. "He's just down for a nap," she whispered.

"A nap?" By Villiers's estimation, this child had to be twelve years old. He hadn't napped at that age. Well, as far as he remembered.

"We'll have to be quiet," she said. "They all sleep together, of course."

"Do you take in many children?"

"I've five at the moment, four girls and he. He's a sweet one." She stopped and turned, her arms crossed over her bosom. "Did someone tell you aught about the way I'm raising these children? Because it's a lie. I never take more than five, and they have their own beds. They go to church of a Sunday, and wear a clean pinafore every other day. There's no—"

"Absolutely not," he said. But she seemed to be owed an explanation, though it irked him to do so. "I have decided to rear my son in my own house."

"In your *house*?"

He allowed a flash of annoyance to cross his face, and then stated, "I shall rear my baseborn children under my own roof."

"Goodness me," she said, looking not the least afraid. "That does make me feel better about letting him go. I've come to love him." She opened a door to a sitting room full of rather faded but clean furniture. "If you'll wait here, I'll tiptoe in and bring him out. I'm afraid he'll be a mite crotchety."

"I am frequently crotchety," Villiers observed, sitting down. "The boy wouldn't be my son without the trait."

The boy was not his son.

This child was as plump as a sofa, if sofas came in baby sizes. His eyes were like little dark currants peering out from all that fat. Villiers felt an instant dislike for him.

The baby apparently felt the same, given his bellows.

Villiers came to his feet. "I'm afraid there's been some mistake," he said to the woman, who was energetically patting the fat piglet and whispering things to it. "My son is twelve years old, and his name is Tobias." It wasn't a name he would have chosen, but it wasn't terrible.

"What?"

He raised his voice over the child's blubbering.

"My son is nine years old. Perhaps even ten," he added, being rather uncertain about that matter himself.

She plumped into a chair, staring at him as if he'd shocked her to the bone. "You're Juby's da. *You're* Juby's da? I never knew more than that he was a gentleman. Templeton promised that."

"A duke *is* a gentleman," Villiers informed her, resisting the temptation to take out the sheet of foolscap in his pocket and consult it. "And my son's name is definitely not Juby. It's Tobias."

"We all called him Juby."

"Ah." That was regrettable. It sounded like the name one might give to a racehorse who would almost win the Derby, but not quite. "Could you please call Tobias, and we shall be on our way?"

"He's not here," the woman said, still staring. "I do think I see some resemblance. He's got a way about him and you have it too."

"If you would be so kind as to call him?"

"He doesn't live here anymore. Templeton said as how he had to go to school." Her face darkened. "I don't mind telling you that I don't like your man Templeton."

"Because he sent the boy to school?" Villiers inquired, wondering in the back of his mind why Templeton had provided this address, rather than that of the school.

"He would come here and look about the place as if he were a duke himself," she said, scowling. She'd managed to get the little lump on her shoulder back to sleep. "And he never gave the slightest bit toward a name day present or anything of that nature. Not Twelfth Night either. And then one day he ups and takes Juby off to school, without as much as a by-your-leave."

"I placed no limitations on the child's support," Villiers said. "I regret that Templeton did not interpret my instructions to include appropriate gifts." He had never thought of such a thing himself. He made a mental note to have a generous amount sent to Mrs. Jobber on the morrow.

"I can see from the sight of you that you didn't know of it," she said resignedly, rocking back and forth to keep the babe asleep. "At least you're here. There's many a man never even touches his child in the whole of his life, you know. The babes go from my house to an apprenticeship, and that's the end of it."

"Could you give me the address of the school?" Villiers inquired. The fat baby was drooling on her shoulder, and he felt a strong urge to leave the premises.

"He took him to Grindel's in Wapping," the woman said. "I wouldn't have chosen it myself. Not for Juby. He's a smart one. He could be anything. You could have apprenticed him to a goldsmith, or even the rag-and-bone man, and he'd be mayor of London someday. That's what we always teased him with. That he'll be mayor of London, just like Dick Whittington."

Villiers sighed inwardly. She followed him out, still talking of Juby. Just before the door he paused. "How many years had you the care of Tobias?"

"He was brought to me at just a few weeks," she said promptly, "and Templeton took him from me two years ago. Horrid little thing he was as a babe, as thin as you can imagine." She lovingly caressed the plump back she held. "Not like Edward here. Edward is the son of a baron, you know." She drew herself up. "I take in only the best."

"Were you adequately paid for your trouble?"

"Four guineas a month, just as I requested, and I thank you for that. Plus all doctor's expenses, though Juby wasn't one to get sick. Once I managed to get him plumped up, nothing stopped that boy."

Villiers groaned inwardly. So he was looking for a junior-sized sofa who went by a dubious name.

"You'll love Juby," she said. "We miss him so. He made dolls for the girls, you know. Out of string and bits of wood. They were always hanging on him, begging for a story."

Villiers had one thought in response to that information: Juby couldn't be his son. Impossible.

"It's an odd thing, you taking him in. Will he be in the stables? He does like horses."

Naturally he would, with that nickname. "Madam," Villiers said, "he will not be in the stables."

"He won't be good in the kitchens," she prophesied. "The cook will have a fit. That boy likes to eat." She beamed proudly.

"I shall do my best to keep him fed."

She put out a hand and touched his sleeve. Villiers froze. He greatly disliked being touched. "Will you let him visit me now and again? I've seen him only two or three times since Templeton took him to Grindel's. He ran away once, but they took him back again. I do miss him."

"Of course," he said courteously, stepping back so her hand slipped from his arm. Then he bowed again and left her there on the doorstep, baby sleeping on her shoulder.

He had a biting headache and a strong inclination to forget this whole idea. He couldn't have a child named Juby. It was inconceivable. He was *Villiers*. A duke.

How did he know this child was actually his? A gentleman's son, she'd said. Surely Templeton would have mentioned that the child's father was a duke?

Everything in him recoiled from the distastefulness of the entire visit. The slobbering child, the ridiculous nickname, the shabby house.

Gentlemen didn't worry about this sort of thing. A child born on the wrong side of the blanket was no *real* child of his.

Even he couldn't rationalize that assertion, though.

Tobias was his child. He remembered the mother, Fenela, well enough. She was a luscious girl, an Italian opera singer, who had been enraged when she found herself with child.

She had screamed, and he had laughed, and in the end he promised to care for the child when Fenela traveled on. As he recalled, he supported the entire opera company for some seven months. They continued their entirely pleasant nightly encounters until she declared that she hated both him and her swollen ankles.

Eventually Templeton had informed him of the existence of a son, and the child's settlement in a good establishment, and that was that.

He even knew why Tobias had the name: because

Fenela had been singing the part of an innocent maiden, seduced by the dastardly baron, Tobias. The baron courted the maiden's affections and lured her to an adulterous doom.

Except that the evil baron had turned into the flourishing, fat Juby.

Juby.

Villiers shuddered as he got into his carriage.

Chapter Twenty-one

Later that morning

Elijah woke with the distinct sensation that something was wrong. But what could be wrong? He and Jemma had finally fallen asleep as the first morning light was creeping through the curtains. Now he was lying behind her, her curvaceous bottom tucked against him, his arms around her.

He felt a pulse of joy . . . and yet the terrible sense of unease lingered. After a moment he slipped out of bed. Jemma made a little moue as his arms left her, and then she rolled farther into the pillows. Her hair was tousled and silky, the color of drowsy sunshine, just as he had told her.

The unease appeared again. Normally just the sight of Jemma fired his loins. But not this morning. With that realization came another.

His heart was misfiring. It had actually woken him

up, which had never happened before. He sprang from the bed and walked a few steps. Sometimes even a small amount of exercise was enough to correct the timing. But his heart still bounded in his chest, as if it had forgotten the proper rhythm.

He would have to go for a ride; that often calmed its rhythm. He eased out of Jemma's chamber and retired to his own rooms.

He had finished his bath and was pulling on a coat when a footman scratched at the door. After a whispered exchange, his valet came back and said, "Mr. Fowle is very sorry to disturb you, Your Grace, but the Honorable Howard Cheever-Chittlesford is waiting below."

"Oh Christ," Elijah said. "Sent by Pitt?"

"He didn't say, Your Grace." Vickery handed him his wig. "He is accompanied by another gentleman, Lord Stibblestich."

Elijah groaned inwardly. Cheever-Chittlesford was a petty bureaucrat who prided himself on his eloquence, yet Elijah seemed to be the only one to notice that the man's eloquence was always employed in the wrong tactics. Cheever-Chittlesford was the sort who would comment, for example, that the slave trade had its place, and that Pitt shouldn't push too aggressively to abolish it.

Blackguard or no, Cheever-Chittlesford was a close advisor to Pitt, and Stibblestich was the liaison to the chief magistrate, so Elijah straightened his wig and prepared to go downstairs. Thankfully, his heart had settled down and was now dancing to a milder, if irregular, beat: not exactly steady, but not frightening either.

Cheever-Chittlesford was standing at the window;

Stibblestich had accepted a glass of brandy. In the morning.

Elijah strode into his library. When he was one of Pitt's advisors, he felt divided between himself and his rank. In the presence of Pitt, he was more an advisor than a duke.

Now he felt every inch the duke. And Cheever-Chittlesford, wily statesman that he was, realized it immediately. His bow was lower and more respectful than it was when they met in the House.

"Mr. Cheever-Chittlesford," Elijah said briskly. "Lord Stibblestich. What can I do for you?"

Cheever-Chittlesford was not a man to rush into speech; Elijah had seen him allow others to instigate conversations thousands of times. Even better, he would provoke a flagrant battle, during which both sides would pour out their best arguments. He would listen silently, saying nothing, and then decide precisely when to seize control of the subject.

Stibblestich, on the other hand, was the perfect man to launch an argument. He rarely thought before he spoke, and therefore his words were invariably insulting. "It's the hulks," he said importantly. "We've been tasked by the king himself with coming up with a solution to those floating monstrosities."

Elijah kept his expression pleasant and uninterested. "A difficult problem, as we've already admitted," he murmured.

"I've suggested that we fire them," Stibblestich said. "That's the best solution. Fire 'em!" He gave a couple of vigorous nods. "There's none but bloody-minded criminals aboard. They're a floating pestilence for the city, like rats . . . like—like—like *rats*," he finished, apparently unable to think of another word.

Elijah turned to Cheever-Chittlesford. "Of course, removing the warships from their current use as prison barges is an excellent idea."

Cheever-Chittlesford looked discomfited, which was unusual. Elijah's eyes narrowed. "Precisely what do you mean by 'fire them'?" he asked, turning back to Stibblestich.

"Burn them down," he said promptly. "It'll take care of all our problems. We'll start over with the same problem, of course, but we can find somewhere else to house the new ones. The king himself was in danger during the riots!" He opened his eyes so wide that his whole face seemed to stretch.

Elijah's heart gave a great thump. "Do I take you to mean that you are considering burning the ships *with prisoners inside*?" He could hear the pendulum clock behind him ticking very hard, as hard as his heart was beating. It was inconceivable . . . it was barbaric. He could feel, deep in his body, the frown that had formed on his face, the fury that was making his back rigid.

Stibblestich started to bluster, something about pestilence. Elijah turned to Cheever-Chittlesford, who looked at him with the shadow of an apology in his eyes, so Elijah knew that indeed the government was entertaining that thought. Something in him raged and despaired at once. They were so stupid, so stupid and violent.

With an effort, he summoned up the logical, calm voice that he used to show madmen the error of their ways. "You intend to burn the hulks."

"That's right," Stibblestich said. Satisfaction reeked in his voice.

"Burning them where they are currently anchored?"

"That's the whole point! We need to make a lesson out of this uprising. We can't just let it pass: the king's own yacht was violated by dirty, criminal hands. The king's noble subjects were fired upon. But that was not the worst."

Elijah frowned. "What was the worst?"

"The Duchess of Cosway was on that yacht! She was caught by those criminals, manhandled, perhaps violated—"

Cheever-Chittlesford interrupted. "They held her briefly; she was rescued by her husband."

"They pushed the Duke of Cosway into the water!" Stibblestich said, his voice rising even higher. "The duke and duchess had to swim to shore."

"Dear me," Elijah said, wondering if his wife knew that her friend Isidore had taken an impromptu bath in the Thames.

"We've had uprisings on the hulks in the past," Stibblestich said, "but as I've told you before, this time they've *gone too far*! We must make an example of them! They touched—nay, they assaulted—a peer. Two peers!"

Cheever-Chittlesford cleared his throat again. "Of course, the duke and duchess do appear to be unharmed."

"By the grace of God, who looks out for the just and innocent," Stibblestich said. His breath smelled like brandy and pickled eggs, and Elijah's stomach lurched.

"And also because the Duke of Cosway was able to knock those holding his wife to the ground," Cheever-Chittlesford added.

"If we don't make an example of *this*," Stibblestich said, "there'll be no end to it. People will be free to assault the highest in the country, to molest those of the highest blood. We cannot allow such an abomination!"

"The argument is that firing the one boat involved in the uprising would serve as a warning to other prisoners," Cheever-Chittlesford said, rocking back on his heels.

He wasn't a bad man. But he was a pragmatic man, and Elijah surmised that he was facing considerable pressure. Nothing else could explain Cheever-Chittlesford's appearance at his house. Nothing other than the fact that Elijah had served as something of a conscience for Pitt, the one man who wasn't motivated enough by money or power to lay aside all sense of principle.

"It is wrong to burn those men inside the boat," Elijah stated. There, the decent truth of it was on the table. "It's against God's law and ours."

"The Parliament makes the laws," Stibblestich argued. "Together with the king. And sometimes the harshest remedies must be chosen for the good of all. Of course, each man would be allowed to make his last confession. We are not barbarians."

But of course they *were* barbarians. The appeal to decency had to be made, as Elijah saw it. Cheever-Chittlesford knew. He *knew* it was wrong. But that wasn't the argument that would sway them.

"You intend to burn the ship with the men manacled inside," Elijah said. "There, in the presence of all London. Will you advertise this fact?"

"Certainly," Stibblestich said promptly. "How else can we ensure that the criminal element understands the serious consequences of laying hands on a peer? Of rebelling against the punishment meted out to them by a thoughtful and understanding judiciary? It will serve as a lesson to all restless criminal minds who plan such riots."

"Most of those prisoners, as you know, served in the Royal Navy," Elijah said. He let that comment hang in the air for a moment. "There are former sailors in the hulks who stole as little as a loaf of bread because they were starving."

Even Stibblestich knew that returning soldiers were a vast problem in England. "Their home counties should care for them," he said lamely. But the counties from which these men came could not afford to feed and clothe a man on crutches, or a man with only one eye and one hand.

"Let's just imagine," Elijah said, "what the citizens of London will think and feel as they watch the boat burn."

Stibblestich seized that, of course. "Londoners love a good execution! We've had hundreds watching around Tyburn when a murderer is being hanged—or better yet, drawn and quartered."

"These are not murderers, of course," Elijah said. "The murderers have already been hanged, with their cheerful audiences. Murderers do not find themselves in the hulks. These prisoners are the poor, those who stole."

"Robbers," Stibblestich said, the word exploding off his tongue. "They beat and they rob. Generally the elderly. They will rob an old woman as soon as look at her!"

"Londoners will watch from the shores, no doubt," Elijah continued. "They will hear the screams."

Cheever-Chittlesford's eyes flared, just slightly.

"The men will be trapped below, as the smoke

begins to creep down. I imagine it will be something like the burning of witches, that happened back in un-civilized times . . . say in the realm of Queen Mary, she who is now nicknamed Bloody Mary. I'm afraid that history does tend to dwell on this sort of event."

Stibblestich said, "I doubt—"

But Elijah spoke straight over him. "The men will begin to scream. The flames will lick onward. And every person on the shore will know someone who knows someone on that boat. The mothers will likely try to throw themselves into the water at this point. They will begin to shriek."

Cheever-Chittlesford's mouth was a thin line.

"Oh yes, they'll scream," Elijah said, folding his arms over his chest. "I expect that the ship burning will be the one event that marks the entire reign of King George III. No one will ever forget it. No one on that shore, who watches that wholesale slaughter, will ever stop talking of it, not in his or her lifetime." He turned sharply on Cheever-Chittlesford. "Does the king realize that he stands to create his legacy by this single act?"

The question of Pitt's legacy hung in the air, not to mention Cheever-Chittlesford's.

"I doubt it," he replied.

"Well, *I* doubt it would be anything near as dramatic!" Stibblestich blustered. "You'll have us all in tears, talking of mothers and such. But the reality is that Londoners like a good hanging!"

"That they do. A man who's been fairly caught and confessed—for they always appear to have written their confessions, even the ones who can't sign their own names—London does enjoy a good hanging of that nature. But men chained to the walls, forced to die slowly, in terror and excruciating agony, for the *crime of stealing a loaf of bread*?"

Cheever-Chittlesford cleared his throat. "I am sure another solution will present itself."

Elijah knew better than to show the slightest sign of satisfaction. He'd lost arguments, after winning them, by exhibiting pleasure in the outcome.

Cheever-Chittlesford's eyes looked like old metal coins, dull and impenetrable. But Elijah knew he had him. Cheever-Chittlesford would not allow the firing of the hulks. Elijah looked deliberately at Stibblestich, and then back at Cheever-Chittlesford. "Statesmen are likely to be judged by those they have around them. Men of the highest integrity are a bulwark against depraved decisions."

"Nothing depraved about it!" Stibblestich said. His voice was quieter now that he'd lost. He looked disappointed. He, for one, would have enjoyed standing on the riverbank and watching the ship burn.

"I suggest you investigate sending such petty criminals to Australia," Elijah said. "It's a large country, and far away." Cheever-Chittlesford didn't look convinced, so he added, "In years to come, it may be a thriving colony, capable of being taxed."

That made Cheever-Chittlesford look even more thoughtful.

Suddenly Elijah wanted nothing more than for these men to be out of the house, with their ability to discuss burning men alive, as if such a thing could ever be a reasonable proposition. As his rage receded, exhaustion followed in its wake.

He bowed. "I'm afraid you must forgive me, gentlemen. I have a previous engagement."

"Of course," Cheever-Chittlesford murmured.

Finally, they left the library and were in the entry. Elijah heard Stibblestich's voice, sharp and scornful. "Of course Bawdy Beaumont has an appointment. I hear he's caught the whore's disease. And you know where he caught that. Like father, like son. I always said it." His voice faded as he and Cheever-Chittlesford walked out the front door.

Elijah didn't even care.

There was a sound in his head, like that of a stream rushing downhill. He was so tired that his legs felt like bars of lead. He had to go back to bed.

But the distance between himself and the bedchamber upstairs seemed insurmountable.

Jemma could not see him like this. He forced himself to move, feeling his heart thump angrily in response. The only thing his body wanted was to lie down, to slip into the blackness that waited at the edges of his vision.

He walked up the stairs steadily, by an enormous effort of will. At his door, he slipped through and closed it behind him, leaned back, head against the wood. Something was wrong with his vision, though, and the walls seemed to undulate.

The thought crossed his mind that he might not wake up this time. He had felt this terrible only once, after fainting in the House of Lords a year ago. A wash of regret went through his mind, but he pushed himself upright. He had had one wonderful night with Jemma.

He put a foot forward, and then another. It wasn't so far to the bed. The walls were turning gray and foggy, as if the solid wood were dissolving. He could feel his heart stuttering, dropping a beat, another beat.

He pushed himself forward. If he were going to die now, it would be decently in his bed. He could have been climbing a mountain, given the effort it took him, but he finally was at the side of his bed. He put his hands out and allowed himself to fall forward.

Then he thought about turning over for what seemed like a long time before he managed to do it.

It was only when he was lying there fully clothed, and the familiar darkness was gathering and billowing around him, that Elijah thought of his father. He had spent the greater part of his life hating his father for dying in the manner he did, for living his life in such a wayward fashion. The facts of his father's death had shaped his life.

Yet if his father had not been immoral in such a flagrant fashion, would he himself have become a person whom statesmen visited for advice when they were considering a leap into cruelty?

He would have been merely another duke, trundling from his country estate to his town house, marrying the woman designated to be his duchess, going from cradle to grave without considering the impact of his own words, of his own life.

With that thought came a feeling of peace. Because his father had died young, Elijah had always felt time at his shoulder. And that drove him to work hard. It allowed him to sometimes intervene before a great injustice was served on the weak and needy.

It even drove him to bring Jemma back from Paris, to give them the indescribable joy they had shared the night before. His father had never found the love that he and Jemma shared.

The late duke had lived in a house full of portraits of beheaded men. Whereas he had lived, if only for a year, in a house graced by Jemma.

He slipped into the darkness, smiling.

Chapter Twenty-two

Elijah was rather surprised to wake up, but not surprised to find Jemma standing at his bedside, her eyes huge in her stricken face.

She said his name on a sob.

"It's all right," he said, the words coming with difficulty. "I'm back."

"I thought the attacks came – I was a fool," she said, clutching his hand. "I put it out of my mind. Was it because we—"

"No!" he said quickly. "Stibblestich visited this morning."

She swallowed, and he could see her make a visible effort not to renew her plea that he leave the Parliament. "Give me some time," he murmured. "I'll have that potion Vickery doubtless has ready-made, and take a short nap."

Jemma's lips were trembling, but she set her mouth and put down his hand. An hour or so later he was up, his headache gone, just the ache of regret in his chest.

He found Jemma in the library, staring at an empty chess board. He didn't think she was playing a game in her head. He dropped a kiss on her hair. "Would you like to take a walk with me?"

She looked up. Her eyes were glazed with tears. "I'm so sorry," he said helplessly.

"I'd like a walk, but not here. I don't want to see Lady Lister next door, or anyone I know."

"How about the gardens of the Roman bath?" he suggested. "We said we would go back, someday."

The truth of that stood between them silently. If they didn't go now, they might never go.

Servants have a way of knowing when it's the right time to be invisible. Without meeting anyone's eyes— not Fowle's, not a footman's—they were in the carriage. Jemma huddled under his arm like a wounded bird. And then they were at the baths.

It was raining: not hard, just enough to make spring look even greener. Every leaf appeared new, as if its paint was not yet dry, the color still vivid and glossy. Even the light looked green.

The little monk let them in, incurious as ever. He wore his hood over his face so all that could be seen was his nose. The nose nodded when Elijah said they would walk in the gardens, and the man hurried away, disappearing between the broken pillars.

"Who *is* he?" Elijah asked, breaking the silence. "Do you have any idea why he tends the baths?"

"There are five of them," Jemma said. Her voice was too controlled. She needed to cry, he guessed. "Caring for the baths is all they do."

"They certainly don't bother with the grounds." The gardens were as dilapidated as the baths themselves. They wandered down a path lined with overgrown shrubs. Flowering vines hung like horse blankets over the low walls, dragging down stones and tumbling them to the pavement.

The tree trunks were shiny black with rain, their leaves reflected in puddles at their feet.

"I believe they spend their time in prayer," she said, when so much time had passed that he had forgotten the question.

"Prayer to Apollo?"

"The God of Healing." Her hand curled suddenly around his. "Oh, Elijah, would it be madness to ask them to pray for you?" She started to turn about.

He dropped a kiss on her nose. "Yes, it would. I don't think people ask Apollo to grant favors. He gave humans the art of medicine, but he didn't promise to cure Lord Piddleton's gout."

"You're not suffering from a mild case of gout," she said tensely.

"Well, you can always ask."

But she was thinking about it now. "The problem is where does one stop? If I ask the monks here, I'd have to ask someone in the church."

"The archbishop, at least," Elijah suggested. Against all odds, he was starting to feel oddly happy.

She scowled at him. "How dare you smile at me!"

"I didn't die today," he said cheerfully. "I'm walking with you, and you don't have gloves on, so I am feeling a pleasantly irresponsible wish to kiss your fingers." Which he did. "And your mouth." Which he did.

"You have the most lovely mouth, Jemma," he whispered sometime later. "It's soft and full. It makes me want to bite you."

Her smile was so beautiful that he kissed her again, and then because a man can't kiss a luscious woman and simultaneously feel despair, he started to feel something quite otherwise.

Jemma had her arms wound around his neck and didn't seem to take it in when he unbuttoned her pelisse and ran his hands inside.

He almost groaned aloud. The lush weight of her breasts, plumped in his hand, made him feel mad. It was the work of a moment to pull down the delicate pleated material hiding their beauty.

The gardens were utterly still. They had walked long enough so even the baths were out of sight. He couldn't hear a sound from the road, just the high clear song of a lark, rejoicing in the end of the rain shower.

If there was ever a moment since the world began in which a man ought to play Adam, and make love to his own Eve, this was it. Without further ado, Elijah spun Jemma to the side and plumped her down on a narrow bench at the edge of the path. She let out a little shriek that might have had something to do with the rain glistening on the marble seat.

But Elijah fell to his knees before her, ignoring her protest. He traced the curve of her breast with his hand and then followed that caress with his lips. She certainly protested: she even tugged at his hair. But he felt primitive and alive, suckling his wife with a passion bred by grief and joy intermingled. He knew her body, knew her soul, and so he wrapped his hands around her waist at the very moment Jemma surrendered. Her head fell back and a ragged cry came from her throat.

The smooth skin under his tongue tasted like milk and honey, like the most delicious food the world has to offer. He gave her a little bite; she gasped and the sound stoked his belly, sent fire raging up his legs.

"Sweetheart," he said, wrenching her bodice even

lower so that he could give the same ministrations to her left breast, "you're killing me."

Her body went rigid.

He gave her another little bite. "Not literally, you fool." And licked her to ask forgiveness for his offense.

"Don't you dare call me names," she said, but her voice was syrupy and he knew he had her. He wasn't dead yet. *He wasn't dead yet.*

He stroked and nibbled until her whole body was trembling and she was clutching his shoulders closer, rather than trying to push him away—and then he stood up. "Time to be on our way, sweetheart." He caught her hand and brought her to her feet, loving the look of her. The contrast between her lush skirts and bare breasts, between her dazed eyes and ruby mouth.

"Wh-what?"

He loved it when his sophisticated Jemma got that look in her eyes, as if she were bereft because he had stopped touching her. As if her need for him was so great that she couldn't think about chess pieces or logic or any of those other things she did so well. So he kissed her again, just to make sure she was agreeable, and then pulled her down the path.

There was mist hanging in the air from the morning's shower, but he could see that the path ended in a little circle with a statue. Perfect. He couldn't give her time to think, so it was the work of a moment to have Jemma flat on her back, cushioned on his coat and her pelisse. He threw off his boots too, though she hadn't quite noticed.

"Just a kiss," she said, starting to wake up. "I don't mind kissing, Elijah, though this is terribly—"

He had to move quickly so he put a hand under her skirts. She was soft and wet, and the little noise that came from her mouth replaced all those anxious words she was trying to say. Every time she started again he changed his touch from light to deep, from a brush to a stroke. She did manage to gasp ridiculous things in between pants. Like "We shouldn't," and "Is that rain?" and "No!"

But he took his time, his fingers dancing, his mouth stealing her moans until she started bucking against his hand, twisting from side to side.

Still he waited . . . waited . . . moved his fingers in the kind of languid stroke that his own sweet Jemma could not resist, could not fight.

It started to spit rain again, just enough to cool them both off. She had stopped saying no, and was breathing his name over and over, like a song. There was something in the sound of it that made him feel such a wave of tenderness that he instinctively shook his head. Rather than say something foolish, he threw up her skirts and slid down so that he could feel with his fingers *and* his mouth every shudder that raked her body. Her hands wrapped into his hair and she gave a little scream, a cry of pure pleasure.

"Elijah!" she cried. "I—" and she came with a force that shook her body from her toes to her fingertips.

It was his moment. He wrenched down his panta-loons and eased into her. She was swollen and silky, like milk wrapped around him. A thick groan broke from his lips.

But: "I'm worried about your heart," Jemma said. He looked down and her eyes were wide open, anxious—terrified.

He brushed her lips with his own. "I've never

been better. Do you know what I love, Jemma?" He moved slowly forward, sliding into her, stretching her. She squeaked. "You didn't think you'd be naked today."

"Of course not." She arched up against him so that he nearly lost his train of thought. "We *shouldn't* be naked," she pointed out. But there was no real conviction in her voice.

"You wear perfume when you think you're going to be naked."

"Yes," she breathed, pushing back against him at just the right moment.

"I love it when you don't wear perfume. You smell so good," he whispered, nuzzling her. "You smell like clean rain, and hot woman."

"Elijah!" She was trying to sound scandalized, so he ignored her.

"Now I'm going to—" He lowered his mouth to her ear again and told her in detail what he meant to do. And then because his language had been thrillingly rough, he followed it up with kisses so sweet that he felt another pulse of nervousness. Making love wasn't supposed to be so—so loving.

He shook the thought away, threw his head back, and pumped. But even as Jemma squeaked when he filled her, her hands clutched his shoulders, and her moan was of fear.

He opened his eyes. "Jemma?"

"I'm afraid for you," she gasped. There was rain on her nose, and shining in her curls, and she was so beautiful that it took everything he had to stop the movement of his hips. Even so, he couldn't stop himself, and nudged forward just a bit. Just enough to make sure that she was with him.

She was, because she took a quick breath and her fingers bit into his shoulders.

"I'm covered with sweat," he observed, stilling again.

"Is that bad?" Her eyes went wide again.

"No! It's good. Remember, I told you that regular exercise has helped my heart?"

"Yes, but this isn't—"

"It is. If you stop me now, it'll be a terrible shock to my body," he offered.

She scowled at him.

"My heart's steady," he said. "Here, feel it."

Her little hands came up to his shirt and pressed. "I can't feel anything," she cried, frustrated.

So with a groan of regret he pulled away, stood up and pulled his shirt over his head. She liked to look at him. He could tell the way her eyes darkened, just a bit. In a flash he was back where he needed to be.

"Now you're going to monitor my heart," he said, grinning because he couldn't stop.

She swatted him. "Elijah, we're making love in the outdoors, in case you didn't notice that. What if that little monk comes along?"

"In the rain?" He snorted. "The man is snuggled up next to a fire somewhere drinking a toddy. That's what monks do. They certainly don't engage in gardening."

"As if you know!" But she looked better for a little jousting: more like herself, and less like a frightened, white-faced woman he didn't recognize.

"Now as I said, you're in charge of monitoring my heart, not that anything will happen."

"How can you know that?"

"Because, I never faint when my heart is pumping. Exercise seems to make it go in a steady rhythm. It's only when I'm resting or fighting with Stibblestich that it skips a beat now and then."

She clutched him. "Oh my God, you're resting right now."

"That's right," he said, enjoying every evil moment of it. "I'd better stop resting. For my own good."

Her eyes narrowed. He knew he had her. So before she could start arguing, he slipped back into the cradle of her thighs.

Sure enough, she protested. She had starting thinking in the two minutes it took him to remove his clothing. "Elijah! We really shouldn't do this. We're—we're outdoors."

"Stay put," he told her. The sight of her had peeled away all his niceness, and now he was just one growling male again. "I want you."

Rain was falling like an uncertain melody, just one drop here or there. One fell on her breast, glistening like a diamond.

He licked it off and then gave her a little bite and she apparently forgot that she was outdoors, because even a monk behind stone walls could have heard that shriek. Then he blew on her skin, and gave her another sweet, deep caress.

It seemed that this particular duchess liked making love outdoors.

Finally, when he had her just where he wanted her, he came up on his knees and drove into her with one powerful stroke. She came. Just like that, with a wild cry, and a convulsion that damn near sent him over the edge too.

Being Jemma, she hadn't even recovered when she began patting his chest, trying to find his heart. He didn't stop; his whole body was intent on one mission, and one mission only.

"Where is it? Where is it?" she moaned, patting him all over the right side of his chest.

"Wrong side," he managed. She was never going to settle down, so he took one of her hands and plopped it on top of his heart. Which was beating so hard that he could feel it in his ears—but with perfect rhythm.

"My heart," he said hoarsely, "is happy, Jemma."

Her fingers pressed his chest, and then he saw her start to smile.

"Enough," he said, pulling back.

"But—"

"We're making love, Jemma. I'm—" But he couldn't shape the words anymore. Instead he just stared at her as he thrust, at her beauty, at the deep goodness of her. She couldn't resist either. Her eyes squeezed shut and her arms flew restlessly around his arms, his shoulders, his chest, caressing him, leaving trails of fire, sliding down his back, clutching his rear.

He pumped harder and harder, until neither one of them had a thought for the rain. Not for anything but the two of them: God's creatures, lucky enough to experience His greatest pleasure.

Elijah lost control. The world narrowed to just the sweet smell of his wife, the taste of her skin, the movement of his hips.

Still, he waited to be sure that her fear was gone. Waited until she cried out and surged against him. And then he flew. The world dissolved into such acute pleasure that his bones flamed with it.

Blissful moments later, he rolled onto the slick stones, enjoying the cool, wet stone against his buttocks and back. His heart beat steadily.

"What are you smiling about?" Jemma asked, but there was a smile in her voice too.

"My body's happy," he said, stretching.

She was already sitting up, pulling her bodice into place.

Elijah just folded his arms behind his head and watched her. It felt wonderful to lie there, stretched out in the warm rain. He didn't give a damn if the monk came along. In fact, he didn't give a damn if the whole House of Lords decided to go for an afternoon stroll, happened down this particular path, and saw the Duke of Beaumont, lying naked on an old stone path.

No one told you that almost dying was so freeing. "I could live here," he said dreamily. "In my house the birds would sing day and night."

"Where will you sleep?"

"Under that huge horse chestnut. We'll have a bed of eiderdown and make love every morning before the birds rise."

"I shall miss my morning tea," Jemma said. She had managed to wrench her bodice up just enough so that it covered her nipples. The plump tops of her breasts looked ready to fall out at any moment.

"That gown will never be the same," he said, watching her. "That yellow part, that pleated cloth on top, looks as if a dog has chewed on it."

"One did," Jemma retorted. "At least it covers my nipples now." She looked over and seemed to realize that he was making no attempt to dress. "Are you going home like that? Or are you truly planning to sleep under the horse chestnut?"

He was too happy to move. "Why not? My blanket could be made of those little green hearts it throws out in spring, the ones with little crimson centers."

Jemma being Jemma, she didn't break into a chorus of little remonstrances. Instead, she surprised him. Again. She turned around and lay down, her head on his bare stomach as the rain spattered her face.

"I never imagined, ever, a duchess lying on the ground, being rained on," he said, after a time.

"It's not really raining. But you're right. I suppose duchesses don't lie about in the rain."

"With their naked husbands," he added.

"That makes it even worse," she agreed. Her hair was all rumpled and fallen from its nest of curls, so he picked a spray of flowers and started poking blossoms in it.

"What are you doing?" she asked, twisting her head so she could see him.

"Turning you into a pagan goddess," he murmured.

"Why?"

"See Apollo there?" In the center of the little stone courtyard was a statue of the god wearing little more than a shawl. He stood on a stone pedestal, its latticework woven through with knot grass and other weeds.

"Poor soul. What's happened to his arms?"

"Knocked off," Elijah said. "He kept his fig leaf, though. A man—even better, a god—likes to keep some things covered through the centuries."

"He looks a bit scrawny," Jemma said critically. "I like your legs better. Who knows what's under that fig leaf? You would need a fig leaf twice that size."

"Hush. You'll insult the god, and right in his own backyard. There." He poked in a last few flowers. "I'll have to be very lucky or Apollo will come to life and claim you for his own."

"If you remember, Apollo had no luck with women. Didn't Daphne turn herself into a tree rather than be with him? And now we know why. It was undoubtedly due to those bony little knees of his, not to mention the tiny fig leaf." Jemma started to sit up, so Elijah got up and pulled her to her feet. "I am ready to return to being a duchess, if it means that my bottom can warm up."

"I can do that for you," Elijah said with an exaggerated leer, cupping his hand over the part of her body in question. Her skirts were soaked, and he could feel her intoxicating, soft curve. "God, I'm so lucky."

Her eyes contained such a beautiful smile that he had to stop and kiss her. "And happy," he said a moment later.

She leaned her head against his chest. "I love you," she said, but not: *I'm happy.*

"I love you," he said, the words rising from his heart naturally. "I love you, Jemma. I love you."

The joy in her face shamed him. "To find all this bliss, at the end," he said, holding her tightly. "I don't deserve it, Jemma. God knows, I don't deserve you."

"Maybe it's not the end," she said fiercely.

"If it is, I've had more joy in the last week than in the rest of my life."

Her arms tightened around him and she said something, so low he couldn't hear. But he thought she said she loved him, and he knew that already.

He dressed, and kissed her a few more times, and they walked back to the little door where the carriage waited.

Chapter Twenty-three

That evening

Elijah had banished Fowle and the footmen, and there were only the two of them, down at one end of a long mahogany table with a great deal of silver reflecting the candlelight.

"I don't know how to live like this," Jemma said after a few minutes of moving her food around her plate. Every time she looked at her husband, her throat tightened and she felt ill.

"I don't think about it," Elijah offered.

He was eating. How could he eat? How could anyone eat, sleep, think in his situation? There had to be some way, someone, who could help Elijah's heart.

"Have you seen a doctor?" she asked.

"There's no point."

"But have you seen one?"

Her annoying, stubborn husband shrugged. "Villiers dragged me to a physician who studies hearts. The man said I may live for years."

"Or not."

"There's a doctor in Birmingham who's apparently doing miraculous things with hearts like mine. Villiers sent a carriage up there to get him."

"How uncharacteristically generous of him," Jemma said, ringing the bell. "Fowle, send around to the Duke of Villiers and find out when he expects his carriage to return from Birmingham. Wait for a response, if you please."

Fowle disappeared with all the efficiency of a man who recognizes a woman on the verge of hysterics.

"Darling—" Elijah said.

"Don't. Not now." Her mind was racing. "There must be a way to cure this. There must be. The doctor in Birmingham will come here and cure you."

"Eat your supper," Elijah ordered.

She shook her head. "When did Villiers send the coach? I heard of a very good doctor the other day. Siffle, I think his name was."

"It was in the *Morning Post*," Elijah said, taking another bite of asparagus. "He's doing miraculous things with broken limbs."

"Well, perhaps he—"

"Come here," Elijah said, pushing back his chair and holding out his arms.

She responded, then sat nestled against him, only to feel her heart beating furiously in her chest. Regularly. A scream threatened at the back of her throat.

He was stroking her hair as if she were a cat. "It's all right, Jemma."

"No, it isn't." She forced out the words.

They were both silent a moment. "Well, it's not all right, but it is—"

"Don't tell me it's acceptable," she said fiercely. "This is *not acceptable*."

"There's nothing I can do about it." The raw pain in his voice silenced her. "There's nothing you can do about it."

"Why didn't you tell me as soon as I returned from Paris?" She whispered it into his chest. "You've known . . . alone. You could have told me!"

"You had the chess match with Villiers. And I wanted to *win* you, Jemma."

"You already had me," she said painfully. "You always had me, Elijah."

"I wanted all of you. When you made the match with Villiers, I seized the opportunity to try to win you myself."

"You could have just told me."

"And then what? Would you have fallen in love with me again, as you have?" She said nothing, and he gave her a little shake. "As you have, Jemma?"

"I loved you already," she said.

"I wanted you in love with me."

"That was selfish. You didn't think that I wanted time with you."

"Forgive me?"

She sniffed and buried her head in his shoulder. "No."

"I've never been so happy as the last days. When you were wooing me, Jemma. When you were loving me. When you were laughing at me, or letting me make love to you. When you were making love to me."

Huge tears were burning in her eyes. "I could have done all that a year ago."

"We may have another year. My faint in the House of Lords occurred over a year ago."

She heard the slightest note in his voice, knew he was lying. He knew, he knew. There was saltwater on her cheeks, the taste of it on her lips.

"You've given me what I thought I'd never have," he continued.

"Don't talk as if you're dying tomorrow," she said. "I can't bear it. I can't bear it!"

"You're my Jemma. You were strong enough to leave me when I had to be left, and strong enough to come home when I needed you. You will care for my house, and my lands, and my poor Cacky Street men. You can bear it."

"No."

His arms tightened around her. "Don't cry."

"I shall cry if I want to," she said fiercely. "Oh God, I suddenly understand widows' weeds."

"You mustn't—"

But she didn't listen to him. "Because if you die, I shan't want to wear anything but black," she said, a great sob rising in her throat. "I shall cry for a year and a day in my blacks, and no one can fault me. I didn't understand why Harriet was still grieving for her husband although it had been almost two years."

"No!" He was almost shouting now, but Jemma was convulsed by grief, bending at the waist, ugly sobs tearing through her lungs. Elijah bent over with her, his strong, warm body curved over her back, holding her, warming her.

"It can't be true," she sobbed. "It's not true, it's not true, it's not true."

He picked her up then and carried her away to bed, and they lay there together while sobs shook her body. Because it was true. He was leaving her.

He had to leave her unless some sort of miracle happened . . . and neither of them believed in miracles. They were chess players. They were logical, and rational.

And thus, brokenhearted.

After her sobs had quieted, Elijah said, "Jemma, I think you should leave me."

She sat up, her eyes burning, and stared at him incredulously. "What did you just say?"

"It's horrible that you should have to live through this with me. You—"

He broke off because she was slapping him, great, open-handed slaps to his chest. "You don't get to send me away again, Elijah! Don't you understand? Why don't you understand?"

She was sobbing again. *"You never get to send me away again!"*

"I'm sorry," he said, pulling her into his arms. "I'm a fool, Jemma. I'm sorry, I'm sorry."

Her face was stricken but her eyes blazed at him. "You made a mistake and you broke us in half," she said. Her voice was quieter, but still passionate. "You keep saying that I'm yours, Elijah, but the truth is that you are *mine* as well."

He heard the urgency behind her voice and he suddenly understood. She loved him. Loved him enough to forgive him for his mistress, for not following her to Paris.

But there was one thing he had to know. He cupped her face in his hands, noting absently that his fingers were shaking. "Will you forgive me?"

She blinked. "For what?"

"For not being able to stay with you forever. Because I would, Jemma. I promise I would."

"I know," she whispered, brushing his lips with her own. "I know."

Chapter Twenty-four

April 2

The next morning, Jemma retired to the morning parlor and began trying to understand how one lived with this kind of knowledge. It wasn't healthy for her to follow Elijah about, nervously demanding to listen to his heart. He disliked it. Besides, every time she listened to his chest, she heard skipped beats and her own heart felt as if it were filled with hot coals.

Yet she was wrung with fear. Her fingers trembled as she picked up the chess pieces. She was on the point of giving up, and joining Elijah in his study, when Fowle entered, a grim look on his face.

She sprang to her feet so quickly that she knocked over the chessboard. Pieces rolled on the ground. "Is he—"

Reading her mind, a look of deep sympathy crossed Fowle's eyes. "He is fine, Your Grace. Should His Grace faint again, I shall call you from outside the room, as I approach."

She sank back down into her chair. "Thank you, Fowle." Her fingers were shaking like leaves in a high wind.

"The dowager duchess has arrived," he announced.

She'd forgotten that there had to be a reason for his entry. "The—The dowager? The duke's *mother*?"

"I have placed her in the rose chamber," Fowle said. "She expressed the wish that you would join her immediately. Apparently she intends to return to Scotland very shortly."

"Return to Scotland?" Jemma asked. "That's impossible! I am certain she will change her mind. She will be making a prolonged stay with us. Please inform Mrs. Tulip."

Now Jemma understood the grim look on Fowle's face when he first entered. Her own memories of her mother-in-law were distinctly unpleasant. The dowager duchess was tall and angry. She carried herself like a man, and Jemma found her alarming.

Jemma had lived the first weeks of her marriage in a house full of portraits of Judith holding Holofernes's head (minus his body) because she was worried about the dowager's reaction if she removed them.

Of course, when she returned from Paris, she ordered all paintings removed without thinking about it twice.

"Your Grace," Jemma said respectfully a moment later, dropping into a curtsy. As she raised her head, she realized that the dowager had hardly changed. She was still tall, and although she leaned on a cane, it gave her no air of weakness. In fact, the cane seemed more like Villiers's sword stick: an affectation that could serve as a weapon.

She had Elijah's beauty, with sharp angles and sweeping lines. But on her the angles looked enraged, and what was calmness in his face was irritation in hers.

"Jemma," her mother-in-law said. "I am grateful that you returned from Paris."

That was an auspicious start.

"We must sit," she continued. "My hip is quite troublesome these days."

"I am so sorry to hear that," Jemma said, seating herself opposite the dowager. "Did Elijah write you?"

"No."

"But you know." There was something in the dowager's face, a version of the same dread that she was feeling.

"I knew the moment I heard that he fainted in Lords. You don't appear to be with child."

"I fear not," Jemma replied, wincing inwardly. "That is, there is a chance that I am with child, but I don't know yet."

"I suppose Elijah's foolish second cousin will inherit after all. The man pads everything, you know, from his thighs to his chest. But he is, at least, a discreet creature. A foolish lust for admiration is better than the alternative."

"Of course," Jemma said, not at all sure what she was agreeing with.

They sat for a moment in silence. "I came to ask you something," the dowager said, her fingers twisting the diamond cornucopia she wore on her bosom. Her fingers were swollen with rheumatism, and Jemma felt a pulse of sorrow. She remembered her mother-in-law sweeping through the house like a whirlwind, her voice as stinging as smoke in the eyes. Back then the dowager had few wrinkles and her fingers were strong.

"Of course," Jemma said again. The dowager fixed her eyes on Jemma's face, and they were so identical to Elijah's, like a dark flame, that Jemma added, "Anything you wish."

"I wish," the dowager said heavily, "no, I *insist* that you cease all marital relations and maintain separate chambers." Her face was at once both mournful and belligerent.

Jemma swallowed a gasp. "I—"

"My husband was known as Bawdy Beaumont," the duchess said. "Were you aware of that?"

Jemma nodded.

"He died in the very act, wearing a frilly lace chemise and tied to a bed," the duchess said. There was no particular rage in her voice as she recounted the facts. "He was attended by several women wearing leather who were engaged in spanking him. I gather he took pleasure in something children strive to avoid, which says a great deal about his character."

Jemma murmured something. Her mind was racing, wondering if she should assure the dowager that Elijah showed no interest in wearing a chemise.

But the dowager was continuing. "He was always a greedy man. One nightwalker wasn't enough; he had to have three or four. We did our best to keep the details a secret. I paid hundreds of pounds to the procuress in charge of The Palace of Salomé."

She raised her eyes to Jemma. "I waited a year, and then I had her arrested. She was stripped and marched through London for prostitution, left in the stocks for a day, and then sent to Bridewell. She died a few months later." There was unmistakable satisfaction in her voice.

"Elijah has no interest in such practices," Jemma said, hurrying into speech before her mother-in-law could say anything else.

"I brought him up to be *virtuous*," his mother said. "But it didn't take."

"It didn't?" Jemma said, dumbfounded. There wasn't a person in England who wouldn't say that the Duke of Beaumont was virtuous. And they didn't even know about the Cacky Street Glassworks.

The dowager duchess looked unblinking at her. "I know why you left for Paris. My son inherited his father's deviant tendencies. It was good of you to return, and attempt to produce an heir. If I hadn't already had a son, I would have left the country as well."

"It's customary for a man to have a mistress," Jemma said desperately, hardly able to believe that she was defending Elijah, after all her years of resenting that same mistress. "Your son has no interest in the more . . . exotic practices that the former duke enjoyed."

The dowager curled her lip. "I don't care about a mistress any more than you would have. But he couldn't keep the woman discreet, as other men do. He brought the woman into public. His own offices." She straightened her back and said calmly, "Revolting. I gather that my husband also enjoyed being watched on occasion."

"Elijah wasn't being *watched!*" Jemma gasped. "He was only trying to prove that his tastes weren't as deviant as those of his father. He was very young, Your Grace. By engaging his mistress to meet him in his chambers, he proved to all those who knew that he enjoyed normal intimacies. There was nothing deviant about it."

The smallest noise made her lift her eyes. Elijah was standing in the open doorway. His face looked terrifyingly calm.

"All I'm asking is that you refrain from marital intimacies," the dowager said, her voice tired and irritated. "If Algernon Tobier inherits the Beaumont dukedom because the current duke drops on the floor of the House of Lords, it will be unremarkable. But if a second Beaumont dies in bed with a woman, even if that woman is his wife, we will never live down the reputation. The Bawdy Beaumonts will go down in history."

"I'm afraid that you cannot choose the hour of your son's passing," Jemma said, her voice shaking, so shocked that she actually forgot Elijah was listening. "If Elijah dies in my bed, in a pleasurable moment, that is something I would welcome."

"You are a fool," the dowager said heavily. "We duchesses live on, you know. My husband took his dissolute, frivolous self to the grave, but he left me to live through the titters and the veiled comments. He left his son to weather the debacle. He made me a laughingstock, and my son will do the same to you."

"We needn't worry about a son since we have no children," Jemma said. She was so caught by inarticulate anger that she couldn't continue.

Finally Elijah stepped into the room. He bent down and kissed the hand his mother held out to him. "I suppose you've heard our subject," she said, her voice calm. But her fingers were twisting on the diamonds she wore on her chest.

"I see my responsibilities to the line rather differently than you do, Mother," he said, seating himself next to Jemma. "My wife and I shall continue to attempt to create an heir."

"I beg to differ," his mother said.

But she couldn't keep her face as fierce and still now that her son was sitting opposite her. Jemma saw that and her anger fled.

"Elijah's heart is stronger than his father's was," Jemma told his mother, speaking to the grief, and not to what the woman was saying. "And we've heard of a doctor in Birmingham who is having excellent results with a new medicine he's developed. We're—"

Elijah put his hand over hers and she stopped. "I shall be very sorry if I leave you ashamed of me in any way," he said to his mother.

The dowager's fingers were clenched over her diamond. "I can't stay here. I cannot. I shall depart for Aberdeen immediately."

"You can't mean that," Jemma said. "At least spend the night."

The dowager's eyes skated to hers. "You will inform me when—"

"I'll take care of him," Jemma said gently, standing up and pulling Elijah to his feet as well.

The dowager stood, looking up at her son as if from the bottom of a well. "You were a beautiful baby."

Elijah held out his hand and she clung to it. "And you have a beautiful smile," she said. "You have always had a beautiful smile."

Jemma felt hot tears pressing in her eyes.

Elijah smiled his beautiful smile, as if his mother hadn't just said he was deviant, and bent to kiss her cheek. "I may well live for years, Mother."

His mother's eyes met Jemma's, and they both

knew the truth. His mother closed her eyes for a long moment, her fingers tight on those diamonds.

"I shall stay for luncheon," she announced, hunching a bit over her cane. "Then I shall begin my journey."

They talked of nothing over the meal. The dowager was clumsy, her swollen fingers causing her to drop her fork repeatedly and knock a glass of wine to the table. But Jemma, watching, thought that it was a heavy heart that made her so awkward.

That night, Elijah came to her room. She held out her arms, and he came over to her, warm and hard, his hand sliding up beneath her nightdress. "We should talk," he murmured. But his hands were already setting her aflame.

Jemma realized that in truth, she'd been waiting all day for this. In bed with her, Elijah's heart beat strong and true. She didn't have to worry.

"Later," she said, her hands sliding lower on his body.

"But—"

"I want to taste you," she said. And then his eyes were like dark flames, like his mother's, but she pushed that thought away and kissed her way down his chest. Her fear was gone, blissfully gone, because she could feel the blood pounding through his body.

He said something, scrambled and inarticulate, but he arched toward her and she laughed and opened her lips.

He was hers, and he was alive, and that was good enough for the moment.

Chapter Twenty-five

April 3

Jemma kept Elijah in bed most of the next day. In the early afternoon, they found themselves lying on their backs, panting, the sheets twisted around their legs.

"I need a bath," Jemma said groggily. She felt drained and happy. She had one hand on Elijah's chest, and his heart was beating strong and true. "It's as if we repaired a clock," she said, changing the subject.

He had his arms thrown over his head and was smiling up at the tapestry hanging over the bed. "My heart can beat normally when it remembers to do so."

"We'll make love every day," Jemma ordered. "Twice a day. Morning and night so that your heart remembers the correct pattern."

Elijah laughed. "If you tell your friends that plan, every man in the kingdom will be pretending to faint."

He rolled to his side, propping his head on one hand. "I heard what you said to my mother."

She tried to pull her mind back from that hot, happy place. "Hmm."

"I didn't think that you guessed why Sarah Cobbett came to my chambers."

Jemma raised her head. "So that *was* the reason? I used to think that it was just a question of saving time."

"I couldn't get anyone to believe that I wasn't sneaking off to The Palace of Salomé in the evenings. God, I was sick of being called Bawdy Beaumont. There was always scorn to it, just under the surface. I knew they were making jokes about spankings behind my back."

Jemma wound her fingers into his.

"I didn't even really want a mistress. Oh, I wanted to bed someone . . . at that age, all you see are women, and each one is succulent, and delicious in her own way."

"You thought every woman you saw was 'succulent'?" Jemma asked, utterly fascinated.

"They had breasts," he said, as if that was all the explanation anyone could wish for. "And other parts."

She giggled, imagining Elijah walking down the street peering at women's breasts. It seemed so unlike him.

"But I didn't have time. I was so determined to mend my father's damage, to change the reputation attached to my name."

"Your mother shouldn't have told you," she said, sorrowing for the eight-year-old boy who was told those details far too early.

"She is obsessed with the reputation of the Beaumonts, as you heard. And, of course, it was much harder for her. She knew he had mistresses, but she had no idea about the storm of scandal that would break over her head when he died."

"It was bad luck that he died at that moment," Jemma said.

"I used to think about it a lot as a boy, puzzling over it. Why the woman's chemise? Why the spanking? Finally I grew old enough to realize that eccentricities of an intimate sort can't be puzzled out and explained. It gave me a passion for logical facts," he added.

"I'm sorry. It sounds like a terrible burden."

"So I found Sarah Cobbett," he said, staring up at the tapestry. "At first I thought it was enough to have a mistress, but then I realized that no one cared what I did when I wasn't in my chambers or in the House. They just assumed I was wearing lacy gowns and begging my mistress to spank me. So one day I told her to come to my chambers instead."

Jemma ran circles over his chest with a finger. She didn't like thinking of Elijah with another woman. But she could hardly be jealous of Sarah, under the circumstances. And Elijah's heart still beat smoothly under her palm.

"It was terribly awkward," he said, turning his head so he could see her. "The desk was uncomfortable. She wasn't pleased, but what could she do? After a while she got used to it and so did I."

"Did it work?"

"Oh, yes. After a month or so, everyone knew. They all slapped me on the back and said they thought it was a marvelous idea. Everything calmed down. But I was cautious, and I still had Sarah come to my chambers twice a week."

"When we married," Jemma said, wondering if she should even voice it, "why didn't you let Sarah go?"

"I didn't think of her in those terms. That is, I didn't think of the two of you in the same way. You were charming and luscious and soft under the covers. I know we weren't terribly good together, but I thought about you a great deal."

"You *did*?"

He grinned at that. "If you remember, we made love every night. I found you horribly distracting. I would be trying to listen to a speech in the House, and I would start thinking about how soft your mouth was, or about the curve of your bottom, and I would lose track of the argument entirely."

"We had made love that very morning," Jemma said. "That was what hurt the most. You turned from me, as if I were nothing more than an hors d'oeuvre, and then you took *her*." Despite her best effort, a thread of pain ran through her voice.

Elijah groaned. "I can't say anything to make you feel better about it. I remember feeling sated by you. I didn't want to bed her. But at that age, if a woman lies in front of you with her legs spread, you can manage it, even if you are tired. How could I have explained to Sarah if I didn't continue? There she was, and it had become part of my responsibilities in the House. If that makes sense."

In a male sort of way, it did. After all, she and Elijah had hardly known each other when they married; the marital contracts had been signed by their fathers years before. She had been in love with him, but he had no reason to feel the same emotion for her.

Suddenly he rolled over on her, and she felt him

against her leg, urgent and hard again. "You are the most succulent of all."

"I am?" But his hand was on her breast, a rough caress, and he didn't answer in words.

That morning they had spent hours making love. He had kissed her shoulder blades and the backs of her knees. He had kissed her eyebrows and the tips of her toes. Now he took her fast and hard, without preliminaries.

Jemma kept her eyes open, and watching his face, loving him, felt again like a young bride in love with her husband.

"I love you so much," she whispered. The heat was building in her legs, starting to cloud her mind and pull her into some other place, a place without fear.

Elijah cradled her face in his hands and said something hoarse that she couldn't hear, but she knew what it was because their love was there between them. It hardly needed to be said.

Chapter Twenty-six

April 4

Fowle entered the study and bowed before Jemma. "The Duke of Villiers regrets to tell you that his carriage has returned from Birmingham empty; the doctor has apparently moved to London but did not leave a forwarding address."

"I might also add that Mr. Twiddy and his two daughters arrived this morning, and I dispatched them to the country estate, as you had instructed."

Elijah nodded. "Thank you, Fowle."

Jemma heard the news with no more reaction than a tightening around her eyes. He wrapped his arms around her and tried to warm her up. "We never expected the doctor to come to anything," he said, wishing she'd never heard of him.

"I want to read his article," she said, stepping out of the circle of his arms.

"Villiers has it; I'll—"

She turned. "I'll fetch it."

"Wait! You can't—"

She was gone. Elijah gritted his teeth for a moment and returned to his work. He was cataloguing the estate: going through it item by item. If Jemma wasn't with child when his heart gave out, then his hairless, brainless second cousin would inherit. He needed everything to be as clear as possible.

An hour later, he was writing a letter, instructing his cousin in clear language about how to oversee crop rotation, when Jemma burst through the door.

"I have the piece. The doctor's name is William Withering. I'm going to hire a Bow Street Runner to find him."

He looked up. "A runner?"

"Why not? I've already sent Fowle to fetch one. Withering's work is rather interesting, Elijah," she said, sitting in a chair opposite him and waving the sheets in the air. "Withering extracted a medicine from a flower. If you take an overly large dose, it acts like a poison. But in small amounts, it seems to cause an irregular heart to change its pattern and . . . " Her voice died out.

Elijah laid down his pen. "He extracts this poison from *a flower*?"

"The market at Covent Garden!" She jumped to her feet.

"There must be many poisonous flowers that have medicinal properties. Do you remember what that old man was growing?"

"He called them Dead Men's Bells." She scanned the article again. " But Withering discusses a flower called foxglove or *digitalis purpurea*. I can't tell from that."

But Elijah's tutors hadn't drilled him in Latin for naught. "*Purpurea*," he said, "means purple. And the flowers were purple."

"Let's go," Jemma cried.

But Elijah stayed behind his desk. "I don't want you to become hopeful."

"I am not overly hopeful. I am determined. I will not sit by and simply wait for you to die next to me. I will *not*!"

When they reached Covent Garden, the flower stalls were closed.

"The market is open Tuesday, Thursday, and Saturday," their footman said, after making inquiries.

"Stay with the carriage," Elijah told him, walking after Jemma. She was moving through the stalls at top speed, heading for the place where the old man sold his flowers. He hadn't had a proper stall; he'd simply put out a few buckets of flowers for sale.

He rounded a corner to find Jemma staring at the back wall where the man had sat. "There's his stool," Elijah said. "We'll come back on Saturday and find him."

"That's three days."

Elijah didn't like the implication that he might not live three days, but he could hardly protest. Jemma turned in a slow circle and then set off, like an arrow free of its string.

He walked after her. The closed-up stalls of the market had a melancholy aspect, as if they had grown tired and shut their eyes for the night.

Finally he saw where Jemma was going. She had spied one stall with an occupant and was bending over the counter, talking to a little old lady wrapped in woolens.

"Do you know which gentleman I'm referring to?" he heard as he walked up.

"That's not a gentleman!" the woman said with a gentle string of giggles. "That's Stubbins. Ponder Stubbins."

"Of course. Could you possibly tell me how to find Mr. Stubbins?"

She giggled again. "It does sound odd to hear a 'Mister' attached to Stubbins's name."

"Does he live close to the market?"

"Oh no," she said. "You'll have to wait for the market again. Just a few more days, that's all. I'll be here with daffodils, oh so many daffodils. And tulips. Do you like tulips?" she asked Elijah.

He bowed and said, "Good afternoon, ma'am. I do like tulips." Though in reality he hadn't the faintest idea what they were. Certainly his cook, Mrs. Tulip, had nothing flowery about her.

"I hope you don't mind if I tell you something. I'm that old that I allow myself a leeway now and then! You look," she said, leaning on the counter, "czactly like my idea of a duke." Giggles once again burst from her mouth. "Now isn't that something for both of us to laugh about! As if a duke would be coming down to the flower market to find old Stubbins."

He smiled at her and she actually turned a little pink. "My saints, but you've got a pretty face," she added. "I always says to my husband that someday I'll meet a duke. It's our joke. The duke'll take me away, see, give me a carriage with gold wheels to it, and make me his beautiful bride."

"And what does your husband say to that?" Jemma asked.

"He says as how what he gives me is better than

a gold wheel any day," she said, giggling madly. "But here, even as you're not a duke, you won't want to find Stubbins until the market opens. He lives in a bad area. I don't even go there unless I has to."

"Where?" Jemma asked.

"Spitalfields. I can't see the two of you there."

"We were there less than a week ago," Elijah said. "Could you give us his direction? Does he live anywhere around Cacky Street?"

Her giggles stopped and she narrowed her eyes. "You're missionary types, aren't you? I know your sort. You'll be trying to turn Stubbins into some sort of churchgoer and make him wear a hat and the rest of it."

"That would make me a miracle worker, not a missionary," Elijah pointed out.

"Well, at least you know that much."

"We just want to find the doctor who uses Stubbins's flowers for medicine," Jemma said. "It's terribly urgent, so could you please help us?"

"Stubbins lives in Wiggo Lane," the woman said. "You'll find him there or behind the mews, most likely. That's where he grows all his stuff. I think he even sleeps there sometimes." She didn't look like laughing now. "You're from the Watch, aren't you? You jist look like a duke, but you're really the law."

"No, not at all," Jemma protested.

"You're going to drag him off to the workhouse and it'll be my fault. I wish I'd never told you."

"I would never put Stubbins in the workhouse," Elijah said mildly. "And I've nothing to do with the Watch. As it happens, I *am* a duke."

"You never!"

Elijah gave her an extravagant bow. "The Duke of

Beaumont, at your service, madam. I would take you away with me, but—"

"His gold wheels are just made of brass," Jemma said, taking his arm.

"Oh my, and isn't it just like a fairy tale," the flower seller said. "The duke and duchess, and you loves each other, just like a tale, don't you?"

Jemma felt her smile waver. "Yes, just like that."

"And do ya have a carriage with gold wheels?"

"No. But I have a beautiful bride," Elijah said promptly.

They found Wiggo Lane without a problem. It was one of the narrow channels that led off Cacky Street, not far from the glassworks. In the afternoon, Spitalfields looked utterly different than it had in the morning. People were sitting on stoops, and children were dashing everywhere, howling and shrieking with laughter. Laundry was hanging out to dry, nothwithstanding the fact that smoke billowed onto the clean cloth from cook fires in the street.

Finding Stubbins wasn't as easy as finding the lane.

"He used to live here," one man said, giving their footman an extremely unfriendly look. Most other people wouldn't even answer, but just backed away or stared at the coach with grim dislike.

"This isn't going to work," Elijah said, watching James approach a man who looked as if he might knock the footman down before he gave out any information. He leaned forward and called, "We'll go to Cow Cross, James!"

The door was unlocked, as usual, the hallway dim, and Knabby came toward them squinting. "It's the duke again," Elijah said, "with the duchess as well."

Knabby was clearly surprised. "It's a pleasure to have you again so soon! Everyone's in the courtyard." He turned around and started bustling away.

"We're trying to find someone who lives in Spitalfields," Elijah said, but Knabby was already through the door to the courtyard.

It wasn't nearly as lively this afternoon. "Cully's sleeping," Knabby announced. "Sophisba's husband took her away again, and Mrs. Nibble went to stay with her sister, as has a stomach ulcer."

After greeting everyone in the circle, Elijah said, "We're trying to find Ponder Stubbins, who lives in Spitalfields and raises flowers. Does anyone know him?"

There was a moment of silence. Then Waxy said, "'Course it is the duke." But it was clearly a struggle between Spitalfields loyalty and glassworks loyalty.

"We don't mean him any harm," Jemma put in. "We only want to find a doctor who buys his flowers."

"Oh," Knabby said, sounding very relieved. "In that case, Stubbins is just around the corner. He lives somewhere, maybe on Wiggo? But he's never there as his wife is a proper terror. He sleeps behind the mews in Fish Street."

"Excellent. We are most grateful for your help." Elijah made the rounds of the circle again, shaking the wavering hands that were held out in his direction, and they left.

The mews were a two-story wooden structure. The ground-story rooms were occupied by horses, busily producing manure, which made it easy enough to find Stubbins. They had only to follow the smell. It was a particularly rich, brown type of smell, perhaps because the back of the mews faced east, and sun struck the manure piles all morning.

Stubbins had everything neatly arranged. To the left were flower beds, and to the right were fresh piles of dung.

"Oh, it's you, is it?" he said, leaning on a shovel. "I thought you'd be about."

"You did?" Jemma asked, shocked. "You thought we'd follow you here?"

"Not you, ma'am, but your husband here. I reckoned he was curious about the manure, and I was right wasn't I?" Without waiting for an answer, he started showing Elijah his arrangements. "It can't be too hot. Fries the flowers, I suspect. So I rakes it here, and then I give it, oh, four or five days. Sometimes I pour fresh milk on it."

That would explain some of the pungency, Jemma thought.

"Then I pile it over here and mix in a little o' that and a little something else. Then I plant my seeds."

He showed them the shack where he kept his seeds, and Elijah looked at everything gravely and asked just the right sort of questions, and Jemma knew exactly why the Cacky Street Glassworks was doing so well. It was Elijah. He was grave and compassionate, and so honorable that people longed to be near him.

A few minutes later Elijah led Stubbins to the question of the doctor.

"He used to live in Birmingham," Stubbins confirmed. "And then he went to one of them far-off countries, but it didn't do the doctor's lungs any good, so he's back in London now. He has rooms on Harley Street, I think. 'Course I never go there because he just sends a man to pick up my flowers."

Jemma's heart was pounding in her throat. "It *is* he," she said, clutching Elijah's hand. "Dr. Withering! He's the one, Elijah, he's the one!"

A moment later they were back in the carriage and racing to Harley Street.

Chapter Twenty-seven

April 4

"Grindel's in Wapping does not appear to be known to the headmaster of St. Paul's," Ashmole said, appearing like a bird of prey in Villiers's study. "In fact, the headmaster believes there *are* no schools in Wapping."

"Any word from Templeton?"

Ashmole's eyes glinted with the fascinated delight that servants always display when one of their own goes bad. Villiers had seen it before. There was nothing more carnivorous than a household that had discovered a maid with child.

The butler drew himself up to his full height—approximately that of a twelve-year-old boy. "Mr. Templeton has vacated his premises."

Villiers generally prided himself on his lack of reaction to unpleasant news, but he surprised himself with a hearty Anglo-Saxon oath.

"Precisely, Your Grace," Ashmole said, bobbing his thin neck in a gesture of solidarity. "That bird has flown."

"Why?"

"It's always money." Ashmole hadn't been head of the duke's household for years for nothing. "How much did you give him?" He cackled. "Shall I let the gardener go and tell Cook to economize in the kitchen?"

"I don't suppose he could get at a great deal, but he certainly had means to feather his nest." He followed up with a few more oaths.

"We can have a Bow Street Runner after him," Ashmole said.

"That won't get the money back." But there was something darker in the back of his mind. "Why now? Why did he run now, Ashmole? It must be something to do with the children."

The old man stared at him, perplexed.

"The devil take him," Villiers said. He'd given Templeton far too much rein. "Get a Runner after him, not for the money—because I'll never get that back—but because I want to know about those damned children."

"Yes, Your Grace. Shall I send a footman over to Wapping to locate the school and fetch the boy?"

Villiers pulled out the list Templeton had sent him just before he decamped to parts unknown. "We'll just stick to the one problem at the moment. I'll go to Wapping. Fetch me a carriage. And I need to see both Plammel and Philaster this evening, whether they're free or not." Those two lyrical names belonged to the unlyrical men who handled his business affairs.

"*If* they're still in London," Ashmole cackled.

Villiers gave him a look.

"They'll be here," the butler said grudgingly. "Templeton wasn't a man to share his profits."

Villiers was in a carriage five minutes later. Generally, he spent at least a half-hour with his valet before leaving the house. Since he maintained the affectation of never wearing a wig, he demanded perfection in his hair, not to mention gleaming boots, a shirt the picture of snowy perfection . . .

Today he simply left the house.

What the hell had happened to the children?

The children, an obstinate little voice in the back of his mind reproached him, those same children whom you didn't care a fig for a month ago.

Yes, *those* children. Why had Templeton run? Mrs. Jobber was kind, and had obviously provided a good home. But then his eyes narrowed. Why didn't Mrs. Jobber have the other children? There were five more of them, after all. Why were they not placed together?

And what had happened two years ago, when Templeton had taken the oldest boy away to school? Villiers was quite certain that he'd never delivered any edicts about school. He'd avoided speaking or thinking about the children, in fact. He'd never asked Templeton for a report, the way he did on his wheat fields, or his tenants.

Guilt was such a tiresome emotion.

The village of Wapping seemed to live on the River Thames. Other places had houses and perhaps a river to the side. In Wapping, everything started at the river, and then jumbled up the bank any old how. There was a charming breeze, smelling of mud and dying fish.

The door to the carriage opened. "Your Grace, Ash-mole suggested that we go to the church. Would you like me to make inquiries?"

Villiers waved the footman on and sat back, door shut. He felt like a fool, peering out of his window, but Wapping was fascinating. It wasn't exactly poor—it was too lively to be contained by that paltry adjective.

Just out his window was a great flight of stairs lead-ing down to the Thames. It was thronged by a mess of boys, breeches rolled up, playing in the mud. Appar-ently the tide had covered the steps and then rolled back, leaving a thick coating.

Villiers watched them for a time and then leaned back against his seat. He and Elijah had once larked about in the river that used to run between their es-tates. He corrected himself. One ought to surmise that the river was still there and not refer to it in the past tense.

Just because he never chose to visit his estate didn't mean that it had ceased to exist.

The footman opened the door again. "The priest is not in residence, but the sexton reports that he knows of no Grindel's School for Boys." He hesitated.

"Out with it," Villiers said.

"There's apparently a dissolute man by the name of Elias Grindel, who runs a pack of five or six mudlarks. Orphans, the sexton thinks. But he can't be the man you're looking for, Your Grace, because—"

"Did you get his direction?" Villiers cut him off.

"Yes, Your Grace."

Villiers gestured for the door to be shut. He would find Templeton and have him thrown into the Clink to rot. The carriage trundled off again, stopping after a mere five minutes. He stepped out onto a street that fell away on one side, plunging down toward the river with all the abruptness of a sawed-off board. There were more steps, and more children.

Villiers felt disgust twist in his gut.

They weren't playing in the mud. They were *mud-larks*. Boys who scavenged in the mud and the sewers to recover whatever they could for sale. And his son, Juby or Tobias, was likely down there as well. Some bit of his ducal bloodline was down there larking around in the muck.

Though "larking" was an altogether too pleasant word.

Grindel, once Villiers located him in a dingy house facing the river, was as belligerent a man as his name would lead one to expect. "I don't have no boy named Tobias, nor Juny either," he said, lower lip jutting out so he looked like an obstinate hedgehog.

"Juby," Villiers corrected him.

Grindel just glared. "I ain't had no dealings with a man called Templeton. I don't run a school for boys. You have the wrong man."

Villiers swung his sword stick casually in front of him, as if it were a cane and he were testing its weight.

"I hear there's another Grindel, down in Bagnigge Wells. Mayhap he's started a school for boys," the man offered.

Villiers twirled his sword stick in his hand. The sheath gleamed with the promise that the rapier inside was designed to inflict damage. Finally, he placed the point downwards, and it sank into the rotten wood at his feet.

"Dear me," he said gently. "And that was just the sheath."

Grindel's eyes narrowed.

"I want the boy named Tobias, sometimes called Juby. I want you to send someone to get him, now."

"Or what?" Grindel asked. "You're planning to slice my gizzard because I'm not running a school for boys? I don't even like boys. I can't stand having them around me."

Villiers looked around the filthy room that Grindel had labeled his "study." It was a study without books. In their place were warped wooden buckets, barrels, and wicker baskets. A bucket at Villiers's feet was brimming with buttons, all shapes. He could see the open top of a basket full of coal, and a large barrel that seemed to be half full of wood chips.

"So what do you do for a living?" he asked genially.

"There's no call for you to show interest," Grindel said, not moving. He was short and sweaty, and wore a yellowed wig. Strands of greasy hair poking out from under the wig confirmed his remarkable indifference to cleanliness.

Villiers poked with his rapier at another basket, precariously balanced on the sideboard. It toppled, and out fell a cascade of teeth. Human teeth, Villiers thought. He took a step back as the teeth rattled to a halt around his toes.

"I collect things," Grindel said. His face was a miracle of blandness. Villiers prided himself on maintaining an expressionless face, but he had clearly met his match. "I'd rather Your Grace didn't overturn more of my things. A man's home, so they say, is his castle." His insolence was in the open now. "Even to those who consider themselves above the rest."

"I'm proud to call myself above collecting the teeth

of dead men," Villiers said. He had poked off the top of another basket with his stick, and found it to hold a small collection of silver teaspoons. It was hard to tell through the muck, but many of them seemed to be engraved with initials or even a ducal crest. "You are planning to return these to their rightful owners, are you not?"

"What's lost to the river is lost, and that's the waterman's law," Grindel said.

The door at Villiers's back opened and he moved to the side just in time to avoid being touched. He was already mourning the fact that he had chosen to wear the rose velvet coat again. It would be a miracle if he managed to leave Grindel's study without touching anything.

"What the devil do you want!" Grindel roared, his eyebrows turning into a solid line across his forehead. Villiers allowed himself a small smile. It seemed that Mr. Grindel was not quite as indifferent as he appeared.

It was a small boy, quite thin. He stamped into the room without showing much fear and said, "Fillibet's cut his foot so badly that part of it hangs right off. Not the part with the toes, the bottom part."

"What's that to me?" demanded Grindel. He turned to Villiers. "I'm friends with all the neighboring boys and they do come to me for advice." Then he turned back to the boy with a ferocious grin. "There's nothing I can do about a wound, son. You'll have to take him to the surgeon."

The boy looked quickly at Villiers and then back at Grindel. "You said we shouldn't go to the surgeon anymores, but Juby says if you don't take Fillibet, he'll die, and the parish constable will take you up for it."

"Take me up for it?" Grindel roared.

But the moment he heard the name Juby, Villiers had unsheathed his sword. Now the blade gleamed with a dull cruel brilliance as the tip just nudged Grindel's grimy Adam's apple.

"*Juby* says," Villiers repeated softly. "It seems you do know of a boy named Juby."

"Everyone knows Juby," Grindel said. "I never says as how I didn't know him. I said I didn't have a school for boys, and I didn't have no Juby living in my house."

"We don't live with him," said the boy, eyeing the sword with great interest. "He says we stink. We mostly sleep down by the river or sometimes up in the churchyard. Juby likes it up there."

Villiers put just a touch of pressure on his sword. "I will ask you one more time," he said quietly. "Are you acquainted with Mr. Templeton?"

"I might as have met him," Grindel said. The sword seemed sure to pierce his throat, especially when Grindel swallowed nervously. He added: "He sends me a boy now and then."

"For what purpose?"

"Nothing debauched! Nothing like that around here. There's them as has boys for shameful purposes, but I ain't one of those. I run a clean house and I've always said so. You ask the Watch. They don't—"

"Juby says that the Watch never does a thing to you because you give them coin for it," the boy said. He was clearly delighted by the unfolding drama.

Villiers looked sideways at the boy. He had a miserable mouselike face, streaked in dirt. "Fetch Juby for me, would you?"

The boy took off promptly.

"I can't think what you want that boy for," Grindel said. "It's shameless, the way that you swells use boys for depraved purposes."

Villiers smiled, and then exerted just a trifle more pressure. Grindel's eyes bulged as the tip of the sword bit his skin. "I'm not the depraved one. No more surgeons? And how much money did you accept from Templeton for Juby's schooling?"

"Naught even a shilling!" Grindel squealed. "I takes boys as a bit of charity work. Because otherwise they'd be in the poorhouse and the parish'd have to pay for them. You can ask any of the parish constables hereabout. They know what work I do. I pay the boys fair and square for what they get too. I might give 'em as much as three pence a day. That's over a shilling a week."

Villiers withdrew his sword so suddenly that Grindel nearly lost his balance.

A single drop of blood made its way down his throat, but Grindel didn't bother to swab it. "I know your kind. You're having a charitable moment, aren't you? Thought you'd come out here and rescue a poorhouse boy, make him into a decent citizen. I wish you luck with that. Juby is a born criminal with a mind like a sewer. He's as corrupt—"

Villiers's smile seemed, unaccountably, to frighten Grindel into silence. "I would expect no less."

"Why?" Grindel demanded.

"This poorhouse boy? The born criminal with the mind like a sewer?"

"What of him?"

"The boy you insisted that you knew nothing of? The boy whom you clearly were forcing to work for you under merciless and cruel circumstances?"

"Say what you like." Grindel's jaw jutted out again. It resembled the jawbone of a wild animal.

"My son," Villiers said. He took out a beautifully embroidered handkerchief and delicately wiped the blood off the tip of the blade. With a shudder he dropped the cloth on Grindel's table. "I expect you can get at least eight pence for this. That's Belgian lace."

Grindel didn't even spare it a glance. "Your *son*?"

Villiers dropped his sword back into its sheath. "I'm taking him, of course." Making a lightning-quick decision, he said: "I'll be taking all the other boys as well."

"You *are* a depraved son of a—"

"It's for your own good," Villiers said sweetly. "You said yourself that you dislike boys. They're so messy underfoot. It would do you some good to go rooting in the mud; you might lose that belly of yours. It seems that you, at least, have had plenty to eat."

Grindel would have lunged from behind his desk, but he was afraid of the sword. Villiers saw it in his eyes, just as he saw the raw hatred trembling in his fingers.

"I might add that Templeton seems to have run off to a rat hole somewhere. If I find him, his next residence will be the Clink. For life, Mr. Grindel. For life."

"Dear me," he said, knocking over another basket with one swift kick. Coals rolled across the floor. "What a mess. I apologize for my clumsiness." In short order he upended four or five more.

The floor was littered with chunks of coal. They cracked under the feet of the boy who entered.

He was indescribably dirty. And there was a smell. But Villiers took one look at the boy's nose and his lower lip and knew. The facial details weren't even important: it was in his walk, and the unyielding tilt of his chin. Juby walked straight over to the desk and cast a cold eye on Grindel.

"You'll pay for Fillibet to go to the doctor," he said, "or I'll have the constables on you, you fat sodding excuse for—"

Definitely his son, albeit with a greater concern for humanity than he had ever managed to summon up.

Villiers just watched for a moment. Juby was so thin that he would give Ashmole a run for his money as the resident vulture. But his shoulders were held back firmly. Villiers could see the wings of them, poking through his ragged shirt.

He cleared his throat.

The boy gave him a look out of thick-lashed eyes. "Where's your sword stick?" he demanded, by way of greeting. "Toad said that a nob was here and about to cut the throat of this disgusting grubber."

"Here you, watch who you're calling names," Grindel said, glowering at him. His fingers were twitching as if he longed to deliver a blow across the table.

The boy laughed at that—and in his laughter was the final evidence, if Villiers needed it. Grindel actually flinched at the sound.

"You don't dare strike me again, Grindel, remember?" His face was positively alight with glee. "After what happened last week?"

"Take him," Grindel said, spitting on the floor. "The city is full of lads who'd be more than glad of my rates and my hospitality, as any of the boys will tell you. I'm known for my fairness, I am."

"I'm taking all of them," Villiers said again, speaking for the first time since Juby had entered the room. "Fetch all his boys," he said, meeting his son's eyes.

"Who are you to say so?" the boy asked, jutting out his jaw precisely the way Grindel did.

Grindel barked with laughter. "You got more than you bargained for there!" he said, his voice suddenly buoyant.

The boy slanted another glance at Villiers from under his thick lashes. "What do you want us for?" he demanded.

"Not for that."

"We're not good for much. And you don't look like the type to be looking for an apprentice."

"Is that what you'd like to be?" Villiers felt as if he were operating outside his own body, watching himself speak to this boy who was a shadow of himself, a weedy, nasty, evil-tempered version of Leopold Dautry, Duke of Villiers. The only real difference being that he himself was muscled rather than skinny.

But the boy wasn't going to give an inch. "We ain't got nothing you would want."

"Stay with me, *son*," Grindel said, chuckling like a maniac. "I'll treat you right. I'll even pay for Fillibet's doctor if you ask me pretty-like."

Villiers found himself in the unusual position of being unsure of what to say.

"I forgot Fillibet," the boy exclaimed, turning around. He jerked his chin at the smaller lad, who was waiting outside the door. "Fetch all the boys." The child ran.

Then he turned back to Villiers. "If you're one of those with a taste for the nasty, you will regret the moment you met me." His eyes were as cold as a November rainfall. Villiers knew those eyes; he saw them reflected in his glass every morning.

"He don't want that," Grindel said, hooting. "Ain't you gonna tell him, then, Duke?"

Villiers cast him a glance and Grindel shut his mouth.

"You're my son," Villiers said. "I'm taking you home. I'll send the others where they'll be clean and well-cared for."

Tobias didn't say a word. Villiers felt a creeping amusement, and, to his surprise, even a streak of pride. He couldn't have known what to expect in response to that announcement, but he would have loathed an excited shriek of "Papa!"

Instead, Tobias silently looked at Villiers's white-streaked hair, then at his rose-colored coat. His eyes lingered on the elaborate embroidery of yellow roses around the buttonholes, slid lower to his perfectly-fitted pantaloons, then to his boots, now slightly scuffed from toppling Grindel's baskets.

Tobias's glance might have shown some approval of his sword stick, but it wasn't hard to read the utter distaste in his eyes for the rest.

"Are you certain of your claim?" he said finally, as proud as if any man would be lucky to claim a filthy, odiferous boy nicknamed Juby as his offspring.

One might not wish for an exuberant display of filial excitement, but rank disappointment wasn't what Villiers would have envisioned either.

"Don't be a fool," Grindel cut in. "You're the spitting image of the bloody-minded bastard, and it's bastard you'll be called from now on, and rightly so."

"Better the bastard of a duke than a bastard by nature," Villiers said. He kicked a surfeit of teeth and buttons from under his feet and strode over to the desk. The family reunion was over, and he had one final piece of business to attend to.

Grindel inched back in his greasy chair.

"My son has a bruise under his eye," Villiers said. For the first time he heard his own voice—its measured—cold tones, and knew it to be a more mature version of that which he'd just heard. He had passed on his most useful trait.

"Could be he got in a tussle with the boys," Grindel said, slanting an eye toward Tobias. Grindel knew as well as Villiers did that the boy would never tattle about an injury. He wasn't the type.

Villiers sighed inwardly. His gloves were immaculate, or at least they had been that morning . . .

Grindel went over in a crash, taking two more baskets with him to the floor. He let out a squeal like a stuck pig from behind his desk. A final basket teetered, then tipped to its side. A torrent of silver spoons poured forth, the fruit of the boys' labors in the river and sewers.

When he turned about, the door was thronged with boys. Five, maybe six of them, staring silently. They were as dirty as newly-pulled radishes and their thin legs were marked with scars.

Grindel groaned from the floor but didn't seem disposed to move.

"Someone take that basket and pick up all those spoons," Villiers said. "There's another collection of spoons on the floor there."

"And the silver buttons," Tobias said, without even the slightest flicker of an eyelash to show appreciation for the blow to Grindel.

"Take them," Villiers said. "They'll pay for apprenticeships for you lot," he told the boys.

They didn't seem to understand, but Tobias scooped the spoons back into their basket with a few swift movements and thrust them at a boy. "Go!" The other basket of spoons, a box of silver buttons, and a third box with a lid, were out of the room before Grindel managed to lumber to his feet. "Here you!" he roared. "What's happening to me stuff?"

To Villiers's satisfaction, Grindel's right eye was fast swelling shut. "You're thieving from me! You're nothing more than a fleagler, duke or no. I'll have the constables on you!"

"You'll do nothing of the sort," Villiers said softly. "You'll find some other way to make a living. I'll be watching, and if I ever hear that a boy has set foot on these premises again, I'll have it burned down. With or without you," he added dispassionately.

"I see the resemblance," Grindel spat.

"You do me an honor," Villiers said. Then he said, "That last was for my son. This one is for the rest of them." And his fist smashed into Grindel's other eye. Over he went, and this time Villiers strode out without pausing.

"Where's the injured boy?" he asked.

Tobias gestured toward a boy lying on the side of the street. Blood was running sullenly from a dirty cloth wound around his foot.

Villiers jerked his chin at the groom standing by his carriage. "Pick up this boy and carry him to the nearest surgeon. Then get a hackney and take him to Mrs. Jobber, in Whitechapel. The coachman knows the street."

Then he turned to the five remaining boys. Tobias stood in front of them, shoulders back, chin raised. He had a defiant look in his eye.

Villiers gestured at one of his footmen. "Find a hackney and take this lot to Mrs. Jobber. Get the address from the coachman. Beg my forgiveness, but ask her to wash and clothe them, as best she can. I'll set Ashmole to finding an appropriate school for them immediately. And give these to Mrs. Jobber." He gave him a handful of guineas.

"A school," one of the boys muttered, his eyes bugging out.

Tobias seemed to relax a bit. "We'll do well there," he said. Adding, rather reluctantly, "sir."

"I'm not a sir," Villiers said. "You may address me as Your Grace." He sounded like a pompous fool. "And you're not going to Mrs. Jobber's house, Tobias. You're coming with me."

Tobias's face didn't change even a whit. "No. And my name is Juby."

"Your name is Tobias. You are my son, and you're coming home with me."

"I will live with Mrs. Jobber. I will not live with you." His lip curled. The boys were watching, slackjawed.

Villiers thought for a moment about the advisability of designating Tobias to his remaining footman. It pained him to think of all that mud—to give it a charitable label—in his coach. But a hackney and a footman didn't seem right. It would put Tobias in the wrong footing in the household, though he'd be damned if he knew what that footing should be.

"You will enter the carriage now," he stated.

"No."

There was nothing for it. His gloves were already a dead loss, and now the rose-colored coat was going the same way. With one economical movement Villiers picked up the boy and slung him over his shoulder.

The footman whipped open the carriage door, and

Villiers tossed him in. Then he followed, slamming the door behind him.

The boy pulled himself upright instantly and sat there, uncompromising eyes fixed on Villiers's face.

Villiers saw no reason to continue the conversation. He sat down opposite and peeled off his ruined gloves.

There were two things going through his mind. One was the wretched realization that he had five children left to find. And the second was that he needed a wife.

Now.

Perhaps a woman would know how to talk to a younger version of himself. He certainly didn't.

He needed a wife today, or tomorrow at the latest.

Chapter Twenty-eight

$\mathcal{D}$r. William Withering had a terrible cough. Elijah and Jemma entered his anteroom only to hear, from the inner chamber, the truly distressing sounds of someone gasping and coughing at the same time.

"The doctor is dying," Jemma cried with some alarm.

Elijah had jumped to the conclusion that a patient was in his last throes, but he thought it wouldn't be a good idea to mention it. Jemma had that still, terrified look about her eyes that only really left her when they were making love.

He himself felt strangely happy. Ever since they'd made love in Apollo's garden, he was at peace with his future, no matter how short. He escorted Jemma to a chair and then sat down himself.

She picked up a published article lying on the table and began to read. "He's experimenting with Jamaica pepper as a cure for lung problems," she said a few moments later.

Dr. Withering appeared before Elijah could reply. He was a tall man with vivid bushy eyebrows that contrasted sharply with the tight curls of his powdered wig. His eyes glittered under the eyebrows, as if he were thinking fiercely, or suffering from a fever. "Your Grace," he said, bowing. And then, seeing Jemma, he bowed again, even more deeply. "And Your Grace."

"I came to consult with you about your work with *Digitalis purpurea*," Elijah said.

The man's eyes brightened even more, if that were possible. "A fascinating subject! I have cause for reasonable optimism in my research."

"I have a heart ailment," Elijah said. "I should like a consultation with you, sir, if you can spare the time."

"It would be best if you came to my inner chamber so I can examine you thoroughly. The heart is a complicated organ, and I'm afraid that *Digitalis purpurea*— or foxglove, as it's commonly called—has a narrow range of applications. Though I have a colleague who is . . . "

His voice trailed away as he led Elijah through a door. He had not given Jemma a second glance after establishing that he had a patient who required his attention.

Jemma removed her pelisse and bonnet and sat down again. She was quite alone, for the first time since she had learned of Elijah's illness.

Her mind skittered over the fact that should he die, she would be alone a great deal of the time, and she forced herself to stop thinking of it.

She had never been in a doctor's chambers before. (If medical attention were needed, the doctor always came to her, as was proper.) One entire wall of Withering's antechamber was taken up by a massive walnut cabinet, comprised of hundreds of small drawers. Some were pulled open and others closed, so the whole presented a chaotic appearance, as if it were a messy pile of blocks stacked by a child.

She got up and walked over, thinking an upright posture might make it easier to breathe. Each drawer was labeled in a quick hand, as if the writer hadn't taken time to shape the letters. Some of the contents had straightforward medicinal uses. A drawer marked LAUDANUM was filled with little vials, as she discovered by pulling it open and peeping inside. TOAD STONE read another. She gingerly opened it to find a small pile of pebbles.

BLACKB FEATH turned out to contain two dusty blackbird feathers, and RIVER WATER had a number of little vials. Some had only a drop or two inside, and others had dried up altogether.

Numbly, she made herself look in more drawers. Many were full of powdery leaves. MUSTARD PLANT made her sneeze just by opening the drawer, and eventually she wandered back to her seat.

It was as if the clock had stopped moving. She sat in the dusty silence, watching the sun move across a harpsichord which occupied one part of the room. One had to suppose that the doctor was a musician.

Ordinarily, she was never bored. During idle moments, she would simply replay a chess game in her head, correcting herself or her opponent. But now she couldn't keep the board's construction in mind, and lost track of the play between the seventh and eighth moves.

She tried to read the doctor's treatise on the uses of Jamaica pepper, but found it hopelessly obtuse. The minutes ticked by. Finally she borrowed peppercorns and white allspice from their respective drawers in the specimen cabinet and set up her own makeshift chessboard.

She had just realized that she had completely missed a move by a White Knight that would win the Black Queen when Elijah and Dr. Withering came back into the room. She leapt to her feet. "Are you able to help him?" she demanded, without bothering with courtesies.

The doctor abruptly fell into a series of racking coughs, so deep that he bent from the waist.

"There is a possible treatment," Elijah said, taking her hands. But the look in his eyes made her smile die.

" 'Possible'?"

"Foxglove might help," the doctor said, having recovered himself. "But the consequences for failure are grave, and unfortunately, as I have explained to him, I must decline to treat His Grace."

Jemma paled and her hands tightened. "Because it's poison?"

"Dr. Withering has experienced some remarkable results," Elijah said. "But he is at the initial stages of his research."

"The possibility of giving someone an overly powerful dose is likely. I have advised His Grace not to attempt this remedy." The doctor bowed, obviously expecting them to leave his chambers immediately.

Jemma looked up into Elijah's face. "What do you want to do?"

"Go home with you," he said. "There's no easy way to say this, Jemma. The doctor has seen many heart patients, and he is not sanguine about the time I may have left."

"His heart is thready and irregular," Withering put in. "But I must emphasize that no one can tell the span of a person's life. I've had heart patients whom I considered to be at death's door linger for months, even years."

But she could read the truth in his eyes . . . He didn't think Elijah would be one who lingered.

Jemma dropped Elijah's hands and said to the doctor, "Your medicine has worked for some people, hasn't it?"

"It has. But I have—" He hesitated. "I have had a number of failures."

"Do you mean that patients have died as a result of the foxglove?" Jemma was not in a mood for euphemisms.

"They would have died in any case, from either dropsy or an irregular heartbeat," Dr. Withering said somewhat defensively.

Elijah moved behind Jemma and put his hands on her shoulders. "The duchess does not mean to imply any negligence on your part, Dr. Withering."

"It is hard for a layman to understand the mysteries of science," the doctor said. "I am drawing closer to understanding correct dosages. I recently discovered that the leaves, once powdered, are twice as potent as the flowers. And the other day I made the serendipitous discovery that boiling that powder renders the effect fourfold as powerful."

Jemma could interpret that comment. Some unlucky patient's death proved the potency of his boiled medicine. "How did you discover the properties of foxglove?" she asked.

"I advised a patient of mine that there was nothing more I could do for him," the doctor replied. "He was as swollen as a ripe plum, and I'd tried everything I knew to cure his dropsy. He didn't agree with my assessment, and made his way to an old Gypsy woman known for her healing arts."

"A Gypsy!"

Withering nodded. "She gave him a potion, and the symptoms of dropsy went away. Even more interestingly, his heart steadied. The moment I heard about it, I went around to find her, of course."

"And the drink was made from foxglove?"

"There were some twenty herbs in the potion," Withering said with a trace of pride in his voice. "It took me nearly a year to narrow my study to foxglove, and then to begin to understand the remarkable qualities of this plant. It seems to have the ability to cure tumultuous action on the part of the heart."

"Tumultuous action?" Jemma asked, confused.

"Irregularities," Withering explained. "Skipped beats. Just as it soothes an overly rapid heartbeat, it also speeds up an overly slow one."

"We must find the Gypsy," Jemma said, picking up her bonnet.

Elijah laughed—he actually laughed. "If we find the Gypsy and I drink the potion, I would need to keep taking it. Do I spend the rest of my life chasing a Gypsy down country lanes? She's a traveler."

"You would have a life in which to chase her, Elijah!"

He just looked at her, and there was something in his eyes . . . She turned to Withering. Not many people could withstand Jemma at her most formidable, and the doctor wasn't one of them. He actually flinched. "In your opinion, does my husband have insufficient time to find this Gypsy?"

"I would not advise travel."

"I asked you a question," she said steadily.

The doctor fidgeted and then said: "In my opinion, your husband does not have much time."

Elijah intervened. "My heart lost its rhythm repeatedly in the time that Dr. Withering was listening to my chest, Jemma. Of course, I was lying flat, and that's the worst possible position."

She nodded. It seemed that Elijah had only a few days to live. She turned to the doctor again. "Have any of *your* patients survived, or only the Gypsy's patient?"

He bridled a little. "I would not keep working with foxglove had I not had successes. There are a number of people, a significant number, who are thriving." He saw the look in her eye. "But I cannot give it to the duke. It's far too dangerous. You don't understand."

"I thoroughly understand. You have been experimenting with the poor," Jemma said, stepping closer to him. "You have been choosing your patients in Spitalfields, and who's to argue when they die in your chambers?"

"It's for the benefit of science," he said with a sort of gasp. "They come to me desperate. No one else can help them. I have done considerable service with the poor. I don't merely treat heart ailments: I have done my best with everything from dropsy to scrofula."

"But a duke of the realm is a different proposition," she said.

"You must see that I am simply not at a stage in my research at which I can sufficiently—"

"You will give the medicine to my husband in the morning," Jemma stated. "I will not allow him to die when there is a possible remedy."

"My last patient expired," Withering gibbered. "Within an hour of trying the remedy. It's too strong, you see. Boiling the powder gave it the power that I needed, but it went too far."

"Make sure you don't go too far tomorrow morning," Jemma said grimly. "Perhaps you can spend the night calibrating the proper amount by reconsidering the case of your lost patient. We shall be here at eight of the clock."

"I cannot!" Withering cried. "I cannot! You do not understand, Your Grace! If the duke were to die here, in my chambers, I would be hanged. They wouldn't listen to me. And my work—my *work*!"

"He's right," Elijah said. "He's right, Jemma."

"He is not right!" she cried.

"His work is important. He has lost some patients, but his discoveries seem to me critically important. If we were to force him to give me the medicine, and I were to die, he would be hanged, merely because I am a duke." He said it flatly. "I cannot allow a man to be hanged on my behalf, Jemma, nor stop research that has the potential to help so many people."

"Don't *be like that*!" she half screamed at him.

His face was like stone. "I cannot be other than I am."

"Stop being so bloody good! Think of yourself for once, Elijah! Don't you want to live? Don't you want to stay here? What if I am carrying a child? What if—" Her voice cracked and she half turned from him.

"I would give anything to stay with you." He took her shoulders in his hands, gripping her so hard that it hurt. "I would give my dukedom, every penny I ever had, my right arm, to stay with you. To stay with our child if we have one. How could you even ask?"

She looked into his beautiful dark eyes. "Then—"

He shook his head. "*My* money, *my* dukedom, *my* right arm, Jemma. But not another man's life and his work. Even if I were to somehow arrange it so Withering were exonerated, he couldn't continue his work. I would give anything that is *mine* to stay in the world. Anything!"

His face twisted, and she knew—knew with her deepest heart—that he meant it. "I cannot risk another man's life to save my own," he said, and in his eyes, despair warred with honor.

She could love Elijah for who he was, or she could wish that she'd married another man altogether. "Oh God," she whispered, falling into his arms.

"I am sorry," Withering said helplessly. "In another six months I believe I will have a much better understanding of the properties of the drug."

Jemma's mind reeled like that of a drunkard. "I can't let you die," she said into Elijah's coat.

His arms tightened around her but he said nothing. She could feel his lips on her hair. It was over. They would go home, and tonight, or tomorrow morning, soon, too soon, Elijah would leave her.

She straightened, and pulled away from his arms, turning back to Withering. "What are the symptoms of a patient dying of an overly potent dose of your medicine?"

"He becomes nauseated and vomits," Withering said. "He sees auras, lights around ordinary objects. The end comes very quickly thereafter."

She nodded. "I will thank you to write down in detail the amount of boiled powder that you gave the man who recently died. We shall take the details with us along with the medicine."

"I couldn't allow—"

"No one will know. Our entire household is well aware of the duke's heart ailment. He and I shall be alone tonight. Should the worst ensue, everyone will assume that the duke's heart has given out, which will be, in fact, the case. I will never say a word to anyone." She held Withering's eye. "I do not *ever* tell untruths. I say to you now: I will not betray you."

"If only I had six months!" Withering cried, wringing his hands.

"Might you perhaps gather some notes in case we decide to try this remedy?" Elijah said to the doctor.

Withering looked at him blindly. "I wish you had not found your way to my chambers!"

"We wouldn't have," Jemma said, "but Elijah is as well-known to the poor in Spitalfields as you are."

"Doctor, will you give us a moment alone?" Elijah asked.

"I'll write it down, but I don't approve; I don't approve!" The doctor trotted from the room, still wringing his hands.

"You're determined, aren't you?" Elijah asked Jemma.

She looked up at him. "It's your only chance."

"What if, in years hence, you come to doubt your actions?"

She was so frustrated that she actually reached out and tried to shake him, except that he was so large as to be unshakable. "We're both in this marriage, Elijah! You and I are *both* here. I will be with you. You don't have to make all the decisions yourself. Please!"

"It seems to me that *you* are making this decision."

"Rule number three of marriage," she said, "is never to allow an ocean to come between us again. Death is a great deal wider than the English Channel, Elijah. I am fighting for that. For that rule."

His face eased. "I know."

"You may die tonight," she continued steadily. "But I will be with you. And if you die, I will live knowing that we tried every single remedy we could to steady your heart and to give you more time on this earth."

They just held each other until Withering came back in the room. And they left with a scrawled sheet of paper and five small vials containing a boiled solution of Dead Men's Bells.

Chapter Twenty-nine

Jemma moved through the next hours as if she were in a dream. Fowle had a meal waiting, so they ate. She felt curiously observant. The fish tasted of the sea. There were pickled peaches that tickled her tongue with the memory of summer.

Her lips kept parting, as if she had something to say to Elijah, and then closing again, stiffly, the words unsaid.

At last the meal was finished. She heard Elijah telling Fowle, as if from a long way off, that they would retire early. And then he asked for a bath.

Jemma knew what he was doing. Elijah would not want to put his servants to the work of washing his dead body. He would prepare himself.

She walked upstairs and felt their decision burning fiercely in her heart.

"I believe I should drink half a vial," Elijah said on entering her chamber following his bath. He was wearing a dressing gown, and had brought a small brandy glass with him.

"Didn't Withering give his last patient a full vial?" They had read the doctor's scrawled description in the carriage.

Elijah nodded.

"Then why don't we start with a quarter vial?" Jemma suggested. "If it has no effect, you could take another quarter."

"That seems reasonable," Elijah agreed. He poured a quarter of the vial's contents into the glass. The concoction looked cloudy, and seemed innocuous. Jemma found herself wishing desperately that there were more ingredients—perhaps a magic feather, or a touch of dew. It seemed preposterous to entrust one's continued existence to a single flower.

Elijah set the glass carefully on the mantelpiece and then pulled her into his arms. "I am fortunate to have loved you."

"*We* are fortunate. I am just so sorry that I—"

His hand gently covered her mouth. "We have already made our apologies for the time we lost." Then he cupped her face, his strong fingers gentle on her cheeks, and looked into her eyes before bending his head. They spoke to each other in that last kiss. Jemma tried to give him a lifetime's worth of love and devotion. She felt the same fierce love burning in his tender touch.

Too soon, he pulled back. "You may feel nauseated, but you *will not die*," she told him.

"Because you won't allow it?"

"I am a duchess," she said, not even smiling.

He kissed her again, fleetingly but so sweetly that her heart would have broken except that it had turned to something strong and like stone. Wordlessly, he emptied the glass.

They sat down together to wait. Jemma kept a hand on his chest. Two or three times she began to hope, and then would feel a double beat or a missed stroke.

"I think I should take another quarter vial," Elijah said ten minutes later. "Withering's patient, the one who took a full vial, is described as a plump man. Unless he was very tall, I am quite likely to weigh more than he does."

"But you are not plump," Jemma protested.

"Muscle is heavier than fat," Elijah said. "I've observed it among pugilists. A fat man weighs less than a muscular man of the same size."

He poured another quarter vial into the brandy glass and drank it before she could protest again.

Almost immediately he said, "I am faintly queasy."

"Nausea is good," Jemma said quickly. "It shows the medicine is working. Do you see any circles around this candle?" She ran to the mantel and snatched one up.

"Who can tell?" Elijah asked. "A candle has a natural aura."

"Well, look at my head then," Jemma said. "No, look at me! Do you see light around my head?"

"Are you trying to find out if you have angelic status?" he inquired, his mouth quirking up in a smile. He squinted at her. "Yes! I see feathery wings as well!"

"How can you make fun at a time like this!"

"If you can't laugh in the face of death, when can you laugh?" Then he added, casually, "My heart feels quite steady."

She couldn't speak, just put her head against the chest that housed that wonderful, regularly beating heart. A second passed, and another, and another. It continued to beat steadily.

"It's not skipping," she said, awestruck.

"The foxglove has forced it into a normal rhythm," he said. "Just like making love to you. Medicine in a bottle instead of a bed."

Jemma chewed her lip. "How will we know when you should drink more? We forgot to ask."

He stood up and stretched. "There's only one way to test it."

"How?"

He grinned, the wicked lively grin of a man without fear. "I have to exhaust myself. Drive my heartbeat up."

Jemma backed away, shaking her head. "No, Elijah, I don't think that—" But he seized her. She managed to say, "Only if you allow me to feel your heart whenever I want."

"I'm going to tire myself out making love to you. And then I shall drink a glass of cognac and lie flat on the floor."

"That's too risky."

But he had her on the bed, her own great warm beast of a man, pushing her flat, kissing her. "I'm fine. Feel." And he pressed her hand to his chest.

There, under her hand, was the most wonderful miracle of all: Elijah's heart was beating strongly, steadily, as if it had never missed a beat in its life, and they hadn't even begun to make love.

Tears came to her eyes. "Oh, Elijah . . . "

But the tears couldn't fall because his hands—his lips—he was *everywhere*. He had no shame.

At some point in the evening, after the household was in bed, they wandered down to the library. Jemma's hair was down her back and she was wearing only her nightdress, with a blanket wrapped around her shoulders.

Elijah poured himself a great glass of cognac. And then he poured one for her, since he didn't feel like drinking alone.

The warmth of the cognac seeped to her toes, but she kept walking around the room, unable to settle down. "We have to send a note to your mother first thing in the morning," she said, chattering. "And Villiers, of course."

"And Dr. Withering," Elijah put in. He was lying on the floor, just as he had threatened to do.

"How's your heart?"

He just smiled and drank more cognac.

She came and stood over him. "Drink faster. This can't be considered a proper test unless you are tipsy."

"I have an idea," he said, and his voice sounded so sleepy that she thought he meant to return to bed. His hand wrapped around her ankle and gave a gentle tug. "Kiss me."

"Oh, Elijah . . . " But she came to her knees beside him. His kiss was more joyful than desperate, more honey than lust. It banished her fears, replacing them with something stronger: faith that her husband would live.

Slowly those kisses changed to something else and fire crept up the back of her legs. "We can't do this again," she gasped.

"O ye of little faith!" He laughed at her, and sure enough the evidence of his ability was more than obvious. "Of course, I must remain on my back. Exhaust me," he commanded.

Jemma shifted, moving to hover over him, allowing him to stroke her. Then with one powerful thrust of his hips, he lunged upward. A cry broke from her lips.

"Did that hurt?" Elijah gasped.

"No," Jemma whispered. "Do it again— Oh!"

She tried leaning forward and leaning back. She tried teasing him, and teasing herself. She let him kiss her breasts, and then sat back again so she could do some caressing of her own.

Finally she found herself beginning to shudder, driven to ride him with a steady, pounding beat. "Beg me," she said, nipping his bottom lip with her teeth. "Beg me to go faster, Elijah."

His fingers tightened on her hips. "I love it when you growl at me."

She rose to her knees and teased him by withdrawing. "Beg me." She slid downwards with a wanton twist of her hips.

"I—never—beg," Elijah gasped.

Jemma would have laughed, but she had to concentrate to keep desire from overwhelming her. She drove him mercilessly, dancing to the brink and then stopping just before he toppled into pure pleasure.

"I can't—" He spoke through clenched teeth, his body bowed in an effort to force her compliance.

"Are you begging now?" she asked, pushing his hips down so that a hoarse gasp came from his throat—and then sliding away just as easily.

"*No.* Begging is shameful and you won't—" His voice broke off because she was reaching behind to caress him. "God," he said, his voice breaking. "Jemma!"

"Mmmm," she said, moving so slowly that her nerves danced with fire. Every inch of her body longed to drive him home, to ride him as fiercely as she was able.

But in a marriage, a true marriage, she couldn't be the only one who knew how to beg.

He was gasping now, his muscled chest heaving, but she was relentless, using her body, her fingers, her lips to drive him mad. Finally, reluctantly, he threw back his head and a guttural moan came from his throat. "All right. I'm begging you!"

Before she could even react, as if the very hint of submission was too shameful to bear, he lunged up, flipping her over and driving deep. She clutched him desperately, gasping in his ear: *"Please, please, please."*

Elijah braced his hands on the floor and stroked forward with a primitive force that made her shriek. "Say it," he said, between clenched teeth. "Say it!"

"I'm begging you," she sobbed. "I love you . . . "

"And I love you."

They fell together into a place where there were only their two bodies, and their two hearts.

Beating together.

Chapter Thirty

April 5

Villiers couldn't sleep. He kept thinking about that *boy* up in the nursery. If you could call him a boy. And then there was Elijah. Was he still alive? Surely he would have heard if Elijah had died.

He rose at the first light of dawn and strode around his chamber, unable to settle his mind. He didn't know what to do next. Should he fetch another child? The idea was—frankly—terrifying. Perhaps it would be better to get a wife first, and bring a woman's hand into it. How long could it take to find a wife?

And then there was Elijah. He turned so quickly that his heel slipped and the rug crumpled behind him. He kicked it flat again.

Finally he cursed and rang the bell for his valet. He required a woman's advice about matrimony. Jemma was a woman. And Jemma was married to Elijah:

he needed to know how Elijah was. In any case, he couldn't bear to be in his house anymore, not with that boy upstairs. One had to suppose he should go upstairs and say something to him. He shuddered at the very thought.

Villiers arrived at the Beaumont town house at the grotesquely unfashionable hour of eight o'clock, fully expecting the butler to deny him entrance. By the grace of God, Elijah's butler wasn't at his post. Instead a round-faced footman informed him that the duke wasn't yet awake. "Fine," he said brusquely, throwing his greatcoat into the man's arms. The footman caught it reflexively, and Villiers strode around him. "I'll be in the library. When the duke awakes, inform him that I'm waiting."

He threw open the door to the room and stopped, frozen on the threshold. Then he stepped through the doorway and closed the door behind him.

"Well, well, well," he said.

"Don't wake her," Elijah said.

Jemma looked utterly delectable, of course. She appeared to be wrapped in little more than a blanket, and was sleeping as soundly as a babe in his friend's arms. At least Elijah had a dressing gown on. Somehow Villiers found himself able to view the scene without more than a faint pang of envy. The whole experience of rescuing his son made his feelings for Jemma seem far in the past.

"You're up and about very early," Elijah observed.

"I had an interesting day yesterday," Villiers said. Then he narrowed his eyes. "You look—"

"The foxglove works."

"It *works*?"

"My heart beat steadily for approximately thirteen

hours after taking a dose," Elijah said, a huge grin breaking over his face. "When Jemma wakes, I'll take another dose, as I only just started missing a beat or two in the last few minutes."

"I'll get the medicine," Villiers said. "Where is it?"

"Nonsense," Elijah said. "Dukes don't *fetch* things. Jemma dashed over to your house to fetch the article on foxglove, and now you're the same."

"We're not living up to your ducal expectations?" Villiers said.

"In some ways, yes," Elijah said. "What has happened to you? You look as altered as I. Did you know that your hair ribbon does not match your coat?"

Villiers had grabbed it from the table and left his valet bleating something or other.

"Just to demonstrate that dukes do fetch things, yesterday I went to fetch my eldest son."

"Were you successful?"

Jemma murmured something and turned in her sleep. Bright hair spilled over Elijah's knees. Villiers realized with some surprise that he felt nothing.

"The boy had been consigned to a grotesque personage who ran a group of boys as mudlarks."

Elijah frowned instantly. Of course he, of all the dukes in the realm, would know precisely what a mudlark was, and how perilous their lives. "Has he been injured?"

"His legs are somewhat scarred, but he seems well. Another boy appears likely to lose his foot from a great cut."

"The mortality rate is very high."

Villiers felt that like a punch to the stomach. "Ah. Well, my son appears to be alive. Very alive. In addition, he seems to be a hellion."

"Imagine that," Elijah said. "Who would have thought?"

Villiers ignored his sarcasm.

"Where is he?"

"I handed him over to Mrs. Ferrers, my house-keeper."

"You handed your son over to the housekeeper? You don't know where he is sleeping?"

"What housekeeper?" Jemma said, straightening up and yawning. "What time is it?" With a groan she collapsed back onto Elijah's chest.

"Who else could take care of the boy? He was filthy. Was I supposed to *do* something with him?" But it was a question he had been asking himself. Should he go up to the nursery and say something? Take the boy somewhere?

Jemma sat up again and threw back her hair. "What the devil are *you* doing here, Villiers?" She blinked and clutched her blanket a little higher.

"I came to hear your good news," he said blandly.

"Oh." Then she beamed at him. "Isn't it wonderful?"

"Yes."

"But what were you saying about your housekeeper?"

"The housekeeper has been assigned to care for one of my children," Villiers said. "I have five more children to find, and God knows what sort of living arrangements my solicitor made for them. He's gone missing, by the way, and I expect he's taken a quantity of money with him."

"Have you put a Runner on him?" Elijah inquired.

Villiers nodded. "Not for the money, but in the event that I can't find one or more of the children."

"You must go look for the rest of them," Jemma said. "What are you waiting for?"

"Advice," he said flatly.

"I know nothing of children," she replied. "Perhaps you should hire a nursemaid. In fact, you will need more than one, as well as a governess. Your house-keeper can find them for you."

"Not that," Villiers said, picking up his sword stick and examining it as if he'd never seen it before. "I need a wife. That is, I suppose I do need a nanny or two, or three. But I need a wife. And I've lost two fiancées so far."

"You need someone of a generous temperament, of course." She hesitated. "Are you certain that you wish to bring up these children in your own home, Leopold? You could place them in the country, with a good family, and visit them often."

"No." He didn't know why it was, but he couldn't have Tobias sent away, where he might not be safe. Never again. Even though he was a repellent little monster. "I was under the impression that you were quite enamored of your brother's illegitimate brat."

"But last year Elijah threw a tantrum at the mere idea that the boy would be staying under our roof, and he was just the one child, rather than six," Jemma said, elbowing her husband.

"I was trying to be effective in Parliament at that point," Elijah said. "And I was going about it the wrong way." He dropped a kiss on her hair.

"You need a woman who won't be terrified by the very idea of your children," Jemma said, "which I think excludes the greater number of debutantes, don't you agree, Elijah?"

"The problem," Elijah said slowly, "is not how to handle these children *now*. It's what will happen to them when they reach marriageable age."

"I shall dower them," Villiers said. "I am one of the richest men in England, and much of it is unentailed. They shall marry whomever they please." He heard the arrogance of his father, in his voice, and his father's father—and didn't give a damn.

"That's not going to be easy," Jemma said. "Perhaps a nice widow?"

"No," Elijah said slowly. "The duchess would have to be of equal stature to Villiers."

"I see. If we could find a duke's daughter," Jemma agreed, "between the two of you, you might be able to compel the *ton* to accept the children."

"I doubt that the Puritanical will ever accept the children," Elijah said.

Villiers felt a wave of rage in his chest. "They are *my* children," he said tightly.

"Illegitimacy is well-nigh impossible to overcome."

"So I need a duke's daughter," Villiers said, ignoring his doubts.

"The problem is finding eligible ducal offspring," Jemma said. "Not to mention ones who might be convinced to marry a man in your situation."

"You show me an eligible woman, and I'll take her," Villiers said softly.

"You can't just *take* her," Jemma said, scowling at him.

"Watch me."

"There's the Duke of Montague's daughter," Elijah offered.

"Actually, Montague has three daughters," Jemma said. "The eldest one is Eleanor. She's apparently quite proud. I've heard tell that she won't even consider those of a rank below an earl."

"I am above an earl," Villiers said. "Are the other two as superior in their thinking?"

"I've met the youngest Montague daughter only two or three times, but it seems to me that she was as full of her own consequence as her sisters. I believe it's a family trait."

"Doesn't the Duke of Gilner have a daughter?" Elijah asked. "I always liked him. He comes infrequently to the House, but he's thoroughly intelligent."

"Her name is Lisette. But she's ineligible," Jemma said.

"Why?" Villiers asked.

"She's mad. Quite mad. She has never had a season. And everyone says it's because she can't appear in public at all."

"There must be others."

Jemma shook her head.

"Then I shall choose among the Montague daughters. Did you say the eldest is called Eleanor?"

Jemma nodded. "Eleanor, Anne, and Elizabeth. They're named after three queens. I don't believe they're in London at the moment, but I shall invite them to the house for tea upon their return."

"I would appreciate that," Villiers said. He was beginning to feel worried about Tobias, as if the boy might flee if he left him alone too long. "I'm happy to find you so well," he said to Elijah. "Now you should have a footman fetch that miraculous medicine."

"We owe you thanks, since you found the doctor who directed us to Withering."

"I shall take that as confirmation that I no longer need feel guilty about the fact you saved my life last year, after that duel."

They didn't embrace. English dukes didn't flaunt affection, even under circumstances like these. But Elijah accompanied him to the door and their shoulders jostled together, just as they had in their boyhood.

The Duke of Villiers walked into the watery morning sunlight, thinking about duke's daughters named for queens.

Chapter Thirty-one

*Two months later, mid-June
1784*

All of London was talking about the Duchess of
Beaumont's benefit costume ball for refurbishment
of the old Roman baths. It was rumored that at least
four duchesses would attend, and perhaps even the
King himself. Everyone, of course, would be dressed
in proper Roman attire.

Mrs. Mogg and her friends were waiting outside
the gate of the baths hours before the ball was due to
begin.

They watched as scores of footmen carried in count-
less garlands of flowers.

"They'll wrap them around the trees, I've no doubt,"
Mrs. Mogg said importantly. "The Duchess of Beaumont did just that at a party she had in Paris." Her
friends all nodded. Mrs. Mogg was considered some-

thing of an expert on the Beaumonts. After all, she'd talked to the duke himself twice. And she seemed to know everything there was to know about the couple.

"That was when they were living apart," she continued now. "The duchess was over in Paris, by herself, see, and the duke was here. But then she came back and they fell in love, just like a fairy tale."

"She's the best chess player in all England," Mr. Mogg put in. He had discovered that if he didn't go along with his wife's obsession with the ducal family, they had nothing to talk about. So in his own way, he had become an expert too.

"Nay, you're wrong there," a bystander said. "The Duke of Villiers is the best chess player. They just had in the paper as how he is the number one ranked player in the Chess Club."

"But that's only because the duke and duchess refuse to play each other for a ranking," Mrs. Mogg said. "I had a shilling and sixpence riding on the duke winning the game with the duchess, and he sent a footman to my house to tell me the match was off."

"Cor," the man said, looking at her again.

Mrs. Mogg drew herself up, her fox head stole shaking with excitement. "He sent that footman right to my house, to tell me that."

"Well, why won't they play each other?" someone asked respectfully, as befitted a conversation with someone who knew a duke personally.

"I expect because of love," Mrs. Mogg said. "They're in love, you know. She calls him Elijah. I heard her, clear as I hear myself. 'Elijah,' she called him."

"Are they really all going to be wearing sheets?" someone asked her. He had a little notebook. "I'm reporting for the *Morning Post*, madam."

Everyone looked at her with respect. "That's what I heard," Mrs. Mogg said, watching as the reporter wrote down *sheets*.

There are some people for whom the command to wear a toga is anathema. The Marquise de Perthuis, for example, received her invitation, shuddered, and dropped it in the fireplace. Wearing a shapeless white gown held no interest for her. Besides, she was packing to return to France. Having heard nothing from Henri, she had decided to shock him (and the French court) with the glory of her new chemise gowns.

Lord Corbin was similarly discomposed. How did one wear a proper wig with a toga? And what about shoes? Weren't ancient Romans prone to wearing roughly-made sandals that displayed one's toes? He went to the opera instead.

But most other English peers were braver than Corbin, or more curious. "It's held up on only one shoulder," Roberta, the Countess of Gryffyn, complained. "What was Jemma thinking of? What if my gown falls straight to the ground while I'm dancing?"

Damon, the Duchess of Beaumont's brother, dropped a kiss on her bare shoulder. "She was thinking that you would look utterly ravishing in a toga," her husband said huskily.

Roberta met her husband's eyes in the glass, and unfortunately that particular couple arrived quite late at the ball.

It wasn't until some hours later—after Mrs. Mogg, Mr. Mogg, the *Morning Post* reporter, and a small stalwart crowd had been standing long enough to be truly weary, and all the footmen and cooks and the rest had gone through the little gate—that Mrs. Mogg really achieved fame.

The Duke and Duchess of Beaumont were the first to arrive. That made sense, since they were hosting the affair.

The reporter started writing busily, for here was a couple for whom the very design of the toga seemed to have been invented. The duchess wore her unpowdered hair in simple curls, with a lock or two falling over her bare shoulder. She had jewels in her hair and on her slippers. The duke looked like Socrates himself, the reporter scribbled, stopping for a moment to wonder whether Socrates was Greek or Roman. Well, it hardly mattered.

"Mrs. Mogg," the duke said, stopping with a bow.

The reporter stopped writing to stare. Did the *duke* just bow to Mrs. Mogg?

Sure enough, she was bobbing a curtsy and talking to him as if he were of no better rank than a dockworker. The reporter shook his head. There was no point in writing this down; no one would believe it.

A few hours later, the gardens of the Roman baths were thronged with Roman nobles—or so it seemed. The trees were festooned with flowers and strands of pearls; twinkling small lanterns lit the darkest corners.

"It's a triumph," Elijah whispered to Jemma.

She smiled up at him. "Did the king tell you that he's going to undertake restoration of the baths himself? They should be a national treasure, he said."

Elijah's arms tightened around her. "I'm a bit sorry to have lost our secret place, but he's right. The mosaics need to be restored."

"I know." And then: "Why do you have that naughty look, Elijah?"

He dropped a kiss on her nose. "After the ball is

over, Duchess . . . " He ran a finger under the single knot that held up her toga.

She laughed. "Yes?"

"I have a surprise for you."

A drawling voice said, "Should I return, or are you two going to continue making an exhibition of yourselves?"

"Piss off," Elijah said, turning his back on his oldest friend to gather his wife in his arms.

"I need Jemma," Villiers said, sounding amused. "Or rather, I need a wife and she promised to help."

"Oh!" Jemma said. "Do let me go, Elijah. I promised to introduce Leopold to the Montague sisters. I just saw Eleanor, dressed as Caesar's wife."

Elijah reluctantly let her go, just pulling her back at the last moment. "Later," he said into her ear.

And then watched her walk off with Villiers, knowing that the high flush on his wife's cheeks had nothing to do with face paint.

As the night wore on, the gardens gradually emptied of revelers. Some of the lanterns winked out, giving the paths the air of a wild bacchanalia. Carriages drew up continually outside the little stone wall, taking away groups of chattering noblemen. The hems of their togas were black with dirt; they themselves were replete with gossip; it was accounted a brilliant night by all.

Finally, Mr. and Mrs. Mogg were the only two people still waiting outside the gate. "But the duke and duchess haven't come out!" she wailed.

"We've been here for hours, Marge," Henry said. "You know I love you, but I'm done with this here waiting. We must have missed them. Or they left through another gate. Look, all them servants have left, and the place is dark now."

Mrs. Mogg finally allowed herself to be drawn away, though she could hardly believe it. "I couldn't have missed him. There must be another gate."

"'Course there is," Henry said stoutly. "They probably left early. Too many people in that there garden, if you ask me."

But in fact not all the lanterns were out. There were still glowing lights hanging from the columns of the baths themselves, and the duke and duchess were wandering hand in hand in that direction.

"We've never been here at night," Jemma said. "It's magical, Elijah. Just look at all the stars."

"I have a surprise for you," her husband said.

They walked between the dilapidated columns, turned right and descended the stairs to the baths. Jemma stopped. "Oh, Elijah!"

In the golden light of the lanterns hanging around the baths, the pool looked like a purple sea. The entire surface was covered with hundreds and hundreds of floating violets. "It's so beautiful!"

"Every violet Stubbins was able to force in his new frames," Elijah said with satisfaction, "and more sent in from the country."

She smiled up at him. "Extravagant man!"

"I've been waiting to do this all evening." He slid the knotted cloth of her toga off her shoulder. It fell to the ground, leaving her in nothing but an extremely naughty pair of cherry-colored stays.

"I didn't expect to find *that* under your toga!" Elijah said. His voice darkened at the very sight of her slender long legs topped by stays that pushed her breasts forward, as if they longed for a man's touch.

Jemma took a step toward him with a sultry swing

of her hips. "Your toga, Duke." With one finger, she pushed it off his shoulder.

Unlike the duchess, the duke had chosen to wear nothing under his toga.

Jemma broke into laughter.

"It was a good idea," Elijah said, grabbing her. His hands slid down her back, over her stays, shaped her bottom. "Unfortunately, every time I caught sight of you I had to turn away and think hard about chess, because the front of this damned toga tented in the most obvious manner."

He picked her up and carried her straight into the water. They made a little path through the violets, as fragrance drifted into the air. "Oh, Elijah," Jemma said, "this is the most romantic night I could ever have dreamed of."

"Do you know what interesting fact Stubbins told me this morning?" he asked, striding through the violet sea.

"Does it involve manure?" she asked, leaning her head against his chest, just for the reassurance of hearing the steady beat of his heart.

"You can eat violets." He placed her carefully down on the edge of the bath, where he had arranged for long cushions to be placed on the cold marble, just as the Romans had.

"What on earth are you planning?" Jemma said. She stretched languorously, loving the way his eyes ran greedily along the lines of her legs.

"I'm going to turn you into a pagan goddess," he said, nimbly pulling out the pins that held up her curls, and then turning to the ties holding up her stays.

Jemma lay back and smiled at the open sky. Far

overhead, stars were shining, though the roofless bath seemed like the most protected room in the world. Elijah was tucking flowers in all her ringlets. He stood back and looked at her. She rolled over on her side and propped up her head with one hand. "How do I look?"

"More like a debauched Roman matron than a goddess," he observed. He reached forward again.

Jemma squeaked. "Not there too?"

"Everywhere," he said with satisfaction. "In fact, given that violets are edible, we should consider your body a banquet. Put a violet everywhere that you would like me to . . . taste. Do you see what I am doing, Jemma?"

"Turning me into a flower bed."

"No, I am having fun. Just as you taught me."

She leaned over to give him a kiss.

"I'm being extravagant," he continued. "I'm risking bankrupting the duchy to blanket you in flowers. I'm flirting with you, and now I'm going to make love to you."

"Hmmm . . . " Jemma rolled to her back and held out her hand for violets. "Here," she said, dropping them onto the slope of her breast. "Oh, and here." She loved it when he kissed her stomach. "And . . . "

The next hour or so was delicious from a culinary— and a personal—point of view.

It was only when they were sitting twined together on the steps leading down to the pool, enveloped by the warm water, that Jemma said, "Elijah."

"Hmmm," he said. "Look at those broken tiles over there, Jemma. I do believe there used to be a mosaic depicting Apollo and Daphne on that wall."

"I have a surprise too."

"You do?"

She looked up at him. "I taught you how to have fun. And you taught me something just as important."

"I love praise," he said, nuzzling her. "Tell me more."

"You taught me that not all games need to be won. And that I don't always have to be in control."

He nipped her ear. "That's true." There was a deep, male satisfaction in his voice. "You've become quite used to begging."

"I have a gift in return."

His eyes were grave now, looking into hers. "What gifts haven't you given me, Jemma? Besides my life?"

She kissed him again, loving him. Then she picked up his hand and put it gently on her belly. "This is my gift."

He froze.

"Jemma!"

She started laughing at the look in his eyes.

"You're joking," he said hoarsely.

"Never."

"You're—You're having a baby?"

"*We're* having a baby," she corrected him.

He had both hands on her tummy now, spanning her with ease. "Are you certain, Jemma?" he asked. "I've seen pregnant woman and you're very slim."

"I am not!" she protested. "You simply haven't noticed. Look!" And she stood up. She thought her stomach formed the sweetest, most delicate curve she'd ever seen.

Elijah rose from the water, drops flying from his muscled body, and without pausing fell to his knees and put his lips to her stomach.

"Oh, Elijah!" Jemma said, putting a hand on his dark hair.

"I love you," he said huskily. "You've given me my life, Jemma . . . twice over."

In the end, she cried.

He was too happy for tears.

Epilogue

An appalling number of years later

There were times when the Duchess of Beaumont felt quite irritated about growing old. Her right ankle hurt sometimes. Her hips were a little rounder than she would have preferred. Her hair was emphatically no longer pure gold.

Even now, for example, as she bent over to adjust the knot of pearls on her slippers, something creaked in one knee and she straightened quickly.

"Why the frown?" Elijah said, entering the chamber and stripping off his riding coat. He had been in Hyde Park with Evan, their eldest. Without waiting for an answer, he continued, "I have to tell you what happened while we were riding. Your friend, the Duchess of Cosway, stopped me because she wanted to know more about the Cacky Street helmets. She had the idea that perhaps their village smith might use something of the same nature."

"Oh, how is Isidore?" Jemma asked with pleasure. "I haven't seen her since our Twelfth Night ball."

"She seemed the same," Elijah said, pulling off his boots. "Beautiful woman. Not as lovely as you, of course. But more importantly, I think she has a good point about smiths making use of something to protect their eyes."

Jemma picked up her manuscript. She had been working all morning on her latest project, a treatise entitled *The Beaumont Chess Series: Complex Problems for Master Players*. "That's wonderful, darling. I've been writing all morning. I thought I'd stow this in the library and go for a walk. Would you like to join me?"

"But I haven't told you what happened yet," Elijah complained. He took off his shirt.

Jemma put her book back down and sat to ogle her husband as he undressed. Even now, at sixty, Elijah was still lean and muscled. She had grown a little plumper, but he maintained the exercise practice that he insisted was half of the reason his heart was still— even now—beating as steadily as the pendulum of a clock.

"Isidore was accompanied by one of her daughters. The younger one, with the extraordinary eyes."

"Lucia has her mother's eyes," Jemma said. "Isidore's eyes tilt up at the corners in precisely the same fashion."

"Well, between us, Lucia looks like a harem dancer," Elijah said. He was down to his smalls now, and Jemma thought he looked delicious. His legs were as powerful as they had been at thirty-five. It was such a pleasure to still desire her husband, these many years later, that she couldn't stop smiling.

"You sound a little moralistic," she teased. "Lucia is a very nice girl and no harem dancer. When she debuted last year, she had at least four requests for her hand, and one of them was from the Earl of Derby's heir!"

"That's my point," Elijah protested. "Any normal unmarried man—except for Evan—would have gravitated to Lucia's side like steel to a magnet."

"Evan ignored her," Jemma said resignedly.

"He's just like me," Elijah said, for perhaps the fourteen-thousandth time since Evan was first put in his arms. It was undeniably true that their eldest son's grave, intelligent eyes looked exactly like his father's. "He's so passionate about furthering his study of heart ailments that he can't stop thinking about his latest experiment, even when a woman as beautiful as Lucia shows interest."

When Rosalind was born, Jemma happily recognized a bit of herself in one of her children. Rosie's bright hair and laughter had kept Evan from being too solemn as a little boy.

But it wasn't until their third, Marguerite, came along that Jemma saw herself and Elijah combined in one child. Marguerite would passionately argue one minute for the life of a frog that Evan planned to dissect, and then turn about and argue just as passionately for the right to wear Spanish blue rather than white for her debut.

"I know, darling," Jemma said. "Evan is just like you."

"He's—" Elijah looked up. "Laugh if you like. But that boy is twenty-five years old, and he shows no signs of being interested in looking for a wife. Perhaps we should have arranged a marriage for him."

Jemma got up and wrapped her arms around Elijah's chest. "He'll find his own way."

"An arranged marriage worked for us. At this rate, he'll never get married. And I think that Cosway might welcome the suggestion for Lucia. Perhaps I'll ask him."

"No," Jemma told him. "Marguerite is going to force Evan to accompany her to balls this season. He'll find someone on his own."

Elijah snorted. "Did you hear that Marguerite slaughtered poor Villiers at chess again last night? He's going to refuse to pay us visits at this rate."

"Mmmm," Jemma said. "You know, Elijah, I think your heart may be missing a beat."

"Really?" He looked unconcerned. "I doubt it."

"No, I mean it," Jemma said. "And you know what resets this particular clock in the best possible fashion."

The smile on his face was positively wicked. "It is two in the afternoon," he said with mock severity. "Are you trying to lead me astray? I had plans to work on—"

She turned her mouth to his chest and his voice broke off.

A moment later he picked her up and laid her on the bed. "You shouldn't lift me," Jemma protested. "I'm too plump for that."

"I love carrying you," Elijah said. "Have I told you how grateful I am that you stopped wearing all those panniers and petticoats?"

"Yes," she said, gasping a little because his hands were wandering.

"And you are not plump. What you are is delicious, Jemma. Every time I see you, I want to make love to you."

"Oh, Elijah," she whispered.

"Last night at supper," Elijah said, pausing for a moment and looking down into her eyes, "Marguerite was nattering away with one of Villiers's boys, and you were talking to Rosalind about a new *modiste*. And I couldn't concentrate on what Villiers was saying at all because I kept looking at you and thinking about how you taste, and how you smell, and how soft you feel . . . "

He stopped talking, but only to give her a kiss.

Historical Note

To be absolutely frank, when Elijah first fainted in the House of Lords some years ago (in both my writing life and in Georgian time), I had no idea how to cure him. So I was fascinated to discover the work of Dr. William Withering (1741-1799). Withering discovered the drug *digitalis*, exactly as described in *This Duchess of Mine*, by tracking down a Gypsy remedy, isolating foxglove, and figuring out how to distill the active ingredient. The depiction of Dr. Withering as taking bold risks with the life of his poor patients is not true; the doctor dedicated much time to charitable medicine.

One fascinating aside: Withering was one of the first victims of academic plagiarism. Erasmus Darwin (Charles Darwin's grandfather) asked him for a second opinion on a patient with dropsy; shortly afterward Darwin submitted *"An Account of the Successful Use of Foxglove in Some Dropsies and in Pulmonary Consumption"* to the College of Physicians in London, noting Withering's experiments only in a footnote. Withering was furious, and for good reason! But Darwin went on with his life, and while his discoveries were nothing akin to those of his grandson, he did invent an organ that could recite the Ten Commandments (one has to hope that he dwelt on the eighth).

Unfortunately, the floating prison ships called the hulks also existed. In the Georgian period, these prisons were moored in the Thames, and as Elijah points out, the mortality rate aboard them was fearful. The riot I described is a figment of the imagination, although I borrowed details from the Gordon Riots that took place four years earlier and resulted in the burning of London's notorious prison, the Clink, to the ground.

And finally, I want to acknowledge that the most ratlike character in the book, the Duke of Villiers's solicitor Templeton, is indeed named after a famous rat. The rat in *Charlotte's Web* is greedy but I may have maligned his character here. After all, the original Templeton saves Charlotte's children, albeit for a price, whereas Villiers's Templeton does the opposite.